CLAWS

The Legend behind Texas's Most Bizarre Unsolved Murders

TIMOTHY GENE SOJKA

Black Rose Writing | Texas

ISBN: 978-1-68513-499-0 (Paperback); 978-1-68513-563-8 (Hardcover)
PUBLISHED BY BLACK ROSE WRITING
www.blackrosewriting.com

Printed in the United States of America
Suggested Retail Price (SRP) $23.95 (Paperback); $32.95 (Hardcover)

Claws is printed in Minion Pro

*As a planet-friendly publisher, Black Rose Writing does its best to eliminate unnecessary waste to reduce paper usage and energy costs, while never compromising the reading experience. As a result, the final word count vs. page count may not meet common expectations.

Praise for
CLAWS

"A master of intrigue, suspense, emotion, and wit. Sojka evokes laughter, despair, fear, suspense, and thrills."
–Sublime Book Reviews

"Sojka's writing style is engaging, providing a compelling reflection on the human condition, with themes of mortality, destiny, and the complexity of personal relationships."
–Readers' Favorite

"A rip-roaring trip back to 1970s trailer park Texas, where a fantastical team of evildoers meets its match in a rule-breaking detective, a pair of 12-year-old terror twins, and a plucky little girl who uses her wits to survive. CLAWS is magical reality at its rollicking best."
–Regina Buttner, author of Down a Bad Road

"It was kind of a *Sixth Sense* feeling, where my mind was racing to pick out all the hints and allusions throughout the book."
–AJ McCarthy. award winning author of By the Book

"Teeny, a child of abuse, gifted with a unique guardian angel, takes you on a thrilling adventure."
–Stephen W. Brings, author of
Beside Us and Family of Killers: Memoirs of an Assassin

"Sojka's mute eight-year-old heroine, Teeny, etches her place among warriors."
–John Netti, award-winning author of
Cupid, The Glades, The Ledger, Jacobi Park,
and soon-to-be-released, Pieces

Dedicated to Denise Kingham
Test Reader Extraordinaire
To all the millions of things you do for all the people around you.
I know you think no one notices.

ac·knowl·edg·ments

Many writers excel at editing and grammatical brilliance. I've met them, I am just not them. So, blessings to my patient and incredible editor Dione Benson.

To Margaret Sojka, for being the first to believe in me and gifting me a love for stories via our trips to old movie palaces like the Pines in Silsbee Texas. To Linda Migura, my sage advisor for each book so far. To Myrtis Gilmore for dragging me along on vacuum cleaner sales calls which taught me more than you know.

To my wife, the beautiful, intelligent, and determined Lori Sojka, the only woman I will ever love. To my brother, Jeff Sojka, the bravest kid I ever met, our adventures still inspire much of what's inside each book (especially this one).

Thank you, Abigail Sojka, for still going to ballgames with your dad, and for being wise beyond your years (we both know you did not get this from me).

Thank you to the incredible teachers at Silsbee Elementary, Jr. High and High School for molding but not breaking a kid with rampant behavioral issues (I'd bet I was not the only one – so kudos.) To Gary Keller and Jay Papasan for your incredible book The One Thing, which reinforced the path forward.

Thank you to my unbelievable test and support readers, Denise Kingham, Linda Migura, the Smiths (Brett, Mary, Steve, and Patti), the Joyners (Jenni and Troy), Kathy Girgenti, Karen Norwood, Kristen Mann, Beez Beasley, Ed Wiesner, Mary Bell, Robert Anthony, the Kilcommins (Joey and Jennifer), Misty Gonzalez, Jim Bob Stuckey, the Bishops (Lori and Alan), Scott and Christy White, Charlyne White, Brian Varvel, Linda Garrett, Tracey Ross-Watmore, Paul Crandall, Ed Kamph, Zack Kampf, Bill Holt, Joel Matthews, Kem Sandifer, Gaye Lokey, Diane Morgenroth, Mary Voigtman, Leroy Johnson, Heath Hardin, Geoff Hinkson, Lorraine Bennick, and Jeff Erwin.

I bet I forgot someone, so if I did, call me! I will set you up with a free book or mention you in the next novel. Unless of course you decide to duck your contributions, … smart.

Thank you to *Payback Jack*, *Politikill*, *39*, and *Claws* publisher, Minna and Reagan Rothe of Black Rose Writing. Your partnership is invaluable. To fellow writers A.J. McCarthy and Luke Swanson for your advice on each book.

Readers can follow me or reach out to me at timothygenesojka.com

Book clubs – Let me know if I can hang out with your crew one day.

My goal for *Claws* is different than past novels. I want readers to feel the whiplash, to say What the Hell did I just READ? That was NUTS. Who can I talk into reading this $h!+sh@w, so I can discuss how batsh!t it was?

So, you can't say you haven't been warned. But, if you're willing, it's more. Much, much more.

Definition

Human trafficking: the unlawful act of transporting or coercing people in order to benefit from their work or service, typically in the form of forced labor or sexual exploitation.

A Note to Readers:

For decades, Interstate 10, NEAR MY HOME has served as an active roadway for human trafficking. Next to borders, ports, rivers, bayous, and backroads, easy-on/easy-off for evil. Americans think slavery does not still exist in the United States – it does. That's what human trafficking is, a different label, for an old evil.

This novel is my (FLAWED) attempt to entertain while educating others about how to spot and stop child abuse and human trafficking and increase donations for organizations that already do. But real heroes are not in my novel, which by nature is fiction.

Be assured, real heroes exist. They do. **And you can be one**, by donating your time or money to great organizations that have already joined the battle to stop and / or rescue the victims of human trafficking.

While I always recommend you research local organizations near you, here is a Houston based organization doing GREAT work. I can tell you more about them, but you can read their story below.

Elijah Rising – https://elijahrising.org/

or simply donate here
https://elijahrising.org/donate/

CLAWS

1

2:22 a.m., Wednesday, May 5, 1976, Beaumont, Texas
Rumbling tractor trailers, drag racing Trans Ams, and honking horns hounded out the croaks of bullfrogs and chirps of crickets, the opera of Texas night. Bordering residents, accustomed to the ear-rape of Interstate 10, flip-flopped in bed or punch-fluffed pillows. Car exhaust choked out the fragrance of star jasmine and honeysuckle.

Aside from the cagiest stray mongrels, mid-sized wildlife was rare. Deer, feral hogs, raccoons, armadillos, turtles, snakes, and skunks—pancaked road-kill—sacrificed at the altar of the all-mighty interstate, the local economy's lynch pin. Two blocks off the interstate, near Beaumont, Texas, eight green, slime-coated mobile homes sat on mismatched cinderblocks along a scrub tree lot.

The "mobile" part of mobile home presents as a stale joke. Each single-wide trailer's tires rotted eons earlier. No double-wide trailers in the mix; double wides offer glamour unavailable here.

Inside the rattiest of trailers, Teeny Voix twisted in bed, half asleep. Dried tears coated her cheeks. A bloody dog collar wrapped her left wrist like a bracelet.

No unicorns or rainbows painted her dreams. No princess fairy tales awaited her awakening. Teeny's home, Trailer #2 (the actual number, not because it's the shittiest trailer) of Trail's End Mobile Home Park, was not the place miracles happened, it's where dreams died … most nights.

An only child, Teeny slept on the bottom bed of a bunk bed. Sissie, Teeny's momma, scouted yard sales after 4 p.m. when bone-tired owners surveyed unsold items, dreading toting tables, sleeper sofas, and mattresses to the garage. An ornery, train smoking, wrinkled roughneck allowed Sissie to haul off the hunk of junk bunks for free. So, boom … bunk bed.

An amber night light illuminated Teeny's room. A rummage-sale rescued suitcase sat next to Teeny's bed, packed, sorted, ready for departure.

Opie, her plush, pink-bellied opossum—a gift from Santa—stood guard in the corner, button eyes focused on her bunk. From Teeny's hand-me-down dresser, three plushy Pekin ducks scouted for enemy incursions. An obstacle course of Legos separated Teeny's bed from the door. Jumping jacks sprinkled her patchwork quilt. A mass of tight, curly, brown hair peeked from her covers.

Oafish footsteps approached her door … again. Teeny Voix stirred from troubled sleep. She listened and registered the next step, familiar with his routine. Teeny's eyes fused shut as she burritoed her blanket around her. Flick would not knock, never knocked—might wake Momma. The door *creeeeaaaaaaaak*ed open.

"Ya awake?" he whispered through busted lips, a reminder of his lost battle hours before.

Teeny remained casket-rigid. *Maybe he'll go away this time.* Flick took the first step toward her. "What the hell …?" Flick flopped assward as Legos spiked into his instep. The trailer trembled as the 375-pound, 6'4" man's butt bounced off the peeling linoleum.

"Damn, Teeny. Told ya to pick this shit up."

Opie watched, but remained still. Flick listened, no sounds. The rest of the house slept … or ignored.

Teeny's stepfather refocused, using the night light to spot Legos and map a path to the eight-year-old's bed. He stood and navigated past Lego landmines toward her.

"Teeny, ya awake?" Flick repeated.

Flick plopped on the edge of her bed. Jumping jacks, camouflaged by the quilt's patches, skewered into his blubbery buttocks. He jumped. *Thunk!* Banging his noggin on the top bed.

"What the hell, Teeny? What the hell?"

Teeny remained wedged into her blanket. *Wake up, Momma, wake up,* she prayed silently.

Flick gathered himself, then listened. No sounds. He brushed jumping jacks from the bed. He groped, testing for soft spots, then sat. His hand moved to Teeny's shoulder.

"What's the suitcase for? You aren't leaving." Teeny started multiplication tables in her head. 4x1=4, 4x2=8, 4x3=12. Anything, anything to distract her from impending horror.

Sounds of giggling children echoed through her room. "Hee, ha, hee, hee, ha, ha, ha … "

The giggles, new to Flick, but familiar from hours earlier to Teeny. The giggling originated from outside the trailer and inside her brain at once. Then the *tap, tap, tap,* on glass.

"What the … " Flick stomped toward the window. Another *tap,* followed by children's footsteps racing away.

Giggling again, outside, inside, in her head. "Hee, ha, hee, hee, ha, ha, ha … "

Teeny's door flew open as Flick raged toward the trailer's front door.

"Flick, what is it?" Sissie called from the other bedroom.

Teeny, unsure of why, climbed out of bed, following Flick, dodging Legos. Once outside, Teeny watched Flick disappear into the scrub trees. Cottony clouds coasted across the inky sky, parking in front of the crescent moon, smudging the night's light source.

No more giggles to guide her, Teeny shuffled across the grass, tender feet assaulted by sticker-burrs. The eight-year-old stopped to dig out assailants.

"Whoever you are, you got no business wakin' my family!" Flick screamed. "Get your ass out here … NOW!"

Porch lights flipped on behind Teeny.

"AHHHHHH!" Flick's scream pierced the night, rising over road racket. Dried bush branches splintered, signaling her stepfather's sprint toward her. Teeny heard a roar, *an impossible roar*.

Seconds later, Teeny's mom, her neighbor Pru, and half-asleep trailer dwellers poured into their postage-size lots. Each to bear witness.

Flick Hurt breached the tree-line as giant jaws clamped his skull and hoisted him into the air, shaking him as easily as goose down pillows. The 375-pound couch potato jiggled, fat bouncing. His shorts flopped lower, and his wife-beater T-shirt raised, exposing his swollen, hairy, purple, stretch-lined booze belly.

Flick's arm swung, trying—failing—to free himself, as jaws whip-snapped him forth, then back, releasing him before claws towed Flick Hurt into the scrub-woods. "Help, help me!"

Another roar reverberated the night, echoing—as if bouncing off the crescent moon. Neighbors quivered in unison. No heroes arose to rescue Flick Hurt. Each cowering witness greeted with the distant sound of the beast's deep gurgle, clamping jaws, crunching skull, and Flick's final whimper.

No one noted Teeny silently mouth, *"Thank you."*

2

Two weeks before

"Mornin', Teeny," Sissie Hurt said as her daughter yawn-stumbled into the trailer's galley kitchen, book bag in one hand, Opie, her stuffed opossum, in the other. An ancient runt terrier circled the girl's steps, yapping.

"Quiet, Peanut, Teeny's feedin' ya," Sissie said. "For God's sake, don't wake Flick." Teeny heaved her book bag and Opie onto the breakfast table, then ferreted under the sink, finding the white and black generic DOG FOOD bag. She poured a half cup into the runt's bowl and dutifully, by rote, filled his water bowl.

Peanut, the sawed-off terrier, struggled to chew the colossal kibble created for Mastiffs, Great Danes, and Dobermans. The dog's old, rotted teeth further complicated the task. Peanut held one kibble in his mouth, letting saliva soften it, before gnawing a corner.

Knock-off store-brand fruit cereal filled Teeny's bowl when she joined Opie at the table. No milk this morning. Just cereal. Teeny shrugged. It happens … bunches of times.

Flick's farting, moaning, belching, and burping in the trailer's *master suite* torpedoed the mood of the kitchen. Momma and daughter locked eyes. Teeny lowered her head.

"Sissie, SISSIE," Flick bellowed.

"Good morning, baby," Sissie answered.

"If I hear that yippie mutt again, I'll rip 'im in half."

"Okay, baby," Sissie answered.

"Get ya skinny ass in here with a cup of coffee."

"Sure, baby."

Sissie snatched the pot from the ancient Mr. Coffee—the only "Mr." in the house that performed a useful function—and filled Flick's mug, hustling out of the cluttered kitchen.

Teeny considered her uneaten breakfast, deciding to leave it so, as her mind returned to her letter. She snatched the letter from her book bag, hopped off her chair, blocked her mother's return path, and shoved the envelope forward as Sissie returned.

"Teeny, told ya yesterday, ain't gotta stamp."

Teeny's hand remained extended.

"Keep your arm hangin'. Still ain't got one."

"Mmmm."

"If you used your words, I'd borrow a stamp from my bossman."

Teeny's face wrinkled, lips twisting to one side.

"How long's the silent treatment lastin'?"

Teeny held up fingers.

Sissie counted. "Four."

The girl spread her hands further and further apart.

"For a long … " Teeny motioned to her momma's Timex. "Time. For a long time."

Teeny could say, "Until you ditch Flick, kick his useless butt out, until Flick stops … ," but she stayed silent.

"Your choice, but I ain't mailin' nothin' if you ain't askin' pretty. Made your lunch. It's in the fridge." Teeny's lunch contained two pieces of white bread slathered with mayo and one piece of meat, thin enough to watch *The Flintstones* through. Months earlier, when Teeny talked, she labeled the culinary calamity her "sad-wich." Most days, Teeny's lunch contained chips or pretzels from Sissie's cafeteria lunch the previous day. Sissie got a free lunch when she got in before 7:30 in the morning. Sissie's bossman promised—a gold star deal.

Some days an apple or grapes joined the sad-wich in the brown paper bag. If her momma caught Flick sneaking out of Teeny's room,

Sissie nabbed a muffin, cookies, or cupcakes, and swore Teeny to silence. Some days, Flick pilfered Teeny's lunch—before she left for school—and scarfed the good stuff.

He always left her sad-wich. Flick had plenty of time to snatch Teeny's treats, 'cause he wasn't working … again.

Sissie started, "I gotta leave early. Flick'll take you to school."

Teeny shook her head violently.

"Well, how you gettin' to school?"

Teeny motioned to the left, toward Pru's trailer. "You'll hop a ride with Pru again."

Two thumbs up. "Okay, but give her this for gas." Her momma palmed Teeny a coin, holding her daughter's hand a second longer than necessary. Teeny smiled appreciatively, knowing Sissie sacrificed her afternoon Coca-Cola quarter.

Teeny snatched her lunch, kissed her momma, grabbed one handful of dry cereal, pocketed the quarter, grabbed her book bag, tucked Opie and the letter inside, then blew kisses to Peanut before jetting out the trailer. Peanut yipped on Teeny's exit.

"Shut that damn dog up!" Flick yelled.

Teeny jumped the trailer steps, landing on the ground, facing the scrub and trash tree lot. She privately celebrated the coolness of her exit, then skipped toward Pru's trailer. Behind her, Teeny smelled singed grass and recognized the familiar sound, **Whiiish**.

Knowing before turning, Dex and Lexi Wexler, the twelve-year-old-terror twins, played nearby.

Both kneeling, Lexi sprayed her bottle of Aqua Net toward a fire ant mound. Dex held a stainless-steel long-handled lighter in place, creating a redneck blowtorch. From her spot, Teeny could not see ants shrivel like raisins and die, but she witnessed the sandy ant bed turn dark-chocolate brown. Distracted by the flames brought to life by the aerosol can, lighter, and unsupervised children, Teeny stood, mouth agape.

"Hey, Teeny," Dex said, waving with his non-lighter-wielding hand.

"Riding with Pru today?" Lexi asked without looking from the flame.

Teeny nodded. She counted seven reclamation projects parked near the Wexler's trailer, one hood up. A blush blue 60s Chevy Nova station wagon. A cooler of beer posted near the front bumper of a yellow Barracuda.

"Have a great day at school," the two yelled in unison. Teeny missed riding to school with the Wexlers, but they attended junior high now, not close to her elementary campus.

Teeny waved before hurrying to Pru's trailer and banging on the door. Pru was a teacher, but not Teeny's teacher. Still, she toted Teeny to school every few days.

"Be right out, Sunshine," Pru said through the trailer's window.

Pru's door squeaked open, and a Cinderella smile greeted Teeny. Teeny attempted to match Pru's radiance, but missing teeth turned Teeny's smile into a work in progress. The teacher shouldered her warped door shut, mussed the girl's hair, and ushered Teeny toward a rolling wreck. Pru greeted Dex and Lexi, still enraptured in pyromania. Neither acknowledged her presence.

Teeny skipped in front of Pru, beating her inside the teacher's poop-brown 1971 Ford Pinto. Feeling at home, Teeny placed her backpack between her feet.

"The Wexlers will burn my trailer to the ground one day."

Teeny nodded.

The drive started in silence. Teeny did not talk, and Pru proved quiet for a teacher. At the first stoplight, Pru turned on the radio, past Teeny's favorite, the Captain and Tenille's *Love Will Keep Us Together* and Frankie Valli's haunting *My Eyes Adore You* before settling on *Rhinestone Cowboy*.

Teeny approved, although Pru did not check. Minutes into the drive, Teeny spotted the billboard again. Looming letters over a rundown theme park. The local church-sponsored billboard announced, **Speak Out Against Child Abuse.**

From her seat, Teeny inspected the rundown theme park, Santa's Summer Village. A sign proclaimed the site as "Santa's Summer Residence."

Pru smiled. "Like Santa would pick that dump for his summer home." Pru pulled onto the interstate, directing the car toward the two's school. Five minutes later, the Pinto sputter-glided into the school parking lot and died before coasting into Pru's "Teacher of the Month" spot. The two gathered their belongings.

All at once, Teeny remembered her letter. After bounding out of the car, Teeny dashed to block Pru's entrance to school. First, Teeny presented Sissie's quarter.

"Sunshine, I told Sissie you don't have to pay me for gas. I'm driving here anyways."

Teeny's arm stayed out, quarter displayed. "Okay," she said. Pru took the quarter reluctantly. A millisecond later, Teeny presented her letter. "Sure, I'll mail it. Got stamps in my purse."

Teeny offered a huge grin and hugged Pru.

"Why thank you, Sunshine. You shined up my morning."

Teeny wondered what Pru would think if the teacher read the letter's plea.

3

Tuesday, May 4, 1976

Teeny noticed Mandy shoe-staring again. Never looking up at her tablemates. Every few weeks Mandy became interested in her sneakers. Some days, after Flick ... well ... when Sissie's not around ... umm, Teeny got real interested in her sneaks too.

The cafeteria bustled. Teeny opened her lunch, finding a whole brownie. Sissie probably caught Flick sneaking around a few nights earlier. Teeny scooted next to Mandy and tore off a third of the brownie. Mandy grinned ear to ear, more for the scooting, than the brownie.

Teeny's heart wanted to share more brownie with her classmates but lost the vote to her tummy. She scarfed the rest, while boy-sharks circled. Teeny burped brownie all afternoon, but two words bounced through her brain. WORTH IT!

Mandy seemed happier, briefly, but an hour after lunch she remembered her shoes needed watching. Brownies might make you unremember momentarily. But, baked goods do not solve the world's problems.

Teeny checked her book bag. Opie seemed fine, so she joined the class working multiplication tables. She worked diligently but trailed most kids. Teeny missed school every time Sissie ran away from Flick. Flick stunk at finding jobs but excelled at tracking down his meal ticket when Sissie escaped.

Teeny guessed the White Van People spotted Sissie and told Flick her location. Even Flick, the worst person Teeny knew, got scared when the white vans entered the mobile home park for a house call. Teeny wondered why others failed to recognize the white vans' monsters.

She concentrated on her multiplication tables, struggling with eights. 8x1=8, 8x2=16, 8x3=26, wait, that's not right.

Teeny remembered 8x8 because of the rhyme Mrs. Calderon taught her. 8x8 fell on the floor. When it got up, it was 64. After thirty minutes of multiplication worksheets, Mrs. Calderon had an announcement

"Today, we have a guest speaker; she's a volunteer from … " Mrs. Calderon turned to the guest speaker to answer.

"Oh, the agency doesn't matter, these beautiful children do," the volunteer offered.

The guest speaker shimmered. Older than Mrs. Calderon, but classically pretty. Her eyes twinkled. The sparkly woman's margarine yellow-blonde hair featured gray streaks wrestled into a loose bun. Much of the speaker's hair escaped cascading around her face, creating a heart shape.

Teeny felt the margarine-haired woman's eyes lock on her, making Teeny warm.

"And what's your name again?" asked Mrs. Calderon.

The speaker answered. "I'm Ms., well Mrs., ahh, I see someone's hand up." The class turned to Theodore, nicknamed by classmates "Tinkle" or "Tink." The boy jammed together his legs. "Why, yes, Theodore?"

"Tink, just go to the bathroom," Mrs. Calderon said. Tink danced the *I gotta tinkle two-step*, hand jammed between his legs holding 'it' tight, upon exit.

"What a pleasant start," the sparkly speaker said. Her twinkling eyes returned to Teeny. "I'm here to address a sensitive subject. Child abuse." Her eyes dimmed. "More importantly, how to stop child abuse. Children, explain child abuse to me."

Lester raised his hand. "When adults hit ya. So as it leaves marks on ya. Like a black eye or busted lip."

"Yes, Lester, that's definitely child abuse. Anyone else?" Again, the guest speaker turned to Teeny. "How about you, Teeny?"

"Oh, Teeny doesn't talk," said Mrs. Calderon.

"Doesn't she?" The speaker raised her eyebrows.

From the back of the room, Teeny's friend Riley yelled. "Leavin' kids alone without supper."

"Yes, Riley, excellent. But back to you, Teeny?" Teeny stared at the guest speaker, horrified. The child, eyes big as Texas, dropped her head, before competing with Mandy in the shoe-staring contest.

Mrs. Calderon reiterated. "Look, Teeny doesn't talk."

"Are you sure?" The speaker addressed Teeny, not Mrs. Calderon.

Teeny covered her ears, but failed to muffle the woman's voice. "Not even if a friend's in trouble, Teeny?" The volunteer's head swiveled to Mandy before returning to Teeny. "Not even then?"

Teeny's world imploded. She shook, sweat gathered above her lip. Her eyes begged the sparkly woman to stop. The woman breathed deeply, turning back toward the class, disappointment obvious. "Let's talk about spotting child abuse ... "

Teeny failed to remember everything the twinkly woman said, but she mentioned poor concentration, getting scared lots, nightmares, kids wearing long clothes even in the summer, bed wetting. The margarine-haired woman failed to mention staring at your shoes.

"Finally, and most importantly, what can you do to stop child abuse?"

Riley offered, "Tell someone, like a teacher ... "

"Yes, Riley, who else?"

"Your kinfolks or a poe-lease man," another child offered.

"Perfect." The volunteer smiled—and Teeny felt surrounded by her gaze. Relief showered over Teeny when the woman thanked everyone and opened a shoe box containing homemade white frosting cookies. The boys gobbled them. Teeny, still brownie-bloated, tore a page from her coloring book, wrapped the treat and placed it inside her desk for safekeeping.

The volunteer hovered while the children exited. Teeny overheard Mrs. Calderon remark, "I never got your name." The margarine-haired woman ignored Mrs. Calderon, but the teacher continued. "And how did you know each child's name?"

As Teeny scuttled out, avoiding contact, the sparkly woman followed. Over her shoulder, the tiny girl heard, "Teeny, I apologize. I can't do this alone. I need your help … "

Teeny raced away, running from the words.

4

9:45 p.m., that evening

Teeny watched Tex Wexler, Lexi's and Dex's dad, guide the twins into the woods, on another late-night expedition. The neighbor in Trailer #6 hickory-smoked a pork butt outside, and the scent sauntered through the oppressive evening air. Mosquitoes flit through the humidity hunting blood donors.

Sissie worked her second job, so only Teeny and Flick occupied the trailer. Pru entertained her boyfriend this evening, or Teeny would have watched TV at the teacher's trailer. As sun surrendered sky to stars, Teeny and Opie hid in the heights of the magnolia tree that abutted her momma's trailer. Teeny's T-shirt and pajama bottoms stuck to her, skin moistened by humidity. Teeny suffered sticky clothes and vampiring mosquitoes, both offering less concern than sharing the trailer with Flick.

Magnolia trees long ago became the girl's favorite. Once on TV, Teeny oohed and aahed over a Chinese beauty wearing a white magnolia in her hair. So Teeny decided her trailer's magnolia tree connected her to the greater world. The tree offered hope Teeny could visit China ... one day ... without Flick.

To Teeny, magnolia flowers smelled of sweet candy swirled with lemonade. Still, the magnolia's scent paled in comparison to the tree's best trait. Magnolias featured huge, waxy, dark-green leaves, perfect for an eight-year-old who doesn't want to be found, especially after dark.

Magnolias offer limbs aplenty, easy to climb … for children.

Even better, the higher you climb the thinner and more tender the branches become. Midway up—and under stress—the branches snap easily, like bird bone. Adults—especially bulbous, buttcrack scratching, jobless men—cannot climb after you. To date, Flick failed to find Teeny's hiding spot. The child prayed Flick's ignorance continued.

From her treetop, Teeny spotted a petite figure emerge from the lot of trash trees next to the trailer park. Teeny spied the figure inching toward the nearest trailer.

Teeny squinted, divining the shadow figure's female form. Even from her vantage point, Teeny understood the woman's incongruency with the surroundings. Teeny turned to check. Opie, her plush opossum, offered no opinion. The shadow slunk from her spot to the next trailer. After pausing two minutes, the woman tiptoed closer to Teeny's hiding tree.

The silent girl's eyes remained riveted to the female's movements. The shadow moved again, this time behind Pru's Ford Pinto, within ten yards of Teeny's front door. The figure stood and surveyed her surroundings. A light from Pru's trailer window lit the margarine-haired woman's face. The woman wore black, shoes to toboggan. Still, her distinctive hair escaped her hat. Relief rolled through Teeny's body.

Then Teeny heard the laughing, or, more so, children's giggling for the first time, originating from the trailer park's trash tree lot. Giggling reverberated around her brain and everywhere. "Hee, ha, hee, hee, ha, ha, ha … " The woman turned, shushing the children in the trees. Teeny wondered why the volunteer speaker brought children near Flick.

The crushing of shell and gravel under tires tore Teeny's attention from the woman. The girl's first thought, *Thank God. Momma's home.*

Teeny's emotions morphed from disappointment to terror when she identified the vehicle negotiating the drive to Trail's End Mobile

Home Park. Teeny's inner voice repeated, *Do not scream, do not scream.*

Teeny turned to Opie in horror as the margarine-haired woman hunkered behind Pru's Pinto. On cue, summoned by approaching evil, Flick emerged from the trailer, stained T-shirt, cutoff blue jeans, hairy buttcrack on display, revolver gripped in his hand.

Peanut circled Flick's heels, yipping at the approaching white van. Flick kicked Peanut, who yelped before retreating under the trailer, growling back from a safe distance. As the van rolled to park, Peanut scampered off to do number two.

Teeny turned back to the margarine-haired woman, hiding in shadows. Retreat no longer an option, the woman pasted herself to Pru's Pinto.

The **thunk** of three slamming doors twisted Teeny toward the White Van People. A behemoth wearing tight jeans and tighter T-shirt stood back, allowing the other two men to advance. A slender, Greyhound-looking man in nuthugger running shorts and tank top followed the scariest of the three, a Hawaiian-shirted man.

The man appeared handsome, but Teeny detected the sticky-icky underneath. White linen shorts and huarache sandals, more suited for a yacht deck than a trailer park social visit, completed his ensemble. Flick Hurt, a massive man, shuddered when the Hawaiian-shirted haole hailed, "Evening, Flickster."

The man seemed as out of place as the margarine-haired woman hiding behind Pru's Pinto. The van's threesome circled Teeny's stepfather.

The man laughed. "Ahhh … you brought a gun. How sweet."

"Look, Vance."

"People who abuse my hospitality use my last name."

"Mr. White, still gonna get you the … "

"Flick-baby, stop mouthing about money you ain't got."

"Well, it's just … well …"

Vance raised his hand, stopping the babble.

"I'm not here for the money. That ship left port, Flickirino."

"But—" Flick offered.

"Besides, I assumed you would never come up with the money. I'm here for your daughter. That's our deal."

From her magnolia tree, a squeak squirted out of Teeny.

5

Responding to her squeak, the four men surveyed their surroundings for a sixty count. Teeny mashed herself to the magnolia. The margarine-haired woman rose behind Pru's car, but not enough for Vance's crew to see. The woman shook her head toward Teeny, signaling the girl to stay silent.

"But she's not even my kid, she's—"

"Ohh Flick-honey … that's not what you implied when you asked for credit to ahh … rendezvous with our last crop of … well—"

"Sure, sorry. But she ain't my kid. Besides, I don't know where Teeny runned off."

"'Ran off' is proper English, Flickipoo." Vance turned to the Greyhound man. "Search the trailer."

The Greyhound man in nuthugger shorts considered Flick, with obvious disgust, then strolled inside followed by the lumbering behemoth. Flick towered over the sticky-icky man, but, even from Teeny's vantage point, the Hawaiian shirt-clad man radiated threat.

"Flickmeister … "

"Yes, Mr. White."

"If you're not using the gun, return it to your predictable hiding spot, behind the saltines. While inside your … castle, make a tuna fish sandwich. Bring it to me."

"I don't think we got any—"

"Make a tuna fish sandwich, you lazy, lecherous Neanderthal."

"Yes, sir."

The trailer shimmied under the weight of the behemoth rifling through each room. Next, sounds of Flick bungling about the kitchen.

The Hawaiian-shirted man reclined against the porch railing. Peanut yipped from the trailer's underbelly. "I hear you, puppy. Come greet your uncle," the man paused, as if searching for his own name, "Vance."

Teeny prayed Peanut ignored the man's prod. Vance White's companions emerged and shrugged. "Search the property," he ordered. The two men prowled the trailer park grounds, even behind Pru's car. Teeny guessed the margarine-haired woman slid under Pru's Pinto or snuck away.

Peanut growled from the shadows, but did not approach Vance. *That's my boy,* Teeny thought.

The men returned as Flick exited the trailer, tuna fish sandwich in hand. Teeny's stepfather passed the sandwich to Mr. White.

"Disgusting."

"I thought you wanted to eat—"

"No, life's too short to eat food from a can, Flickarillo."

"Okay," said Flick, confused.

"What do you know about your dog?"

"Sorry?"

"Your dog, idiot," Vance enunciated.

"Fucking mutt."

"Not so. Gangly, but full-bred, a direct descendent of the Mini Foxie from Australia. They arrived with the First Fleet in Australia in 1788— after Australia became a penal colony for the Brits. Anyway, the Mini Foxie worked as ship ratters. Ahh, such spirited dogs." Vance White paused, seemingly lost in nostalgia.

"Like Fox Terriers?" Flick asked.

Vance looked annoyed. "Not as inbred. The Foxie proved pure of purpose, perfect seadog." Vance paused before ending with flourish, "A sailor's friend."

Teeny watched Peanut circle closer to the four men but remain at shadow's edge.

"You talk like you were there," Flick said.

Vance chuckled at the ridiculousness of the statement, before raising his hand again to hush Flick. "As seadogs, they ate the day's catch, shrimp, crab, and tuna. Seafood, even this canned crap, irresistible to a Foxie." He dropped the sandwich at his feet.

Peanut stepped into the light tentatively, distrustfully at first, until the siren smell of tuna overcame him. Peanut, not needing to chew, devoured half the sandwich in one bite. Peanut's final meal.

Vance White's leg rose swiftly, slamming his sandal into the dog's torso. A crunching sound ravaged Teeny's ears. Next, a soft, pained whimper escaped Peanut before Vance's huaraches rose again and pummeled Peanut's skull.

His actions, viper quick, practiced, precise, perfected. The animal died quickly, without seeing the final sandal drop. Flick's nervous eyes skittered from Vance White to poor Peanut, back to Vance.

Every ounce of Teeny's strength poured through her, forcing her to remain still. She hugged the magnolia as tears streamed from her face.

"Well, okay," Vance said cheerfully. "My regards to the wife. I'll return for her daughter in three days."

"But … "

"Here're your options. I'll return when your wife's working. One of you must work, huh." Vance said, not hiding disgust. "You'll hand the girl over to me, tell everyone the girl ran away. Or … " Vance White waited.

No one spoke.

"I'll castrate you, then filet your wife, while you watch. I'll take the girl, either way. You're doing your wife a favor."

Flick nodded.

"Your stepdaughter interests me; from what I've heard, she ahh … " Vance paused, shook his head, before redirecting his conversation. "Well, time to go. I assume we've reached an agreement."

Silence.

Vance's leg swung from the ground into Flick Hurt's groin. Flick crumpled in pain. In one motion, Vance's left hand pushed Flick's head down while raising his knee. The knee crashed into Flick's teeth. Flick flopped backward, blood spraying from his mouth.

"So, then," Vance paused to stretch. "Full understanding."

Flick nodded.

"Good for you, Flick-to-m'-lou."

Vance White spun to leave, offering relief to the small tree-bound girl.

As he opened the van door, a soft night wind trickled through. The breeze swept low, leaves and dust twisted on the ground. Teeny noted the most peculiar thing. Vance White sniffed the air like a connoisseur. "Hmm … " Vance White stopped in place. "Anyone else catch that?" He sniffed again, relishing the moment. Vance's head snapped toward Pru's Pinto.

"Impossible, she hasn't stuck her head out in … "

The margarine-haired woman rolled from under Pru's car, stood, paused, shook her head in Opie's and Teeny's direction, before sprinting toward the trash tree lot.

6

The woman's pause cost her. An expensive second to send the girl a signal. Stay quiet. Not a peep—no matter what.

Teeny stared down, understanding her and Opie's role. Witnesses. As the woman raced away, the Hawaiian-shirted man said casually, "Do catch her before she gets to the trees."

Like a dog, released from "STAY," the Greyhound-built man in nuthugger running shorts bolted. The lumbering behemoth reacted a second later but found himself yards behind his compatriot. The margarine-haired woman's speed surprised Teeny, but she lost time clocking her pursuers over her shoulder. The Greyhound covered yards with each footfall.

Almost there, *hurry, hurry, hurry,* Teeny screamed in her brain, as the woman closed on the wooded lot. Feet short of her goal, the Greyhound man tackled, spun, then stood over the margarine-haired woman in one practiced, predatorial motion.

The lean man's foot pinned her throat until the behemoth arrived. The behemoth hoisted her, bent her arm behind her back, while covering her mouth with a hulking hand. He guided the woman, whose feet barely touched the ground, toward Flick and Mr. White. In her too-brief life, Teeny relived the surgical capture hundreds of times in nightmares.

The behemoth approached, delivering the woman like an offering. The Hawaiian-shirted man bowed overdramatically. "To what do we owe the pleasure?"

The woman jerked and twisted, but failed to wiggle from her captor.

Vance looked around, considering each trailer, "No need to cover her mouth. She won't scream."

Everyone paused, but the behemoth's mitt still muzzled the woman's mouth, doubting Vance's directive.

"We live by mandates, she and I. She chose to operate in the gray of her directive tonight. Still, she understands … if she screams," he paused, placing his face directly in front of hers, "every soul that exits their trailer dies tonight."

The woman nodded before the behemoth obliged. Vance considered her, "Been a while."

The woman stayed silent.

"I'm filing through memories. You were never much of a runner."

Vance smiled. "Next time, pump your arms; that helps." He jogged in place, swinging his arms in demonstration. "More momentum."

The woman shook her head.

"But, overall, great form for someone of your advanced age."

Nothing from the woman.

"A little out of your depth. This isn't in your job description. Quite a conundrum."

Teeny grasped, despite his bravado, the wolf in Hawaiian apparel lost a hint of his cockiness. The woman's appearance shook him.

"I can't execute you, of course."

He looked at his minions. "There are rules," he sighed, "even for me." Vance seemed trapped in the past, reveling in it, enjoying each victory, then despising each loss. He shook his head, turned back, embracing his time on stage. "But still, the fun we can have together, old girl."

Vance considered the night sky, the stars, the droning of the interstate. Vance paused as clouds drifted past the moon, brightening the sky, lighting the scene, resetting the view.

Vance considered Teeny's magnolia, focusing on a spot inches from her. Teeny's breath seized in her throat. The Hawaiian-shirted hyena studied the tree. Teeny stared back as Vance stood silently, deep in observation.

"Hmm," he sounded. The next cloud bank drifted in front of the moon, and the moment passed. Darkness consumed Trail's End Mobile Home Park.

Vance, obviously tired of the situation, ordered, "Toss her inside."

The behemoth guided the woman toward the white van. The Greyhound stayed with Vance.

"Well, see you soon, Tricky-Flicky," Vance said before turning to leave.

The white van backed onto the grass and dipped into the ditch. The van tires spun in place, squealing, struggling to escape the ditch's grasp, spitting grass. Finally, the van popped forward as the tires gripped.

Flick lifted Peanut, and turned toward the wooded lot. He stopped short of the brush and pitched Peanut's body. The carcass crashed through dead branches, wild azaleas, and privets before bouncing off hardened dirt. Flick returned, trudging toward the trailer.

Flick stopped under the magnolia, his head rotated, considering each trailer, each hiding spot, looking for her. Only after Flick rumbled through bedrooms, searching for her, quit, then collapsed in front of the TV, did Teeny and Opie descend from her magnolia. She and Opie traveled through the clumpy grass, avoiding sticker burrs. She paused at the lot's edge. Nothing, no voices, giggles, or movement.

Opie in tow, Teeny pushed past the obstacles to find Peanut's broken corpse. She kneeled, committing to stay strong for Peanut. The little girl removed her dog's collar, wrapping it around her wrist. She prayed over Peanut, hoping he understood she yearned for a proper service and burial. For now, she covered him in pine straw, dead leaves, and loose dirt. Teeny, dirt under her fingernails, wiped tears from her cheeks before comforting Opie.

After completing the ad hoc funeral, Teeny tiptoed to her tree. She gripped the first limb, tugging her and Opie up to their spot and crying herself to sleep. An hour later, a car expertly traversing the potholed drive woke Teeny. *Momma*, she thought.

Teeny ached to mourn Peanut, but understood packing—and convincing Sissie to pack—came first. She hopped from her magnolia, dropped Opie, and raced to her momma, hugging, holding, squeezing her, allowing a moment of relief, before she tried to explain.

"Love you too, Teeny," Sissie said.

Teeny released Sissie, the girl's arms twisting, turning, miming, imploring, and executing advanced charades. Sissie watched for a full minute before begging, "Not tonight, Teeny, I'm whupped. Let's try in the mornin'."

Sissie turned. Taking bags of groceries from her car, she handed one to Teeny, then guided the miming girl to the trailer.

7

4:45 a.m., May 5, 1976

Police detective Pedro "Paunch" Perez's sedan bumped down the gravel, shell, and potholed road twenty minutes after the black and whites arrived. Every porch light—some amber, some white, some yellow—glowed. Orbiting red and blue bounced off moldy trailer siding mixing with shadows, offering optic overload. Most residents of Trail's End Mobile Home Park gawked from their porch or spoke to the badges already on the scene.

Paunch paused to study the strain, terror, and panic highlighting each resident's expression. The detective's duties demanded he witness mankind's worst offerings. Still, Paunch never fielded a call like the one taking him to this location.

Paunch mentally noted each resident, cataloging them, per his practice, but his attention got stuck on one family. A mechanic, covered in oil and grease—using a hand lamp hooked to the hood latch of a beefy Plymouth Barracuda—worked on an engine, pretending not to notice. His actions communicated, maybe too clearly, *Nothing over here to see, folks; turn your attention back to the main attraction.*

Paunch checked his watch, not 5 a.m. Strange time to tinker under a hood. The mechanic's boy and girl, possibly twins, studied the proceeding, but not like other residents. The boy and girl sprawled on the hood of a blush blue Chevy Nova wagon, blanket under them, sharing a bag of Ruffles and French Onion Dip, watching the proceedings like a Saturday night Godzilla marathon. *Interesting*, thought Paunch. *Must meet that family.*

Paunch manned the graveyard shift alone, between partners. Or, more so, abandoned again. His last three partners retired or asked for reassignment. Most of the force treated the 5'2" potbellied police detective like a leper with a raging case of gonorrhea. Detectives considered partnering with Paunch or offering the slightest courtesy political hara-kiri. The portly detective breathed deeply, prying himself out of his vehicle into the maelstrom. A white, short-sleeve, too-taut, grease stained, button-down shirt struggled to cover his expanding frame. A cheap, polyester clip-on tie announced his divorce, even to the uninformed.

Dozens of voices added to the overload.

Paunch overheard the word, "Screaming." Pretty standard for crime-scene investigations. "Sissie and her girl split town." Not unusual. Paunch worked dozens of cases where witnesses got scarce.

"Animal attack." Paunch chuckled at those two words strung together. Doubtful. Few surviving southeast Texas beasts presented the heft or hutzpah to take down humans. Coyotes avoided mankind; bobcats maxed out at forty pounds.

Alligator? Paunch scanned the surroundings, ditches sure, but no ponds, lakes, creeks, or bayous abutted the trailer park. Not a gator. Then someone spoke the impossible into being. "Hank heard it roar." There's a new one. Paunch spun, spotting a spark plug of a woman, hair set in rollers, wearing an inappropriately-revealing night shirt. His ears shut out the surrounding soundtrack and calibrated to her voice. Again, "Roar."

Cooper, the police chief's son-in-law and most recent promotion, scrutinized Paunch, head to belly, and rolled his eyes. The new sergeant strutted to Paunch. "Dressing for the ball today, 'ey Paunch?"

Paunch ignored the jab. "What da we got?"

"Definitely an animal attack. Most gruesome thing I ever saw."

In your 15 months on the beat, Paunch squeezed down. He asked instead, "Type of animal?"

"The current guess, cougar. It's the only big cat around. Several people heard it roar."

"Wrong," said Paunch, without explaining.

"What?"

"I went to University of Houston."

"So?"

"The school's mascot is the cougar. So, a professor, for grins, lectured on big cats and their differences."

"Your point."

"Big cats, lions, tigers, leopards, and jaguars roar."

"And."

"Smaller cats can't."

Cooper looked confused.

"Cougars can't roar, jackass."

Cooper stared, stunned, angered. "You don't need to be pissing on your buddies."

"You're not my buddy, will never be my buddy. My buddies deserted me after the divorce. For the record, I ain't shopping at the station for new ones." Paunch shrugged. "Coop, if your father-in-law could fire me, he would. She won't let him. So, there's that at least."

"You smug … "

"Let's admit our mutual disdain and get to the case. A man died. But it wasn't a cougar."

"Well, according to everyone here. Something roared."

"Body still here?"

"Yea, no one's touched it."

"Give me the two-bit tour," Paunch said.

Coop strutted toward a grouping of trash trees. "The vic is Flick Hurt. Real asswipe. No job. Sponged off his wife." Cooper checked his notes, then continued. "Sissie. Sissie's gotta daughter, everyone calls the girl," glancing at the pad again, "Teeny. Different last name. Voix. According to neighbors, Sissie worked two, sometimes three, jobs, to support fatass."

Coop and Paunch pushed past the brush. Once they reached Flick's body, Paunch asked, "Vic have a record?"

"According to Fraley, Flick beat child molestation charges around '71 and again in '73."

"Fraley's here?"

"Yeah. Poking around the vic's trailer. Fraley remembered Flick's indictment. Someone misplaced evidence both times. Fatass got a free pass."

"Well, 'til today," Paunch said.

Flick Hurt's corpse rested against a pine, tossed aside. An afterthought. Paunch approached the dead man, skull perforated with teeth marks; a claw mark tore into his midsection.

"Weird," said Paunch.

"What?"

"Whatever killed the schmuck, it … a … didn't eat him."

"Child molester probably tasted nasty."

Paunch laughed, before corralling himself. Not the place. Coop smirked, pleased with his joke, then said, "Probably something scared it off."

Paunch considered the statement proof of Coop's ignoramus status.

Coop read Paunch's face. "What, someone coulda fired off a shotgun."

"Any witnesses say they fired a weapon?" asked Paunch, turning from the body toward Coop.

"Nope."

"Whatever did this," Paunch's hand waved toward Flick's carcass, "ain't scared of anything not toting a shotgun."

"Positive it's not a cougar?"

"Not a cougar, wolf, alligator, bobcat, nothing from around here."

"Okay, what was it?" The crack of snapping, dead tree branches shook the two officers. Both jumped at the sound, followed by a shuffling of feet to hide the fact.

"A bear," Fraley stated, as he stepped into the clearing.

"Bullshit, no bears in Texas," said Coop.

"Coop, try keeping your mouth shut … sometimes. Test run the concept. That way you wouldn't be wrong all the damn time."

"Screw you, Fraley."

"There ARE bears in West Texas, black bears, mostly in the Chisos and Guadalupe Mountains."

"So, a black bear killed him." said Coop.

"Coop, again, I'm begging you. No, a black bear didn't kill him. But a bear did."

"How do you know that?" Coop pressed.

"Because, boys, I'm a twice divorced, no girlfriend, pickup-driving redneck who blows his paychecks big game hunting in Alaska."

"Explain away, Fraley," said Paunch.

"West Texas is an eight-hour drive. Also, black bears knock things down, take a bite'r two off the arms or legs, then go for the neck or head. There're claw marks, but only a few. No neck wound."

"And?" pushed Paunch.

"Texas bears weigh 200-300 lbs. Getta 'bout 5 or 6 feet tall. A black bear could take out shit-for-brains over there, no sweat." Fraley stared at Flick Hurt's corpse. "But … not like this. "

Coop decided to add value. "Witnesses claim whatever killed fatass lifted him two or three feet off the ground."

"Bullshit," said Paunch.

When Paunch turned back to Fraley, the investigator's eyes remained locked on Flick Hurt's crumpled body, like he needed to reconfirm his opinion. Fraley's lips pressed together, his brow wrinkled as his head ticked back and forth.

Paunch studied Fraley, before asking, "What's wrong?"

Fraley emerged from his thoughts. "Boys, you're gonna think I'm an idiot."

"Too late," Coop said.

Fraley did not respond to Coop, but continued. "I thought they were exaggerating. The witnesses." His eyes turned from Flick to Paunch. "Traumatized people say crazy shit." He paused. "But these witnesses, especially that teacher chick, seemed pretty composed, considering. More importantly, every statement aligns."

"Okay," Paunch said.

"Still, I'm thinking bullshit. Nothing in Texas could toss a vic of his size around. Oh, and I'd be correct. But then I examine Flick here." Fraley stops. He bends down near the carcass and points to the teeth marks in Flick's scalp Paunch examined earlier. "Something huge bit this guy around the noggin."

Paunch stooped beside Fraley.

"Want to know something hilarious?" Fraley continued.

"Sure."

"That's how bears kill seals. Bear waits on an ice pack for a seal to come up for air. Seal pops up, bear bites it around the head, lightning quick. Over in seconds."

"No seals around here," said Paunch.

"Or ice packs, for that matter," adds Coop.

Fraley nodded. "No shit."

"But?" pushed Paunch.

"But … only a few bears kill that way," Fraley answered. "The big Kodiaks."

"Funny," Paunch said.

"And polar bears," Fraley tossed in.

"BULL-SHIT," said Coop.

"Yeah, I thought so too. Most of me still does." Fraley's head rotated from the body to a brush trail, then back. He put a hand on his knee, pushing himself upward.

"Follow me," said Fraley, waving as he turned. He pushed through bushes to a muddy trail.

"What the hell's that?" asks Paunch.

"Bear print," stated Fraley, now shaken. "There's more. Few feet up."

Fraley led Coop and Paunch to the next print. He stood as Paunch and Coop kneeled. A minute later, Paunch rose with some effort.

"I'm going to need a second opinion," said Paunch.

"I'd like that too. Because I feel nuts for—"

"Spit it out," Paunch said.

"Usually, only aggressive, young, male bears hunt humans. Even that's rare. Mature bears seldom interest themselves in human prey."

"Okay."

"This," Fraley pointed to the paw, "is a mature bear, male for sure."

"Since we're talking fantasy, keep talking," said Paunch.

"I've seen bear tracks. Never one this big. Never."

"And?" Paunch asked.

"I'm looking at this print, thinking I'm an idiot. But I see the next paw print, then the next." He pointed. "They're a ways apart."

"What the hell are you saying?"

"The bear was 11-, 12-, hell, 13-feet tall."

"Impossible."

"Yep." Fraley answered. He breathed out, his head ticking back and forth again.

Paunch studied him. He recognized Fraley's stance, not from his years as a detective, but from his too-brief stint as a father. Fraley was stalling.

"Something else?" Paunch asked.

Fraley nodded.

"Show me."

Fraley shook his head.

"Fraley, I need you to show me."

Fraley replanted his feet. Paunch understood Fraley's body involuntarily reacted while his brain calculated scenario after scenario. Paunch walked to Fraley. The top of Paunch's head, inches below Fraley's chin. Paunch put his hands on Fraley's shoulders, looking up, offering comfort.

The big game hunter, force veteran, and the most experienced crime scene investigator in five counties failed to return Paunch's stare. Fraley shuddered.

Paunch whispered, "Frales, it's okay." He comforted his former friend. Fraley glanced at Paunch before his eyes skittered away.

Regret coated the taller man's face. "Sorry, after your divorce, I … ahh, wasn't much of a … "

"Let's address that another time, Frales. I need you to show me."

Fraley nodded. He turned, following the bear's tracks for thirty yards.

Paunch crunched information in his head. In thirty years, Fraley, the ice-cold professional, found dismembered bodies, dead children, bloated three-week-old corpses. Never once, in Paunch's memory, did Fraley offer an ounce of emotion, repulsion, or fear. Paunch braced himself for what lay ahead.

Lost in his thoughts, Paunch bumped Fraley when the investigator stopped. No dead children, no ripe corpses, nothing. Paunch and Coop studied the scene, confused.

"I don't get it," Coop said.

Fraley, who earlier crushed Coop for opening his mouth, stayed quiet. Fraley raised an eyebrow.

"What?" Paunch asked.

"The trail ends," said Fraley, pointing to the final bear print.

"There has to be—" Paunch started.

"Nope, I looked. Everywhere."

"A 12-foot bear showed up in Southeast Texas, killed a man, and, ahh, vanished into thin air?"

Fraley concentrated on the honks, roars, and bumps of the interstate, noting each cirrus cloud decorating the sky, even embracing the stench of car exhaust, delaying his answer. Until he couldn't.

Fraley nodded.

8

November 19, 2026, MD Anderson Cancer Center, Houston, Texas
Heels click-clacked confidently on the floor in a tight, rhythmic pattern. Val, petite, a bit too lean, marched toward her destination when the purple-scrub attired nurse recognized her. The nurse—rocking a power ponytail—swiveled, surveying coworkers, expecting someone else, everyone else, to recognize the legend walking toward her. Tears leaked from the nurse's eyes.

"It's you," the young nurse gushed toward Val. The name sewed on the young nurse's purple scrubs identified her as Chelsea Lance.

"Sorry?" Val answered.

"It's really you," Chelsea grabbed Val's stringy, muscled arm, stopping the petite woman in the hospital hall. The nurse spun around, looking, begging, for reinforcements. "It's her, it's really … " The nurse's shift captain hustled over.

Val received this greeting before, seldom, but it happened. Most kids failed to recognize her after hurdling into adulthood. Val, like Easter egg hunts, waiting up for Santa, and Halloween's scariest stories, faded over time into the outer recesses of memory. Still, occasionally, adults remembered.

Val paused, shifted stance, adjusting to the situation.

"This is her?" the shift captain asked.

The nurse, mascara running, snot bubbles forming, nodded; her verbal skill lost in emotion. Sobbing now offered the power-ponytailed nurse's only communication channel.

"She talks about you like a superhero, reads every news clipping," the shift captain continued.

Val stared at her stilettos, before glancing toward Dr. Arthur's receptionist, steps away.

"Wait," the shift captain asked, catching the interaction. "Why are you here?"

Recognizing Val, Dr. Arthur's receptionist clunked a clipboard on the counter. The sound rattled through the hall.

"Oh," the shift captain said. A thundercloud passed over her face. Chelsea shook in reaction to the clues.

Val placed her hand on the young nurse's shoulder, gripped, and turned to walk away. Not satisfied with the goodbye, Chelsea chased Val and swallowed the tiny woman in an all-encompassing embrace. The sobs continued, more pronounced now, but for a different reason.

Val's gaze swung to the shift captain, then the receptionist, uncomfortable with unwanted attention. Chelsea sobbed on her shoulder.

The shift captain dislodged the young nurse from Val, with, "There, there sweetie, it's okay, baby. Woman's got an appointment, give her space, Chelsea." Val cleared her throat, adjusted her blazer, one shoulder damp with tears and snot, and finished her walk to the receptionist, who offered tissues.

Val nodded thanks, wiped her coat, and tossed the snotty tissues trashward. She grabbed the clipboard, turned toward the seating area, when Dr. Arthur's receptionist asked, "What's that about?"

Val shrugged, selected her usual chair, and sat to complete her test paperwork.

·   ·   ·

That evening

"Hello, idiot," April said, opening the door, little-black-dressed-to-perfection.

"Hey, brat," Harold countered, but the words got gluey in his mouth.

A script forged over decades failed him for the first time. Harold, forced by their book club, wine club, country-club tennis-doubles partners' mothers into the role of April's babysitter in childhood, caught hints of Lancôme Poeme, as April Andrews, no longer a child, exited her apartment.

"Something wrong, Harold?" April asked. "Off your game?"

Since April's birth, Harold's mother, Eunice, chose this girl as the ideal daughter-in-law—ensuring April Andrews represented everything Harold did not want. "Thinking about a case," he said.

"Em, hmm," she countered. She turned and locked her door, and he found himself staring at her bare back. He shook his head, righted himself, holding out his arm as he directed her to his midnight-blue Porsche 911.

"How was NYU?" Harold asked.

"Brutal, incredible. Limited mom-meddling. So … perfect."

He studied each softly sculpted muscle in her legs as she flowed into the Porshe's leather seat. She grinned, catching him. "Been a while," she said.

He stressed, "Didn't need a date for this, or I'd of already … "

"Happy to see you too, idiot."

He walked around, opened the driver's side, muttered to himself, before sliding in and starting the sports car. He backed out before reengaging the conversation. Distracting himself, even for a second, seemed important.

"How long's it been … since," he pointed from her to him.

"My eighteenth birthday. Water-skiing trip, after your senior year of college, but before your deployment."

Harold remembered that trip, her water skiing … the accident. *New subject*, his brain begged. "You've been back in town?" he led.

"Five minutes before your mom-ster bullied and my mom-zilla bribed me to set up this date."

The bribe comment knifed Harold, clawing old wounds; he tried to fight the resentment—battling to stay with April—but lost. Harold's internal protector stepped forward, firing the only weapon in his arsenal to survive this situation, to protect himself. **Harold Edgard Reginald Oxford the Seventh** or just **H7**, now occupied the car with April.

H7's privileged asshole-face, THE FACE, the personality, the avatar mandated to survive Oxford family expectations and more importantly to hide **THE SECRET,** curled his lips, flared his nostrils, narrowed his eyes, and lowered his eyebrows. **H7's** eyes riveted to the route. Conversation concluded.

In the passenger seat, April studied Harold, accepting blame for her clumsy words. She alone recognized THE FACE, remembered the timing, if not understanding the cause of H7's origin. Only she saw past the mask. April rallied to rescue the evening she unintentionally savaged. "Sorry, just a joke, idiot."

Too late. Her former protector, Harold, checked out, left the building, went for ice cream. By her own hand, or words, she must now survive the evening with her least favorite person, H7.

•   •   •

Banquet Tent, outside of Houston's Youth Museum

H7's metal banquet chair leaned back precariously. The back two chair legs teetered on the ground, the front two legs returned to airborne, as H7 flirted with tumbling into the row behind him. Better to take a peek at Tamara, the new forensics tech, or, honestly, anyone not bribed to attend the event by their moms.

"She's cute, I could wingman, if you wanted," April offered.

"Funny you think I need one."

"Harold, stop leaning back like a seventh grader in study hall. I'll be embarrassed when you fall."

H7's chair's front two legs touched the ground; he winked at April, before tilting back again.

"Harold, I promised to play the perfect date to help secure your promotion."

"Call me H7; everyone does."

"Harold, look, I'm sor—"

"You mentioned a ... bribe," he bristled. He stared, raised his eyebrows, waiting for an answer, concurrently winking at a brunette, third row, fourth chair. The brunette smiled back.

"Unimportant," she said. She snapped, demanding his attention, "Play your part. Your boss hit on me, so we're off to a strong start. Let's make tonight a win for you." She half-smiled her *please forgive me* smile.

Her half-smile almost pulled him back. He wanted to believe, but the scars cut too deep. H7 remained. He leaned back again before turning to the stage. The mayor boasted about his accomplishments. He paused. *Time to introduce the speaker,* H7 hoped. Instead, more bragging.

Ten merciless minutes later, the mayor motioned toward the reason for this beating of an evening, a veiled statue. Finally, he nodded to a fit, tan, tiny, chic 50ish woman in 4" heels. "To do the honors tonight, may I introduce Val ... "

H7 breathed out. The front feet of his chair clank to the ground. Two neighbors shushed him. Harold asked one of the shushers. "Who's the high-heeled chick?"

"Harold," April's voice begged for decorum.

"H7," he corrected.

The shushers doubled down on shushing.

The end of the mayor's introduction drowned out by the shushers. H7 knew one thing: he needed to be somewhere else—anywhere else—but here.

"Pisser," H7 said, pointing to the bathroom sign. April kicked his shin and stared bullets through him, beseeching him to remain in his chair.

H7 ignored.

Exiting the tent, Harold Edgard Reginald Oxford the VII turned back as the speaker positioned herself at the podium. For some reason, the high-heeled woman watched him.

"Strange." He looked at his watch. 7:37 p.m.

•   •   •

H7 cleared his texts before exiting the Youth Museum's bathroom. A pro at turning bathroom breaks into piss-sabbaticals, H7 glanced at his watch. 7:58 p.m. Twenty-one minutes—not H7's personal best.

Before he reentered the tent, a twosome passed through his periphery, just a glance, a father? and daughter? leaving the museum together, hand in hand. Probably nothing. The girl glanced back over her shoulder, pointing, like she wanted to see one last display or …

H7, his protective armor, his avatar, vanished. Harold turned and jogged over to the two as they exited the museum.

"Hey, guys," Harold said. Perfectly generic, no lead, only an opening.

The man dropped the girl's hand. "Ahh … no, I was just … hi," the man offered back.

"Hello," the little girl bubbled.

Harold understood everything about the girl in one word. Bold, would wander off on her own. Outgoing, precocious, would talk to children, adults, *strangers*. A target for certain …

Harold kneeled to her eye level. "This your dad?"

"No, I'm not … ah … trying to help her … ah … find her parents," the man said.

"What's your name?" Harold asked.

"Ah, Joe," the man replied.

"Tell you what, Joe, I'm a police officer," Harold said, staring up at the man. "How about I take it from here?"

"No, yeah, I mean, ah … probably … best, yeah," mumbled the man.

"Want to see my badge?" Harold asked the girl.

"Yes," she said, jumping as he pulled it out. "Wow!" she exclaimed.

"Always ask to see a badge if someone tells you they're a police officer." Harold scanned the people leaving the museum, and turned back to the banquet tent, noting everyone. Then Harold clocked him, a second man, watching the situation while engaging the security team.

The second man pointed, making a scene ... or distracting the guards. The second man caught Harold's inspection, turned, apologized to the guards, and scurried away. Harold noticed Joe shaking his head.

"Joe, wait here, while I take ... " he paused, looking to the little girl.

"Lily," the girl finished.

Harold ordered, "Wait here, while I locate Lily's parents. Then I can ... thank you for helping." Harold took the little girl's hand. "Stay right here, Joe," he ordered.

Harold and Lily explored the museum; he kept his eye glued to Joe, but had no luck finding Lily's parents. Harold led Lily toward the tent. A few steps inside, a disheveled, young woman, dragging a three-year-old boy, hurried toward them. "Lily!"

"Mommy!" the little girl bubbled. Harold watched the two embrace. "He's a police-o-man, Mommy. The coolest, right?"

"The coolest," the mother answered.

Harold smiled, happy for the reunion, but battling uneasiness. He turned, starting toward the banquet tent exit, back to the museum, to find Joe. Two steps away, Lily's mother grabbed Harold, smothering him in a hug.

"Thanks so much," she said.

"Ah, sure."

"Divorced, in case you're wondering," she whispered into his ear.

"Yeah, okay," Harold said, wiggling away, "I need to find someone." She released him, and Harold sprinted from the banquet tent to the museum. Joe and the second man vanished. Harold burst through the museum doors and paced outside, studying sidewalks, parking spots, and departing cars. Vanished.

He shook his head. "Damn." He vented, turned, stepped inside the museum, taking another look before returning to the tent. Understanding his responsibilities, he needed to return to the banquet.

Reentering the tent, H7 took over again, pushing Harold deep inside, to protect him, just in case. H7 located April standing ten yards inside the tent's entrance.

As expected, Harold's boss and three SWAT Team members surrounded the beauty. Harold understood the four men established their positions for when the presentation ended. April stepped to him, took his hand, and led him to their chairs. H7 smirked back at the four failed suitors and winked.

"Why did I see another woman hugging you? I'm your date."

"Pretend date," H7 said. "Paid engagement."

"Play your role, idiot," April whispered.

As they sat, no longer able to distract himself, H7 tuned to the presenter.

"And now, time to unveil the statue of a hero," the high-heeled chick promised from stage. The mayor and other dignitaries posed for pictures in front of the covered statue. In unison, the dignitaries tugged the veil.

9

"That's one plump bastard," H7 said before April's stiletto staked his foot. "Damn, April, no one heard me."

April rolled her eyes, then examined attendees. "She did."

H7 turned to spot the presenter, glaring. The salt-and-pepper-haired woman forced a 'tired-of-this-world" breath. Harold Edgard Reginald Oxford the VII swore the woman mouthed, "Why him?" before marching off.

H7 approached the statue as April read the epitaph.

Pedro "Paunch" Perez, 1942 to 2022

Detective, Hero, Child Advocate

The statue featured the bronze depiction of the plump man, shirt buttons battling to bind his belly, sitting on a park bench reading to an admiring girl. The tiny, bronzed girl beamed at bronze Paunch. The sculptor etched a small #1 into the girl's dress.

Other bronze children assembled at bronze Paunch's feet, listening. Each bronzed child faceless, except the bench girl. Each child wore the same number engraved onto their shirt, like a sports jersey:

#562

"Hmm," H7 vocalized.

"If you paid attention to her presentation—" April said.

"Why, Amazing April," the two heard the warm, burnished baritone behind them.

"Mr. Mayor," she said, before spinning and hugging the mayor.

"How are Patricia and Carl?"

"My parents are fine, Mr. Mayor. Thank you for asking, sir. How are Emily, the boys?"

"Amazing. I've not seen you since the ribbon cutting."

April nodded respectfully. H7 snuck a peek at Tamara again.

The mayor continued. "Wow, you two—

"It's new. Just started dating," lied April.

"Would be the wedding of the season if—"

"A little early to plan the reception, but thanks," April said.

"H7, how are Eunice and the Senator?"

H7 nodded, smirked at April, and leaned into his moniker. "Eunice and H6 occupy separate states at the moment. So, they are fantastic."

The mayor chuckled uneasily, scanning the crowd for escape routes. He spotted his exit and waved her over. "VAL, VAL," he shouted. "Over here."

The salt-and-pepper-haired presenter nodded. As the woman finished her ongoing conversation, the mayor remained mute. Relief washed over his face as Val arrived. "Val, this is—"

"April Andrews," April said before the mayor concluded, offering—and accepting—a firm handshake. Val's eyes surveyed the woman, bangs to stilettos. Val nodded, as if a check mark clicked.

The mayor started, "And this is—"

"Harold Edgard Reginald Oxford the VII," Val finished. "The son of Senator Oxford, grandson of Secretary of Defense Oxford, great grandson of Governor Oxford, and so on back through eternity."

"Well, since you are acquainted," the mayor said, executing his escape.

"Made quite an impression, if the mayor chose not to shake the Oxford's and Andrews' money tree, Harold."

"It's H7."

"I'll stick with Harold."

"Thank you," April added, offering a broad smile.

"Put away the smirk, April. You're as guilty of hubris as dipshit here."

"Excuse me?" April said.

"Hey," H7 stated.

"Harold, stand down, I'll deal with you next."

He stood dumbfounded.

Val continued. "I did my research when I reviewed the guest list. You're a fine young lady. Eight international mission trips. Graduated Summa Cum Laude, double major. You should take over your dad's company. Sadly, he'll turn the reins over to your sycophantic brother."

"How—"

"Hang in there, April. Take the offer from Blake-Towers. They're clean, solid financially, and strong community players. They have serious plans for you."

Val paused, nodding to the younger woman. "April, this is beneath you. How much did his mommy pay you to attend the ceremony with the putz?"

April's head tilted back, and a full laugh engulfed her body.

"Look, lady, who do you think you are—"

"Your new boss, Harold. Shut up. Adults are speaking."

April, still giggling, composed herself.

"My guess, Caribbean vacation," Val said, staring at April.

"A shoe shopping spree," April said, noting her inquisitor's stilettos. Harold steamed next to her.

Val softened, then surveyed April's shoes. "Magnificent, vintage Prota Fiori?"

"Great eye," April said.

"Yes," Val responded. "Now, I need a moment with Harold. Please, grant me that?" April nodded before departing. Val watched a crowd of gentlemen ride April's wake.

"You're actually foolish enough to screw that up?"

"She's not my type."

"Bright, beautiful, amusing …"

"She's like a sister to me," H7 said, reminding himself, or telling Val.

"What a dipshit. How long have you known April?"

"I babysat her for a decade. Our moms required both hands to two-fist Cabernet."

"For reasons only God fathoms, that remarkable creature fancies you."

"You heard her. Our mom's set this up—"

"She said yes, you fool. Do you think April needs more shoes?" Val turned from April's gaggle of gawkers, shifting focus to the statue. Her right cheek pulled into a wry smile.

"Was he really that chubby?" H7 jabbed.

Ignoring the insult—or not considering it an insult—Val replied, "The sculptor embraced reality. Paunch would have appreciated that."

Annoyed he failed to generate a reaction, Harold studied his new boss. Val, trapped in the moment, stared at the statue before returning to her obligations. "So, tomorrow, meet me at Simos Diner on Shepherd at 7 a.m., for the interview."

"Interview? You said you're my boss."

"Not yet." Val said.

"You're interviewing me?"

The woman brimming with confidence seconds beforehand wavered. "Yes and no."

"What the hell does that mean?"

"Harold, he … well, a … they … or, I guess, the team selected you."

"So, you're recruiting me?"

"Technically, yes."

"Well, you'll be dining alone tomorrow morning."

"I doubt that, Harold," Val said to the back of Harold's Armani suit as he departed.

10

November 20, 2026, Simos Diner, near Garden Oaks, Houston, Texas

Scents of sizzling bacon slapped H7's senses as he entered the renowned Houston diner. He hesitated at the door, ambushed by olfactory nirvana. Yes, bacon, sausage, hash browns, and egg smells originated from the grill, but, the young detective accepted, the essence of those foods—over time—fried into the diner's walls.

The Formica table tops, high-backed booths, and hodge-podge décor complimented the perfectly prepared plates H7 watched dropped to neighboring tables.

H7 glanced right. Most tables crowded with characters worthy of Cormac McCarthy novels. A wrinkled WASP spinster prayed with a young Black man. An ancient denim-vested biker's silvery, braided beard hung to his belly as he stood to settle his bill. Coarse gray beard hair escaped the braids as his gut threatened the bottom reaches of his worn ZZ Top T-shirt. Two gentlemen dressed in black suits and stingy-brimmed fedoras entertained neighboring tables. Harold wondered if they served as small parish preachers or planned on attending a funeral later. Their dress perfect for either endeavor.

A waitress dropped five steaming cups of coffee at the closest table. Each mug stamped with the diner's logo and tagline:

SIMOS
Where the Working People Eat

H7 never ate at Simos before. He wagered his father, H6, and his clan skipped the place. H7's gaze followed a waitress toting coffee and two enormous omelets packed with Feta cheese and black olives. Confusion crossed his face. "Weird."

The waitress dropped the omelets in front of Val. He walked over and stood beside her table. She glanced up from her work. "Sit, Harold." Not certain why his body complied before his brain could muster a smartass response, H7 found himself seated.

"You ordered for me?"

"Did you a favor. The Greek Omelet's the stuff of legend. I went with the sausage over bacon, half hash browns/half grits. Try both. Oh, I ordered you the biscuit."

"I don't want olives in my omelet—"

"Shut up. Try it. Your stomach will thank me, but your inner prick will keep your lips sealed. Quite the conundrum."

"You don't know me."

"But I do, Harold."

H7's face reflected doubt, so she continued.

"Model student, perfect grades, great conduct scores until about the third grade. Then, **IF** I believe your grades, you stopped caring."

H7 nodded, before he could stop himself.

Val said, "You attended the finest private schools, passing because your parents were the school's most generous benefactors. Despite your parents' influence, school superintendents suspended you seventeen times for truancy or unruly conduct. You fought in the Muay Thai national championship, third place, I think. You excelled partially on the merits of your ability but also because daddy spent thousands of dollars on private coaching."

"You attended your father's college alma mater because the dean lacked the huevos to tell daddy you were unqualified. You joined ROTC at granddaddy's behest. You served in the Army for the minimum term. Powder-puff assignment arranged by your family, so you could check that box."

"Now you'll serve on the police force long enough for your next promotion. Daddy's pressing for law school, but you've won that battle so far. Once you give in, and you will," Val paused, savoring caffeine before continuing, "because they'll leverage you with your inheritance and mommy will secure a job in the DA's office for you. When you run for congress, which she planned before your birth, you can recycle the tough-on-crime platform daddy and granddaddy used. About right?"

"Yeah," Harold muttered, feeling strangely safe, despite the harsh critique. For reasons he failed to decipher, Harold wanted to be here and pushed H7 aside.

"Eat the damn omelet."

Harold succumbed to the strange, but unnamed, kinship. His eyebrows rose. "Wow."

"Told you."

"What do I call you?"

"Val's fine."

"Val, why am I here?

"A few reasons."

"Okay."

"You took three child welfare classes as electives. Aced them. Your professors said you're a pretentious prick but possess a heart for children."

"Doesn't matter, my family will never—"

"Allow you to work in child welfare. Guessed that. Second, despite being a prick—"

"Every time, really?"

"You're a damn fine detective. You gotta nose for it. The McCluskey child trafficking bust surprised everyone. McCluskey rolled on his clientele; nice work surprised everyone. Eleven arrests so far, more to come."

"Thanks."

"And … well." Harold's investigative brain studied Val. She considered another point, something important to her, set it aside, or skipped it, then moved to the next one. "They want you."

He ignored the omission for now and played along. "Who?"

"The people I work for."

"That's a lie."

"Sorry?" Val grinned, intrigued.

"You're the Director of the National Task Force to Stop Child Trafficking and Abuse. You receive substantial Congressional funding. Oh, and you are the boss, the head of the department."

"We all have bosses, Harold."

"If you had a boss, which you don't, why'd they want me?"

"Maybe they selected the most cynical bastard on the force. A nonbeliever."

"In what?"

"In anything, Harold."

"There's more. You work with several agencies, dozens of cooperating officers, but you're the only paid member of the task force. You're the Lone Ranger. Still, with over 700 convictions, 1000-plus kids saved, your one-person task force proved damn effective."

She nodded thanks.

"Why keep it so quiet, so close to the vest?"

"We collect intelligence from a nontraditional source. We—"

"You mean you."

"Yes, protect my source."

"Then what's next?"

Val held up her hand, and a server dashed over with a coffee refill. She nodded as the woman topped her mug. Val stared at the steaming cup before opening. "Did you know I-10's the most active corridor for human trafficking in the U.S.? Been so for decades."

Harold added. "Next to borders, ports, rivers, bayous, backroads. Essentially, easy-on/easy-off for scum."

"Correct. Ever heard of the I-10 Corridor Killings?"

He chuckled. "Who hasn't? Freaky 1970s murders, the vehicular fatalities, the log cabin slaughter."

Val nodded.

"They're unsolved. Despite dozens of columns, two documentaries, three true-crimes books, and numerous failed internal and private investigations. Started with a bear attack. Victims died in bizarre ways."

"Not victims, Harold, molesters, rapists, criminals, human traffickers died."

"Okay."

"Want the whole enchilada? How they died? Who executed them?"

"You know?"

"Of course, Harold."

"But you've told nobody?"

"Traditional law enforcement lacks the … capacity to believe me."

"And I possess that capacity?"

"I doubt it."

Harold laughed. "You're telling me anyway?"

"That's my orders, yes."

"Why?"

Val raised cup to lips, emptying her coffee before responding. "We need you, Harold."

"You and your imaginary boss."

"We do."

Harold looked over and pointed to his coffee. As the server approached, he said, "What the hell. Make it entertaining at least."

Val chuckled, despite herself. "I will do my best, Harold."

11

May 26, 1976, East Texas, near the Louisiana Border

Teeny Voix clutched Opie while peeping through cheap, metal motel blinds to the rundown pool. The water, ogre-green more than aqua-blue, offered swimming for the young, naïve, or, more often, inebriated. Forty yards north of the pool, big rigs rumbled past on Interstate 10. Long ago used to road-noise pollution, Teeny made no notice.

Her former mane of brown curly hair gone. Teeny sported a tight, red, pixie cut. Her momma, Sissie, sunbathed in black panties and bra—the closest thing packed to swimsuits. No problem, no one else occupied the pool. Sissie's formerly lily-white skin now a suntanned reddish-brown, out of necessity, not vanity.

Sissie's polyester house-keeping frock draped over a nearby plastic chair. Sissie's shift ended twenty minutes before. She shared the same cut and color as her daughter, since the two split the bottle of Clairol weeks before.

Teeny scrutinized each car occupying the parking lot. No white vans.

She hopped backwards, shocked by spotting HIM for the first time. The blinds snapped shut as Teeny tripped over her momma's bed, fumbled Opie, tumbled onto the cheap carpet, hyperventilating momentarily, breathing in and out, resetting.

She wrung her hands, stared at the blinds, afraid to peek through. Teeny counted to ten, collected Opie from the floor, consulting him for confidence. Seconds later, Teeny stepped to the blinds, bucked up her courage, and peered through.

The oldish, massive—but fit—man wore woodland green swimming trunks and no shirt. Coarse gray hair covered his chest and stomach. Tattoos decorated his howitzer arms. He toted an Igloo cooler, wore black sunglasses, and strolled barefoot over blistering concrete toward the pool.

A cropped beard and mustache covered his face, and tight, gray stubble covered his skull, like he shaved his scalp days beforehand. Thick-ribboned old-man muscle encased his frame, offsetting his slight belly.

The graybeard dropped the cooler and turned, lobbing his towel over the chair. When he settled into the lounge chair, Teeny studied his tattoos. Giant bear tracks engulfed bulging biceps and triceps on his right arm. Interlocking antler tattoos mixed with the musculature of his left, commencing above his wrist, and ascending to muscle-capped shoulders.

Even though she glanced through a slit in the blinds, Teeny swore the sunglassed graybeard studied her.

Curious. Teeny consulted Opie for his opinion. He agreed. She peeked through again, reexamining the potholed parking lot.

Still no white vans.

After passing time gawking at the man, her momma, and the parking lot, Teeny abandoned her stakeout. She bounded onto the bed to begin her favorite activity. Hotel bed springs complained as Teeny hopped, reaching for the yellowed water blotch on her motel room's ceiling, her tiny fingers falling short of the ceiling each time.

She watched each failed attempt in the cracked mirror affixed to the hotel room dresser/TV stand combo. Then, she felt it; one fingernail tipped the cottage cheese textured ceiling, knocking chalky white residue, like snow onto her bed. A huge smile filled her face as she tried again.

Approaching steps and the jiggling of keys ended her game. Teeny butt-dropped to the mattress, snatched *A Wrinkle in Time* from the bedside table and started reading. Sissie Voix Hurt, or Sally, per her motel nametag, opened the door, now dressed in a powder-blue polyester housekeeping frock.

"You weren't jumpin' on the bed again, were you?"

Teeny shook her head.

"Teeny ... "

Teeny studied the shag carpet and nodded. Then she turned excitedly, pointing out the white chalky residue on her bed.

"You did it, you touched the ceilin'!"

Teeny hugged her momma excitedly.

"Okay, congrats, but no more jumpin' on the bed, okay?" Sissie held out her arms, displaying her tan. "How do I look?"

Teeny held her thumbs up. "Thanks, Teeny, but what I mean is, do you expect anyone would recognize me?"

Teeny shook her head.

"So, good disguise?"

Teeny nodded.

"Well, you're pretty darn disguised yourself." The girl's cheeks pulled to a broad gum and toothy smile.

Teeny walked to the window, sneaking another glance through the blinds. She glanced back at her momma and raised her eyebrows.

"I haven't seen him 'fore either. Must be a guest."

Teeny flexed both biceps like Superman.

"Yeah, he's E-normous."

Teeny pointed to her right arm.

"I spotted the tattoos too. Strange, huh?"

Teeny agreed, before twitching her mouth, silently posing the key question.

Sissie continued. "Pretty positive he ain't with 'em. Just some muscled-up old fella."

Teeny peeked through the blinds again, and he still sunbathed. With his dark sunglasses, Teeny could not confirm, but she swore she caught the graybeard inspecting her room. The blinds snapped shut when she removed her fingers. Teeny heard the shower dribble behind her—and turned as the bathroom door shut.

She breathed deeply, relaxed, rejoicing in her momma's presence, before peeping through the blinds again. The muscled graybeard now stood closer, near the boundary of the pool deck, holding his cooler, ready to depart. This time—no mistake—he stared back at Teeny. Just when Teeny determined she must be paranoid, the graybeard waved.

12

Later

Teeny dropped to her knees, jammed her hands together, mimicking prayer, eyes imploring.

"Teeny, I gotta go," said Sissie, or Sally per her job application at the motel. Sissie/Sally dressed in her slinkiest jeans and tight, striped top. Bright red lipstick adorned her face.

Teeny knee-walked, wrapping her arms around her momma.

"Teeny, I told you. Bud." Teeny looked confused. "Bud, my new bossman figured we were on the lam. He keeps his mouth shut, pays me cash for housekeepin' and gives us a free room. He lets me park our car in his garage. But, in return, I hafta … " Sissie glanced down in shame. "meet 'im for coffee after shift sometimes."

Teeny jumped from kneeling position and rushed to the window. She pointed outside.

"Teeny … "

Teeny pointed again.

"The big old guy's not with 'em. Or at least I'd bet he's not." Teeny glared.

"You're right, I don't know for sure. Teeny, I've tried to play along. And I get you tried to splain to me with your signin'. Ain't no group of evil men out to get you. Can't believe Flick sold you off. You made that up. No such thing as slavery anymore."

The girl gritted her teeth, spread out her fingers, puffed up her body, and monster-walked across the room, reminding her bone-tired momma of their circumstances.

"I know, Teeny, somethin' big and creepy kilt Flick. So, I ran off 'cause I was scared too. I've been thinkin', Teeny. Maybe it's best if I call my old bossman, see if I can get my job back, and we turn back home. The police'll protect you, Teeny. Nobody's gonna sell you."

Teeny ran at her momma swinging, her small fists bouncing off Sissie's stomach. The momma let her daughter swing until she tired and collapsed onto the bed.

"So, here are our options. One, go back out on the road. Two, stay in this crappy motel. In which case, I gotta go ... out for coffee. Or, three, go back home."

Teeny held up two fingers.

"Okay, settled."

The girl crossed her arms and plunked onto the bed. Frustration, fear, anger poured out of her.

"Teeny, don't you miss Pru? Your buddies at school?"

Teeny nodded.

"We can go home. It'll be better without Flick."

The girl shook her head sadly.

"Why not?"

Teeny holds up one finger.

"First," Sissie said.

Teeny transforms into a combination of a zombie-Frankenstein.

"The monsters?" Sissie asks.

The girl's head shakes.

"Okay, your white van stalkers."

Teeny nodded as her left hand circles.

"Are all around there."

Thumbs up. Then Teeny holds up two fingers.

"Second."

Teeny points to Sissie.

"Me, no, no, that's not it. I'll—"

Teeny nods, then pretends to be an explorer.

"Look for … "

Teeny picks up a pen and acts excited to hold it.

"I'll find." Two thumbs up from Teeny.

Teeny raced to her momma's makeup kit and snatches three cotton balls. Sissie looked perplexed. Teeny displays the two cotton balls before adding another.

"I'll find another … "

After nodding, Teeny contemplates. Her mom observed as the girl searched for the final clue. Sissie concluded the sentence for her girl.

"I'll find another loser. Another freeloader to replace Flick. That's what you think?"

Teeny nodded. The slap came swiftly, too fast for Teeny to prepare, her jaw ripped to the right, and she sank to the floor. She squatted on the stained orange shag carpet, familiar with the sting in her left jaw. She watched her mom storm out of the room.

"Ain't nothin' I do good enough for you?" Sissie slammed the door.

Teeny allowed herself a hundred count to cry, pout, and complain silently to Opie. She turned to her suitcase and contemplated choices. She packed slowly, smelled her momma's perfume and work frock, put on her sneakers, before stepping to the rust-stained sink to wipe her face.

While Teeny stared in the mirror, her brain considered the big, intimidating graybeard who watched her room. Images of him displaced by the true nightmare, the White Van People. She hoisted her suitcase, Opie, then slowly opened the motel door.

She quick-checked the pool, no one there. Teeny peered down the corridor to the vending machines. Nobody.

Next, she inventoried every vehicle in the motel's parking lot. A challenging task because multiple light posts featured flickering, burned out, or shattered bulbs. Still, she confirmed, no white vans. The humming of the motel's faulty neon sign and the cricket's cadence colored the soundscape. She half-stepped into the night, her conviction wavering, but the door's momentum tapped her backside, bumping her into the night. The sound of the door click-locking behind her upped the stakes. In her hurry to pack, Teeny left her room key on top of the TV.

No turning back.

Teeny toted her suitcase toward the interstate. She stuck up her thumb, like in the movies, and waited for cars to slow.

An eight-year-old girl, dressed in pink, holding a stuffed opossum, alone, at night, on I-10, one of the busiest traffic corridors in the United States.

Whoooooosh. Macks, Peterbilts, and assorted big rigs blew past, not noticing her. Gusts whipped Teeny's hair. She inspected the big, green interstate sign a few yards away.

Lake Charles 33 Miles

New Orleans 237 Miles

More headlights, miles away, approached fast. After regripping her opossum, she held up her thumb, determined to be spotted. The stars twinkling above caught her attention; she smiled softly at them, considering the night, when movement across the highway snatched her attention

The tattooed graybeard, without his sunglasses, stepped from behind a pine tree abutting the interstate. Teeny made eye contact with him. Graybeard shook his head, glaring down the highway toward the expanding headlights.

Teeny knew, just knew, the White Van People were coming.

Coming for her.

13

Teeny spun, darted, and dove with her suitcase and Opie behind a row of pink oleander. She peeped from behind the bushes; the graybeard vanished. Did she imagine him? No time to ponder her sanity, Teeny shook off the thought as three white vans whooshed past.

Teeny toppled backward onto her bottom and butt-scooched from the street. Shaken, she surveyed the van's taillights fading into the horizon. Almost gone, almost gone, almost gone. Then the last van's brake lights illuminated.

The van drifted to the shoulder, stopped, turned, and started a return toward her. Teeny scanned the spot graybeard stood earlier. Gone or never there.

Teeny snatched her suitcase and Opie, before sprinting toward her motel room. Once there, she dropped her suitcase and Opie, before yanking the door handle, once, twice, thrice. Locked, or, more precisely, locked out. Teeny jerked the door handle again, again, again, again.

She slammed her tiny shoulder, then backside, against the door. Nothing, nada, not an inch. Fear-tears streamed down her cheeks, her back slid down the door, considering her fate. Headlights flooded the lot.

"Hee, ha, hee, hee, ha, ha, ha … "

The giggling again. Teeny's head whipped right, then left. No one. Horror filled her tiny body. The giggles last harbingered Flick's brutal death.

"Hee, ha, hee, hee, ha, ha, ha … " echoed behind, in front, beside her, and inside her head. The van turned into the motel entrance.

"Hee, ha, hee, hee, ha, ha, ha … "

Click.

Teeny spun back to the door, jerked the handle. The door opened immediately. She ripped the door open, tossed her suitcase and Opie inside, locked the latch behind her before bolting behind her bed.

·   ·   ·

Sissie stared into the mirror of Bud's room, vigorously brushing her teeth. She turned to his sink, spat, rinsed her mouth, before gargling with Bud's Listerine and spitting again.

Bud snored, rip snorted, grumbled, turned, then snored more, a stupid, contented grin covering his face. Sissie shoved her lipstick in her jean pocket, shook her head, then opened Bud's door to escape.

Three white vans idled in the parking lot. Sissie wondered how long the vans occupied the space. The drivers and passengers made no effort to exit the van, instead studying the surroundings. Sissie jerked the door back, peering through the crack.

"A coincidence, there's lotsa white vans, fluke," Sissie reassured herself.

Finally, one van door opened and two men stepped out of the vehicle, one a behemoth in white shirt and blue jeans. The other man possessed a 5-foot-nothing fire hydrant build, wore a striped, blue velour shirt and white polyester pants. Thinning, blond hair—slicked back—topped his pink head. The two examined the parking lot, searching for something—someone. Neither moved toward the motel office. Sissie drew the door shut as the behemoth's head rotated in her direction. The behemoth motioned to the other vans to stay put.

Sissie held the door shut, gripping the handle tight. A deep breath later, Sissie moved to the window and sat under it, watching the second hands tick, tick, tick on Bud's Lone Star wall clock.

Sissie gathered her courage, moved to her knees, and peeked outside as a lean man in nuthugger running shorts stepped from the second van, signaling the third van to pull out. He seemed to be in charge. The cracking gravel under tires confirmed the third van's exit.

One gone, she thought to herself. "Maybe they're leavin'," she whispered.

"Uhh, mmm, ahh, ehhhh," Bud answered, flipping over in bed, before returning to snoresville. Sissie stared at him, shaking her head, breathing out regret. "Useless." She returned her attention to the drama outside.

Sissie clocked three men now wandering the property. Two stayed near the vans—the man in nuthugger shorts and a man in a cheap three-piece suit. Sissie gasped.

The back door of one van inched open, and a boy's tiny sneakers stepped onto the asphalt. As Sissie watched, the towheaded boy silently lowered his second foot. He glanced right, then left. So far, his escape went unnoticed by his captors.

Sissie silently cheered each step the towheaded boy made, one, two, three, four, before passing the van's rear bumper, five, six, seven silent steps. The boy's escape buoyed Sissie's heart.

Then a fatal mistake. The towhead ran. The boy's captors clocked the sound; irritation covered their faces. The man in nuthugger shorts turned, sprinted, and scooped up the boy seconds later. He covered the towhead's mouth and barked orders at the man in the cheap suit. Sissie could not hear his words but saw his frustration. The man in nuthugger shorts carried the towhead back to the van, then, with the help of the man in the cheap suit, duct taped the boy's hands, mouth, and feet. Their cargo ready, the two tossed the towhead into the van. When the van door opened, Sissie choked a scream. A half-dozen children, some bound, some not, populated the van.

"Oh, God," she whispered, dropping to the carpet in terror. She looked to Bud's bedside phone and considered calling the police. But—right now—she needed to get to Teeny. Still, exiting Bud's apartment unnoticed seemed impossible, unless …

After minutes of formulating her plan, Sissie wiggled out the bathroom window, clearing her head, shoulders, and waist. She stared down at the walk below, planning her drop. Almost to freedom, when her jeans caught on the window crank. "Damn't." She tugged and twisted but could not clear her hips.

Frustrated, she pushed backward and returned to Bud's bathroom floor. She considered her narrow shoulders and waist, then examined her hips. "Mmm," she sounded.

Needing to get to her daughter, Sissie eliminated option after option before removing her jeans. She tugged her shirt kneeward, bent over and collected her favorite jeans, then stepped to the window again. First, she lowered her jeans quietly to the ground before shimmying through the window.

A pantsless Sissie slid silently onto the ground below. She snatched her jeans, tugged her shirt kneeward again, before glancing around the corner.

"Great, how'm I gettin' to the room?" she muttered. She started to step back into her jeans when steps approached. "Shit!" Her head shot right, left, and forward. No hiding spots.

Tanned of leg, snow white of ass, jeans in her hand, Sissie foraged for a hiding spot. She spotted her only option. Sissie squeezed betwixt snack and soft drink machines, wedging near the wall, her bare backside chilled by the refrigerated sodas. Flickering corridor light supplemented her cover.

Footsteps. Sissie judged by the frequency and rhythm of footfalls two men neared. "One for the road," a voice said.

"Sure, yeah."

Coins clinked into the machine, and a drink dropped. The "Pssssspt," of the tab popping, then soda spiraling down a man's throat.

"Whatta we do next? Can't toss the rooms," said voice one.

"We keep looking. Might satisfy 'em," said the second.

Another set of coins clinked through, but this time Sissie recognized the clunk of a soda jamming, not dropping. "Son of a bitch," she heard, before one of the two men karate-kicked the machine, which rocked across her bare backside. Sissie slinked to the rear, now wedged between wall and snack machine.

"Zip it, asshole. Want to wake the place? We got vans loaded with kids out there. Cops catch us, they toss us up-under the jail."

"Sorry."

The two rocked the machine. Finally, the soda dropped. The second "Pssssspt," followed, and the two walked off.

"Huuuuuuh," escaped her seconds later; she dropped to the cold pavement, balled up and bawled, tears, running mascara, and bubbling snot covering her face.

Twenty minutes later, tears still streaming, Sissie heard motors crank. From her hiding spot, she watched headlight beams cut across the motel facade. Sounds of gravel and shell cracking under tires coaxed her to exit her hiding spot. Sissie surveyed the parking lot. The white vans, gone. She raced back to her room, jeans in hand.

She attempted to open the door, but someone—Teeny, she guessed—jammed the desk chair against the door. The door budged a few inches. Sissie toggled the door before reaching through the crack and shoving the chair aside. No sounds of life.

"Teeny, Teeny," she whispered. Nothing.

Sissie felt a presence behind her. She peered over her shoulder and there he was, the graybeard, sitting on a pool recliner. Not reading, eating, drinking, or listening to a radio. Sitting.

Graybeard made no movement, nor offered assistance, or explanation for his presence. Sounds of Texas night expanded around him. The song of bachelor mockingbirds, crooning all night for brides, echoed through her ear. The soliloquy of crickets, the hum of streetlights, even the rhythm of passing cars seemed amplified by his presence … or his silence.

Goosebumps covered Sissie's legs, arms, and buttocks as a chill passed through the air. Strange, she thought. Chill in Texas in May. Remembering her wardrobe issue, Sissie tugged her shirt, collected herself, and pushed into her room. She locked her door before sliding the desk chair back, blocking the front of the door. She peered out the window. Graybeard—vanished.

Shaken, Sissie searched for Teeny. Every light in the motel room blazed. "What the?"

Teeny's back rested against the far wall. Her head dropped to her chest, yielding to exhaustion. Dried tear canals striped the girl's face. She made no movement, completely comatose, her packed suitcase on the bed.

Sissie sank to her knees. Her daughter held Opie, Sissie's aerosol hair spray, and a book of motel matches.

14

Morning

Sissie lifted Teeny and Opie onto their bed before wiggling back into her jeans. Teeny's momma packed within minutes. Despite her terror, glances through the blinds convinced Sissie of Teeny's safety. For now. Sissie marked time until sunrise, needing the courage daylight delivered.

Once the first glimmers of morning cracked through the blinds, Sissie retrieved her Vega, pulled the hatchback in front of their room, and loaded her and Teeny's suitcases in seconds. Enlightened to her dark circumstances, Sissie, like her daughter the day before, scanned the parking lot.

No white vans, hulking graybeards, behemoths, or men in nuthugger shorts. The smells of diesel and asphalt, the rhythms of rumbling diesels, racing cars, busy bug zappers, and the crackle of the motel's neon sign registered to her heightened senses.

Sissie shook Teeny. "We're leavin', girl."

Teeny sleep-nodded, rustled awake, then measured her momma's eyes. Spotting terror not present last night. The girl snapped awake, bouncing into action, reliving … the vans, the bearded man, the locked door, the giggling, the …

"Now, Teeny, now," Sissie urged.

The idling Chevy Vega's muffler pumped exhaust through the open door, offering a stench and Teeny's next clue to her momma's newfound urgency. Teeny snatched Opie, raced outside, and hopped into the hatchback's back seat. Seconds later, the Vega traveled west along Interstate 10, Teeny's momma repeatedly glancing into the Vega's rearview mirror.

"I'm so sorry for not believin' you, Teeny," Sissie said. Her tired and terror-filled eyes begged forgiveness via the same mirror.

Teeny nodded back.

"I saw 'em."

Teeny made muscles.

"No, not the big, gray bearded dude. I saw 'im too, but that's not what I meant."

Teeny squeezed Opie.

"The people chasin' you, I saw 'em."

Teeny's expression mixed terror, excitement, and relief. Relief her momma believed. "But we snuck away. They ain't followin'."

Teeny understood truths her momma missed. They ain't "followin'" … but something was.

·   ·   ·

Three hours of senses firing, nonstop, not even to pee, glancing in the rearview—both hands on the steering wheel—smelling every dead skunk, clocking every white van, hearing every car horn—shit, now it's raining, high-stress driving delivering Sissie and Teeny to the Columbus/La Grange exit.

Relief washed over Sissie when she spotted it, an abandoned silver Chevy Impala. Sissie drifted beside it, her head swiveling—surveying the surroundings—before turning off her engine.

"Stay here," she said to Teeny.

Teeny wiggled in her seat, but nodded. Sissie opened her trunk, rifling through a rusted toolbox—a long-ago gift from her grandfather. Inside, she located the grimy screwdriver.

Teeny stepped outside and performed the pee-pee dance. "Teeny, stay inside," Sissie barked.

The girl performed the dance's next steps before pivoting from Sissie to the tallgrass. "Okay, pee-pee if ya have ta. I swiped toilet paper; grab a roll." Teeny snatched a roll, then darted into the bushes.

Sissie completed her task as Teeny emerged from the bushes, relief on her face, toilet paper roll in hand. Sissie snatched the TP from her daughter, retracing Teeny's steps. "Stay put."

When Sissie returned from her nature call, Teeny stared skyward. "Whatcha lookin' at?"

Teeny shrugged.

"Let's get goin'," Sissie said.

When Sissie pulled out, the abandoned Impala sported a Texas license plate, and a *Mountain State West Virginia* license plate decorated Sissie's Chevy Vega. Not a perfect disguise, not perfect at all.

15

May 27, 1976

Detective Paunch Perez smoldered. He glanced at his Seiko, then the wall clock, which concurred. Two hours, butt stuck in chair. Flick Hurt's case file rested on the cigarette-burned, food-stained coffee table.

The detective no one wanted as a partner, the living cautionary tale, inhaled. Paunch fathomed the fortitude required to endure his appointment.

His pudgy palm slid into his back pocket, extracting his Moby Dick of a wallet. He unfolded the frayed, brown, leather wallet, flipped to the photos and sighed. His ex-family. A much thinner him next to two beauties. His ex-wife, Guillory—electric green eyes, strawberry hair, freckles. His daughter—the perfect combination of Paunch's black hair and Guillory's cream skin and blazing light-green eyes. Perfect. Perfectly preserved by Olan Mills Portrait Studio … forever.

No homecoming dances, no proms, no trips down the aisle. Paunch mopped a tear before wedging the wallet into his pocket. Why, why, why? howled Paunch's inner voice.

To distract himself, Paunch replayed the investigation in his head. The auto mechanic, Tex Wexler. His twins pointed investigators to Teeny's dog's crushed carcass. Tex remained mum, obviously knowing more than he admitted. Strange, but how did a silent mechanic and dead terrier tie to the events that followed?

Sissie's former boss spoke highly of her, but Sissie's former coworkers implied she received special treatment. Interviews with Sissie's daughter's teacher recounted Teeny's decision to quit speaking months earlier. Her strange attachment to a stuffed animal—he checked in notes—an opossum. The registrar and principal overviewed Teeny's missed classes, erratic grades, hints but not proof of abuse. Every adult Paunch interviewed referenced the compassion and darkness the girl toted like luggage. How and why did those facts lead to a bear attack?

Paunch predicted the outcome of today's appointment. Others assigned to the case prompted Paunch to compose every memo, issue each statement, and complete all reports. Even with Paunch's Mexican ancestry, he detested cabrito. Funny, considering his forthcoming role as scapegoat du jour.

A ringing jerked Paunch from reflection. Irene, the chief's ancient admin, picked up her phone. "Okay, sure." After she rested the receiver in the cradle, she studied Paunch sadly. Her lips pinched.

"He'll … ah, see you." Paunch registered Irene tried to be brave for him. For this. Finally.

Paunch smirked at another former friend and coworker. Another deserter. He retrieved the Flick Hurt file and trudged toward Jack Ash's office. "Paunch, look, I'm sorry," Irene said.

"Cram it up your crusty ass, Irene," Paunch countered before entering the office. Smell of Old English wood polish, Pine Sol, and testosterone monopolized the room. His former best friend waved him to a seat.

Pictures of the chief, Jack Ash, with middling local media personalities, area politicians, and multiple mayors dotted the office. Paunch memorized each photo forever ago. He glared at a shot glass from Bermuda—Jack's honeymoon—and the picture on Ash's desk.

Jack with his new family. Paunch tried to look away. But Ash's new wife's electric green eyes, strawberry hair, and freckles enchanted him. She held Jack Ash's newborn son.

"So, Paunch," Chief Ash said.

Stuck in the past, Paunch failed to acknowledge the chief.

"Paunch."

The detective concentrated, forcing himself to the present. "Chief Ass."

"What?

"Yes, Chief Ash. How can I make your job, career—heck, your life—complete today?"

"Resign," Ash answered.

"No thanks, Jack. My presence annoys you. Which, strangely, comforts me."

"Screw you, Paunch," said the chief.

"You're screwing my wife; isn't that sufficient?"

"Ex-wife, Paunch."

"So sweet of you to comfort Guillory, when we hiked through hell."

Jack looked away first, lifting a report from his desk. "A peer committee read and reexamined Flick Hurt's file. I'd have called you in earlier, but—"

"But you lacked authorization from legal," Paunch said.

Ash's eyebrows dropped and his lip quivered. "You put in a police file a bear killed a man … in Texas. Preposterous."

"Fraley floated the idea," Paunch said.

"Fraley didn't file the report. You did. The other detective at the scene—"

"Your son-in-law," Paunch added.

"Disagrees with your assessment. Someone—"

"Again, Cooper, your son-in-law."

"Leaked the report to the press." The chief continued. "You come off like a dumbass. You've read the headlines."

Correct, Paunch had, "The Blockhead of Beaumont, the Dunce Detective, Idiot Investigator." The Associated Press and United Press International picked up the "bear" story. Papers printed details of Paunch's ineptitude in New York, Chicago, Los Angeles, Philadelphia, and Houston.

"The committee agreed you'll be suspended …"

"With pay," Paunch stated—not asked.

Ash stood, unraveling his 6'2" frame, attempting to dominate the room. Paunch remained seated.

Paunch smirked, understanding he—despite divorce, death, and years apart—resided under HER protection. "She won't let you suspend me without pay."

Ash slammed both hands on the desk. "I'm the chief, not you, not your ex-wife, or your former father-in-law, not … "

"Just hand me the form."

Seething, the chief continued. "First, your service weapon and badge."

Staring bullets, Paunch banged his badge on the desk before pulling his service pistol from its holster. He slammed down his SW19, already feeling naked without it. Paunch stared at his Smith and Wesson a beat too long.

"Ahh, hmm," Jack vocalized.

Paunch's eyes shifted from his SW19 to the dolt he daydreamed about emptying it into—Paunch would never do that to Guillory.

"Let's get on with it. Gotta get back to running this place," the chief said.

"Show me the damn form."

The chief spun the form. Simple enough. Detective Pedro Perez suspended: twelve weeks. He checked the only two boxes that mattered:

Without Pay

X With Pay

Then, a barrel laugh. Paunch signed the form, fighting final chuckles. Guillory still loved him, despite everything. As he exited, celebrating twelve-week's paid suspension, Paunch pitched a passive-aggressive fastball. "Thank your wife for the paid holiday."

"Mother fu—" started the chief.

"Nice to see who wears the pants 'round your house, Jack Ass."

The chief's Bermuda honeymoon shot glass sizzled past Paunch's ear shattering into thousands of pieces.

16

2:29 a.m., Saturday, June 12, 1976, La Grange, Texas

Now bleach blonde, hair trimmed to mimic a boy's crew cut, Teeny bolted upright in bed. She understood they located her. But how?

During their stay in La Grange, Teeny remained in her room, exiting infrequently, wearing baseball hats and boys' clothes. Sissie procured books for Teeny at garage sales, retrieved magazines from dumpsters, and sticky-fingered paperbacks from the offices she cleaned. The motel room resembled a literary hurricane, reading material scattered from floor to table to bed to bureau.

Before she left for her shift, Sissie drew the drapes. Only an inch gap remained. "Now, Teeny, I'll be back from work 'round 8 a.m. My new bossman moved me to the graveyard shift. Pays better."

Teeny mimed confusion.

"Graveyard shift sounds spooky; it ain't. No one died. Means I'm workin' midnight 'til 8 a.m. Funny name, huh?"

Teeny and Opie agreed.

"Also, we ain't seen the scary old fella or white vans. We're safe here, I reckon. I'm on Main Street, few blocks away. 'Member how to get there?"

Teeny nodded. At the time, no big deal.

But now, hours later, alone, after her momma left for work, blocks felt like a billion miles, because the behemoth peered through Teeny's window. Even with his face masked by drapes, Teeny recognized the monster.

She glanced at her momma's bed. Teeny Voix occupied the motel room alone, almost. She snatched Opie before spinning and dropping behind her bed. Behemoth and girl locked eyes as she crawled to the bathroom, pulling the door behind her. Teeny hated what this situation demanded. She railed against her mind's defense mechanism.

The rotating knob—then the jerking on her motel door—forced **the split**. A skill necessitated to survive Flick's late-night abuse.

Public Teeny split into two Teenys. *Scared Teeny* and her protector, *Thinking Teeny*. The behemoth bucked his shoulder into the door, the threshold "CRACKED", but held. *Thinking Teeny* needed a plan, *fast*. Another *CRACK*. She peeked out of the bathroom as wood splinters and shards of the threshold showered the bedroom.

Scared Teeny screamed inside her and *Thinking Teeny*'s head, *Need an answer NOW!*

The splintering door offered the kernel of *Thinking Teeny's* plan. The behemoth could not observe her movements through the window and batter the door concurrently. *Thinking Teeny* exited the bathroom, shut the bathroom door behind her, but squeezed under her momma's bed, adjacent to the motel room's splintering door.

She and Opie stayed put, as the doorknob twisted again, holding again. A thunderous *CRACK* this time, the wet sound of wood yielding but not surrendering.

A muffled shout demanded, "Be quiet out there; we're sleepin', stupid." *Thinking Teeny* understood. The motel guests—all three of them—would not save her.

Thinking Teeny calculated the door's acquiescence with the next behemoth blow. *CRUSH!* The behemoth bowled into her room, crashing to the floor, focusing on the closed bathroom door like a bull enraged by the matador's cape. He stood, grunted, and bulldozed the bathroom door, crashing inside. Only when the bathroom door shattered did *Thinking Teeny* roll from under the bed, turning the next phase of the escape to *Scared Teeny*.

Time to RUN.

Gripping Opie, *Scared Teeny* sprinted from the motel room, past the behemoth's white van. "Hey!" he hollered. The behemoth lumbered behind her.

She scampered toward the two-lane street hoping to wave down cars. Nothing. She followed the street's shoulder before bolting toward a massive oak, when everything changed.

"Hee, ha, hee, hee, ha, ha, ha … "

Frozen, baby bb-sized pellets pelted her and the landscape. Hailstorm? Her shock, and the questions racing through her head, fell to the wayside as she raced for her life.

Hail clinking off cars—ricocheting off rooftops—overwhelmed the Texas night. *Scared Teeny* ran despite the frozen stings inflicting her face. Grass crunched under her feet, frozen.

"Hee, ha, hee, hee, ha, ha, ha … " Behind her, in front of her, and in her head.

"What the?" the behemoth started.

Smoke exited her mouth with each gasp. Goosebumps coated her arms. "Whaaaa," her pursuer enunciated, then Teeny heard tumbling. *Scared Teeny* peered behind; the behemoth had slipped, and lay cursing near the streetlight.

As she sprinted, *Scared Teeny* returned focus to the live oak. Luckily, no one groomed the 200-year-old brown and green goliath for a decade. Low-lying limbs abounded. The girl pumped her arms, jumped, snatched the lowest limb, pulling herself and Opie up, up, up.

As she shimmied, the behemoth belted out, "No! Shit, nooooo … ahhhhhh, ahhhhh, ooohhh … "

Scared Teeny gripped one limb, then the next. The chilled air—present a minute before—dissipated, as humidity reclaimed the night. The atmospheric anomaly caused sweat beads to sheath her body as she climbed.

Her head whipped around, confused. A standard Texas summer evening greeted her inspection. Only after she and Opie settled on an oak limb, thirty feet above, did she turn toward the streetlight, where she last heard the behemoth's cry.

"Ahh, ahh … " he moaned. Dying, but not dead. The behemoth kneeled in the grass, his torso leaning back from his knees. His hands gripped something, some projectile shoved through his body, just below his rib cage, binding him to the ground. Stuck like a pig at a luau.

The behemoth's death, positioned perfectly under the streetlamp, on display for anyone nearby, which—currently—meant Teeny.

The girl repositioned herself, now eclipsed by the oak's trunk, hidden from view.

"Hee, ha, hee, hee, ha, ha, ha … "

She closed her eyes and squeezed Opie. Tears ran down her cheeks.

"Hee, ha, hee, hee, ha, ha, ha … "

17

Paunch Perez pulled the smoking Banquet chicken pot pie from the oven, wielding his lone oven mitt. He positioned the burnt offering on the only TV tray in his bachelor pad. Although, labeling the unkept, dusty, dirty clothes cluttered apartment a bachelor pad stressed reality's limits. To be fair, a single-guy-with-zero-dating-options-pad lacked a certain ring.

Paunch turned on the TV and tugged his tray before him. The News at Noon team greeted Paunch on KFDM, Channel 6. While listening, Paunch spoon-punctured the blackened pie crust. The yellow gravy near the top bubbled. Paunch never mastered the calculus of proper pot pie preparation. He used his spoon to dig to the pie bottom. The peas and carrots remained frozen. The crust from the bottom gummy, raw, not crisp—uncooked.

Paunch stirred the uncooked bottom and boiling top into a united, lukewarm offering as the television's dialogue demanded his ear. "In a bizarre story from La Grange, Texas, police found a dead man a few hundred feet from a local motel. Parts of the dead man's body ... "

Briiiinng, briiiinng, briiiinng, the phone blared. "Not now, not now." Paunch pushed the pie aside and pressed toward the television. *Briiiinng, briiiinng, briiiinng.*

"Shit, missed it." Irked, Paunch lifted the receiver. "Hello!"

"Hey, ah ... "

"Spit it out, I'm eating."

"You Paunch Perez?"

"Sure."

"Yeah, well, I'm, ah … Chief Kurt Witkowski."

"I'm suspended. Can't help." Paunch started to hang up his phone.

"Wait, wait! Don't hang up, Detective. Fraley told me you're suspended. But he said you were friends and that I—"

"We WERE friends, not so much now."

"Okay," the Chief said, "Well … ah … Frales and I got history. He said you might be keen on helping me."

Paunch chuckled. "Why the hell would he say that?"

"Because I'm the police chief of La Grange." Paunch glanced at his TV screen, the story supplanted by a weather report. "97 degrees last night here."

"Okay," Paunch said.

"I gotta dead guy, outside a local hotel, with a rap sheet longer'n *War and Peace*. Someone impaled this S.O.B with an icicle."

"Bullshit."

"Don't hang up," the voice begged.

"Okay."

"The motel's missing two guests. Mother and little girl. They match the description of Sissie Hurt and her daughter."

•　　　•　　　•

"Can I examine the body?" Paunch asked, standing at the site of the icicle murder. He studied an ancient oak behind him. Cars slowed as they passed, trying to divine the reason a police car and Paunch's battered personal car—a green Ford Galaxie—were parked along the shoulder of N. Jefferson Street.

La Grange Police Chief Witkowski answered, "Sure, I'll take you. But we got stuff to show you first." The chief motioned to a man smoking a Pall Mall on the tailgate of a gold and white 1973 Chevy Cheyenne. The man nodded, snuffing the cigarette and placing the stub behind his left ear. The Cheyenne's chassis scarcely creaked when his skinny butt vacated the tailgate and boots hit the ground.

Paunch walked and greeted the man halfway. The stringy, strong man towered over Paunch. A vice-grip handshake and calloused palms communicated decades of farmwork. The chief introduced them. "This is Jimmy. Our night-shift officer. Found the body on a drive-by. Forgive his dress, he's off duty. Here to answer questions."

Dressed in a purple LSU ball cap, paint-spattered overalls, and a yellow LSU T-shirt, Jimmy nodded.

Paunch asked. "This is where you found him?"

"Yep."

"When?" asked Paunch

"I'z patrolling Main Street, before resolving to hook dis way. I 'member zactly when I spotted 'im. Made an impression. I'z eating an andouille po-boy Lucy—dats my lady—made me."

The chief twirled his finger, signaling Jimmy to speed it up.

"Wuz 'bout 5:45 a.m. I saw 'im. Never forget it." Jimmy pointed to the streetlamp, "Body 'uz spotlighted, like dem window deezplays at 'de shopping malls." The skinny officer wavered, lost in the past. Then Jimmy looked to his chief and regrouped.

"He uz sitting like dis." Jimmy kneeled like he was praying, then leaned backward. He put his hands to his midsection and mimicked holding a massive pipe. The chief and Paunch pondered as Jimmy dusted his overalls and stood up.

"Impaled with an icicle?" Paunch asked.

"Not zactly," Jimmy said. "It wuz smoking hot, and dis old boy been dead a bit. De icicle melted. Dere'z a sliver left, laying on de ground."

"How'd you decide someone impaled him with an icicle?"

"Old boy 'uz sporting frostbite on his finger, and hiz innards." Jimmy signaled a hole in his chest. "Most his insides didn't leak out, stiff from kissin' up to de ice. Also … "

"Yes?" led Paunch.

"Dere'z dis." Jimmy pointed to a six-inch-deep hole in the ground, about three inches in diameter. "Whatever went through him pinned him to dis spot."

"Bullshit," said Paunch. "The force to shove—"

"Look cuz, I'd agree with ya if I didn't see it myself. Like I said, the icicle uz melted down. But I peeked through the crater in his gut, and lined 'er up with dat dere hole in de ground."

Paunch studied the cars in the parking lot. "Which vehicle belonged to the vic?"

"Not tough to figure, only a few guests. The ugly-ass white van." The chief pointed.

"What do we got on the white van?" Paunch pressed.

The chief answered, "Nothing, stolen plates, serial numbers obliterated, no way to track it."

"White van. Weird. Anything else strange?"

"Yeah, one guest overheard a commotion. He and another mentioned a hailstorm last night. Hundreds of dents in cars support that."

Paunch considered, before asking. "Jimmy, you worked the night shift. See any hail?"

"Yep. Get 'em all de time. March ta August mostly. Not dat unusual. Hailstorms in Texas in de summer are a dime a dozen. A giant icicle, pinning a growed man to de earth, now dat I ain't seen."

The chief nodded, but Paunch continued, unimpressed. "The chief mentioned a mother and daughter when he called me."

"After I woke up de chief, I eyeballed things." Jimmy pointed to the motel. "One door 'uz wide open. Lights a'blazin. Walked over 'n found drawers ajar, books slung about. I woke Lester, the motel manager. He'd met de momma once or twice. Didn't know de woman got gone."

"What's the woman's name?"

"She used Sadie Hawkins. Lester figured dat wasn't her real name. But she looked harmless, so he kept 'iz mouth shut. Said she 'uz trashy pretty too. Sure, dat didn't hurt with de decision making. Also, she paid cash. Lester probably 'uz planning on hiding de income from de tax man."

"The girl and the mom. How do you know they were Sissie Hurt and her daughter?"

Jimmy answered. "Don't for sure. But the momma worked for de local housekeeping service. She cleaned shops on Main Street at night. Worked cheap, but only for cash money."

"And … "

"She gave her boss de same fake name. According to de cleaning crew girls, Sadie's kid showed up scared shitless, and de two left lickety split. No splaining, nothing."

The chief added, "Never saw the two. Lester said someone sheared the little girl's head. The momma tried to pass her off as a boy. No one bought what she was selling. The kid always carried around a toy." The chief checked his notes. "A stuffed … possum?"

"Weird." Paunch raised his eyebrows. The stuffed possum reference set off fireworks in Paunch's head, but he tried to appear unaffected.

"The girl and mom you're searching for went missing after a bear attack, right?" the chief asked.

"Ain't no bears in east Texas," Jimmy added.

"That's what everyone keeps telling me," Paunch said.

"This mom and girl are about the same age; they hid their identity, and they're on the run. They got scarce after a murder, like your case. Who else could it be?"

Paunch remained quiet, fighting a nod.

"Look, man, Jimmy and I go way back. I trust every word out of his mouth. I called because you're the only person who MIGHT believe us. The press and other police forces'll label us clowns. My own family thinks I'm full of shit. Just need one person, besides Jimmy, to believe me."

Paunch nodded as the three measured each other. "Speaking of our victim, who is he?" asked Paunch.

"Clint Wirst, scum of the earth, recently got outta Huntsville lockup. Our mutual friend Fraley says Clint works—"

"Worked, past tense," corrected Paunch.

The chief continued, "As muscle for anyone with a budget."

"Why'd someone with money want anything from Sissie Hurt?" Paunch asked. "She rented a ratty trailer near Beaumont."

"Dey didn't want de momma," Jimmy said.

"What?" Paunch asked.

"Well, de momma 'uzn't home when Wirst came knocking at de motel."

The chief nodded.

"Dat piece of shit, or whoever funded 'im, dey'z after dat little girl."

18

Simos Diner, near Garden Oaks, Houston, Texas, November 20, 2026

A shotgun blast ripped Harold from the story. He rose, ready for action, but Val's firm grip stopped him. Harold blinked, stunned to find himself standing in Simos Diner, coffee cooling in his mug.

"Just a dually backfiring," Val offered.

"Oh," Harold said, regaining his bearings.

Val allowed him to sit and sip his coffee before reengaging. "Paunch and the chief examined the body before Paunch drove home. I imagine him, sitting behind the steering wheel, worrying, stewing, hell, obsessing, about a little girl on the run. Common sense and Paunch's suspicion suggested Jack Ash preferred Flick Hurt's murder out of the spotlight. Paunch loved his police brethren, even if they spurned him. So, he considered their position objectively. Sticking to facts, dismissing emotions."

"Fact #1 - Even if **B**eaumont **P**olice **D**epartment possessed the prerogative, they lacked resources to track down Sissie and her daughter.

Fact #2 - The La Grange police chief dealt with a homicide investigation, perhaps the first one in years.

Fact #3 - Although the La Grange team showed sympathy for Sissie and her daughter's situation, they possessed fewer resources than the BPD.

Fact #4 - Most police forces—hell, few civilians—place priority on locating a mother not committing crimes.

Fact #5 - The big one. Besides sharing head-scratching causes of death, the cases shared few connections at first glance."

"Except Sissie and Teeny," Harold replied.

"Investigators ignored or missed that connection, except maybe Paunch."

"Sissie could just call the cops?" Harold asked.

"I may sound like a bitch," she paused.

Harold lifted his coffee cup, encouraging continuation.

"You're an Oxford, born into privilege. You trust the system because your forefathers formed the system to perform for individuals like you." She continued before his protest. "People with money, yes, but also citizens who operate within the borders defined by law and, well … common sense."

"Sissie lived outside those borders. Insufficient education, poor judgment, and a lecherous husband ensured that fact. Her neighbors included law-abiding citizens like Pru, but also pot dealers, a black-market mechanic, and a family of small-time gun runners. When Sissie needed cash, a boss's favor, a new job, she, well … you can guess. Life taught Sissie to avoid the cops."

"Also, this case happened in the 70s. Amber Alerts and the proliferation of agencies protecting children came later. Paunch was a suspended cop. His ex-wife married Jack Ash, Chief of Police. When the BPD cops picked a side, they sided with the chief for job security."

"Rough patch for Paunch. His mom and dad died in a car wreck. Paunch and his wife lost their daughter to cancer. He needed more time to grieve. She needed to live again, move on. She did."

"Funny, I knew her. Guillory loved Paunch. Behind her new husband's back, she protected Paunch 'til the day she died. But Guillory refused to stay and watch Paunch kill himself with nachos, burritos, pizza, burgers, fries, and pot pies. In retrospect, Paunch battled clinical depression without the tools and support he needed."

"Wow."

"Hell, you saw me unveil his statue."

Val sighed, resetting. Sipping coffee before continuing. "To pile on, at his rock bottom, Jack Ash suspended him. Paunch's world imploded. Imagine the inadequacy he must've felt. Then, by the strangest quirk, the La Grange police chief called him."

"No one knows what happened on Paunch's drive from La Grange to Beaumont. Maybe he prayed for divine direction. But something clicked. Everyone who remembered Paunch from back then tells the same story. When he arrived back in Beaumont, Paunch Perez was a different man."

"He decided Teeny Voix needed a protector. And Pedro "Paunch" Perez, divorced, childless, suspended, rejected, abandoned by friends; called fat ass, gordo, tub-a-lard, and butterball behind his back, hell, to his face, all 5'2", 200-plus pounds of him, decided *'I'm the man for the job.'*"

19

3:33 a.m., June 12, 1976

Sissie packed in panic mode … again. She checked outside repeatedly, but no one was there. She pulled cash from under the mattress and stuffed it in every available pocket of her cutoffs.

Teeny appeared at Sissie's work ten minutes earlier. The girl's face informed her momma of everything. When Sissie rushed from Main Street to their motel, she witnessed the gruesome display, an ice-kabobbed dead man.

"Who did it?" Sissie asked.

Teeny shook her head but brought her hand to her ear.

"Didn't see it, but you heard it?"

Teeny nodded.

"Any clues?"

Teeny twisted her expression into a monster face.

"The monster that killed Flick."

Teeny's face communicated *maybe, possibly, not sure, but could be,* in unison.

Sissie and Teeny surveyed their room one last time, staring at each other, passing strength between them. Both exhaled before gathering luggage, a few magazines, and Opie.

They headed south on US 77 toward Interstate 10.

Before Sissie pulled into Schulenberg, a soft snore greeted her ears. She glanced at the back seat. Teeny dozed, head bobbing to the roads, bumps, and turns. Seconds before Sissie hit her blinker to turn west, whiffs of BBQ and German sausage wafted through the air. Sissie stared at the Oakridge Smokehouse Restaurant, yearning for a different life. She considered hiding her car, napping until the smokehouse opened, and slipping in for sausage, biscuits and country gravy. Sissie's stomach rumbled, voting for that urge. Sissie's fear vetoed her belly, she drove on.

She glanced at her gas gauge, practically empty. She coasted into the corner gas station. There he stood, the graybeard.

Sissie's mouth hung open as he shook his head. Then Sissie marked it, at the gas pump, a white van. Luckily, the driver who filled his tank stared east, away from her and Teeny. Sissie recognized the man, thinning blond hair and a pink head, the same bad, white polyester pants but a different patterned blue-velour shirt.

Sissie zipped from the gas station lot, pulled to the intersection, and ran the red light, not even tapping her brakes, heading west on Interstate 10, and away from white vans and scary old men.

A few miles up Interstate 10, she looped back and headed east toward Houston. The White Van People realized Sissie was on the run, expecting her to push farther from home. *But what if…*

Sure, heading home proved problematic. However, escaping to the Piney Woods of Southeast Texas, the safety and comfort the soaring pines presented, the back trails and dark woods her parents bore her into, comforted her. What if she remained on the run, but closer to home?

Sissie realized poor life choices led to the White Van People's hunt for Teeny and recognized failure today may prove fatal. Sissie stared at herself in the mirror, too weak to leave Flick, even when she suspected … knew.

Sissie, pregnant at seventeen, the girl next door, knocked up by the thirty-seven-year-old married insurance salesman who got her stoned at the neighborhood Christmas party. The salesman, Teeny's father, divorced his first wife, abandoning five kids to marry Sissie. In stereotypical fashion, the insurance salesman 80-proofed himself into a six-foot hole and budget headstone, leaving zero life insurance for his ex-wife, Sissie, or his half-dozen children. Sissie remembered crying at the funeral home, branded "home wrecker" and "widow" at nineteen. Funeral bill in her lap, cruel whispers in her ear, and Teeny the only things the lout left behind.

The insurance salesman and Flick, the two bookmarks of her romantic life, were no worse than the idiots inhabiting the between. Sissie understood now. Green highway sign after green highway sign passed, reflecting the mileage home. Marking her voyage east.

Columbus, Sealy, Brookshire, Katy, then Houston, Channelview, Winnie, Beaumont, before her final destination, Silsbee, Texas.

In the back seat, Teeny slept. Sissie prayed her daughter dreamed of sugar plums and gumdrops, but understood the naiveté of her wish. Seconds later, Sissie glanced to the back seat. Teeny's eyes fluttered open. She stretched—then torqued—her head to stare out the back window. Sissie checked the rearview mirror.

"No white vans back there … " Sissie started.

Teeny nodded agreement.

"No one's followin' us."

Her daughter's face scrunched up. Teeny torqued her body again, staring, studying the woods on either side of the freeway and the cottony cloud-covered sky. Teeny turned back repeatedly and Sissie understood her daughter disagreed with her momma's last statement.

"Think someone's followin'?"

Teeny turned to Opie, he agreed with her; she pinched her fingers together, close but not quite touching.

"I'm close, but not quite there."

Teeny pointed to her cranium.

"You know someone's followin' us."

Teeny nodded.

"Okay, then. I need to make a stop tomorrow. You ain't goin' like it."

20

7:15 a.m., June 13, 1976

Yesterday, Sissie drove through Houston—Garden Oaks to River Oaks, Oak Forest to Piney Point, Alief to Aldine—constantly consulting her rearview. The girls remained on alert. After ensuring no one followed them, Sissie dashed into an EZ Mart, bought a loaf of bread, mustard, and Carl Buddig lunchmeat. The momma and daughter ate while parked in a downtown parking garage and spent a tense night under flickering fluorescent lights.

Sissie used the time to evaluate her plan and count allies. She pulled out before dawn, settling on strategy. Teeny snored in the backseat, snuggled with Opie.

Sissie, head swiveling, left, right, left again, steered toward her past. The potholes and crackle of shells under her tires welcomed her home. Eight slimy trailers awaited. Most trailers dark, residents recovering from a date with a six-pack or twelve-pack the night before, men dreaming of Linda Carter's Wonder Woman, and women pining for Burt Reynolds, Al Pacino, or Paul Newman. Young girls slept under their Leif Garrett or Robby Benson posters, boys dozed surrounded by Led Zeppelin, Cream, or Pink Floyd albums.

One trailer, the home of terror twins, Dex and Lexi, shined like the July 4th night sky, because they could not create early morning chaos if they slept in. The twins, born into crazy, the offspring of local eccentric Tex Wexler and an incarcerated mother.

Teeny, who dozed in and out of sleep moments earlier, bounced to full awareness, awakened by familiar bumps and puddles on approach. Teeny kicked the backseat, communicating her fear.

"Told you you wouldn't like it." Sissie turned off her engine and glided to the Wexler's front yard. Teeny's head whipped around. "Teeny, I checked. Nothin' suspicious here."

Teeny unbuckled, and beat her mom out of the car, guiding her back into the driver's seat. "Look Teeny, they know my car. And we ain't got no defenses."

Sissie stood, pushing her struggling daughter aside. She considered the menagerie of used cars in various states of repair. Three hoods stood open: an AMC Javelin, a yellow Barracuda, and a Pontiac GTO. Tools scattered across an ancient Ford Fairlane, a beer cooler occupied a place of honor near a blush blue Chevy Nova station wagon. After making her selection, Sissie climbed the stairs.

Lexi answered before the knock. "Crap, oh sorry. Cops been looking for you two … "

Dex announced, "This is awesome!"

Two meat hooks jerked the twins from the trailer's threshold. A thick-necked titan, in a dirt- and oil-stained blue workshirt and greasy Texaco ballcap, pulled the door back. Tex studied the other trailers before waving Sissie and the child inside. "Shit, Sissie, what the hell you thinking?"

Within seconds, the twins snatched Teeny away and ushered her to their room.

"I need Flick's gun and cash stash," Sissie started.

"You think I snuck over there before the cops and took 'em? Damn, Sissie, who do you … "

Sissie's hips tilted to the left, both arms crossed over her chest.

"Yeah, okay. I still got the gun." He removed the Texaco ballcap and wiped sweat from his forehead, before placing it back on his curly-topped head.

"And the money."

Tex studied the blue shag carpet on the floor.

"That's okay, 'cause you're makin' it up to me."

Minutes later, Sissie's backside buffed the blush blue Chevy Nova station wagon's driver's seat. Flick's dusty Colt Python sat in the passenger seat. Teeny sat in the back with Opie the stuffed opossum and new toys from Lexi's stash. Sissie rolled down her window. "Tex, dump my Vega, fast!"

"Okay, okay."

Sissie slapped the side of her new car. "This ain't a chance to turn a buck. Don't sell my car, ditch it. You owe me this favor. For lotsa reasons."

Tex shuffled his steps. He knew Sissie long before Flick moved in. "Yeah, yeah, it'll disappear."

"You better, or you're puttin' my life … " Sissie looked to her back seat. Tex's eyes followed. "And Teeny's life at risk. Bad men are after her."

"Why'd bad men be after Teeny?"

Sissie turned to her old trailer, shaking her head in disgust. A tear trickled down her cheek.

"What'd that idiot do?"

"Promise me, Tex."

"Sissie, I got it."

"And Tex … "

"Yeah?"

"Whatever you do, don't let Dex and Lexi near the White Van People."

"White Van People?"

Sissie shook. "Just don't, okay?" She rolled up her window, reversed the Nova, crushed gravel spit from her tires as she drove away.

Lexi, Dex, and Tex watched Sissie's new Nova exit Trail's End. They waved, not knowing—but feeling—they would never see Sissie alive again. Tex barked instructions to the twins, then sardined himself into Sissie's Chevy Vega. He pushed the seat back to accommodate his frame, then drove away.

Unseen to everyone, a finger held back a curtain's edge. Curious eyes watched everything, noted everything. The finger disappeared as the lace settled into place. Inside the trailer, the same hand lifted the receiver of the cream-colored rotary Southwestern Bell phone as the other hand dialed.

21

11:11 a.m., June 13, 1976

Tex Wexler trudged over shell and gravel, almost back to Trail's End Mobile Home Park. He considered his trailer. Tex smiled, pleased and surprised the twins did not burn his home to the ground before they disappeared. Dark sweat stains intermingled with the oil and dirt on his workshirt.

Tex's head swiveled trailer to trailer; something's amiss in the Trail's End Mobile Home Park ecosystem. A pebble crunched under his feet, Tex turned to trailer #5, Buckshot Blackburn's trailer. The blinds flipped back and forth. Buckshot, who headed a small-time gunrunning clan, signaled Tex. *Get away, run, something's not right.*

Tex pondered making a run before considering his home. No matter the danger, the twins needed him there. He continued onward, as Buckshot signaled again.

"Whew," Tex calmed himself. He remembered Sissie's warning considering Teeny's safety and, now, Dex's and Lexi's. His trudge transitioned to gallop. As he rounded the corner of the first trailer, he ground to a halt. Neighbors packed in their yards. A car parked directly in front of Tex's trailer. A man Tex met once before, and hoped to be rid of, sat on his stoop waiting. Cop.

The short, portly man stood. Tex walked by Pru's trailer. The substitute leaned against her Ford Pinto. Tex whispered, "Stool pigeon," shaking his head, stepping past her and the nosy neighbor contingent.

"Hello, Mr. Wexler."

"Tex's fine. How can I assist Johnny Law this fine Sunday morning?"

"We met briefly, I'm Paunch. A few neighbors say your twins are missing."

"They ain't."

"They're not here."

"Correct."

"Where are they?"

"Zactly where I want 'em." Tex jammed fingers to lips, unleashing a high-pitched whistle forcing Paunch to muffle his ears.

"Shit." Paunch complained.

"It's a gift," Tex said. Seconds later a return whistle, not as loud, but a clone of Tex's. "They're safe."

"Okay. Can you call 'em back?"

"Am I under arrest?"

"No."

"Then, nope. They're safe together. Not positive the world's safe with 'em in it." The father paused in proud reflection. "Hey, 'fore I answer questions, can we thin the herd?"

Paunch turned to the trailer park's inhabitants gathered in their yard. "Police business. Everyone return to your home."

Pru and a few residents returned to their trailer, but a majority loitered. "Hey … "

"I got this," Tex offered. "Back to your trailers—or no free oil changes." More turned, but a resolute few maintained positions. "Leave, asswipes, or the twins'll test their new aerosol grenades up under your trailer." The remnants scurried home.

"You a full-time mechanic?" Paunch asked, inventorying the impressive collection of American metal.

"Nah, I deliver groceries to restaurants and such. Tinker nights and weekends."

"Any good?"

"Not under the hood Monday to Friday. Must not be that good. I deliver can goods, flour, cornmeal and such, late nights mostly. So, I can wrangle my kids during the day."

Tex went to his cooler, pushed it back, and pulled out an ice-cold Pearl Beer. "Psst," escaped the can as he popped the top. Four gulps later he tossed the can aside, burped, and pulled out another two, opening one. He reclined onto the hood of a Ford Fairlane and gulped. "Ahh."

Tex offered a cold one to Paunch and showed surprise when the cop gripped it and sipped it. "Nice." Paunch pushed the Pearl to his temple, cooling down, before relishing a second, third, and fourth gulp.

"Thought you couldn't drink on duty."

"I can't."

"Then why are you drinking?"

"Not on duty. I'm suspended."

"For what?"

"Saying a bear killed your friend, then disappeared into thin air." Paunch motioned with his Pearl to Flick Hurt's trailer.

"Flick wasn't a friend. But Sissie's one of my favorite people. Unfortunately, that girl's got superpowers."

Paunch's face exhibited interest.

"If there's a no account, shithead loser in a 50-mile radius, she'll draw 'im. Girl's gotta moron magnet."

"Who'd you think killed Flick?"

"Flick killed himself, brother. Bad decisions, bad acquaintances, and being a miserable human. Somebody stepped up and granted this world a big ole' favor. But you ain't crazy. My kids and I were trekking through the woods that night. Squirrels and armadillos made themselves scarce. Birds scattered to the wind. Something scared 'em. Something big."

"Did you?" Paunch started.

"Yeah, I heard the damn thing roar, and we were miles away. Later, my twins, Dex and Lexi, led me to the bear tracks. That's some scary shit." Tex gulped his Pearl lager, before asking, "If you're suspended, why are you here?"

"Someone called the station. Call got directed to the investigator. He's an old friend. He sent me out here."

"Someone," Tex laughed, staring at Pru's trailer. "You don't gotta cover. I know it's Pru. Good girl, nosy, but a sweetie."

"My source says Sissie and Teeny visited you this morning."

"Hmm, that is mighty strange." Tex long-drew his Pearl, looking toward the scrub trees.

"Source claims you loaned Sissie a car," Paunch looked down at his notes. "Then you drove off in her Vega."

"Weird," Tex responded, offering nothing else.

"Ya, weird. When I find Sissie's car—"

"Good luck, brother."

"I could charge you with—"

"If you weren't suspended, you mean," Tex said, bumping Paunch's beer. He winked, took the final gulp, tossing his can aside.

"My source says Sissie and Teeny drove off in a blue station wagon. A Nova maybe."

"Sure is chatty, your source. Guess you got everything you need. Good luck, brother."

"I could pull the records on the station wagon and … "

Tex raised his eyebrows and smiled.

"There aren't records the station wagon was here," Paunch said with confidence.

Tex shrugged.

"Okay, let's try another tactic," Paunch said.

"Sounds smart."

"Seems you care about Sissie and her daughter. They're in trouble. People dying around them trouble. I can't share the details of an ongoing investigation—"

"Well, you couldn't if you weren't suspended."

"Not letting that go."

"Not a chance, brother."

"Someone tried to abduct Teeny a few nights ago. But that someone ended up dead—"

"Shit. How?"

"Let's just say it's as strange as—"

Tex remembered the news report. "La Grange."

"Can't say." Paunch said, touching his nose and winking.

Tex grabbed another Pearl, popped the top, took another gulp, but seemed stuck, like a snapping turtle on a trotline. Paunch prodded. "I can almost literally see a light bulb above your head."

"What kinda vehicle did the dead guy leave behind?"

"I'm sorry?"

"In La Grange. The dead guy, what kinda car'd he leave behind?"

"We can't track the vehicle. The vin number's missing, the license plate's stolen."

"Yeah, yeah, yeah, don't care. White van?"

Paunch tried but failed to hide surprise. "Ahh …yeah."

"Not saying I talked to Sissie."

"Of course," Paunch agreed. Tex registered the lightness of their approach. The father smiled as Paunch failed to note his twins' emergence.

Seconds later, Dex and Lexi stood behind the Ford Fairlane in full camo and face paint, steps from the suspended police officer. Tex raised his hand, opposite the officer. The two stood at attention. Tex tapped his ear, and the twins disappeared into the brush.

"So, I heard from someone," he winked at Paunch. "Sissie's scared to death of something she called the White Van People."

"White Van People?"

"Yep."

"Who—or what—are the White Van People?"

"Don't know brother, but they scared the piss out of Sissie."

"You don't know me, but you saw me with the cops. So, you know I'm straight."

Tex chortled, unconvinced.

"Tex, I'm a suspended cop. But I lost a daughter. So, I gotta soft spot right here." Paunch tapped his chest. "Give me anything. A license plate number, location, something."

Tex paused in thought, he looked back at his collection of vehicles, each with assorted, untraceable history. His lips drifted to the right side, considering the ramifications of answering the question.

"Can't. But I'll offer something better. Our help, if you find Sissie, and she needs us, we'll be there."

"We'll … plural."

Tex chuckled. "Yep."

"Okay, keep that in mind. But I gotta find 'em first. Sissie and Teeny need protection. And I'm willing."

"Look, officer."

"Detective," Paunch corrected.

"Seems to me someone's already protecting them."

Paunch thought for a moment, nodded, and sipped his beer.

"Or something," Tex said, studying the trash trees where Flick flatlined.

Paunch nodded.

"If I were Sissie, I'd stay close to home. Where I understood the lay of the land. Where the locals spot strangers miles away. That's what I'd do."

22

July 3, 1976, Beaumont, Texas

Perspiration painted Paunch's portly physique as he prepared for her impending arrival. The AC pumped; box fans stationed throughout the house blasted in different directions. Lemon-shaped car air fresheners dangled from each fan. Newly-dusted furniture, recently-mopped linoleum, and freshly-vacuumed carpet would greet her.

Stouffer's lasagna warmed in his oven.

Anyone who visited his apartment weeks before, hell, the day before, would assume they occupied a different dwelling. Paunch grinned. A chance to see her, a wild swing for certain, but suspended detectives only had wild swings.

Desperation transported him to this moment. He stripped, tossed his clothes in the washing machine, and started his last load. He palmed his bulging belly, shook his head, then stepped toward the shower. Twenty minutes later, he emerged from his room clean shaven, teeth brushed, cologne on, in his best, casual outfit.

Being suspended, with pay, proved liberating at first. Paunch did what he wanted when he wanted. Unfortunately, he realized all he wanted was to find Teeny Voix.

Initially, he took day trips to nearby towns. He hit them all—Orange, Bridge City, Mauriceville, Nome, Sour Lake, Lumberton, Silsbee, Evadale, and Kountze—searching for signs pointing him to Sissie. Zilch. Visions of white-lettered, green metal signs marking his progress—nine miles to Nederland, eleven miles to Port Neches—danced behind his eyelids when he slept. Even awake, mile markers flipped through his brain, like diamonds, spades, hearts, and clubs merging between the dealer's thumbs.

Because he had nothing else—no job, no commute, no kids, no wife—finding Teeny dominated Paunch's waking and sleeping moments. Case. Probably not the appropriate word for his undertaking. Personal obsession seemed more apt. No one else searched for Teeny and Sissie.

Except monsters.

Paunch's thoughts strayed to the White Van People. Why did their mention terrify Sissie? Who were they? Why did he know nothing about them? The White Van People remained absent from police files.

Now, Paunch noted each white van, some labeled flower shops, A/C repair, pest control, carpet cleaning, others not labeled. Some business vehicles, others family-style vans. The mass of white vans overwhelmed him. Too many existed to pinpoint which Sissie feared.

Since his return from La Grange, Fraley snuck Paunch copies of active and inactive child murder cases. Paunch pressed Fraley for missing and abducted children's cases, too. Fraley grumbled, but delivered them in dribs and drabs.

The room contained three sections of photographs.

Section One, labeled MURDERS: Photos of young murder victims, when they lived. Paunch chose not to study the dead body or remains. He needed to stare into the victim's animated eyes.

Section Two, labeled ABDUCTIONS: Photos of abducted children. Cases in which someone witnessed the abduction, or parents reported an abduction.

Section Three, labeled MISSING CHILDREN: Photos of missing children, not reported originally as abductions. Police knew little about the circumstances of the child's disappearance. Teeny Voix served as Paunch's centerpiece for this category.

Paunch taped—or thumbtacked—information and photos to the walls—depending on the surface.

He studied his tableau of the missing and dead, focusing on the victims. The victims, the magnetic pull of the case, intoxicated investigators. Paunch worked homicides, so he was familiar with a few of the cases, but ...

Paunch's head jerked from the pictures on his wall to his front entry. **Knock, knock, knock, knock, knockity knock.**

"Coming," Paunch said. He hustled to each box fan, turning them off, snatching the car air fresheners, jamming them under couch cushions. He hurried to the door, took a deep breath, and opened it fake-casually.

She stood before him, electric green eyes, strawberry hair, freckles, his wife Guillory, or, more specifically, ex-wife. Guillory Ash. The woman Paunch would never get over; no man would.

She stood loaded down, grocery bags in one arm, two orange Tupperware containers in the other. He caught himself staring. Guillory rocked back on her heels awkwardly.

"So sorry, come in, come in," Paunch said, waving.

Without receiving instructions, Guillory stepped to the kitchen, dropped the grocery bags on the counter, and placed Tupperware containers in the fridge. Seconds later she unloaded the bags, placing tomatoes, a cucumber, and lettuce in the fridge. She left the bananas on the counter before rinsing purple grapes and Golden Delicious apples. She located Paunch's sole dish towel and spread the damp fruit to dry.

She sniffed, smiled, and inventoried. "Don't clean your apartment for me, Paunch."

"I keep my apartment like this all the time."

Guillory tapped her foot.

"Might be a smidge cleaner than usual."

"Mmhmm. Why am I here, Paunch?"

"I'll explain over lunch." His hand motioned to his dining room table. Flatware, silverware, napkins, and water glasses placed with precision.

"This isn't a date, Paunch. I'm married."

"Yeah, yeah."

"I love you. I always will. But I couldn't stay and watch … " She looked at his belly. She gasped, swallowing hard. "I'd already lost one person I loved. I couldn't … "

"We all handle losing someone differently." Paunch glanced at the picture of their daughter on the wall, the picture of them as a family. "I couldn't get past losing her, still can't."

"Don't for a minute assume I have. Any of it."

They both stood in stasis, uniquely comfortable with the other's presence, but divided by time and circumstance. "I made lasagna. Well, Stouffer's made lasagna, I stuck it in the oven."

"I'll take it from here, sit down."

Paunch sat at the table as his wife … damn't, ex-wife, he forced himself to note, pulled lasagna from the oven, and balanced the steaming tray on his lone potholder. Scents of oregano, tomato ragu, and melted cheese hijacked the room.

"Let's let it cool and set up while we eat a big salad."

"I, ah, didn't make a—"

"I did." Guillory pulled her Tupperware containers from the fridge. Moments later an uber-salad featuring lettuce, tomatoes, cucumbers, olives, onions, red bell pepper, croutons, almonds, and her homemade dressing sat in front of Paunch. Guillory prayed for their food and extra protection for Paunch. He shrugged and started eating.

When he finished his salad, Guillory cut a slice of lasagna, about half the size he planned. "Maybe a bigger piece," he started.

"It's plenty. You're almost full; you just don't know it yet. Eat slowly, chew every bite. Take time, savor it. After you're done eating that slice, sit for five minutes. If you're still hungry, I cut another slice."

"Hmmmffff," he grumbled, but followed directions.

Because fewer bites sat in front of him, he relished each. When he finished, he smiled, rising to retrieve a second slice. Guillory tapped her watch, "Five minutes. Time to ask again, why am I here, Paunch?"

"I need your brain. You're the daughter of a cop, hell, the granddaughter of a cop. You married a cop, now you're married to the chief of police."

"Sure."

"You've been surrounded by cops your whole life; hell, longer than me. I needed someone with history. Here, look at what I got." He stood, grabbed her hand, guiding Guillory into his living room.

She paused, examining the pictures of missing children, abducted children, and young murder victims.

"I won't ask how a suspended cop got these files."

"Probably best," he said, stepping to the centerpiece of his display. "I'm looking for this girl and her mom." Paunch pointed to the picture of Teeny. "No one else is. She's not been reported as missing or abducted because she's with her mom. But … she's in danger."

"So, you want my help finding her? And for some reason, you're studying old cases." He nodded, standing in place as Guillory moved from section to section, hands behind her back, scrutinizing each photo. She looked from the photos to the stack of files filling his corner desk. She stepped back before pacing forward again. "Hmm," she sounded. Guillory circled, closing in on something.

Paunch exhaled, he tried to hold it, but the question exploded out of him. "Has Jack mentioned a group called the White Van People?"

Guillory spun, her nostrils flared, her top lip tightened. "You son of a bitch."

"What?"

"I believed it, that bullshit line." She threw up her hands. "You wanted my expertise, liar." She turned to the kitchen to snatch her Tupperware. "You want me to tell you what Jack's been talking about," she screamed over her shoulder.

"No, no, no," Paunch held up his hands.

"That's what it sounds like. Cops aren't supposed to tell their spouses about cases, but, let's be honest, they do. They're human. You did, Jack does." She stood in the kitchen rinsing her Tupperware.

She cut two huge slices from the lasagna tray and placed them in the Tupperware.

"Wait, wait Guillory, please. I'm sorry. You're right. I shouldn't have asked."

She glared at him.

"I am so, so sorry. Please, I need to find this girl. I'm lost. Insecurities overtook me. I'm sorry, okay?"

They both stood there, both unsure of the path forward. She cracked first. "I loved that about you. God forbid, if I knew a murder victim, I'd want you on the case. You'd do anything to … " she trailed off.

He looked at the food now filling her Tupperware. "Are you taking my lasagna home to your husband?"

"You're damn right. Least you could do, asshole."

"Kinda funny. Jack'll be eating lasagna I cooked."

"He's taken your leftovers before," she smirked, enjoying the harshness of her joke. He started laughing and could not stop. Guillory joined in.

"Wow, wow," he said, when he could enunciate again.

She raised her eyebrows.

"Nicely done. I'm glad I didn't say that." The two stood for a moment. Paunch's brain shifted from the joke to the moment—Guillory seemed onto something. "Before I asked my stupid question, something bothered you."

"Yeah."

"What was it?" he asked.

"Nothing. It's stupid."

"Please," Paunch pushed.

"Just a theory." Paunch's eyes encouraged her to continue. "I think everyone's standing too close." Guillory walked back to the living room. "Look how you labeled your display. By type of case."

"What?"

"Not by victim type."

"They're all kids, so I had to separate them somehow."

"You picked the wrong 'somehow.' The police forces assigned investigators by type of crime, not by victim type. Everyone's standing too close to see the patterns. Cases have two ends."

"What do you mean?"

"Well, there's the victim; everyone gets caught up in the victim."

"Sure."

"But there's also the investigator."

"I don't follow."

"This is my opinion. No one asked me—"

"Until now."

"Okay, until now. Hand me those files, but, before you do, sort them by date, not type, of crime."

"Okay, need a minute." She stepped over and helped him; they finished in thirty seconds.

"Give me the quarter with the most activity." He handed her the fourth quarter of '74.

She scanned the file, "October, 1974, Candy Coglin file, a missing 8-year-old girl. Carl Jones was the investigating officer."

"Also, in October, 1974, a murder, an 8- or 9-year-old. John Doe, you worked that one."

"I did." Paunch remembered every detail. The case remained open, no closer to finding John Doe's identity than in 1974.

"Next, the child abduction, Locke got assigned to that case. J.J. Luis, 7 years old. A neighbor saw him step into a white van."

"White van," they said together, pausing for a moment.

"Next, another missing-child case, Louie Peters; he was 9. Jones investigated that one too."

"Okay."

"Four similar victims," she started.

"Calling missing children victims is assumptive," Paunch interrupted.

"Sure, okay. Two missing children, one abduction, one murder in a month. All the kids the same age group. Four cases, three different lead investigators who report to three different bosses. Cops don't share unless someone strong-arms them.

"Shit."

"Same victim profile, but it slipped through the cracks, because the system assigned them to different departments, different detectives. It gets worse."

"You sure?"

"You guys don't share within the Beaumont Police Department, you can bet your ass Orange and Port Arthur aren't sharing with you."

"I'll call in favors and check that time period."

"Maybe don't mention you're suspended."

"No."

"Here's something else. You asked me about the White Van People. Never heard of them."

"But?"

"What if they understood the cracks in the system? And used the cracks to stay invisible, hitting towns and moving on? If evil operated like that, what vehicle would keep them off the radar?"

"White vans," Paunch answered.

"What if there were five, six—or an army of 'em?"

23

July 3, 1976, Silsbee, Texas

Teeny's curls twisted past her ears, and the bleach blonde of her former buzz cut ambled out to simulate shabby highlights. Sissie abandoned changing hairstyles, as it failed to fool their pursuers. Sissie chose camouflage instead. Sissie wore an Astro's cap. Teeny sported a flowery bucket hat tugged so low it crimped her ears, giving her an elvish appearance.

Sissie and Teeny migrated to Silsbee, Texas, a small town packed with Sissie's people: third cousins, shotgun-toting aunts, insane uncles, etc. Sissie's kinfolk connected her with Molly, an elderly woman who survived alone in a decrepit home near Silsbee's second water tower on an oft-patched blacktop road, Durdin Drive. Vinyl-sided or asbestos-shingled homes with three-tab roofs—sitting unevenly on cinder blocks—filled the street.

Smells of pine and freshly mowed grass, mingled with melted asphalt, dominated the nose-scape. Deep ditches ran up and down the drive. Untamed crepe myrtles, wiry azaleas, and pecan trees abounded. Thousands of unclaimed, unharvested pecans littered the ground, some whole, most cracked under foot traffic, punishing the tender footed.

Sissie let Teeny pick names this time. Based on extensive hours planted in front of their 9" black and white television, Teeny selected Marcia for her momma and Jan for herself. When she passed her momma the note, Sissie laughed, but agreed.

Sissie (Marcia) became Molly's caretaker in return for one room she and Teeny (Jan) shared at the front of Molly's house. The home smelled of rotting timber and mold. Rusted faucets, flickering light fixtures, and squeaky floors accented the outdated decor. Rats, or *squirrels*—Teeny prayed—scampered through the attic nightly. Cockroaches abounded, embracing strength in numbers.

Three fire-kissed sweetgum trees, victims of backyard runaway trash fires, hinted at the lack of oversight the elderly woman's family offered. Teeny's favorite part of the home: the lack of Flick. An added bonus, the woman's family forbade Sissie from bringing men home.

The neighbors accepted Teeny immediately, embracing her silence, as if it checked an eccentricity scorecard needed for residence. The wildlings, or neighborhood kids, included her immediately in kickball, cops and robbers, and kick-the-can. Teeny's hide and seek skills already reached legendary status among the Durdin Drive youth-clan.

The day after they arrived, Teeny discovered the widow across the street ran a yard sale. Not on holidays, sporadically, or weekends, EVERY DAY. Each morning, the widow and her begrudging children pulled tarps back from clotheslines running along the front of the house, from pine to pine. The clothesline's strength was tested by hundreds of castoff blouses, blue jeans, and overalls.

Teeny found her flowery hat there, days after she arrived. She and the old widow negotiated a chores-for-hat contract, comical to witness. The widow, who haggled prices on used jeans and polyester pantsuits to survive, versus a mute eight-year-old who mastered pouty-lipped eyelash flutters.

The agreement? Teeny sorted three bags of clothing donated by the widow's neighbors and friends in exchange for the hat. Teeny discovered, by sorting through donated items, she could set aside the cutest outfits for her and her momma. So, based on the widow's needs, Teeny's proficiency, and her willingness to be paid in other's discards, the one-time arrangement became a part-time job.

For her efforts, Teeny became the finest-dressed wildling on Durdin Drive. Yesterday, Teeny claimed an elegant play dress she could not wait to model but needed a special event.

Yard sale opportunities aside, Teeny embraced the street for numerous reasons. As Molly's caretaker, Sissie received a grocery stipend from Molly's grandson-in-law. Teeny's momma cooked Molly scrambled eggs for breakfast and assembled sandwiches for lunch, alternating between tuna fish and turkey. Sissie prepared Manwich sloppy joes, S.O.S (hamburger in cream gravy), or Salisbury steaks for the old woman's dinner. Sissie's specialties revolved around ground round.

A week after their arrival, Teeny, who occasionally cooked for Flick and Sissie, learned to mimic her momma's middling selection, becoming "chef" in residence. The old woman's family seemed contented to discover a cheap solution to what they considered the complication of their grandmother.

Molly, for her part, acted overjoyed to find someone to nod to her chatter. Teeny and Opie listened attentively to Molly's stories and never talked back. "Great listeners you got there," Molly said to Marcia (Sissie).

To create additional income, Sissie worked five nights a week on a crew that cleaned two local banks, Goodyear , Silsbee's Little Theater, and Birdwell's Department Store. Teeny's momma parked the blush blue Nova wagon in Molly's backyard away from prying eyes. Sissie only drove the Nova at night in case their pursuers tracked down Tex and the twins. She and Teeny borrowed Molly's Schwinns and biked to J&M or Wilson's Grocery, depending on which printed the best flyer in the Silsbee Bee, the local newspaper.

Days after Teeny and her momma arrived, the girl experienced true Texas hospitality.

Myrtis, Molly's neighbor, peddled Electrolux vacuums, and the saleswoman demonstrated her wares every few weeks by vacuuming Molly's home. Myrtis's husband, Selman, a kindly, clean-shaven WWII veteran, church deacon, construction worker, and surprisingly exemplary down-home cook, produced extra food most nights.

Occasionally, Myrtis delivered a plate to Molly. A few nights after Myrtis chatted-up Marcia (Sissie) and her young mute daughter, meals started arriving for all three once or twice a week. Teeny never decoded Myrtis' system for who received a meal which evening. Teeny celebrated Myrtis's knock every few nights. The meals served as a welcome break from the ground-meat rotation.

Selman's specialties included chicken fried steak fingers with cream-pepper gravy, cornbread casserole, and fried catfish with homemade tartar sauce. The steak fingers stood out as Teeny's favorite; she sopped up the gravy with Wonder bread. Well, favorite until today.

This morning, the bespectacled, clean-faced old man, who wore suspenders and a belt, started smoking chicken on his pit. Teeny, even at eight, understood the smoke pit was not purchased, but crafted. Selman welded an abandoned 55-gallon oil barrel to scrap metal parts to create his smoker, which he named *Pride and Joy*.

The aroma wafting from the smoker taunted Teeny all day, dominating her thoughts, teasing her belly. Her tummy began grumbling around 2 p.m. Teeny prayed for Myrtis's visit.

Sissie biked to the Savon RX for Molly's prescriptions. Molly slept most of that afternoon, nose-blind to the events next door. So Teeny suffered alone, sitting next to the fan in the living room rereading *A Wrinkle in Time*, scrutinizing the wall clock. Teeny glanced at Molly's door, occasionally peeking out the window, but 5:30 arrived without Myrtis's steps.

Teeny sighed before grabbing the can opener and a Manwich can. She tugged a cast iron pan from the third cabinet to the left. The pan clanged onto the stove—Teeny's announcement of her disappointment.

Teeny grinned as the unfamiliar feeling settled over her, lazily, then all at once.

Her feeling resembled the first sweat beads on a humid day, barely noticeable. Then shirts dampen slightly, inconvenient, but no problem.

Next, the pit-out—arm pits soaking through shirts—encouraging friends to offer space. Finally, bodies drenched head to toe in perspiration. Dripping faces, sweaty butt cheeks, and sticky socks squishing in shoes. Not immediately, but over a few weeks, the blue collar, hardworking, truck-driving, church-going folk of Durdin Drive offered Teeny something she never experienced, and, if questioned, could not label: safety.

Happily confused by this surprising occurrence, Teeny returned to her task. As she opened the refrigerator, she heard it; her ears microfocused for patio footfalls. Teeny raced to the front door, flinging it open before Myrtis knocked, plates in hand. One of Myrtis's granddaughters, attached to her leg like a koala wrapped round a eucalyptus tree. The granddaughter's blonde ringlets and piggy-tails glittered in the sunlight.

"Why, hi, Jan. Your momma home?" Myrtis asked.

Teeny (Jan) shook her head, staring at the plates, incapable of concentrating on Myrtis's words.

"Let me hand you these plates 'fore you die of a conniption." Teeny snatched the plates from Myrtis's hands, spun, and whisked them to the kitchen. Myrtis trailed Teeny and noted Molly asleep in her chair. Seconds later, Myrtis, her granddaughter—still wrapped around her leg—and Teeny occupied the kitchen.

"The BBQ sauce looks greasy, but it makes the chicken. Use white bread to sop it up."

Teeny smiled and nodded.

"Selman gets the credit, but that sauce recipe's mine. I made them beans too."

Teeny stood, unconcerned with who cooked what, just wanting to shovel BBQ into her belly. The eight-year-old struggled to remain polite. She wanted Myrtis to leave, so she could scarf her plate. She planned her mime-apology to her momma and Molly as Myrtis loitered.

Then Myrtis said "My daughter, Margaret, and her two boys … "

The granddaughter wrapped around Myrtis's leg interrupted, "Those boys'r craaaaaaaaaaaaazy."

Myrtis continued, "Are going to the Bicentennial celebration downtown tomorrow night. There'll be fireworks, food booths, a cake walk. We're meeting 'em down there. I know your mom's working, but would you like … "

Teeny nodded.

"We'll leave around seven. Check with your momma and make sure it's okay."

Teeny smiled and nodded assurance. She would not ask for approval.

Teeny tittered with excitement, a chance to wear her new dress, watch fireworks, and put scary graybeards and white vans behind her.

Tomorrow night promised to be the greatest night of Teeny's life.

24

July 4, 1976, Silsbee, Texas

After kissing Opie goodbye, Teeny traveled to the celebration sandwiched between her kindly neighbors, Selman and Myrtis, in the couple's ancient but fit Ford F-100. Upon arrival, Teeny (Jan) stood next to Selman, in the city square, near Silsbee's library. Firecrackers popped from blocks behind. Toddlers stampeded past, waving sparklers leaving egg and sulfur scented smoke trails. Teeny's nose wrinkled. Sawhorse barricades ensured Silsbee's downtown operated as a pedestrian park.

Myrtis chatted with neighbors and vendors around the town square. Selman palmed Teeny two dollars. She surmised later her cash arsenal matched her companions' for the evening. When Myrtis's daughter, Margaret, arrived, she dropped off a frosted Bundt for the cakewalk, then guided her two boys, occasional visiting members of the Durdin Drive wildlings, toward Selman.

Seconds later, without asking, the boys grabbed Teeny's hand and bolted off, free-ranging the event, bouncing from booth to booth, surviving on food samples and condiments while playing free games.

Teeny's companions, the brothers in freckle, seemed opposite in every other way. The oldest boy, a skinny, moptopped, nonstop chatterbox, stayed at each booth until he wore out his welcome, and the booth's host 'encouraged' or, if necessary, bribed the threesome to test the next booth. His brother, quieter, smooth-haired, with a bulldog jaw, charmed with his gruff seldom-heard voice. When not at war, the brothers complemented the other's skillset.

The two accepted her into their crew immediately, and Teeny (Jan) enjoyed their company, the bulldog-jawed brother ensuring she got the first food sample or played each game first. The moptop repeatedly engaged her in conversation, as if her silence presented an affront to his being. "Your name's Jan and your Mom's Marcia. Like *The Brady Bunch*." Teeny (Jan) nodded. "That's crazy cool."

The barrage continued. "What's your favorite cartoon?" She shrugged. "Franken Berry or Count Chocula cereal?" She held up two fingers; she loved Count Chocula.

Upping the stakes, moptop lowered his Levis, showing off the top of his backside. "Here's where the Gore's dog bit me." Teeny's eyes widened, surprised by the brashness. "You been dog bit before?" Teeny shook her head.

She answered each future question—dozens of them—with nods and pantomime but remained silent. After sampling food booths ran its course, the three decided to find something to eat with their cash-on-hand. They priced food offerings: sausage on a stick, $1, ate up half their budget; BBQ Sandwich $1.50, a no-go to their priorities.

The winner: Frito Pie 75¢, allowing $1.25 for their sweet-tooth priorities. Cotton candy, caramel apples, or funnel cake.

The three sat, backs against the wall of the Pines Theater, a bag of Fritos sliced open, longways, topped with chili, cheese, and onions in one hand, plastic fork in the other. Teeny pinched a napkin between her knees. The boys ignored the napkin dispenser, politicking for second ladles of chili instead, so chili painted their faces.

Teeny studied her glowing hand and smiled broadly. Above her, the midnight blue sign of the Pines Theater dominated the streetscape, accented by fuchsia and lemon shaded neon. The soft, repetitive hum of neon passing through the tube comforted her. After eating, the three scouted the upcoming movie posters, *Rocky*, *Carrie* and *Logan's Run*, then bumped back through the throng, arriving at their destination, the cotton candy booth—adjacent to the library.

While rooting for Myrtis and her daughter to win the cake walk, Teeny picked at her pink cottony indulgence. The boys scarfed their blue cotton candy quickly, then *helped* Teeny finish her pink. They gripped each other's tacky hands, interlocked with dampened sugar, and skipped forward, the boys singing/butchering the Captain and Tennille's version of *"Shop Around."*

The mopheaded brother's voice cracked, and the three giggled. Teeny considered that the happiest, safest moment of her life. No concerns beyond sampling the cupcakes or positioning herself for the fireworks show. No white vans, no ...

She recognized him shouldering through the crowd. The muscled graybeard. He wore jeans, a cut-off camouflage T-shirt, and boots. The tattoos she remembered accented his cannon arms. Teeny froze in place, the boys nearly jerked her arms out of their sockets, skipping forward, before they stopped with her.

"What's goin' on?" asked moptop.

Her head swiveled east then west, slowly, accepting the reality of graybeard's appearance. The old man stood, keeping his distance, but his tilting head, directed Teeny toward Ave. H and N 5th Street. The boys stared at her, not recognizing the old man, or the danger invariably present in his proximity. Teeny pivoted toward the bulldog-jawed boy, then back to graybeard's location. Vanished, tattoos and all.

Her head whipped around to the sound. "Hee, ha, hee, hee, ha, ha, ha .... "

They're here.

Again, "Hee, ha, hee, hee, ha, ha, ha .... "

The boys heard the giggle, but, to the unindoctrinated, the sound washed with the celebrations: laughs, screams, pops, and crackles. Smoke, the entrails of firecrackers, popped just outside the square, rose to waist depth, offering a gunpowder-scented fog. Teeny studied her surroundings. The firecracker fog spread, expanded, offering eeriness to the night's celebration.

Near the corner, just off the square, Teeny spotted a white van idling, generic, blending with the surroundings, concealed by the commonality, posing no visual threat.

In 1976, the year after *Jaws'* release, few things instigated fear more than a shark's exposed dorsal fin. Teeny needled Sissie to see *Jaws* for months; her momma refused. However, based on the movie's trailer, which she watched through pinched eyes and crevices between her fingers, Teeny understood a shark that did not expose the dorsal fin presented more danger. Teeny remembered the beautiful swimmer, Chrissie, jerked at first from below, confused, then horrified, understanding her fate. The attacker's gray-blue skin invisible in the darkened waters.

The white van blended in - the shark without an exposed dorsal.

She studied from a distance as the doors opened and three predators exited. The first she remembered. The skinny Greyhound man once again sported nuthugger shorts. The other two she chronicled. A short man, with a bad blond combover in an atrocious velour shirt, and a 6'8" Swizzle-stick of a man, in blue cutoff jeans and bright yellow shirt, licking a lollipop like a three year old.

The men panned the surroundings, selecting prey. Teeny remembered nature videos she watched in class. Hyena clans circling a herd of zebras, working separately, but finishing prey together. One predator, patiently, systematically isolates a young foal from the herd. Teeny returned her attention to the present danger.

The White Van People, or two-legged hyenas, scanned the crowd, noting young distanced from their herd. The threesome fanned, circling the event. In that moment, Teeny understood the White Van People had not located her. Instead, the predators patrolled their natural hunting grounds.

Teeny's gaze zipped throughout the square, revelers unaware of monsters lurking close to their foals. The young girl knew, somehow she must protect them, warn them. Teeny bit her lip, followed her instincts, gripped her companions' hands, dragging them to the spot graybeard directed her.

She turned right, as a Roman candle fired nearby, the red ball floating into the sky, then drifting down, illuminating a metal ladder, leaning against the building closest to 5th street. The ladder, abandoned, and unseen by most, enrobed in darkness. Teeny jerked the boys toward the ladder.

"Cool," said moptop, climbing the ladder without Teeny's encouragement. "Perfect place to watch fireworks," he said over his shoulder, three rungs up, then finished the climb. "Awesome. You can see EVERYTHING!"

The bulldog-jawed boy smiled at Teeny and motioned for her to climb next. She did, hopping onto the flat roof seconds before her bulldog-jawed companion. Teeny remembered her momma might be cleaning a nearby building, or even the buildings she stood on now. The thought offered comfort. Her companions jerked her attention back to the present.

"We can jump roof to roof!" Moptop started—and sped toward the first building transition. He hopped over the short ledge and plowed toward the next building. The other brother climbed the transition and offered Teeny his hand. She did not need assistance but appreciated the gesture. Once securely on the other side, a Roman candle projectile—green this time—floated overhead, illuminating her surroundings.

Teeny glanced to her left, spotting building materials, long ago abandoned on the roof, forgotten bricks, rotting timber, a weathered pile of nails, an old bucket of paint, and three rusted hammers. Like Teeny's favorite poem, Eugene Fields, *Little Boy Blue*, *"the little toy soldier, red with rust, musket molding in his hand,"* Teeny wondered if hammers awaited the return of their erstwhile owner, the grip of a hand, and frequent dates with nails. Did the hammers ache for usefulness again?

She returned to the action around her. Teeny raced across the roof toward the Pines Theater, studying the festivities. The boys babbled between them, excited for the view. Engrossed in their surroundings, not aware of the trauma cycling in Teeny's head.

A firework, not the small Roman candles held by children, but a full-fledged rocket lit the sky. The boys turned, overcome with excitement for the Bicentennial Fireworks Show.

Forgetting her existence, the boys jumped building to building, back to the roof closest to 5th street, the building they originally boarded. A half mile away, the Silsbee Volunteer Fire Department oversaw the July 4th's firework extravaganza, the biggest in the city's history. The next rocket bolted into the sky, and the boys cheered.

She held her position, staring down at the Pines Theater entrance, understanding the White Van People waited for this moment, when glittering explosions distracted the matriarchs and patriarchs of the pride. "Hee, ha, hee, hee, ha, ha, ha … " The laugh reminded her graybeard placed her on this rooftop for a reason. Her brain processed the key questions.

Whose side was the graybeard on?

Was graybeard a bad man, like the White Van People?

Why did he separate her from the crowd?

Did he plan to kidnap her?

Or …

Did graybeard signal to lead her to safety?

Did graybeard protect her for some reason she failed to fathom?

Or …

Did graybeard position her on the rooftop for another reason … to help him, to be his scout—or apprentice—or to save someone else?

Teeny feared some of the options, but focused on the last one.

Teeny's narrow chest puffed outward, thinking graybeard, with his muscles and tattoos, needed her help. She embraced her assigned task and focused on spotting the three hyenas. She found one, the short man, in the velour shirt with a blond combover, now standing on the corner near the Pines Theater. His thumb-shaped pink head accented by the fuchsia and lemon neon sign above, Velour Man tried to meld into the crowd. Teeny searched for his fellow hyenas, not seeing them.

Velour Man's head swiveled slowly north, then south, scouting prey. As the explosions continued, adults filtered away, searching for unobstructed views of the night sky and the fireworks.

Teeny watched two girls, one in cutoffs and a T-shirt, the other in a bright blue sundress, skip in front of Velour Man—unaware of a hyena in their midst. The predator's gaze stalked the two. Teeny checked where she originally located the white van, not there. Seconds later, she found it idling near an intersection a block away. With most parents filtering toward the fireworks, the hyenas remained the only adults within a one-block radius. Now that the velour-shirted hyena separated the youth, his team members circled to enjoy the capture.

The swizzle stick skinny man stepped out of the van and moved an A-frame police barricade. The van pulled through, and the swizzle stick man returned the barricade to its place before hopping back into the passenger seat. As Teeny watched from above, the van trolled toward the two girls.

Teeny's breath caught in her throat. The choreographed hunt played out below her, each hyena working together to capture their quarry.

The conflagration exploded behind her, soft, foglike smoke settled earthward, the scents of spent fireworks surrounded her. So similar to the smells of war. Unlike any other person present, Teeny understood the cost of this war: lost children.

In the break, after one barrage, before the next, the blue-sundressed girl's voice traveled to Teeny, "Let's cut through the alley, so we can see the fireworks better."

Her companion said, "Okey dokey."

Two words, just two words, ensured the foals' separation from their herd, and placed the girls in the hyena's path. The twosome skipped toward the alley, Velour Man shadowed them, and the white van trolled meters behind.

25

The Battle of Silsbee

No, no, no, repeated in Teeny's brain, her stare tracing the girls' entry into the alley.

Teeny turned, locating her two freckled companions who stood rooftops away in awe of the Bicentennial fireworks show, oblivious to the deadly game playing out below. Teeny's hands fisted, released, then fisted again. Below, the velour-shirted man closed on his two unwitting victims.

The girls skipped through the alley toward the fireworks show, giggling at a glittering crimson explosion. Red fireworks lit the sky, rooftop, and the pile of abandoned bricks and tools. Accepting her role, Teeny raced toward the pile, leaping the transition.

Teeny snatched one hammer with both hands, raised the clawed-tool overhead and slung it. The hammer spun toward the unsuspecting hyena. Whether skill, blessing from above, or pure luck, the hammer struck the man, knocking him assward.

He looked up, dazed, but now aware of his attacker's position. The van halted beside him. Teeny watched the girls skip away … to safety. Teeny allowed herself to enjoy the victory briefly before returning to the fray.

She turned her attention to the downed man. The next firework, green this time, lit the alley. The hammer's claw miraculously locked under the man's collarbone; the handle pointed toward the stars. The stunned man reached for the handle. Pulling, he failed to remove the tool. Taking advantage of his distraction, Teeny risked a peek into the alley.

While she had looked away, the Swizzle Stick, lollipop in mouth, and the man in nuthugger shorts exited the van and studied the roof that served as Teeny's protection.

The man in nuthugger shorts extrapolated the projectile's origins. Staying low, Teeny launched a brick toward the van; the masonry missile bounced off, but half-moon cracked the windshield.

"What the hell?" Swizzle Stick exclaimed. She hurled the second hammer next, and it whizzed by the head of the Greyhound man in nuthuggers. The two retreated into the van's safety and pulled toward their velour-shirted companion.

The van blocked the view of the man she nailed with the hammer. Teeny hurled her fourth projectile at the van, frustrated it bounced off, causing minor damage. She turned, surprised to find her two freckled companions beside her.

"We're throwing stuff at that van?" asked moptop.

Teeny tossed the next brick as her answer.

"Awesome," said moptop, who selected the last hammer and zipped it toward the van. The hammer crashed into the van driver's side window, shattering it. "Bull's eye."

The bulldog-jawed brother shrugged, before joining in, and the three pelted the van with bricks. *Thunka, thwack, thunk, crash, thunka.*

The boys focused on their target, using their limited Little League skills. *Thwacka, thunk.* Out of the corner of her eye Teeny watched Velour Man, the man she maimed with the hammer—dazed, still on his butt—scooch from the barrage, toward the cover of a tree's arbor.

Teeny heard another one of the boy's projectiles, *Crash!.* She turned her attention back to battle, spotting a spider-web crack across the front windshield.

In a moment of inspiration, the bulldog-jawed boy selected the paint bucket. He lifted the bucket. "Humpf." He toddled back—under the bucket's weight—then forth, toward the building edge, drop-throwing the bucket bomb.

The paint bucket bounce-splooshed off the top of the van, popped, before ooze-splattering Sherwin Williams down the shattered front windshield. The idiot driver hit the windshield wipers, spreading the Poinsettia red. Next, the moptop tossed an open box of nails, and the tinkity-tink-tink of them pelting the van mimicked a flash hailstorm.

Facing an unrelenting barrage of bricks, hammers, nails, abandoned contractor tools, and Sherwin-Williams SW-6594, the van reversed, peeled out, spin-turned, and whipped out the way it came, leaving a dripping paint trail. The white van crashed through the police barrier, abandoning the third member of their clan, racing out of town, driven off by eight- and ten-year-old combatants.

Teeny's two companions cheered along the roof line, following the van's exit. Teeny turned back to the tree arbor, and the velour-shirted man emerged, hammer still lodged in his shoulder. He glared at the roof line that hid Teeny. Unsure of why, Teeny grabbed a brick, climbed onto the ledge, and faced Velour Man eye to eye.

She stared, protected by her position on the roof. As the fireworks exploded above, Velour Man looked right, then left. Teeny realized from his angle he could see the ladder. Teeny ran the roof line, toward the ladder, beating the man there by a second, slamming the ladder to the ground, the ladder clank muffled by the fireworks. The man picked up the ladder and started to position it as Teeny fired her brick, which Velour Man dodged. She clanked the ladder to the ground again.

Unarmed, she turned to retrieve three bricks. Her companions still cheered the van's withdrawal.

She returned in time to see the ladder rest in position; she watched as it bounced, marking each rung Velour Man climbed. *Danger, danger, danger* rang through her. She raced to the building's edge, Velour Man climbed halfway up. She dropped the third brick to the ground before flinging her first brick. Miss. But Velour Man retreated a step.

She tossed her second and it struck his fingers gripping the ladder; he cursed, shaking his hand. Teeny attempted to push the ladder straight back and could not against Velour Man's weight. Defeat. He climbed, smiling, foreseeing victory.

Teeny looked over her shoulder; she would not let the White Van People claim her new friends. Instead of pushing the ladder backward, Teeny tilted the ladder sideward, along the roof line, investing all her strength, nothing at first, then an inch, then three, then six.

"Don't touch that ladder you … " Velour Man started. He abandoned his sentence and raced to the top, as the ladder slid from under him. In desperation the predator's hands gripped the edge of the roof. He started to pull himself up.

Teeny saw the third brick, abandoned at her feet. She snatched it and slammed the brick against Velour Man's fingers.

"Ahh!" he screamed. He released one hand quickly, but regripped with both hands again a second later and started pulling himself up. Teeny slammed his other hand with the brick. He grunted but held his grip. Teeny's eyes spotted the lodged hammer, sticking up, hooked under the man's collar bone.

Teeny slammed the brick into the hammer's handle. The man screeched in pain, tumbling backwards and slamming to the ground. Before Teeny could celebrate victory, the man's eyes reopened.

He stood, swaying slightly into the alley.

Teeny looked down the alley. Revelers stood a block away, on 5th street cheering fireworks, unaware of the battle for souls behind them. Velour Man bent to retrieve the ladder when a shadow spread across the wall.

The beast stood proudly in the dark, unafraid, mere yards behind the revelers, arrogantly displaying a head and rack any Texas hunter would proudly center on their trophy wall.

A massive white-tailed buck?

Nope, too big. The shadows must be challenging her perception. This creature resembled *Bullwinkle J. Moose*, from her favorite cartoon character, but stood on four legs, not two, like the cartoon. Teeny studied the creature's rack; not like Bullwinkle's. She processed the creature's incongruence to the setting.

Distracted by the mammoth, Teeny lost track of Velour Man. She turned back to where he stood. He stood stupefied, staring at the moose-buck-mystery beast.

Velour Man looked quizzically at Teeny, confirming she too witnessed the impossible. The beast appeared disinterested in the situation, content to stand in Teeny's admiration.

Then Velour Man unwisely bent and selected a brick.

The antlered beast, noting a threat—or triggered by the salvo of fireworks behind—charged. Velour Man reared back, tossed the brick which bounced harmlessly off the beast's dewlap. With swift, deadly precision, the antlered beast gored Velour Man's midsection before casually tossing him aside.

Amidst the nearby explosions, the beast clippity clopped across the pavement before leaping onto the grass of the adjoining lot, then trotting off.

The mammoth crossed the street and disappeared into the darkness. Teeny turned to find the Velour Man, and watched him bleed out as he crawled toward the outcropping of trees.

"Did you see that deer?" moptop asked in awe, pulling up beside her. "He ran that'a way."

Teeny nodded, understanding he missed the goring below. She held her hands far apart.

"Yeah, huge," the bulldog-jawed boy agreed.

Teeny looked to the ground—and the fallen ladder.

"Bummer," moptop offered. "No big deal, we'll jump." The boys steered Teeny to a low point on the roof. Moptop jumped first, rolled, and popped back up. "Ta-dum!"

The bulldog-jawed boy waited for her to go next; she did. Teeny landed, rolled, rose, and giggled at the moptop, for a moment forgetting her encounter. The bulldog boy jumped, keeping his feet. His audience clapped as he bowed.

Teeny glanced over her shoulder, to the outcropping where the White Van People's hyena lay. As the three turned around the corner,

Teeny stopped the two boys. She held a finger to her lips and eyed them sternly.

"Won't tell a soul," said the bulldog-jawed boy.

"Best night of my life, and I can't tell no one?" the moptop begged.

Teeny shook her head.

"Okay, but when I'm old, I'm telling everyone. I'll write a book or something."

"They won't believe you," the other boy ribbed. Moptop nodded, smiled, and slapped his brother on the back. The boys skipped toward the fireworks and the safety of the assembled crowd.

The girl paused to process the situation as the boys faded into the night, there when she needed, now off on another misadventure. She wanted to stay in Silsbee. She liked the people. Her Durdin Drive clan accepted her.

If the moptop and his brother kept their mouths shut, no one would know she captained the rooftop war. No one could track the dead man to her.

If anything, the White Van People may avoid Silsbee for awhile. They did not know she lived here. She looked toward the now dead velour-shirted man. Well, not the living ones.

As fireworks burst in the sky above her, Teeny calculated tonight's cost. Death leaves footprints, even if you do not play the Reaper's role. Teeny understood nightmares awaited; already such familiar companions, she doubted much change there. Thoughts of Flick's mauling, the shish-kabobbed goliath, the gored Velour Man, and the method of their deaths would weigh on her.

More interesting, her unusual collection of protectors. What were they? When did they find out about her? Where did they come from? How did the graybeard fit in? Why did they select her? How did they stay in the shadows, hidden from others?

As the last thought passed through her brain, the strangest emotion overtook Teeny; she felt like a guest who overstayed her welcome.

She started to shake it off when rocks bulleted over her head— *Pumpff*—bursting the streetlights. Glass shards sprinkle-sprayed to the ground. Teeny shook in fear, head whipping to the dead man's resting spot, now invisible in shadow.

Teeny was trespassing, uninvited, not meant to witness the workers' *behind-the-curtain* efforts to perfect this magic show she just experienced.

She gulped, turned, and sprinted after her companions as the soft hum of the Pines Theater neon marquee 'whirred,' then crackled, then flickered off, leaving nothing but darkness.

Knowing not to look over her shoulder, her racing footfalls drowned out by the next volley of fireworks, she expected and heard the workers *behind-the-curtain* in her head. "Hee, ha, hee, hee, ha, ha, ha …. "

26

5:43 a.m., July 5, 1976

"Hello," Paunch muttered into his phone, still three-quarters bad dream one-quarter awake.

"I'll be parked near Village Creek Bridge on the way to Silsbee in 20 minutes. Get dressed, get there."

"Fraley," said Paunch, but the yelping of a disconnected line served as response. Paunch turned, focusing on his bedside clock.

He rolled out of bed, and shrugged. Paunch's best pants and least-stained shirt inhabited the floor. Minutes later—Thermos of steaming 'wake the hell up' rested between his thighs, two creams, two sugars—Paunch piloted toward Silsbee on 96 N.

Fraley's official vehicle idled, hazards blinking, just before Village Creek Bridge. Fraley reclined on the hood, smoking. Paunch stepped from his Ford Galaxie and walked toward his former friend. He paused, looked over the bridge, admiring the dark, gently drawing waters of Village Creek. Paunch swiveled to his left to witness sunrise crack over thousands of pines. He grinned, welcoming an emotion he missed since his daughter's death, **purpose**. "Riding with you?"

"You can follow me."

"Catch me up on which heap of shit we're traipsing into. Least you could do."

"I'd bet the crime scene'll do that. The deputy who found the body bow hunts with me. I trust him, but I gotta see this shit myself." Fraley paused and reached into his pocket. "Here." Fraley extended his hand, presenting a shiny offering. Paunch stared at his badge.

"Did you get me reinstated?"

"Ffff … no," Fraley scoffed. "Just liberated your badge from Ash's desk. When we get there, flash your badge, keep your trap shut. They know me; I've consulted a bunch down here. They won't question you if you're with me. Also, your ex-wife's new husband ain't got no allies in Silsbee. Ash treats small-town cops like secondary citizens. Lil' chance of our field trip bouncing back to him."

"Okay, I'll … ahh, follow you." Fraley nodded and turned toward his car.

During his windshield time, Paunch weighed what awaited him. Hundreds of bizarre death scenarios danced through his thoughts. He pushed them away, then looked to the heavens. Paunch cradled the long-forgotten rosary that swayed from his mirror. His fingers romanced the beads like a forgotten lover, remembering the route rhythm of Perez family prayers.

"We've not talked for a bit, but I could use your help, Lord. Show me something, anything." He exhaled, slowing as Fraley tapped his brakes.

Paunch's Ford followed Fraley's into the railroad and lumber mill town of Silsbee. Soaring loblolly pines bordered the street until they reached Ave. N. An old-fashioned burger joint, Top Burger, dominated the corner to Paunch's left. His car crept forward, passing First Baptist Church and gas stations before bumping over railroad tracks. A rail yard brimmed with activity to his left.

Fraley's signal flashed; he turned right on Ave. G. Paunch glanced to Farmer Funeral Home on the left before Fraley guided them right again. City workers abounded, cleaning up rubbish from the preceding night's celebration. The two pulled under the Pines Theater sign and exited their car. "Flash your badge, shut your mouth," Fraley reminded.

Paunch identified the corpse of a blond man, body resting under a tree. The body, still uncovered, stared at a circle of four men. The men—gripped in heated conversation—ignoring, or forgetting, the body and the evidence it provided, as it decayed steps away. None of the four turned to address the arriving officers.

"Shut up, dumbass, that's impossible," said a man, obviously not law enforcement, facing Paunch. The cheap suit identified him as a government employee, but not the kind with a badge. The other spectators, both wearing overalls and ball caps, nodded along.

"You're not a hunter. I am, and I'm telling you … " said the officer, Paunch guessed. Even out of uniform, the man's parlance proved his law enforcement credentials. Two patrol officers leaned against the back of a building, awaiting instruction.

"Just 'cuz you're a hick don't make you right, Matthews."

Matthews faced away from Paunch; pressed, tight jeans wrapped his backside. Skoal can ring marked his left butt cheek. Even from the rear, Paunch noticed a spit cup in the man's right hand. Not until Fraley reached the foursome did Matthews, without turning, speak to him. "Fraley?"

"Hey, boys," Fraley said, nodding to each observer.

"Tell this idiot what we're looking at."

"Deer tracks," said Fraley without pause.

"Told ya," said the man in the cheap suit.

Matthews shook his head. "No, shithead, put on your old-man glasses and look closer."

Fraley pulled out his readers, then he and Matthews crouched together. The others remained standing. The two said nothing, but Matthews pointed to four indentions in the ground. The two lingered, knees bent, staring at the print.

"Got any more like this?" Fraley asked.

"Wouldn't have woke ya if I found one."

"They all like this one?"

"Depends on how it was stepping," Matthews said. He stuck his finger into the indention. "Whatever it is, ain't missed a buncha meals. Weighed three-, shit, four-hundred pounds."

"Bullshit," the cheap suited man said. Paunch watched as the overall'd contingent nodded.

Fraley snickered to himself. "Yeah, you'd think so." He sat there bouncing an inch or two, like a catcher working into position, percolating. A minute later he said, "Any chance the tracks disappear into thin air?"

Matthews stared at Fraley, confused. "Yeah, but I thought maybe I lost the trail."

"Matthews, I've been on a dozen hunts with you—deer hunts. Don't remember you losing trails."

Matthews smiled at his friend, and they rose slowly, Fraley's knees crackling, signaling numerous orbits around the sun.

"What the hell is it?" said cheap suit.

"Could be a lotta things … in theory," Fraley said.

Cheap suit offered, "Probably a white-tail deer that gored 'em. Spooked by the fireworks."

"Nope," answered Fraley.

"What's your answer, Mr. … "

"Fraley, just call me Fraley. Not a deer. Not from around here. A white-tail deer leaves two indentions, sorta like two crescent moons facing."

"Well, that matches," said cheap suit.

"Sure, at first glance. Look here, boys. There are two more indentions. Made by the dewclaws. They look like slits. They're extra support to keep them from sinking in the snow. Give 'em extra grip when they're climbing. See here."

"Kinda looks like demon eyes, with horns. That's how I identify their tracks. Also, it's five frigging inches. A white-tail's print goes 'round 3."

"So, what is it?"

"Right now, let's just say, not a white-tail deer. And not from around here. Anyone keeping exotics on a ranch nearby?"

"Good thought, but no exotic ranches keeping one of these," said Matthews.

"Who's the beaner?" asked the octogenarian overall'd observer, pointing to Paunch.

"Don't call him that; that's Detective Perez," Fraley answered. Paunch flashed his badge. "Gotta name for Mr. Rigid over there?" Fraley pointed to the body.

"Not yet," said Matthews, "No wallet, no identification. But I can tell you, ain't local. Never seen 'im. Neither have these old timers." Matthews spit a black stream of Skoal spittle into the cup, then nodded toward the overall'd observers.

"Seems like I'd a recognized that ugly ass shirt if'n it was from round here," said the younger, plumper observer, whose chest, shoulders, and chubby arms squeezed out of the too-tight denim like cake frosting pushed out of a piping tube.

Paunch laughed, despite the situation, then asked, "We're all talking about hoof prints. I'm wondering why a hammer's wedged under the dead man's collar bone."

"Quite the mystery, ain't it?" the oldest man cackled.

"Got a decent idea," offered Matthews, looking down the alley at paint splatters, a collection of bricks, broken glass, and contractor tools.

"Hmm," Paunch vocalized.

Fraley held up his hand, demanding Paunch to stay in place, before projecting his next words. "Matthews, let's clear civilians?"

Matthews motioned to the two badges closest to the alley. They nodded and escorted the cheap suited man and the overall'd men away, walking them toward the library. Matthews leaned into Fraley, "Thanks for that; we had two past mayors there. The guy in the cheap suit's running for office. Not even elected yet. But, shit, small-town politics is a hornet's nest."

Fraley nodded and walked to the body. Matthews and Paunch followed.

"Who found the body?"

"Irony's a fickle bitch. The mortician from Farmer Funeral Home noticed it this morning."

Matthews observed the body. "Don't want to insert my opinion, Fraley. What do the gore marks tell you?"

Fraley stood, stared, blew out air through pressed lips, then spoke. "Don't need to examine the gore marks. The hoof print tells me everything."

"Caribou," Fraley and Matthews said together.

"But … " continued Fraley.

"But?" Matthews asked.

"I've worked lotsa crime scenes, did lotsa hunting. Heard of hunters or hikers getting gored, but never saw it." Fraley leaned closer to the body and pointed out punctures. "Any idiot can see this wasn't a white-tail rack or any native Texas deer."

"So, I'm not crazy?" Matthews asked.

"Didn't say that." Fraley grinned. "But you're right. Caribou."

"Whew … " Matthews spit into his cup, then grinned back. "Thanks for coming, Frales."

"There's a problem with our theory," said Fraley.

"The fact that caribou don't range south of Montana," continued Matthews.

"'Bout sums it up," answered Fraley.

"Like the bear that killed Flick Hurt," said Paunch before he stopped himself.

"I read about that," said Matthews. "I'd love to work that case."

Only if you like getting suspended, Paunch thought.

"Think they're related?" Matthews asked.

"In Beaumont, the vic, Flick Hurt, got indicted but not convicted of child molestation. Charges got tossed."

"Shit," Matthews said.

Fraley continued. "Petty-crime rap sheet longer than Paunch's waist line."

"Asshole," whispered Paunch.

"If this guy's scum," Fraley motioned to the velour-shirted dead man, "could be connected."

"I'll let you know when we find out," Matthews answered.

"There's something else," Fraley started.

"Okay."

"After Flick Hurt's death."

"Yeah?" Matthews asked.

"His wife, Sissie, and stepdaughter split; they're on the run," Fraley stated.

"Happens," added Matthews.

"Yeah, it happens. But … " Fraley paused, setting the hook, reeling Matthews into conspiracy. "There's the other incident, in La Grange."

"Little outsida your jurisdiction."

"Paunch went down on a … day off." He nodded to Paunch.

"Some guy got shish-kabobbed. A hole," Paunch tapped his two middle fingers and thumbs together, "this big went straight through him."

"Wow," said Matthews. "What's it gotta do with this?"

Paunch continued, "Locals are keeping theories to themselves so they don't sound like nitwits."

Matthews's eyebrows floated upwards.

"The victim, also a piece of shit, multiple visits to our state's finest correction facilities."

"Okay, that's a coincidence, but—" Matthews started.

"Just wait for it, Matthews," Fraley coached.

"The vic had frost bite on his fingers and around his innards," Paunch said.

Matthews stepped forward, fully engaged. "That was JUNE."

"Yes, skewered with a giant icicle," Paunch said.

"Bull … shit," said Matthews, enunciating each syllable.

"It's true," offered Fraley.

"How's it connected to the bear mauling in Beaumont?" Matthews asked.

"The dead man in La Grange, he ahh … tried to kidnap or kill a little girl," Paunch said. "The girl's since been identified as Teeny Voix." He paused, looking from Fraley to Matthews. "The stepdaughter of the Beaumont bear vic."

"Shiiiiiiiiiit," Matthews continued.

"Yesterday was the Fourth of July," Paunch said. "Crews are still cleaning up the mess."

"Yeah, I was with the fire department, helping with the fireworks' show."

"Bettin' there were tons of kids here?" Fraley said.

"Yep," Matthews answered Fraley's rhetorical question.

"Wondering if Teeny Voix was one of 'em?" Paunch asked.

"That's speculation, but possibly," said Matthews.

"If so, I'm betting she knows something about the hammer stuck in your vic's shoulder."

27

Paunch studied the clue bonanza in the alley. Even from this distance he spotted another hammer, bricks, paint bucket, and the giant paint splatter.

"What the … " Paunch stepped toward the alley.

Matthews gripped Paunch's shoulders, halting the suspended detective.

"Not yet, I gotta handle the body." Matthews said, thumbing toward the tree outcropping. "Let's evaluate the evidence in the alley together. I want your first response, not contemplations. So, wait for me. It'll take a bit."

Paunch wanted—needed—to walk down that alley, but respected Matthews' request.

For the first minute, Fraley and Paunch watched Matthews oversee the coroner's team collect the "victim's" body. Paunch studied passersby. Fraley took photos of everything around the victim before asking, "Matthews, can I follow the tracks?"

"Sure, but don't disturb anything."

"Wasted words, Matthews, always one for wasted words." He looked to Paunch. "I'll follow the tracks; look around the rest of downtown. See if you can find anything. If—"

"Wasted words," Paunch interrupted Fraley. "Done this before, asshole."

Each busied themselves with separate parts of the investigation. Fraley followed the caribou tracks. Matthews oversaw the body's collection and transportation.

Paunch realized how distracting the caribou tracks, gored body, and pushy local officials had been because, for the first time, he registered the splatter-spotted trail of red paint exiting the alley. He looked at the paint splatters, then caught Matthews' eye, leading the local officers' gaze to the red evidence trail.

Matthews shrug-nodded approval. At first, splashes of red and occasional pieces of busted windshield glass led the way. He noticed a smashed A-frame police barricade twenty yards ahead under a blackjack oak. Paunch guessed the retreating vehicle's size from the damage. In his mind he pictured the white van coated in red paint, the cracked window. He shook his head, trying to erase the image. No proof existed of a white van's involvement.

"Stay objective, stop putting your mental bullshit into this," he said aloud. He returned his attention to the fading paint trail. The splatters, spots, and dribbles decreased—then stopped—yards ahead near a signpost announcing G Street and N 2nd. Paunch imagined the paint shedding from *the white van* in sheets at first, then diminishing to …

"Stop, just stop," he said, before marking the paint trail's end and returning to the scene. He asked city workers, arriving librarians, and business owners if they attended last night's festivities. All confirmed. Did they spot a little girl who matched Teeny's description? Yep, a hundred, skinny, petite 8- to 10-year-old girls munched on popcorn, got snowcone-brain-freezes, and waved sparklers last night.

Next, he asked. "See any white vans?"

"You bet," "The Frito pie booth," "The cotton candy guy," "Ain't one always 'round?," "Kinda blends into the background," were his answers. He did not bring photos of Teeny Voix or Sissie Hurt to show witnesses and kicked himself for that.

Did anyone see or hear what caused the contractor debris, splattered paint, and broken glass in the alley? No one, surprisingly.

Probably happened during the firework show. Did anyone see the broken glass and scattered bricks on their way home? Nope.

A dozen times Paunch asked, "Did you spot the dead man under a tree?" He skipped the hammer hooked under his collar bone and antler gore marks. The interviewees offered recurring answers, "Nope, First I heard of it," and "Ain't that somethin'?"

Fraley had not returned from following caribou tracks, so, after his interviews, Paunch studied residents' reactions to the crime scene. Paunch's plan paid dividends when the Pines Theater manager arrived. The manager greeted the obviously enthralled neighbors and onlookers, concerned by a crime scene steps from his theater's entrance.

The manager glanced casually over his shoulder at his theater's marquee and winced. Paunch chronicled the reaction.

The manager's eyes led Paunch's to a shattered streetlight. The manager twisted back to his marquee, pivoting between it and the streetlight. Panic coated his face. The theater manager whipped out a jingling mess of keys and raced toward the Pines' entrance. Despite the assortment of 25+ keys, the man snatched the right one, jammed it into the door, threw back the entry, and bolted inside.

Intrigued, Paunch followed. A corpse in front of your theater, not an ideal marketing tool, Paunch thought. Still, the manager's mind focused on another crisis. Paunch needed to understand.

When Paunch entered the theater every light shined, some still buzzing, others flickering, signaling the manager woke them from night's slumber. A service door swung on its hinges. Guessing the manager's path, Paunch rounded the corner. The theater manager faced an ancient breaker box, staring.

Puzzlement—then relief—reflected in his expression when he turned to Paunch. He breathed deeply, smiling. The man studied Paunch. Remembering the crime scene, the manager's relief-smile vanished.

"You a police officer?" the manager asked.

"Detective," Paunch answered. The man looked confused, so Paunch offered detail. "From Beaumont."

"Oh, okay."

"Looks like you danced with a ghost. You okay?"

"I am now. Yeah."

"What happened?"

"Feel shitty saying this, 'cause a man died over there … "

"Go on," Paunch pressed.

"My marquee," the manager said, pausing like his answer solved the riddle. He studied Paunch's face, then added, "It was dark when I arrived."

Paunch watched the manager process the situation. After a moment the man continued. "The closing manager leaves the marquee shining all night. I shut 'er off when I arrive each morning."

Paunch's eyes encouraged continuation.

"It was off this morning … "

The manager considered the breaker box again. "I saw the broken streetlight and shattered glass and I thought —"

"You assumed someone vandalized your sign, too."

"Sounds terrible. We're a one-screen theater. Replacing a neon sign's not exactly in our budget." The manager paused and stared at light switches near the hall entrance, then back to the breaker box. Paunch let the man gather his clues. "Weird."

"Been a lot of that lately," Paunch said before he stopped himself.

The manager pointed. "Funny they didn't turn it off at the switch." Paunch looked at the bank of eight light switches. "They flipped the breaker."

Paunch walked over. Someone marked each breaker with duct tape and handwriting. Paunch studied the labels, Lobby, Balcony, Main Theater, Bathrooms … Marquee. The only flipped breaker.

"Huh," the two said together. Paunch followed the manager to the bank of switches. Unmarked, Paunch noted.

"Was the door locked when you arrived?" Paunch asked, out of habit.

"Think so, but I was panicked. So, not positive. Didn't check before I jammed in my key."

"So, someone broke into your theater—"

"Or walked in, if my night manager left the door open," the manager added.

"And that person, the intruder, for some reason, flipped off your marquee sign." Paunch did not add *which darkened the street and hid a body and a crime scene.*

Paunch's eyes locked onto an old, wooden milk crate under the breaker box. His mind raced.

"You okay?" the Pines Theater manager asked him as Paunch stood and stared at the milk crate. *A makeshift step stool?*

"Yeah, I'm okay."

"You're staring at the milk crate, like it solves the world's problems," the manager said. Paunch did not answer, guessing the milk crate promised answers he could not yet translate.

"Anyone on your crew really short?"

The manager considered the old milk crate. "Not short enough to need a milk crate to reach the breaker box."

"Hmm." Paunch's face crinkled.

"Want to make this stranger?"

"Why not," offered Paunch.

"Never seen that milk crate. Hell, I haven't seen a wooden milk crate since my teens. That thing's straight out of the 20s."

"You—" Paunch started.

"Yeah, I'm sure."

"Thanks." Paunch turned to leave. He stopped before looking over his shoulder. "Has this ever—"

"In my 30-plus years managing this theater, never happened once."

"I need to check entrances and exits. See how someone might access the place."

The manager nodded. Paunch started at the back door—locked, barred, and dusty. No one used the door in weeks—or months. He returned to the lobby, no broken glass, busted locks, or signs of break in.

The manager joined him in the lobby. "Are there any other entrances?"

"No ... " the manager paused, deep in thought.

"Your face tells me that's not completely true."

"Back in the 50s ... no, can't be."

Paunch twirled his finger, instructing the manager to continue.

"There's a group a kids, twelve year olds, who climbed to the roof, snuck through the duct system, came out on the balcony—to watch movies for free."

"Can we check?" Paunch asked.

"I guess." The manager shrugged, climbing the carpeted stairs to the balcony, Paunch followed. "We keep the balcony closed most nights. Cleaning crew ain't been up in a spell." The carpet, thick shag, left clues of previous occupants. Cowboy boots, loafers, kids' sneakers, women's pumps, and tennis shoe steps indented in the carpet.

Strange shoe prints—kid's boots, maybe—imprinted over the others.

Paunch felt magic in the air, déjà vu, pixie dust, something indefinable. A presence he experienced twice before. He knew before they reached the balcony. The AC duct stood open; the cover rested on a nearby seat. A dozen small boot imprints scattered from the origin point of the duct and fanned out, like an ant colony, foraging for food.

Or to flip a breaker and hide a crime scene.

"Just kids, pulling a prank, I guess. Strange it happening the same night as that murder," the manager offered.

"Strange. That's an appropriate word."

28

Paunch exited the theater, eyes struggling to transition from darkness to blazing blue Texas sky. He cleared his head before noting the fresh batch of crime scene observers. Paunch wondered if small-town gossip or darker motives hailed them. A gut pang, then nauseousness, overwhelmed Paunch as he studied the whole.

Paunch stepped toward the crowd, needing to be one with the collective, assimilate and isolate his instinct. A voice jerked him from his head.

"You clocked this, right?" Fraley asked. Fraley stood in the street, studying the paint trail.

Paunch nodded. "The paint trail ends right around the corner."

"Save it for Matthews."

Yards away, turning from his conversation, Matthews nodded toward Fraley, held up one finger, before reengaging.

Paunch returned his attention to the bystanders. Some he remembered from earlier. Others chatted with observers Paunch already noted as locals. The detective's gaze narrowed to one man.

A strangely handsome man in a Hawaiian shirt, shorts, and huarache sandals bracketed by a misfit menagerie. The Hawaiian-shirted man's demeanor communicated two words: "PISSED OFF." Paunch studied the man whisper-bark orders to the misfits surrounding him.

Paunch processed each group member, committing them to memory. To the Hawaiian-shirted man's right stood a whippet-thin guy in inappropriately-tight running shorts, and a tall swizzle stick of a man sucking a lollipop. To the Hawaiian-shirted man's left stood a skinny up top/fat-legged man with a wiry, yellow perm.

"Odd," said Paunch.

The grouping galloped past odd—and raced toward peculiar—as the Hawaiian-shirted man sniffed the air like a bloodhound on scent. The man's face crinkled, Paunch attempted to comprehend his expression: confusion, surprise, an upping of the stakes.

Paunch left Fraley's side, marched toward the group, readied his notepad, preparing to question the outliers. The Hawaiian-shirted man clocked Paunch's approach, nodded to his contingent. The group dispersed. Paunch followed the Hawaiian-shirted leader.

Paunch checked his holster and service pistol, remembering they rested in his chief's top drawer. "Damn't" he blurted.

The Hawaiian-shirted man surveyed over his shoulder, grinning, like he and Paunch now shared a secret. Paunch stutter-stepped to speed his pace, "Excuse me," he said, but the man continued his escape.

Before his next step, a hand gripped Paunch's shoulder. "Matthews needs us," Fraley said.

"Did you clock that strange group of guys? One of them had on a Hawaiian shirt."

"No, but I gotta little distracted. Come on."

Paunch turned back; the Hawaiian-shirted man had vanished. Paunch's head pivoted, none of the oddballs remained.

When they joined up with Matthews, Fraley confirmed he, like Matthews earlier, lost the caribou's trail. Paunch overviewed his interviews and the paint trail. Next, Paunch pointed to the broken streetlight; both noted the light earlier as well.

Paunch surprised Matthews and Fraley with the news that someone flipped the breaker at the Pines Theater. Both struggled to hide confusion when Paunch explained someone small—children most likely—entered through the theater's duct system and flipped the breaker.

The three stood dumfounded, rotating from the busted streetlight to the Pines Theater, then down the alley. "Well, shit," sputtered Matthews. "Let's, ahh," he nodded toward the alley, "stroll down and decide if the crazy train jumped the rails."

The three gathered around the scene.

"Definitely a windshield, boys," Fraley said, after bending down and pushing shards of broken windshield glass with a pen. "Something … " He pointed to the roof.

"Someone," he clarified, "from up there attacked a vehicle." Fraley stared over his shoulder and pointed to muddy tire marks that ripped through the grass lot. He stood, considering everything. "Damn war zone."

Matthews offered, "Bricks, hammers, paint, hundreds of penny nails, shattered glass from a … "

"A vehicle that'll be easy to identify. If we locate the damn thing," Paunch finished the thought.

Matthews turned, studying the environment, noticing a key piece of evidence lying on the ground, its end peeking into the alley. "And a ladder."

Matthews' team collected the ladder, committing it to evidence. Minutes later, Matthews scrounged another ladder from the jewelry store owner. Paunch followed Matthews and Fraley up the borrowed ladder and to the roof. As he stepped onto the roof, Paunch heard the call of an approaching train. From his position, he turned and watched blinking red lights on each side of 5th street, the main drag. Two red and white metal arms lowered, blocking traffic, as the train approached. Even from his vantage point on the roof, Paunch could hear the *whoosh, whoosh, whoosh* as Santa-Fe branded boxcars, covered hoppers, and tank cars passed.

"We processing a crime scene or watching the choo-choo," Fraley ribbed.

"We get ten of those a day," Matthews added, discounting the train.

Paunch and the others turned their attention to the roof. Seconds later, the three men gathered around a pile of bricks, rusted nails, and abandoned tools. "Shit's been up here a long while, boys," said Fraley studying the battle's unused ammunition.

"We found their arsenal," Matthews said.

"But whose arsenal?" asked Paunch.

"That's a hell of a question," said Fraley.

"Someone was up here … " started Matthews, then stopped. He turned, staring toward his position the night before. "To watch the fireworks show." He pointed to where he and the volunteer fire department oversaw the celebration. "Hell of a view from this spot."

"Kids, maybe. Vandals. Drunks … " Fraley said.

"No beer bottles, Boone's Farm, or Thunderbird," Paunch noted.

"I've done this a long time. Not as long as you," Matthews lobbed at Fraley.

"Screw you, Matthews," Fraley returned.

Matthews continued, "But usually I'm searching for clues. Here we got clue overload."

Speaking of overload, Paunch stood staring at the cars waiting for the train to pass. A blush blue Chevy Nova station wagon puttered up behind an idling cream '66 Mustang. The Nova's driver, blocked by the downtown buildings, did not note the crime scene yards away.

"Sissie Hurt," Paunch whispered to himself. Paunch turned to the train, still whipping by, estimating—if he hustled—he could catch her.

"What was that?" Matthews asked over his shoulder.

"Nothing," said Paunch, "I got to get something from ground level. Be right back." As Paunch reached the ladder, he watched the faded red and yellow Santa Fe caboose roar past the intersection. Seconds later, the railroad crossing gates opened, and the blush blue Chevy Nova wagon pulled away.

He forced himself to return to Matthews and Fraley, hiding his newfound knowledge.

Paunch acted engaged as the three explored the rest of the roof. Matthews asked, "Any chance the gored body and the attack on the vehicle ... are unrelated?"

Fraley shook his head. "Hell of a coincidence if they are, boys."

"The hammer sticking out of the cadaver's ... " Paunch pointed to the point of the hammer's insertion into the body.

"Yeah, okay," Matthews said. "Related."

Fraley started, "A caribou, a dead man, a broken streetlamp ... "

"A flipped breaker, fireworks show ... " Paunch added.

"And a battle," Matthews said.

"To the death," Fraley continued. "Can't forget that part. A battle to the death."

"What the hell happened here?" Matthews asked, staring into the alley beneath him.

Fraley finished, "And who were the combatants?"

Paunch knew one person, more specifically one eight-year-old girl, who possessed answers to those questions.

29

Simos Diner, near Garden Oaks, Houston, Texas, November 20, 2026

"Teeny stayed put, despite … "

Val nodded.

"And Paunch kept the fact that he spotted Sissie's car to himself."

"Yes."

"But … " Harold paused, unwinding facts in his head. Val studied him, watching him process, check some mental box, before moving to the next line of questioning.

"This shit's missing from the case files."

Val's face dropped into melancholy. Harold studied Val, maybe as a human for the first time. "Can I … ahh, say something?"

"Sure, Harold."

"You're like my mom's age, so take this the right way."

"Where's this heading, Harold?"

"But you're … I mean, for your age, considering everything, I bet, in your time, I'd bet, outside of the job, you were … really pretty."

"I especially like the qualifiers you stuffed in there, Harold. How does my appearance relate to anything?"

"You already dissected me."

She shrugged.

"So, I get to analyze you."

She sipped her coffee, emptying the cup.

"You're smart, direct … were pretty, why choose this life?"

"Like most cops, it chose me," Val answered.

"Your personal file starts at college. No mention of parents. Bet your dad was a cop?"

Harold waited for an answer, none came, but then the strangest thing happened. A tear trickled down Val's cheek. She erased the evidence quickly. "My dad, no."

"Someone close to you?"

"Let's get back to the case," Val said, shutting down questioning.

"If I join your team, you'll tell me about him?"

Val nodded, but remained mum. Instead, she waved for another cup of coffee. Seconds later, the waitress filled her cup and topped off Harold's.

"How much coffee have you had?" Harold asked.

Val stayed on task, adding creamer and Sweet 'n Low .

"That artificial sweetener crap'll kill you," Harold said.

"I doubt it," Val replied. She let her gaze bounce around the diner, taking in the characters, sounds of bustle, aromas of coffee entwined with bacon.

She glanced out the window, escaping questions for a moment.

And there he stood. "Shit."

"What?" asked Harold.

"Stay here. I'll be back."

"But … "

"Harold, whatever you see out that window, STAY PUT."

He nodded, then watched Val storm out of Simos into the parking lot, toward a man reclining against a black Mercedes, donning a $10,000 suit.

30

The door exploded open as Val marched toward him. He looked good. Too good. The quick-clack high heels marked her trek toward Simos Diner's landmark pole sign. His legions and their matching vehicles surrounded him in the restaurant parking lot. Only a narrow strip of grass and ten feet separated him from passing traffic.

Behind him, on Shepherd Drive, a mustard yellow mommy mobile zipped by, followed by a vintage MG MGB, and an Amazon delivery van. A lawn maintenance truck passed next, six crew members stuffed in the cab. The truck's trailer, jammed with blowers, rakes, and wet grass-covered mowers rattled behind. Scatterings of fallen leaves and nubs of manicured lawns wafted in the wind.

The slimy, but handsome, man in the bespoke suit, loitering in the Simos parking lot, acted unaware of traffic behind him.

Sporting a perfectly trimmed beard and mustache this time, he reveled in the day. Limited edition Brunello Cucinelli sunglasses rested on the crown of his head. The slicked-back dark hair, a different shade, but the taunting grin remained the same. Leaning against one of three tinted-window black Mercedes hybrid sedans, he looked around—to include his cohorts.

"Hey, boys, meet my OLD friend Valentina," he said before she reached him.

She continued her march.

"The Valenator," he added.

"No one calls me that."

Each minion checked her briefly before losing interest. The man in the custom suit chuckled, "If they knew your sordid past, old girl."

"I **felt** you were back … " she paused, allowing him to fill in the blank.

"Devlin … " He smiled impishly.

She waited for his finish. She expected and received flourish.

"Devlin Maycare," he finished, then bowed.

"That's what you're going with this time? Just one letter from the truth."

He turned, facing traffic. "Why disguise who I am, Val? Today's parents, the choices these imbeciles make," his snakish eyes traced passing cars. "The slime they elect, the programming they allow their kids to view, ahh, and the video games. Come on, Val. Society summoned me, mailed handwritten invitations. No need for me to hide anymore."

"Guess not." She studied his and his team's sartorial selections. "New dress code."

"Ahh, thanks for noticing. They **say** crime doesn't pay. But, well." His arms flared out, a vulture spreading its wings to collect sunbeams on a cool day. She considered the full show. His minions surrounded him, three chattered in French while smoking Gauloises Caporal. One sat in a passenger's seat clipping fingernails, two others leaned against a Mercedes, arguing. She studied their jackets, each packing heat.

"Bring enough guys?"

"You look old, Val."

"And you … look exactly the same, except for the show-poodle beard and the overpriced suit."

His head tilted back, his body embracing the chuckle. The theatrics seemed forced, too grand. When Devlin finished, he paused as his face shifted to insincere concern.

"Oh, I've missed you, Val. The memories. Shame we don't have more time together or specifically … you don't," he tapped his Rolex, "have time."

"We'll see."

His minions circled. "Father Time's got you on the clock, Val-pal."

"Until the buzzer runs out, I'll find new ways to stop you."

"Keep telling yourself that, Valerino. Who knows, one day, you'll believe it."

One minion stepped forward, inches from her. The slack-jawed man loomed over the fit, tiny woman. He paused, seething threat. He inched his face closer, then closer still. A dark, crooked smile slow-blossomed over his demented face, rust-colored teeth on display. "Woof," he barked, then smiled, turning to his brethren, reveling in his joke attempt.

Val refused to give a centimeter. She waited, staring, imparting her boredom, and, as she suspected, the mongrel returned to his horde, tail between his legs, ridiculed by his mates.

"I stopped you before," Val said, returning her attention to Devlin. "More than once."

"Stopped, that's a stretch. Inconvenienced, interrupted."

"You keep telling yourself that," she echoed.

"Well, you had help. Help that'll not be available today, in this world, I suspect."

He measured her up, then down. "Looking good, Val ... considering. Got the legs of a 25-year-old runway model. Running still?"

"When I can."

"Be honest, not so much anymore."

Val wondered if Devlin's minions staked her out.

"When will you tell everyone?" Devlin reached into the vehicle and returned with a pathology report, CT scans, and MRIs. He presented the file to her, like a gift. "Yours, it would seem." Val did not bother asking how he got it. People—let's say hospital administrators—have secrets, addictions, foibles. People—with secrets—can be leveraged.

Devlin studied the diner's window. Val followed his gaze. Harold eagle-eyed their meeting. "He's not the answer, Val. I know the family;

arrogant, entitled. Unless you're playing for my side, hubris is not an attractive quality."

Studying Devlin, or whatever name he used this time, she caught something. His smile faltered. Her glance moved from minion to minion, the expensive clothes, meeting her unannounced. "You're right," Val said. "Hubris is unattractive and points to deep-seated insecurities."

"Ahh, you underestimate me, Val."

"Sure it's me underestimating?"

"Like I said, you're on the clock." Devlin's stare followed movement in the restaurant, movement she failed to register, facing him. He slid his sunglasses down, masking his face. She noted the dark lenses for the first time. "Well, time to depart. I'll spread your file around."

She caught it again, the insecurity or …

"I doubt it. Or you already would have."

She turned to Simos Diner, her old booth. Harold no longer occupied the window seat; the diner's door jingled, and he jogged toward her.

Interesting, the arrogant putz, running to ensure her safety. Strangely, as she watched Harold's approach, car doors slammed behind her, and Mercedes' tires squealed. She whispered to herself, "Why the show of force? Unless I … or he," Val turned to Harold. She smiled, unsure before but certain now. Understanding her next move, tears of relief flowed. Harold glided beside her as the last of Devlin's convoy peeled away. "Scares you," she whispered.

31

Silsbee, Texas, July 6, 1976

Dark, gluttonous clouds devoured sunlight, as afternoon turned to evening. Porch lights flicked on, one by one along Durdin Drive, beckoning scattered children home.

Ditches dispatched water from the earlier downpour. Rain released its grip on the day only hours before but threatened fresh assault. A car bumped down the slick asphalt street, finding each rain-filled pothole, the driver oblivious to the chase in the damp field twenty yards away.

Teeny's arms pumped, racing from her pursuer. She zigzagged, to throw him off. His footsteps closed, and Teeny understood milliseconds remained. No help offered itself this day. She turned, spotting him, calculating her end.

By diverting attention from her steps, she made the game-ending mistake. Teeny's sneaker clipped a muddy crawdad tower, and she tumbled forward. He cackled before releasing the projectile.

Spoiiink, the red dodge ball slammed into her lower back, before bounding away. She flopped over and moptop stood over her.

"Gotcha," moptop said, laughing, before turning to retrieve the ball.

Teeny represented the final out. Game over.

Half the Durdin Drive wildlings' hands thrust skyward in victory. Half's head hung, if only for seconds.

Teeny took a moment to adjust her hat, pulling it over her ears. She rubbed her lower back with her left hand; it smarted.

Teeny rested on the wet St. Augustine, grass-stained, muddy, sweaty, coated in filth, back-tingling but brimming with joy. Like each kid, overjoyed to escape the boredom of being trapped by the rain with babysitters, mothers, aunts, and/or grandmothers watching *General Hospital, As the World Turns,* or *Days of Our Lives.* She considered each playmate and grinned.

Bulldog jaw boy and three others stood over her. The bulldog-jawed boy glanced to his moptop brother over celebrating and mouthed, "Sorry." He extended his hand.

Teeny accepted happily and the boy jerked her upright.

Moptop raced back with the ball. "Let's play again."

"Can't," mumbled a mud-stained redhead, pointing to porch lights. "Gotta get."

"Just one more," moptop begged, but the crowd parted. Each filthy participant followed their beacon, signaling King Ranch Chicken, fried river catfish and hushpuppies, or Nana's awaiting pot roast. Evening began coloring the sky.

The bulldog-jawed boy motioned to a tired Grand Prix pulling into the driveway. Even Teeny knew the Grand Prix meant Myrtis's daughter arrived to collect moptop and the bulldog. "Gotta go, I guess," moptop begrudged.

Teeny followed the two, as Molly's house sat next to the boy's grandmother's. Teeny collected pecans, from last year's crop, still littering the yard. She avoided rotted ones and found worthy candidates, dropping them into her pocket, then skipped to Molly's. From behind her, "goodbyes," "love ya's", and slamming car doors, as the Grand Prix pulled out, spitting pecan shells upon exit.

She snuck a peek to the back yard and found Sissie's (Marcia's) car parked. *Tuesday,* Teeny celebrated! Dancing, jumping, throwing her hands in the air. Tuesday. Sissie's night off!

Teeny jumped the stairs, bolted across the porch before the swinging door announced her entry.

"Evening," Molly said. "When you starting dinner?" Teeny shrugged, skipping past Molly toward the room she shared with Sissie.

Maybe they could cook together for a change. She stopped in her tracks before reaching the threshold.

One whiff, all it took. The girl's face collapsed. **Perfume**.

Teeny moped toward the bedroom threshold. Sissie, chair parked in front of the mirror, finished applying makeup. Sissie wore the pink dress Teeny earned sorting yard sale donations days earlier. After being ignored, Teeny pounded her foot into the ground.

"Hey, girl, momma's gotta date."

Teeny walked to the calendar on the wall tapping her finger on the day.

"I know it's a Tuesday, but it's your momma's only night off."

Teeny pointed to herself. Sissie huffed, "I spent lotsa time with ya. Momma needs adult time and a stiff drink … or two."

Teeny shook her head, as tears welled. "Come on, I'm wearin' the dress you bought me. And I ain't had a real date in years. He's real nice."

Teeny looked to her momma's bed, unmade, as usual. Her momma's suitcase splayed open on the bed. Three middling outfits Sissie considered but tossed aside littered the room.

Teeny reached up to her hat, then pointed to her mom.

"I spent twenty minutes doin' my hair. I ain't wearin' no hat Tee …" she said," before enunciating loud enough for Molly to overhear, "Jan."

"No one's gonna recognize me," she whispered. "We're headin' to the Steak-n-Ale in Beaumont. Fancy."

Horror coated Teeny's face. "No one's goin' to see me. Besides, I ain't staying here, locked up like a nun forever. And … he's key-ute, wiry, blond hair, nice thick legs."

Teeny's head volleyed to Opie. The plush toy opossum offered no opinion. Teeny gripped her momma's shoulders, begging Sissie not to go. Sissie pointed to the bed. Teeny trudged over.

Teeny's momma finished her makeup, stood, and turned toward Teeny. Teeny's eyes questioned. "He spotted me waitin' on the train, right 'fore I pulled off. I realized I was outta gas, so I pulled over a few blocks down the way. He followed me, pumped my gas. Very romantic."

Teeny shook her head, mime-begging. Then she went to the window looking for the guy's car. "He wanted to pick me up here. But I wouldn't let 'im. I won't let strange men come to the house ever again. Promise."

Teeny held up her hands, encouraging more detail.

"I'm meetin' 'im at the J&M Grocery Store. I'll leave my car in the lot."

Teeny's *are you nuts* expression needed no translation.

"It's just one night. We're safe."

Teeny plunged toward her momma and wrapped her body around Sissie's leg. Holding on for dear life. Teeny stared into her momma's eyes, begging, praying, demanding for her not to go … to leave Teeny behind.

"It's one date, I ain't runnin' off or somethin'."

Teeny collapsed backward onto the floor. She stared at the ceiling. Cataloging faux-fathers fumbling into and out of her life. Drunks, dumbasses, divorcees, liars, loafers, lechers … then Flick (who wrapped the six-pack of loserdom in one fatass package).

Teeny processed. Despite grinding through graveyard shifts, maintaining Molly's home, caring for Teeny, and surviving on the run, Sissie squeezed in time to unearth another candidate for her lifelong loser-boyfriend battle royale. Teeny did not need to meet the louse to know; her momma preserved a perfect scorecard.

"Jan," Sissie said, "How much worse can he be than Flick?"

Teeny stared at the mouse trap in the corner, before shifting to cobwebs above. "Come give momma a hug, 'fore I leave." The young girl refused, holding her spot. "Come on." Teeny flipped over, facing the floor, muffing her ears with tiny hands.

"Okay, have it your way," her momma said. "But at least tell momma how pretty she looks."

Teeny refused.

"Goodbye, my beautiful, tiny, stubborn, tougher-n-nails girl. Love ya."

The echo-click of her momma's yard sale heels exiting offered the room's only sound. Outside, her momma's car started and Teeny watched from the window as the blush blue Chevy Nova wagon reversed from the driveway.

One emotion overcame Teeny. She struggled to identify it. Not fear, abandonment, or even loneliness. Dread.

Teeny's pride, anger, and fear faltered. She popped up, raced out the door, the screen slamming behind her, flying off the porch.

"Who's cooking my dinner?" Molly's words trailed Teeny as the girl sprinted away.

The tiny girl, alone in the darkness, chasing her momma's taillights. Sissie roll-stopped the Nova on the corner of Durdin Drive and Woodrow Street, before disappearing ... into darkness.

32

Silsbee, Texas, July 7, 1976

Surrounded by warmth, Teeny smiled. Sissie climbed in bed next to her last night.

Strange Sissie chose this morning to nuzzle. How bad was her date? Teeny's eyes batted open as memories from last night crept back into her consciousness. After making Molly's Manwich, Teeny and the old woman ate on TV trays watching the *Tony Orlando & Dawn Rainbow Hour* on CBS. The chorus of *Tie a Yellow Ribbon Round the Ole Oak Tree* still rang in Teeny's ears.

Teeny forced herself to remember the rest of the evening's events. After the show and cleaning the kitchen, she vacuumed the living room, guided Molly to bed, then Teeny and Opie waited on the porch together for Sissie's return. Succumbing to exhaustion, the girl and Opie plodded to bed.

Now Teeny enjoyed a warm moment with her momma, cuddled to her. Surrounded by the warmth and safety of her protector.

A moment so rare, she decided to consider each one ...

Teeny reached through the recesses of her mind finding no memories existed of snuggling with her momma. Teeny decided she must be incorrect and respun her mental Rolodex. Diddly squat.

Huh.

Teeny, emerging from dream state, allowing her senses to engage. First, smell. No scent of stale beer, cigarette smoke, intermixed with body sweat, the nose cues Teeny associated with Sissie's nights on the town.

Taste. Teeny smacked her tongue; her staleness of breath offered a clue. Sissie failed to shake Teeny awake to brush her teeth. Next, touch. After three squeezes, Teeny understood; she held Opie, not her momma, in her arms.

Opie, soft, dependable, always present. Before Teeny cried herself to sleep last night, around 2:30 a.m., she surrounded herself with a pillow fortress. The pillows, not her momma, offered warmth and the impressions of safety. Sight. Teeny flipped up and looked across the room at the second twin bed; scattered dresses and the splayed suitcase remained. No one occupied Sissie's bed last night.

Hearing. The last sense arrived cruelly. Molly demanded, "Who's making breakfast?"

Teeny realized the answer to Molly's question. With no ceremony, over the last weeks, she, not her momma, acted as Molly's caretaker. "Jan, Jan, I'm hungry, Jan."

Teeny sighed, no time to cry or worry, only time to steward HER ward. Teeny's tiny feet dropped to the cold floor, she banged her foot, alerting Molly, *message received.*

Worries for her momma pushed forward, attacking her thoughts, threatening to spiral. Teeny slammed her foot floorward again, but this time rallying herself. Fraidy-cat thoughts do not help at this moment.

Thinking Teeny forced *Scared Teeny* to step into the periphery. *Scared Teeny* and her worry, hand ringing, and doubt offered no value in this moment.

Thinking Teeny started her multiplication tables to comfort her and *Scared Teeny.* 7x1= 7, 7x2=14, 7x3=21 …

Unconvinced, *Scared Teeny* tried to seep back to the frontal lobe. But *Thinking Teeny* tossed the emotional wreck into the shadows, relegated her there until *Thinking Teeny* formulated solutions.

Now officially in command, *Thinking Teeny* marched to the kitchen and inventoried the items left in the refrigerator. She counted grocery jar money—$3.17—and created an emergency grocery list in her head.

Teeny marched to the guest bathroom, holding up one finger to Molly, signaling, *Just a minute, please.*

Teeny continued to process as she entered the bathroom, brushed away a wasted tear, removed the cap from an empty tube of Crest toothpaste, rolled the bottom tight, to force out another last-gasp-half-squirt, wet her toothbrush, and scrubbed her teeth.

33

While Teeny brushed her teeth, far from her bathroom a pursuer awoke, sobbing. Tears and sweat stained his pillow and bed sheet. Familiar with the nightmare, recognizing it, pushing it back into his subconscious, he kept his eyes jammed shut and wiped his tears. The operation: familiar, repeated, rote.

Once he dealt with the nightmare, Paunch's eyes opened, and he stared at an unfamiliar ceiling. His first thoughts were not of Teeny, or Sissie. His first thought, *Where the hell am I?*

Each morning at his apartment Paunch woke, staring at a popcorn-textured ceiling and a light fixture missing two bulbs.

This ceiling, smooth textured and recently painted, tested his equilibrium. The smell of a recently Pine-Sol'd bathroom greeted his nose. Not his place.

Someone—him he assumed—tossed off his covers, in the middle of the night, and he lay, belly exposed, sporting day-old tighty-whities, on an ancient but well-maintained queen bed. Soft light passed through the gold curtains, offering an amber glow for him to explore his surroundings. His head drifted right, then left, as he assembled the pieces.

Hotel room.

Paunch sat up and winced, experiencing the type of pain sleep camouflages. Now awake, the injuries reintroduced themselves.

"Crap." He looked down at a large, steering wheel shaped, purple bruise covering his chest.

He rubbed his neck, sore, probably a mild case of whiplash awaited him too. "Fantastic," he said. He spun, allowing his feet to touch the floor, memories flowing back, accompanying the pain.

Images cut through his brain. Yesterday he prowled the streets of Silsbee for hours after he and Fraley parted ways. He guided his sedan up and down major thoroughfares and residential drives of the small town, finding nothing. At each turn, wondering why he chose not to tell Fraley about spotting Sissie's Nova.

He knew—but did not want to admit—he resented Fraley—and his police brethren—for abandoning him after his divorce, while he struggled through the death of his daughter. More so, selfishly, he needed answers to unanswerable questions.

Questions about a bear, a caribou, a roof top battle, an icicle impalement, white vans, and a little girl and her momma on the run recycled through Paunch's brain, fueling him. Still, all fuel tanks run dry.

10:44 p.m. last night, Paunch's personal reserves redlined. Determined, but exhausted, Paunch nodded to sleep patrolling near the Silsbee Tiger's Football Field on 7th Street and Ave. C. He woke, tossed forward, then back, as his sedan coasted into a ditch.

Old timers, who sat shooting the shit on a screened front porch, ambled out to his rescue. The two, happy for distraction from the survey-encroachment-fenceline argument they beat to death nightly for twenty-two years. Disgusted by the disagreement, the old timers' wives banished the topic to the screened porch.

Using an ancient, rusted Chevy pickup, the two locals sparred/argued, offering and rejecting the other's advice, before successfully jerking Paunch's dented Ford Galaxie from the ditch. After explaining, yes, he was a cop, no, he had no experience in survey-encroachment-fenceline disagreements, he departed with firm handshakes from the old men's life-worn hands.

Ten minutes later, he booked this room at Silsbee's Pinewood Inn, then flopped into bed. His Beaumont home lay just twenty minutes away; still, he did not want to risk falling asleep at the wheel again.

Despite exhaustion, once in bed Paunch's thoughts raced, crippling his chances for an early night. Trying to fall asleep, assuming he never would, his body acquiesced after he turned to the bedside clock sometime after 2:30 a.m.

The sore, suspended detective battled back to the present, focused on deep breaths before dressing in his stale, day-old clothing, and plopped back on the bed. The creaks and groans of the bed frame beseeching him to abandon fried foods.

"Another day, looking for a mother and daughter who don't want to be found. This'll be exciting." His last sentence, meant as sarcasm, turned out to be prophetic instead.

He walked to his hotel room's cramped bathroom and looked for something, hell, anything, to brush his teeth. No small tube of toothpaste or brush presented itself. He turned on the water, scrubbing his teeth with his pointer-finger.

34

Simos Diner, near Garden Oaks, Houston, Texas, November 20, 2026

Harold reached Val, catching her wipe her face; 'tears' he questioned. Still, the screeching exit of the Mercedes caravan demanded attention. "Who the hell was that?" he asked.

Val stood, not answering. Harold waited for a moment, processing the events he witnessed.

"Did he threaten you?"

She shrugged.

"Brought a metric ton of assholes," said Harold.

Val's body remained in Simos's parking lot, but, to Harold, her mind appeared galaxies away.

Color exploded in Harold's face, as his brain tickled the wrinkle that stored a favorite memory. "You know that old movie, *Die Hard*?" he asked.

She stayed silent. Harold watched Val sort through emotions, process thoughts, or both.

"Val," he said, demanding attention.

"Yeah," she answered flatly.

"Remember that old movie, *Die Hard*?"

Val said, "Surprised you're old enough to."

"That movie played on repeat my entire childhood. Those guys in the Mercedes looked like Hans Gruber and his crew from *Die Hard*."

She remained mum, so he doubled down. "When Hans stepped off the elevator at the Nakatomi Tower."

A slow grin confirmed she appreciated Harold's reference.

"Dude looked like a half-assed Hans Gruber."

Val nodded to the spot Devlin Maycare vacated. "He'd take that as a compliment." The two stood yards from Shepherd Drive, close enough to the street that passing cars offered "whooshes" of trailing air.

Not the location to revel in moments, Harold watched Val revel anyway. She considered the heavens, then a passing taupe Toyota Tundra, but not her companion. As if in prayer, she closed her eyes, and he swore she whispered, "Thank you."

When Val turned to him, moments later, she smiled, not the begrudging smirk of their first meetings, or the polite halfhearted offering when he arrived at Simos. This smile offered something Harold never received from his driven mother or social-climbing grandmothers. A smile that he, and most men, wait lifetimes to enjoy.

A smile of complete acceptance, complete joy. A smile that shouts to the gods, you're my favorite person in the entire world. Val offered the smile of a mother welcoming a son home from an overseas war, a grandmother embracing grandkids at Thanksgiving.

He paused, realizing the smile said more still. *You are the answer to my prayers.*

He processed her expression, not knowing why his appearance in the parking lot altered their relationship. The moment ended as quickly and surprisingly as it started. The toughest woman he met wiped a final tear, girded herself, then returned to her old form.

"Our table better still be there," she said, turning, marching away, the click clacks of stilettos striking asphalt cutting through the street noise and his laugh.

He hollered after her. "I think we'll be okay," then jogged after her.

She paused at the entrance to Simos, waiting for him to catch up. "Yes, I think so too. Let's finish the story, Harold. You've got a huge decision to make."

35

Silsbee, Texas, July 7, 1976, late afternoon

Teeny peered from behind a mismatched garbage can collection near South 7th Street into the J&M Grocery parking lot. Her bucket hat, pulled down tightly, cropped her ears. *Breakfast at Tiffany's* style sunglasses, snatched from Molly's vanity, masked Teeny's face. Opie's face poked from a yard-sale-rescued black backpack slung over her shoulder.

Hours earlier, Teeny prayed for her momma to stagger through the door, hung over, drunk, stoned, filled with excuses. Teeny willingly accepted all options, just to hug her momma again. After 10 a.m., Teeny's worry blossomed to fear, then terror. *Scared Teeny* nearly ripped the young girl apart, before *Thinking Teeny* regained command of the girl's subconscious, with a plan the two agreed on.

Teeny's makeshift breakfast satisfied Molly. Teeny left Molly's premade lunch, a repeat of breakfast, in the fridge. Myrtis, the next-door neighbor, promised to check up on Molly and deliver dinner.

Next, Teeny worked one hour at her widowed neighbor's yard sale and owed two more in exchange for the outfit she now sported: a man's size small, forest-green T-shirt, which hung to her knees covering black polyester girl's shorts. Teeny's camo-gear. Not perfect, but better than her usual arsenal of pinks, purples, and daisy-yellows.

Knowing her mom left their Nova at J&M Grocery Store, *Thinking Teeny* felt unsafe buying groceries. Sissie's disappearance hinted the

White Van People approximated Teeny's location. So, shopping anywhere, not wise.

Teeny mime negotiated with the yard-sale widow's daughter, to purchase groceries for Molly, in exchange for a 10% service fee. Teeny penciled Molly's grocery needs and handed the list and $3.17 to the girl.

With the basics completed or delegated, Teeny shifted to phase two. Finding her momma. She hiked to J&M Grocery's parking lot. Teeny chose not to ride Molly's bike; instead she traveled wooded paths, staying off streets. She crossed TX-327—a trafficked thoroughfare—when no cars approached, staying invisible … as much as possible. Sweat glistened over her exposed, twig arms and legs as the sun beat down on her.

From her vantage point, Teeny could not see her momma's Nova. She watched Copenhagen spitting roughnecks, grandmothers with gaggles of grandchildren, and young, pregnant, former small-town beauty queens enter and exit the store. She inspected each car and studied the changes in her view of the parking lot as vehicles exited and entered. From her hiding spot on 7th, she could survey half the lot.

She noted each white van. Three arrived, one delivering small cakes, another chips, and a third Wonder bread. Product advertisements covered each vehicle. None of those vans alarmed Teeny. The vans' drivers hopped out quickly and loaded carts with boxes of products.

But … a fourth white van, this one unmarked, remained parked near the lot's center. Teeny sweated, studying the van from behind her trash-can blind. The fourth remained parked. A man with tightly-curled, permed, blond hair occupied the driver's seat. His head swiveled back and forth, then back again, scrutinizing the lot.

Teeny remembered her momma's description of her date and wondered if the van's driver acted as her momma's suitor. She lacked evidence, but the driver gave Teeny the heebie-jeebies. The girl considered options.

Sneak to the parking lot's opposite side now, in daylight.

Or wait here, sweating—Texas heat bearing down—until dark to make a move.

Thinking Teeny took over, deciding for her. Yes, she wanted answers, but abandoning her spot risked everything. Darkness offered an empty parking lot and answers to her questions with less risk.

Over the next hours, drifting clouds blotted out the sun, offering relief from the heat's pounding. Teeny repositioned herself and moved one trash-can lid to block the sun's rays. Steadfast in her watch, as cars cycled through the lot, Teeny eyed the back edge of her momma's blush blue Nova.

Still, she confirmed color only, not shape. As the day droned on, she slapped assaulting attackers. Dozens of welts and splattered mosquito guts covered her tender skin. A neighborhood tomcat visited her trash-can fort, purring, rubbing against her, inspecting her efforts. The cat completed his tour, departing with a flicking tail.

Teeny's study returned to the white van's driver, still there. Early evening took over, sounds of crickets came first, then bullfrogs. Cars exited the lot, but the white van remained. As did employee vehicles, late-shopping customers, and remaining vendors.

Finally, as the sky shifted from blue to pink, the van's driver exited the van and stretched. He possessed a strangely thin upper body, but a thick rear and stocky legs. The man turned, inspecting the parking lot's four corners. Teeny noticed the man's legs jammed tightly together. She recognized the stance. Tink, from Mrs. Calderon's class, squeezed his legs tight and squirmed when he needed to tinkle—the pee-pee dance.

The white van's driver jogged inside, and Teeny's eyes darted north, then south. She abandoned the trash-can fort's safety and hurried into the lot. She ran past high school-aged kids, one boy and three girls, laughing, aprons tossed over their shoulders, leaving work, not a care in the world; Teeny ran toward the blush blue Nova wagon. The boy, a handsome blond, with bright blue eyes and a mischievous grin nodded at her as she passed. "Nice sunglasses, kid."

Teeny waved but kept moving. Once clear of the high school contingent, Teeny focused on getting to the car before the white van's driver returned from the bathroom. Teeny's feet moved faster than her brain, forgetting parking lot's dangers.

"Watch out," the blue-eyed boy called.

Teeny turned to him before …

The high school girls screamed.

Time stood still, the *Urrrrk* just inches from her. Teeny's head whipped back, a Lincoln Continental "uuuuurcked," to a stop inches from her. Approximately 4883 pounds, almost two-and-a-half tons of American-made metal jerked to a halt. The bumper tapped her hip, knocking her forward, but not off her feet.

Through dark sunglasses, now askew on her face, Teeny stared over the hood at a beehive-haired old woman behind the wheel. The old woman seemed as shaken as Teeny. The high school herald who announced the impending danger raced to her. He and his companions took charge, one of the girls shepherded Teeny out of traffic, the boy waved the Lincoln through. Once the situation calmed, he turned his attention to Teeny.

"You okay, kid?" he asked. "That was close."

Teeny nodded, repositioning Molly's sunglasses on her face.

"Where's your mom?"

If Teeny spoke, which she did not, or mastered sarcasm, she might say, *Young man, that's a damn fine question.* Instead, she shook her head and pointed to the Nova.

"Okay, kid, be careful." The three turned and fanned toward their cars. Teeny surveyed the lot again, then jetted to Sissie's Nova, trying to recover lost time.

From the passenger-side back window, her eyes inventoried the car's interior. Empty. She studied the station wagon's back area. No clues.

Teeny jerked the door handle. Locked. Strange, Sissie was not the door-locking type. The young girl bit her lip. What next? She walked around the car, surveying it from other angles. Moving to the driver's-side window. The little girl tippy-toed to see inside. A peek revealed too much for the girl's brain to process.

Teeny jumped backward, bumping the car parked next to the Nova. The little girl shook uncontrollably. Her head darted around the lot, searching for help, for anyone to offer hope.

Alone in a parking lot, abandoned in a town she hardly knew, Teeny gathered herself, *Thinking Teeny* again assuming the reins. Maybe she saw it wrong, or her brain processed incorrectly. She exhaled, removed

Molly's sunglasses, secured them around her bucket hat, mustered courage and stared through the Nova's driver's-side window one more time. Her eyes confirmed what they hinted at first glance. Her momma was NEVER coming back. EVER.

An inch of Sissie Hurt's purse strap peeked out. Sissie never left her purse behind … anywhere. Yet, there the purse sat, jammed under the driver's seat. A purse strap, not visible from any angle but this one. Teeny turned to check the grocery store front door, and there he stood, glaring at her, the wiry-haired blond man.

The skinny-topped, fat-legged, wiry-haired man sprinted toward her. Teeny's head swiveled as she spotted her only escape route and sprinted. Losing a second, she checked over her shoulder. The man raced blindly through the parking lot, focused on her. Teeny's arms pumped as she crossed TX-327. Two cars swerved to miss her, *BEEEEEPPPP*. Her backpack rocked with each stride, sunglasses and hat wobbled on her head with each footfall, but stayed in place.

Then, *Urrrrk*.

Brakes slamming and screams from a parking lot for the second time in minutes. Before disappearing into the woods, Teeny glanced back and saw the wiry-haired man rise from the asphalt parking lot. The man appeared dazed, confused, and pissed off. He slammed his hand on the hood of a green Ford sedan driven by a fat, Hispanic man.

"Watch where the hell you're going," the wiry-haired man yelled. Focused only on intimidating the man driving the green sedan, he lost track of Teeny.

But strangely, the fat, Hispanic driver paid no attention to the screamer, his well-being, or the shoppers running to assess the situation. The fat, Hispanic man's eyes locked onto hers.

Before she turned to disappear, she swore he mouthed RUN. Teeny leapt over a ditch, crashed through a wiry outcropping of ungroomed privets—Opie peeking from her backpack—as she vanished into the thicket.

36

Silsbee, Texas, July 7, 1976, later that afternoon

Paunch remained relegated to his car, feet from where his green Ford Galaxie derailed Teeny's pursuer an hour earlier. He studied the investigation from his vantage point.

Matthews, spit cup in hand, Fraley, and another badge, inventoried Sissie's Nova. Matthews held up a purse and handed items from the purse to the officer beside them to inventory. Even from Paunch's position, he noted the items: hairbrush, lipstick, makeup kit, change purse. His mind understood key items remained missing.

After another twenty minutes of forced exile, Matthews and Fraley strode toward him. Paunch studied the faces of shoppers, recounted the incident in his head—anything to act disinterested—as Matthews inspected Paunch's Ford. Frito bags, burger wrappers, French fry containers, and empty soda cups littered the suspended detective's car.

Matthews death-stared them both, sharing his ire between Paunch and Fraley. "You sonsabitches." He turned to Paunch. "You've been staking out the Blue Nova for … "

Paunch shoved his hands in his pockets and counted yellow parking lot stripes.

"How long?" Matthews demanded. He inventoried Paunch's wrinkled clothes and recounted the trash in the car, daring Paunch to lie.

"Awhile."

"So, you decided to conduct a stakeout in my town without alerting me. A suspended police officer … " He looked at Fraley. Matthews steamed. "Fraley, you didn't think I'd figure out you brought a suspended cop into an investigation on my turf. I got friends too, asshole. After Paunch mentioned the missing girl, I made a few calls. Didn't take lotsa digging."

"Well, ah," Fraley started.

"Shove your 'well, ah,' up my ass. Loop me into everything, EVERYTHING, or get the hell out of my town. Basically, you two decided without me," Matthews started.

Fraley glared at Paunch. "Actually," Paunch interposed, "I kept Fraley in the dark too."

"Shit, shit, shit," Matthews said, running his non-spit cup hand through his hair. "Three jurisdictions are jammed up investigating bizarre murders," Matthews spat a black stream of Skoal, into his spit cup, "so you decided to do the lookin' for the little girl."

"Sums it up," Paunch offered.

"Okay, explain to me why you ran over a guy, and who the hell he's with?" Matthews asked.

"The last person who talked to Sissie Hurt, he's a … let's say, off-market mechanic named Tex Wexler. He ditched her Chevy Vega and loaned her the Nova."

"Okay."

"He mentioned a group Sissie called the White Van People. Sissie told him to protect his kids from them."

"That's all you got? One guy mentioning something called the White Van People?"

"No, Clint Wirst—"

"The guy popsicled in La Grange." Fraley added.

Paunch continued, "He drove a white van. His plates proved to be a dead end. Gets more tangled. I checked everywhere. Nothing on a group called the White Van People. Don't exist in police records, no other mention of them anywhere."

"So … " Matthews led.

"I brought in an off-the-record expert. Her theory—"

"Her?" Fraley and Matthews asked together.

"Yeah, her theory, if you planned to be invisible: what better vehicle to drive? Plumbers, electricians, carpet cleaners utilize white service vans. Familiarity leads to comfort, comfort leads to relaxing your guard. White vans become invisible because they're common."

"What do the White Van People do? Gun running, dope, murder for hire?" asked Matthews.

Fraley and Paunch waited for the other to answer. Paunch broke first. "Not sure. I'm positive they want this girl … not sure how alive or dead calculates into their equation."

Matthews pondered.

Fraley rounded the conversation back to Matthews. "Boys, did we get an ID yet on the caribou victim?"

"You know what I do—no ID on him. Waiting to hear back."

"The damaged vehicle, from the alley?" Fraley asked next.

"Nada," Matthews said. "Still missing."

Paunch said, "We know Flick Hurt was a scumbag, records say Clint Wirst worked as muscle for scumbags. So, let's assume when you ID the guy, he's a scumbag too."

"Maybe. But, back to today," Matthews ordered.

Paunch came clean. "I set up shop here. White vans came and went, most vendors for the grocery store. But one van's driver stayed and parked. Parked where he'd have a sightline to the Nova."

"The van's driver, a wiry-haired blond dude."

"You didn't try to run him off," Matthews said.

"Like you said, I'm suspended. But, I wrote down the license plate," he said, then handed a torn note sheet to Fraley.

"I'll run it."

"There's more," Paunch added.

Fraley and Matthews huffed, shaking their heads. "The guy I bumped into. The guy driving the van. I've seen him before."

"Spit it out Paunch," Fraley said.

"He was at the Pines Theater, with a group of guys. I'll get you a description of each later."

"What the hell, Paunch. You made this guy before, and not a word?"

"Sorry. Anyway, today he jogged inside to take a piss or something. Then I saw her, Teeny Voix. Apparently, she made the guy too, and waited for him to go inside."

"Sure it was her?" Fraley asked.

"Yeah, positive. She wore chunky sunglasses, but I looked at every existing photo of Teeny Voix. It was her. Also, she went straight to Sissie Hurt's car. Inspected it. I planned to follow her home, so I could question Teeny and her mother. But the white van's driver ran out of the store, spotted Teeny and chased her. Forced my hand."

"What happened to the guy," Fraley asked.

"After I bumper-tapped him, he bitched first, but then he made me. Kinda guys who learned to spot cops from the crib. I asked everyone to stay put, but the grocery manager came out to inspect. I got distracted for a minute, then the guy and the van vanished."

"We gotta car that may or may not be Sissie Hurt's," Matthews started.

"I saw her in it. It's her car," Paunch confirmed.

"Someone wiped the car clean," Matthews said.

"What?" Paunch said.

"No prints. There's a purse, but no wallet, ID, or keys," the local cop added.

Fraley turned to Paunch, "These White Van People, you think they're real?"

"I think so, yeah," Paunch said.

"And they operate like a team?" Matthews added.

"Or an army," Paunch amended.

Each man's eyes cut to the *Tiger-Tow* tow truck pulling behind Sissie's blush blue Nova. Matthews asked, "Any chance Sissie and Teeny dumped their car here?"

"Why'd Teeny be nosing around if the two dumped the car?" Fraley said.

"Safe bet Teeny doesn't know what happened to her mother," Matthews said.

"She's alone, in a town she hardly knows, with the worst the world has to offer chasing her," Fraley continued.

"And we're all she's got," Paunch added.

37

Silsbee, Texas, July 8, 1976, early morning

Tic, tic, tic, tic, tic, tic, tic, tic …

Like elevator music, a nonfactor, white noise. *Tic, tic, tic, tic, tic, tic, tic, tic …*

The nightmare returned, the same nightmare, exactly the same, completely different. He stood again watching his daughter die in a hospital bed, life dwindling away each *tic, tic, tic, tic, tic, tic, tic, tic …*

Her essence leaking from her body. *Tic, tic, tic, tic, tic, tic, tic, tic …*

The horror of nightmares is not the dream's darkitecture, or the unfolding drama, but the dreamer's inability to participate, to help the loved one in need.

For years, the nightmare remained the same, Paunch's daughter dying in a hospital bed. The villains rotated, different death dealers arriving to drag her into darkness. Paunch's feet cemented in place, unable to fight the villain *de la nuit.*

Predictably, after his daughter's death in Paunch's dreams, the hooded man with the sickle dragged her into darkness. Later, when his wife left him for his former best friend, Jack Ash, Ash appeared in nightmares and hauled Paunch's daughter off. Over the following months, a parade of monsters from past dreams intermingled in nightmares.

The faceless, long-haired, moss- and vine-covered beast appeared next. An amalgamation of climbing, coiling, killing, kudzu vine and

Bigfoot engulfing his girl. Paunch realized, via nights with his self-appointed counselors, *Don Julio* and *Jose Cuervo*, the kudzu killer represented cancer, spreading, unstoppable.

After months facing the Kudzu Vine Killer, Paunch's dreams turned darker. Much darker.

Paunch remembered his personal monster's origin. His mamá tugged him behind, as she scoured JC Penney's for his kindergarten clothes. Paunch's mamá forced him to try on ensemble after ensemble. In protest, Paunch climbed under the changing room door, snuck past his mamá and the clerk, and raced away, vowing to join Captain Kangaroo's cast of characters.

To begin his journey, Paunch followed a stocking crew member into the back room. Paunch entered and froze in place. The stock girl passed them a thousand times, so made no note of the battalion surrounding her.

An army of mannequins, stripped of their wardrobe, naked, awaiting their next smart outfit and endcap. Dozens of them, all staring at the small, trembling boy.

The stock girl did not turn to spot the boy, warm piss squirting down his pants, terrified. Not knowing he followed her; she switched out the light as she passed from sight.

Five minutes later, the next stocker switched on the lights and found Paunch bawled-up, lying in a piss pool, crying. Paunch and the stock boy found his mamá. Paunch never explained his *accident*. He never told Guillory, his daughter, his best friends about his time in the darkness with the mannequins, or the fact that he still hears them whispering to one another.

Unsurprisingly, for a majority of childhood, female mannequins dominated his nightmares, a naked, strangely beautiful, long-limbed, terrifying creature. Nightmares provided one change, turning the mannequin into a Medusa-inspired she-monster. However, no coiling snakes covered her skull. Instead, rusted nails jutted out.

Each appearance of mannequin-monster in his childhood dreams ended with him waking in his piss. As he matured, the mannequin he called Pincushion fell from his dreams. Not returning for almost twenty years.

But after cancer ravaged his daughter, Guillory married his best friend, he found himself completely deserted, and the other monsters took turns tormenting Paunch's dreams, Pincushion returned. Her reentry into his life smacked of inevitability.

So now, in adulthood, Pincushion's presence dwarfed the other tormentors' best efforts.

Now each night, before the nightmare mannequin dragged his daughter into darkness, her cold, dead eyes found his milliseconds before he woke. And when Pincushion returned, so did the bed wetting.

Each occurrence forced him to launder his sheet. Every six months, the urine stench forced him to purchase a new mattress. The dream tapped into his embarrassment, shame, and loneliness. Each time Paunch prayed for the haunting, dead-eyed mannequin to disappear, to be replaced by the next taunter.

And now, Paunch found his wish … granted.

Tic, tic, tic, tic … The link shared by the real world and dream world added credibility to dreamscape.

Paunch's eyes volleyed wall to wall. The hospital room, exactly the same. The darkness, as always, seeming darker than before, his daughter …

Wait—not his daughter—a sprite he glimpsed once, before she disappeared into the Piney Woods. A girl pursued by monsters. Teeny Voix, strapped into the hospital bed in front of him.

Not sleeping, not connected to tubes and devices, but wrestling, twisting, tugging. A money board behind her, ticking upward, like any television fundraiser. Each time she fought back, the price ticked upward. $2,110, $2300, $2600.

Behind him stood a room full of faceless men; each held a paddle. An auctioneer stood in the corner, driving the girl's price skyward. A different, faceless man raising his paddle each time. $3750, $4800, $5875.

Some faceless men remained involved in the auction. Most turned away, choosing to ignore the consequences.

Paunch turned to the auctioneer, recognizing him. The Hawaiian-shirted man grinned, feasting on the evil in the room.

"Hey, Paunchirino," the man said before reigniting the bidding. The skinny-tall man with the lollipop laughed at his leader's joke. Paunch, however, focused on one man specifically, blond, permed hair, a small upper body and thick legs. The minion moved toward the hospital bed that held Teeny. He loosened her bindings.

Paunch looked at the money board behind Teeny; it flashed, signifying a winner.

$6,666.66.

Tic, tic, tic, tic, tic, tic, tic, tic …

The wiry-haired man finished his task, tossing Teeny over his shoulder. She fought, her fists bouncing off the man, doing no damage. The tiny girl twisted toward Paunch, eyes pleading for help. He fought to move forward but failed … again.

Carrying the girl, the wiry-haired man turned, stepping into the darkness, toward the shadowed purchaser of the child. A faceless man stood, holding out his arms, awaiting his prize. Not buying the girl. Purchasing her innocence, her moxie, the parts of her codified by life's bonfires.

He screamed, unsure if the scream existed in his dreams, or did it pass with him back to reality. **The White Van People** *replaced* **Pincushion** *as tormentor.*

Tap, tap, tap, sounded so close, then far away as the dream wrenched him back.

Tap, tap, tap. Not a knock, his brain clicked into gear, not someone at his door. He experienced the drool on his chin first, "Ehh."

Sorting clues, he recognized the smells—honestly, the stinks—of his car. His memory reengaged. He had pulled over for a second, to nod off, before restarting his search for Teeny Voix and her mother.

Tap, tap, tap.

He opened his eyes, but did not move, to let the tapper know he reached consciousness. Paunch focused on his Seiko, 4:30 a.m. Before he rose to face the situation, he studied the clues of his predicament.

"Shit," he said, as light burst through his front windshield, blinding him. He sat up, now pissed. A truck faced him, headlights blasting into his car.

Tap, tap, tap. "What?" he said, too loudly, before calming from the sensory overload.

Still adjusting to the blinding headlights, Paunch turned toward the annoying sound, as a wrinkled redheaded woman triple tapped his window **again**, using her wedding ring to add veracity to each repetition. He rolled down his window to address the woman. A large man stepped from the idling truck and moved closer.

"Mornin'," she offered.

"Morning," he returned, confused.

"You were screaming, you okay?"

"Think so, yeah, just a dream."

"Hell of a dream." The redhead paused before returning to business. "Saw your car parked out here when my husband started readying for work."

"Oh, okay."

"Came out here, watched you sleeping."

Paunch nodded, not offering clues to his inquisitor.

"Felt your hood, it's cold. Been out here awhile." She paused, giving him time for response. He sat silently.

She turned. The tank of a man behind her nodded at Paunch. "Selman, my husband, said you might be sleeping off bad decisions. But you don't smell like booze, cigarettes, and loose women."

He remained mum.

"Selman's not a fan of people we don't know parking on our street at night. He don't know you, don't trust you. Move on, we got kids 'round here. Don't need no one creeping at night."

He nodded, smiling to himself. This neighborhood's kids had protectors. Every kid deserved that. "If we see you snaking 'round again, no one will find your body."

"What?"

She offered no more, signaling the last statement did not exist, and was hard fact, concurrently. Selman, her husband, returned to his truck, turned off the headlights blinding Paunch, and returned. The imposing man appeared twenty years Paunch's senior, but, more importantly, now held a shotgun.

"Selman'll follow you out. Lots of people we don't trust been creepy crawling 'round lately. We're watching you all."

He nodded.

Myrtis stared into Paunch, wanting him to register each word. "And tell your slimy friends driving around in them white vans, I got my eyes on 'em too."

38

The suspended detective exited the neighborhood, followed by Selman's headlights. Paunch shook himself awake, deciding Teeny lived close. He believed it, brain to bone marrow.

That meant the White Van People circled her. Paunch understood there were more of them than him. Still, he counted Matthews and Fraley as allies now. Matthews promised Silsbee PD would run off suspicious white vans. Hassle them—if they possess criminal records—and document each driver's name.

Paunch occasionally spotted white vans patrolling areas near Teeny's disappearance. Paunch recognized two of the drivers, the guy with the bad, wiry perm and fat legs who chased Teeny and the rail thin, tall guy who sucked lollipops. Both men surrounded the Hawaiian-shirted man in front of the Pines Theater and visited Paunch's nightmare.

Paunch wrote down the license plate number of each van and planned to turn his list into Fraley or Matthews. The men driving the vans broke no laws. The drivers he followed puttered through the neighborhood, never approaching the speed limit, using turn signals and braking for all stops. As a former traffic cop, Paunch understood no one drove that carefully, unless they were eighty-year-old-blue-hairs, had suspended licenses, or a police cruiser behind them.

As Selman's lights guided Paunch out of the neighborhood, he revisited his nightmare. His first in years without his daughter's occupancy. Strange.

Paunch assembled the dream's clues. Teeny Voix, a girl he never met, replaced his daughter. She fought back, understanding her resistance was futile. A strong little girl, who possessed a unique quality, a quality Paunch could not label, but recognized.

Paunch turned his memory from her to the other characters in his dream.

The dream's auctioneer, the Hawaiian-shirted man and his crew from the crime scene. One of the crew parked a white van near Sissie's abandoned car. Still, dreams and parking a white van in a grocery lot failed to represent damning evidence in court.

Strangely, Paunch understood the auctioneer, and his crew—although vile—were not the worst villains in his dream. The true villains, the faceless observers of the vile proceedings, turned away.

39

Silsbee, Texas, July 8, 1976, morning

Molly's grandson-in-law inspected the home. Carpet vacuumed, kitchen spotless, Molly asleep in her chair, an empty plate of food beside her.

"Your mother must be a great cook; Molly never cleans her plate."

Teeny nodded, Opie acted along. The grandson-in-law smiled, happy Molly was someone else's issue. "Well, ahh … give this to your mother." He held out the cash grocery disbursement and Sissie's weekly pay. Teeny snatched it quickly, too quickly, she thought. The girl mustered a relaxed, everything is okay smile.

"Where's your momma?" the man asked.

Teeny pretended to push a shopping cart and take things off the shelf.

"Ahh, shopping. Great, well, see you next week," said the grandson-in-law.

Teeny smiled, *whew*, she thought, *in the clear.*

Then the grandson-in-law paused, remembering his orders. "Sorry. Forgot. I need to talk to your mother in the next day or two. Molly needs to go for her annual checkups. Eyes, teeth, and physical. A general overhaul for the old gal."

He glanced at his watch, obviously already moving to the next appointment in his head.

From behind the grandson-in-law, the old woman's eyes opened, and she started to speak. Molly's breaking character would circumvent their charade. Teeny's eyes begged for the old woman to remain quiet. Molly relented. The act played out behind the clueless grandson-in-law.

He continued, saying, "My wife will arrange the appointments, but she works full time. So, we need your mother to take her. I'll bring the schedule by tomorrow."

Teeny rubbed her fingers together. The grandson-in-law smiled, chuckled, appreciating the moxie. "Fair enough, I did not negotiate doctor's visits as part of your mother's duties. Look, here's twenty bucks." He handed Teeny a wrinkled Andrew Jackson, face-up. Teeny slipped the money into her jean pocket.

"Another $20 after the doctor's visits."

Teeny nodded. Business complete, she followed him outside, standing behind the guard of the screened porch and an overgrown azalea. After his car started, Molly's voice echoed from the house. "Not much of a magic trick. Taking twenty bucks from a sucker." Teeny turned, the screeching door marking her return inside. The two roommates' eyes locked. Teeny once underestimated Molly, an ally she never expected, a luxury in this situation.

"Can't keep this charade going forever," Molly announced, her eyes opened from feigned sleep.

Teeny returned to the living room. She pointed to Molly's empty plate and rubbed her belly.

"Yeah, yeah, you're a better cook than your momma."

Teeny pointed to the lines in the recently vacuumed carpet. "Sure, you're doing every chore your momma was supposed ta." Teeny raised her eyebrows. "And more."

"But we gotta call the cops or something; your momma's missing." A fact Teeny hid from neighbors, so far.

Teeny shook her head.

"Can't keep this up forever," Molly said.

Teeny used her fingers to lie for her. Teeny's fingers mimicked something walking.

"You still think she'll come home?"

Teeny made a B with her hand.

"B," Molly said.

Teeny held up four fingers.

"Four."

Teeny nodded. "Your momma's gone missing before?"

Teeny nodded, then mimed fingers walking again.

"And she comes back?"

Teeny nodded, her mime-lie complete.

"Okay, but I'll only keep quiet a few more days. Aren't you worried about your momma?"

Teeny nodded, pointing to her noggin.

"You're thinking."

Teeny nodded before pointing to Molly's clock.

"Just need some time."

Teeny offered two thumbs up.

Teeny remained under self-imposed house arrest. She rejected repeated invitations for dodgeball, hide-n-seek, and cops and robbers with the Durdin Drive wildlings. She longed to ride one of Molly's bikes into town but squashed the urge. Mostly, she and Opie stared out the shades at passing cars and the potholed, asphalt street.

Four times she spotted white vans pass; twice, she recognized the driver, the Swizzle Stick man, and the Greyhound. The vans circled repeatedly, not slowing. Teeny translated their pattern. The White Van People did not know her address—yet—but surmised her general location.

Once, she saw the chunky Hispanic man passing in his ugly green four-door sedan, patrolling slowly, his head swiveling side to side. She also noticed a few black and whites pass. Strange she failed to note their presence before.

The day drug by slowly, Teeny watched *The Price is Right, Ryan's Hope,* and *All My Children* with Molly, completed her chores, and prepared lunch and dinner. Teeny perused *Reader's Digest* and scanned JC Penney's and Sears catalogs to distract herself.

She snuck to the yard sale and worked for two hours hunched behind a table to repay the widow.

At dinner that night, Molly asked Teeny to pull her chair beside hers while they watched the Walton family's newest crisis on CBS. The old woman kept glancing lovingly at Teeny.

"What're you going to do?"

Teeny shrugged

"We're running out of time together, I guess. I'll miss you."

Teeny put her hand on the old woman's; they both squeezed. The girl felt every arthritis-swollen knuckle and callous on her current protector's aged hands. They stared into each other's eyes, cycling affection between them. The old woman's face morphed from a soft tender smile into wizened counselor.

"Well, if you asked me, which you didn't." Molly smiled, Teeny returned the offering. "I'd say the question is what's up your sleeve next, Houdini?"

Teeny pushed back her sleeves, displaying her twig arms.

"Nothing, huh, poor girl."

· · ·

Beaumont's Southwestern Bell White Pages in her lap, Teeny's fingers searched for news about her momma. The phone rang, once, twice, three times.

She picked it up. "Hello."

Teeny did not speak. Hoping Pru recognized her silence.

"Hello," Pru said again. "Look, you creep, don't call here again." The phone slammed.

Undeterred, Teeny located the next candidate's number, then dialed. *Ring, ring, ring, ring, ring, ring, ring.* Nothing.

She shook her head, breathed deeply before settling on her last resort. She dialed the unlisted number by memory. Someone snatched the receiver on the first ring, before Teeny could question her sanity. "Hello," said Lexi Wexler enthusiastically.

Teeny remained silent.

"Oh, hey, Teeny," Lexi said. "Cop came looking for you and your momma. Fatso Mezcan, I think."

Teeny remembered the man who used his green sedan to bump her pursuer in the grocery store parking lot.

"He just came back, says Sissie's gone missin'. They found her car, but ain't found her or you."

Teeny considered the news.

"We ain't seen her. If that's why you're calling. So sorry, Teeny."

Lexi continued. "The white van creepers Sissie told daddy 'bout drive by sometimes. But they don't hang round. Daddy scares 'em some, I think."

Teeny waited on the line, the voice of her friend comforting her. "Come on home, okay? Daddy, Dex, and I'll watch over you."

Teeny sniffled.

"Ahh, don't cry, Teeny. I'm sure Sissie'll turn up."

Teeny said nothing as an explosion rattled through the phone.

"Gotta go, Dex is testing … " Lexi hung up the phone without completing her sentence. The disconnection tone squawked as Teeny placed the avocado green phone handset back on the matching base.

She allowed herself five minutes to cry while cuddling Opie, then processed the clues as she completed her chores, sweeping the kitchen, vacuuming perfect stripes into the carpet. Teeny set out ground meat for dinner, clipped Molly's fingernails and toenails, before taking her place in front of the blinds. Happily, no passing white vans today.

Maybe her pursuers relocated their search. A small victory. Later that afternoon, the girl left Opie beside Molly, while browning the meat for spaghetti. The sizzling hamburger and popping meat fat distracted her from approaching dangers. Teeny heard creaking from Molly's porch and peeked out the kitchen window.

Teeny recognized the Swizzle Stick man, rail thin, lollipop in his mouth as always, but dressed differently, in dress pants and a white button-down shirt. The Swizzle Stick man carried a briefcase and toted a large book under his arm.

Only a latched screen porch and Molly stood between the man and Teeny.

She tapped the floor before collapsing to the ground. Molly studied Teeny from her position in the wheelchair. The small girl locked eyes with the old woman. Molly channeled Teeny's fear, nodding, understanding the dire situation.

Teeny opened a lower kitchen cabinet door and crawled inside, concentrating on translating the muffled conversation.

"Well, hello there," the Swizzle Stick man said, his voice full of fake sunshine.

"Don't want nothing. Go away," Molly said.

"Well, how do you know?"

"Just do."

The man continued, undeterred. "Well, I brought the gift of knowledge. We can never possess too much knowledge, can we?"

Molly said nothing.

The Swizzle Stick man continued. "You see, I have the world's knowledge bound in an encyclopedia set. The world is yours for an initial payment of—"

"Don't need 'em."

"Well, a woman of your knowledge might not, but what about your children?"

"My kids done growed up."

"Grandkids?"

"Never visit."

"Huh," said the man. "Shame."

"Yep, shame."

"Funny."

"What?"

"If no kids live here, why's a stuffed armadillo … " he pointed.

"It's an opossum," she retorted.

"Why's a child's opossum sitting beside you?"

"I'm an old woman, I'll do whatever I want," Molly retorted. "And I don't want no damn 'cyclopedias."

"Fair enough," the man said, the porch crackling under Swizzle Stick's exiting steps.

From her enclosed hiding space, Teeny heard Molly's reaction. "Creepy."

Teeny climbed from her space, nodded, and Molly signaled for her to stay quiet. Teeny peered through the blinds and watched the Swizzle Stick man.

He marched down the street, not peddling his wares to other homes. Once the man reached the corner, about one hundred yards away, he tossed the text under his arm into the ditch. As he turned the corner, a white van coasted beside Swizzle Stick and he climbed into the passenger seat, looking back toward Molly's house as the van pulled away.

Teeny stared into the kitchen, turned to the TV, then the wall clock, and finally her room. She sniffed, sucking in the moldy, warm, mothball, and hamburger aromas of Molly's home, Teeny's home for weeks. She allowed each smell into her soul, knowing the home that days earlier felt like the safest place in the world no longer offered that illusion.

40

Silsbee, Texas, July 9, 1976, 6:22 p.m.

Hiding her intentions, Teeny finished preparing dinner. If Molly grasped Teeny's plan, the old woman would summon the sheriff. The girl waited for the cover of darkness, backpack ready, Opie on standby, terrified, but prepared for departure. The pinks of evening faded to the purples of night.

Ten minutes earlier, Selman's truck arrived home. The girl embraced the comfort his presence offered. Teeny peered out the blinds of her bedroom window. The yard-sale widow and her family covered their wares.

Teeny spotted it, the white van, this time driven by the curly-haired blond man. Then a distinctive, *Click, click,* a shell dropping into place before a booming blast rattled through her home.

Birds scattered from the tree in front of Molly's home. The yard-sale widow and her family stopped their task, staring across the street toward Myrtis and Selman's home. The van's rear tires squealed as the vehicle sped away.

Teeny crept out of her room, holding her finger to her lips, begging Molly for silence. The young girl peeked out the screen door. Selman stood in his yard, shotgun pointing to the sky, barrel smoking. He watched the van whipsaw the corner, two wheels losing contact with asphalt, as it raced away.

Selman turned, considering the Krylon blue and rusted chair beside him, and walked back to his post. A few neighbors looked out their door, but Selman waved them off. Each returned to dinner, trusting the church deacon. A minute later, Selman resettled into the rusted chair.

Teeny watched him as Myrtis exited the home and hugged her husband. She handed the guardian something wrapped in foil. From experience Teeny remembered a beef patty—slathered in sandwich spread, pressed between toasted pieces of Sunbeam bread—warmed inside.

"You eatin' out here?" Myrtis asked.

Teeny strained to register their conversation

"Yeah," he said, before unwrapping his dinner.

"First van you saw?" Myrtis asked.

"So far," Selman said. "You call the sheriff?"

"No, better. I called his momma."

"Smart," said Selman.

"She'll make sure her boy drives by a few extra times tonight. Said the force's already on high alert since the Pines Theatre killing."

Myrtis drug a chair next to her husband and took his hand. Teeny sat, squeezing near Molly's threshold, and watched her protectors scan the street. Something about the old couple's presence comforted her.

Hours later, Teeny snapped awake, drool hanging from her chin to her shirt, lulled to sleep, she assumed, by Texas night sounds and her neighbors' chatter.

Teeny jumped, Molly hovered. The old woman stared lovingly. "Didn't mean ta wake you. You were snoring. Better get ta bed." Teeny gazed at the wall clock. 11:21p.m. Teeny glanced outside. Selman remained in the front yard, illuminated by the front porch light, shotgun in his lap, snoring. Myrtis returned inside.

Even protectors need sleep.

Still, without his full attention, the human-hyenas approached. Teeny peered out the screen and down the street and saw it, a white van idled at the end of the block, waiting to thwart a southbound escape.

She snuck to her room and peered out the window. Another van waited a block up the street, blocking the northern route.

Teeny breathed in and out, understanding in moments she would undertake the most dangerous journey of her life. Teeny hugged Molly, then rolled the wheelchair-bound woman to the refrigerator, which Teeny stocked with sandwiches, chili, and taco meat.

"Wait, whatcha doing?"

Teeny sighed.

"You can't leave."

Teeny nodded.

"Won't let you. I'll call the police."

Teeny unhooked the phone cord from the wall hours earlier. Her tactic could not stop Molly but might delay her.

"I don't know what's happening, but you can't handle this mess on your own. Just ask me, anyone, for help."

Teeny hugged the old woman again before collecting the backpack and Opie from her bed. She jammed the stuffed opossum into her backpack; like usual, he never complained. Teeny opened the back window, hung out, then dropped to the ground silently. Molly's sobs woke her neighbor.

"Molly, Molly … " Selman called. The rusted chair's squeak alerted Teeny she needed to hide from Selman and the White Van People to execute her plan. Due to her lecherous stepfather, Teeny mastered the art of escaping into darkness. Selman checked on Molly, buying Teeny time to disappear.

Croaking bullfrog calls dominated the night, as Teeny crept into Molly's neighbor's rear yard and toward Ikes Lane. She crossed the asphalt street and disappeared into the wooded field, to a trail the Durdin Drive wildlings used for hide-n-seeking.

The wooded trail offered a route to sneak behind the white van to the south.

Teeny chose not to pack a flashlight, even though she found Molly's in the pantry. She understood the flashlight alerted the White Van

People of her location. Instead, Teeny allowed her eyes to adjust to the darkness, using the porch lights of the neighboring homes.

Teeny inched in the darkness, step by step, along the path near Ikes Lane. She slowed where Ikes merged with Durdin as the van came into sight. No headlights, no interior lights, the van rested in place. The wiry-haired blond man sitting in the driver's seat, his head swiveled back and forth, patrolling.

The trail passed dangerously close to the street, just a thin line of pines stood between her and her pursuer. Teeny slowed, moving from shadow to shadow. She placed each foot in front of the other, one step at a time, carefully calculating each footfall, assuring no human could track her escape.

From the yard across the street, Teeny froze as dogs stirred on a front porch. She stared through trees as the mutts paced back and forth. The girl stood statue still, not moving, waiting for the mutts to resettle. The four-legged porch protectors refused.

Even from the distance, Teeny noted the soft rumble of a growl, then …

A cur from the next yard yelped, ears trained to note night sounds. Another joined in, then another, a cacophony of baying, waking household after household. Adjacent house lights blazed into existence.

Choruses of "Shut up, you mangy mutt," and "I'm sleeping," exited the homes.

The wiry-haired man jumped from the van, and Teeny's body jerked in response, alerting the world to her position. He spotted her.

Teeny turned, sprinting along the trail. The van's door stayed ajar, as the wiry-haired man raced after her. Teeny's arms pumped, but the wiry-haired man's heavy footsteps closed in. Teeny embraced her two advantages. First, her eyes already adjusted to the darkness. Also, her size allowed her to duck limbs that blocked her pursuer's path. His heavy breathing, underbreath cursing, and snapping branches marked the seconds until her capture.

Her backpack jerked as the pursuer took hold. Then *thwack, huuuumfff,* as a limb smacked her pursuer's face, forcing him to trip, lose his grip, and tumble past her. Teeny guessed he tripped over a knobby root, but she chose not to analyze her blessings. She raced on.

The man scrambled to his feet, but Teeny put twenty yards between them before he could correct himself. Teeny glanced to the street as the other white van followed her along the trail, piloted by the Swizzle Stick man. The Greyhound man sat in the passenger seat directing. Teeny processed her only choice: escape into the woods, unknown territory, but away from the van. One pursuer presented better options than three.

She turned deeper into the woods, no longer running, now using shadow, darkness, and the possibility of multiple escape routes to her benefit. Teeny crept behind a fallen, rotting oak.

The wiry-haired man searched.

He no longer knew her position—the fallen oak shielded her—but staying still only delayed her capture. She skittered to a pine outcropping. A light emblazoned into the woods as Swizzle Stick shined a flashlight, illuminating her.

"Get her to the van before the neighbors come outside to shut their mutts."

The wiry-haired man nodded, turned, and raced toward her. Now off trail, both she and her pursuer raced past bushes, trees, and protruding roots in pitch black. Teeny skirted tree to tree, when the sound she prayed for bounced through her ears. "Hee, ha, hee, hee, ha, ha, ha … " All around her.

She continued running as children's laughter bounded through the woods. Her pursuer also marked the new presence. His footfalls stopped; he remained in place. Teeny used the distraction to hop behind a pine, taking a breath, trying to spot the best escape route, when reality warped to insanity.

Footsteps, light as a feather, approached from every direction. No bushes rustled, no twigs snapped, and Teeny failed to spot the disturbance's cause. Her head whipped from one trigger to the next, understanding the unknown crowded the woods.

Whomever, or whatever, shared the woods tonight, mastered the art of traveling in shadow.

From hundreds of yards away, dogs continued to yelp, louder now, and, even from the woods, Teeny heard porch doors swing open. She refocused on her surroundings.

Quick, precise, but inexplicably childlike steps passed her. Converging in one spot, yards behind, near her pursuer's position. "Hee, ha, hee, hee, ha, ha, ha … "

Her ears, not eyes, communicated the night's terror.

"What the hell?" spilled from the man's mouth.

"Hee, ha, hee, hee, ha, ha, ha … " The laughter originated from one place now.

"Hey, put the damn scissors down, or I'll … "

"Hee, ha, hee, hee, ha, ha, ha … "

"Hey, hey, step back, step back you crazy little …" Then the sound of branches snapping and huffing, the fat-legged, wiry-haired man fleeing. The giggling intensified as the shadow dwellers chased.

"Shit, that hurts, stop it" he begged, as crashing branches echoed his continued escape. Teeny registered his gait, different now, slowed, as if … "Stop it, stop!"

Stabbing, repeated stabbing sounds, quick strokes before the man tumbled, "Help me, help me," he huffed slowly.

"Hee, ha, hee, hee, ha, ha, ha …"

Then weaker, "Help me … somebody."

Teeny gripped the tree that served as cover, terrified to move, terrified to run. From a distance she heard the white van piloted by Swizzle Stick reverse down the street. The curly-haired man's van started too, Teeny guessed, piloted by the Greyhound man. Both vehicles peeled away.

"Come back … " the man yelled to his departing companions. The man sobbed. "Please."

His sobs quieted the bullfrogs and crickets, but not the baying dogs. A moment later Teeny heard, "Little girl, little girl, could you … "

Teeny's hands earmuffed her ears, not wanting to experience the man's death. She waited, not moving, understanding THEY waited too.

A voice boomed through the woods and her covered ears. Not the dying man's cries, but a megaphonesque announcement. "Hurry back. We're not supposed to be here."

Teeny's head whipped toward the call, not knowing it, never hearing it, but recognizing the voice's owner. Whomever or whatever attacked the wiry-haired man scampered toward the voice, skirting roots, hopping fallen trees, ducking branches, abandoning Teeny and the dead man.

Teeny pressed to the tree that served as her hiding spot, eyes jammed shut, not daring to look upon the killers who shared the woods seconds before.

41

Simos Diner, near Garden Oaks, Houston, Texas, November 20, 2026

"This seems headed north of crazy," Harold said, not laced with his usual sarcasm, but actual concern.

"Due north," Val answered.

"If I won't believe you, why tell me?"

Val did not answer, conflicted as her listener.

"And why now?" Harold asked.

Why now? That, she could answer. Val turned her attention back to the dinner patrons. An old woman, dressed in a pink flower-patterned handmade dress, stood. Using the table as leverage, she maneuvered to her companion. The old woman wiped the admiring octogenarian's face and smiled sweetly.

The gray-sweatered 89-year-old man returned her gaze, his liver-dotted hands shaking as he reached up, stroked her face, relished her stare. Only after enjoying his view did the shaking man use his walker to wobble upright. He secured his balance before maneuvering toward the door.

Pushing his walker—bumping diner after diner—he plowed forward, leading his beloved to the restaurant's front door. She followed patiently, patting each disturbed diner on the shoulder, mouthing apologies and thank yous. A pair of stoners, obviously controlled by the munchies, drooled over biscuits while dodging the old man's trek to the exit.

He proudly opened the door for his bride. The pair's exit, a show for Simos guests, took two minutes. If the wife forged their path, exiting first, their departure time would have halved. Val, the old woman, and every diner understood the man's pride—every ounce of his soul— demanded he hold that door for his love. Val's heart soared as the old woman kissed her husband's cheek as she passed.

That moment cemented her answer. "Because not everyone gets the fairy tale ending, Harold."

"That's pretty vague."

"Harold, your life's laid out for you. Corporate events, donors, BMWs, limos, reservations at the Ritz, everything. Take it. If you want it."

"I'm offering the opposite. A shitty salary, ridiculous hours, a job that consumes you, nights in budget motels, and a four-door SUV with 173,000 miles. Oh, and nightmares. Because your subconscious gets a nightly chance to process the darkness you chased on the job. Everyone undersells that part."

"But?"

"But you'll have a count." Val said.

"A count?"

"A count, like Paunch. The child molesters, human traffickers, and rapists you throw behind bars, sure. More importantly, a count of children you saved, Harold. A count of girls who become mathematicians, doctors, principals, and mothers. A count of boys who become engineers, teachers, architects, and fathers. Lives saved. What else matters, Harold?"

"What happened to the girl, to Teeny?"

"That's the right question. We'll get to that." She paused. Val meant to save her sales pitch until the end of the story, but now needed to press. "They saw something in you." She reached across the table and took his hand. "Look, I refused to believe them. Mostly based on your last name and the silver spoon parked up your ass. But there's something there, Harold. You know it."

Then the sound, the buzz that ends millions of conversations in the modern world, *Zuuh, Zuuh, Zuuh.* Harold's phone rattled on the table.

Val exhaled, knowing her moment passed.

Harold checked his phone display, his brow dropped when the caller ID displayed. "I, I ahh, gotta take this."

"Sure," Val answered. Resignation settled, understanding the battle's outcome.

Outside the diner's window, Harold argued into his phone. After checking her watch three times, Val pulled a file from her tattered, leather briefcase and laid it in front of her. Disappearing into the dark details of her mission.

To refamiliarize herself with the case, she flipped through the file's heinous photos, not wanting to spread them on the table, protecting her waitress from the images. Next, she reread the unreliable witness testimony and reviewed mountains of forensics.

Her goal remained simple, to save one more, then hopefully another after that, before her time …

His voice pulled her out. "I ah … can't." He stood, not taking his seat, looking down at her.

Val stared up from the file into something darker. "You can't."

"No."

"Or daddy says you can't?"

Anger volcanoed in Harold. "Screw you, Val." Harold tossed twenties on the table before marching off.

After the jingle of the front door confirmed his exit, Val slammed the papers back into her file. "He fooled me for a bit," she said. "But I told you, he's unfit for the job."

The man sitting alone in the booth behind Val sipped hot chocolate before answering. "Yeah, Paunch voted against you taking his place too."

"Go to hell, Nick," Val said, storming out of the diner.

42

Silsbee, Texas, July 10, 1976, 6:16 a.m.

Baying dogs alerted Paunch of hubbub before he noticed the trucks near the junction of Ikes Lane, Marshall Lane, and Durdin Drive. A half-dozen pickups and cruisers, one he recognized as Matthews', sat bumper-to-bumper. Paunch patrolled these streets dozens of times, looking for and finding no hint of Teeny or Sissie Voix.

He feared the collection of vehicles pointed to someone finding Teeny dead. Paunch grabbed his flashlight, took a heavy breath, and wedged from his vehicle. A neighbor, who wore an SVFD hat, asked. "Can I help?"

"Where's Matthews?" Paunch name dropped, cutting to the chase.

The neighbor pointed into the thicket, "'Bout thirty yards thata way." Paunch nodded, entering the woods. Just before Paunch flipped on his flashlight, the man continued, "With the body."

Ten or twelve yards into the dark pines, Paunch picked up the cadence of Matthews' voice, following it to his destination. The sun still hid, moments from cracking horizon. Matthews stood between two men—neither badges—likely neighbors or friends, both holding shotguns near a clearing's perimeter.

"Keep this area clean," Matthews barked. "Don't let anyone pass unless I okay 'em."

Paunch felt relief when his flashlight passed over the body, an adult male, not Teeny or Sissie. The body lay face down. Even from this angle, Paunch recognized the corpse. The fat-legged kinky-haired blond.

Stab wounds covered the man's buttocks and thick legs. The corpse's tattered and shredded jeans allowed Paunch to see the corpse's meatloaf-textured lower remains, a grisly, painful death.

"Weird," Paunch said.

"Ya think?" Matthews asked sarcastically, bending over the bloodied body. "I planned to call you and Fraley, didn't have time yet. How'd you find this mess?"

"I planned to patrol the area today, do more door knocking."

"After you called my office and got permission, of course."

"Of course."

They both stared at the body, using their flashlights to unearth clues.

"Any guesses 'bout a murder weapon?" Paunch asked.

"Weapons," Matthews corrected. "Not sure, but not knives. The incisions tell me shears, scissors, but hard to tell." Matthews shook his head. "Paunch?"

"Yeah."

"Outside of domestic disputes," Matthews started.

"Those are messy," Paunch added.

"No murders in Silsbee for years."

"Hmm," Paunch offers.

"Then Sissie and Teeny Voix turn up, and we get one a week. I'm guessing, based on the bad perm and blond hair, that's the guy you described from J&M's parking lot."

Paunch inspected the body, the splattered blood, the remains of the man's lower body, "What's left of 'im. Can you confirm this is related?"

"Chet called this in an hour ago." Matthews' head nudged toward a shotgun-wielding local. "His dogs wouldn't simmer down. He let one of 'em lead him into the woods. He called me and I hightailed over. Several neighbors snooped 'round before I got here. So, news leaked out."

"After Chet walked me to the body, I ran back to my vehicle to snag my evidence kit. An old redhead brought down pots of coffee, offered some, before asking if the dead body was a little girl. I told her no. She'd find out soon, anyway. I asked the redhead if a girl and mother moved to the neighborhood recently. The woman clammed up. Didn't seem like her natural state. I pushed, told her the little girl's in danger."

"And the old woman asked me, and I ain't shitting, 'In danger, you mean from those scumbags driving white vans?' I almost crapped myself, but tried looking calm. I nodded. She opened up after that. She said a young mother was housekeeping for a wheelchair-bound woman named Molly Atkinson. My officer, Taylor, walked down with the redhead to meet Molly"

"Shit, I'm headed there," Paunch said. He turned to leave, ignoring the corpse and surrounding clues.

"Wait, Paunch. I wished we found 'em. Taylor came back, the woman, Marcia, they called her, fit the description of Sissie Hurt. Disappeared a day or two ago."

"That explains Sissie's abandoned Nova." Paunch said.

"The little girl—never talked according to Molly—musta been Teeny, ran off last night. I'm guessing into these woods."

"I was afraid you found her. Never so happy to see a dead man."

"Don't go crying for this one, had his ID on 'im. Claude Simpkins. Just spent a ten-spot in Huntsville for transporting a truck load of minors 'cross state lines. Woulda spent more time in the can, but got a soft-dick judge. Shoulda put this one under the jail. Got released in March," Matthews said, nodding to his two shotgun-wielding buddies. "Hey, guys, give us some space."

The guardians hiked toward the street as soft, yellow light pierced the pines. The first hints of sunrise fought through the darkness. The receding shadows did not subtract horror, but instead added emphasis. Paunch and Matthews considered the body again. Both switched off their flashlights and kneeled.

"What the hell is this?" Paunch asked.

"Hell if I know." He pointed up and down the dead man's legs. "North of a hundred stab wounds. What's left of the back of his legs is hamburger soup. Muscles not even connected to bone in spots."

"I don't see any stab wounds above his lower back," Paunch added.

"There's not. I rolled him when I got here, no stab wounds in front. He ran from whoever got him."

"And who's that?" Paunch asked, looking at Matthews, a mix of confusion—possibly fear—and kinship passed over his face.

"I spotted 'em first with my flashlight. No one else clocked 'em yet."

"What?"

"The kinda thing I've never seen before; I won't sleep for a while." He paused, nodding to Paunch. "The kinda thing that gets an honest cop suspended." Matthews used his finger to clear his dip, spitting it absently to the side, before realizing he polluted his crime scene.

Paunch stared at the local police veteran, "Tell me."

Instead of answering, Matthews raised his eyebrows. He waited for Paunch's eyes to lock onto his. Matthews' stare led Paunch's to a set of tracks. One set of sneakers, most likely, a young boy or girl.

"Teeny," Paunch said.

Matthews nodded. "Think so."

Then Matthews' eyes tracked to the dead body.

The morning sun now softly illuminated the forest floor, pine straw surrounded the body in spots, hiding clues. Adjacent softened dirt and mud told a twisted story. Paunch shook his head, not trusting his eyes.

"Boot marks, but not work boots or cowboy boots." Matthews nodded agreement. Paunch continued, "Dress boots?" His eyes and psyche suffered from clue-palooza—hundreds of tracks—his brain calculated a dozen-plus assailants.

The disturbing fact: not the number of prints, or even that clues pointed to multiple assailants. Terror creeped into Paunch's subconscious, promising nightmares because of the shoe prints' size, strangely narrow, the prints of a petite child. Correction … children.

Paunch's eyes asked, hell, begged Matthews for any other explanation.

"Like the ones at the Pines Theater?"

Paunch nodded, Matthews' cackling radio leaving their discussion incomplete. "Matthews, Matthews, you there?"

"Yeah, Doris," he said to his dispatch.

"Is some guy named Paunch with ya?"

"Roger."

"Fraley's trying to track 'im down. He needs Paunch in Beaumont."

"Kinda busy here, Doris."

"Tell Paunch Fraley said, sorry, this is a direct quote … "

"Okay," Matthews said.

"'Get his fat ass to Trail's End Mobile Home Park. They gotta dead body.'"

43

Once again, flashing red and blue lights bounced off the moldy trailer siding at Trail's End Mobile Home Park. One uniformed officer stood outside the trailer, but inside the taped-off crime scene. The cop looked confused as Paunch started toward the tape.

"Hey, Paunch."

"Lansky."

"You're suspended, right?"

"Oh, wow, you heard about that," said Paunch, trying, but failing, to wrangle his sarcasm.

Lansky chuckled. "Can't let you pass."

"Okay."

"Why you here?"

"Family friends," Paunch lied.

"Still," the officer offered. Paunch nodded, turning, taking in the rest of the scene. Pru and most of the neighbors loitered outside their trailers, but Paunch looked for one man.

A food truck, sagging toward the back, heavy with flour, sugar, and canned goods parked close to Tex's trailer. The normally animated man leaned against the truck, face dark with gloom. The suspended officer walked over. Tex's children stood mourning nearby. Tears streamed down the little girl's face.

"You see anything, anyone?"

"Nah," answered Tex. "Neither did Dex or Lexi, and they notice most shit that rolls in."

The twins stood dutifully by Tex's side, as if commanded. Still, neither twin seemed mentally present, their eyes scanning the horizon. Paunch assumed they longed to traipse into the woods.

"You called the cops?" Paunch asked.

"Phew, nah. Made Pru do it. Don't like the cops having easy access to my number, brother."

"How bad is it?" Paunch asked, his head motioning to the abandoned trailer.

Tex looked down and shook his head.

"How long's the body been in there?"

"Day'r two," Tex said.

"How'd you … "

"Dex, my boy, noticed the door open yesterday. Critters sneaking in 'n out. Didn't bother to mention it." Tex turned to his other child, the girl. "Lexi collected doodlebugs under Sissie's trailer this morning. Smelled something foul. I went exploring. Found her."

Paunch offered Tex—a man Paunch guessed did not often display emotion—a moment to compose himself.

"Swallowed a bullet."

"Shit." Paunch studied the children, before saying to Tex, "Apologies."

"Gonna give you a pass." Tex pulled up his sleeves. "Knife marks up 'n down 'er arm." He mimicked cuts every few inches.

Paunch stewed on that fact, processing. Delaying added to the misery, so Paunch nodded to the trailer. "Who?"

"Was waiting for you to work your way there," Tex answered. He breathed in and out. "Sissie."

"Okay," Paunch answered, hating to admit relief. Still, a loose end tickled the detective's brain. He processed, waited, forming the idea, assembling the facts. "Someone blew Sissie's head off. No one heard it."

"Been rubbing against the same problem."

"And?" Paunch pushed.

"Silencer, I guess. Not everyone sports one of those."

"No, not everyone does." Paunch sifted thruugh past crime scenes he worked. No memory of an assailant utilizing a silencer. Silencers/suppressors littered cop shows and action movies, but seldom surfaced in Beaumont crime scenes, at least in Paunch's cases.

Paunch started, "Anyone—"

"No one's seen Teeny," Tex answered the unasked question.

Paunch caught a quick glance between the twins, a subtle manifestation of shared secrets.

No one's seen her, my ass, Paunch mused silently to himself.

·   ·   ·

Twenty minutes later, the black and whites departed. Paunch waited. As he guessed, Fraley emerged from Flick and Sissie Hurt's trailer and waved him over.

"Can only spot ya a look-see, the coroner's minutes away," Fraley said from the threshold.

"Bad?"

"Brains-on-the-back-wall bad."

The stairs creaked as Paunch climbed. Fraley continued. "My boys'll be back. Looks like the site's wiped clean, no clue, not one fingerprint. Professional job."

"The White Van People?"

"Could be. No way of knowing. None of the neighbors mentioned 'em." Fraley waved Paunch inside.

Sissie Hurt's corpse sat in a cheap, yard-sale-rescued soda-fountain chair. Her head leaned back, brain matter splattered across the wall behind. Her arms displayed on the table, dozens of marks across each one. An empty saltshaker, top removed, sat between her arms.

"They cut her, put salt in her wounds."

"Yeah," Fraley answered.

"Did Sissie talk?"

Fraley considered for a long minute. "If her little girl is still alive, she didn't."

·   ·   ·

Earlier

Teeny and Opie studied police cars come and go from their hiding spot in the brush, thirty yards from Trailer #2. She pushed her knuckles into her eye sockets, rubbing them, to offer relief. She yawned, bone-tired, but unable to rest, even for a moment.

Teeny started her ten-hour walk from Silsbee to Beaumont last night, her only play. Understanding she needed to find her momma, dead or alive. A mile out—Trail's End Mobile Home Park in sight—sirens approached. She sprinted toward one of the many trails she explored with Dex and Lexi.

Over the last hour, Teeny processed clues: the number of cops on site, officers interviewing neighbors, and the bits of radio chatter. The information removed all doubt.

Someone—or something—killed her momma. *Thinking Teeny*, taking control, allowed *Scared Teeny* to cry, and cry some more, certain of the nightmares that lay inside her home. This night's terror promised to haunt her for the rest of her life. A life, based on recent events, that ended soon.

Those deaths, although gruesome and troubling, were demoted. Teeny mourned her momma. She embraced her grief, allowed emotions to wash over her; dealing with them now, in this outcropping of trash trees, seemed important.

Teeny wiped tears and snotty sniffles with her sleeve, shirt bottom, and Opie. She embraced the pain. *Thinking Teeny* allowed *Scared Teeny* to control the reins as long as possible, but after an hour of grieving, *Thinking Teeny* raised her hand. She asked: *Remember Flick's late-night visits?*

Scared Teeny did. Who else occupied the home when it happened? Who ignored?

Scared and *Thinking Teeny* embraced the anger residue from each occurrence, the hurt, the shame, the abandonment. Palming the emotions, letting them harden her heart. Flick, although vile, shared the blame. No one stopped him.

No one. Name her, name her, *Thinking Teeny* demanded. Momma knew … momma stayed … momma ignored.

Thinking Teeny used that fact to wrestle back control, as a familiar car bumped down the potholed trailer park entry, a green Ford Galaxie.

Teeny watched the portly man in the sedan pull in next to the cop cars. The portly, Hispanic man twisted his girth from his car. He seemed comfortable with these surroundings. Weird.

First, he engaged comfortably with the cop protecting the site. After the uniformed cop shooed him away, the rotund man walked over to Dex and Lexi's dad.

Teeny focused on the exchange, noting familiarity, and maybe trust, between the men. After the patrol cars left, Teeny watched the remaining cop step from the trailer and wave the portly man inside. The cop trusted the fat man too.

After the cop and the chunky Mexican stepped inside the trailer, Teeny distracted herself, calculating why the portly man seemed comfortable in cop world and trailer park world. Teeny pulled Opie close, eyes locked onto her former home.

Neither man emerged for some time, and Teeny used the time to study her surroundings again. Most neighbors loitered outside their trailer; some now bordered the crime scene tape. Her eyes rolled to Tex Wexler; unlike the others, he returned to his normal activity, tinkering with a yellow Plymouth Barracuda.

She scanned the trailer park entry, a van approached. Bumping through potholes, undeterred by the surroundings, more so drawn by death. *Scared Teeny* shuttered, and her body searched for escape routes.

Thinking Teeny held the floor a minute longer, noting one word on the side of the trailer. CORONER.

CORONER = Another confirmation of Sissie Hurt's death.

Teeny's eyes remained glued to the scene in front of her, the chubby, short Hispanic man sneaking out before the van stopped. The last cop on the site, walking out to greet the coroner. The coroner and his assistant unloading the gurney.

Teeny watched, defenses down, emotionally spent, tired, exposed, ears not registering the calculated approach, the feet edging closer, one silent step after another, a familiar game to the stalkers.

44

Beaumont, Texas, Sunday, July 11, 1976, 6:42 p.m.
Paunch felt ridiculous. The suspended detective dressed in camo-gear from his only hunting trip a decade earlier. The too-tight pants pressed his butt-cheeks into a singular cheek and jammed his briefs up his butt crack. His camo-jacket refused to zip. So, Paunch's lone, gray T-shirt filled the opening. Still, some camouflage offered better cover than no camouflage.

From his position behind a pine outcropping near the gravel entrance of Trail's End Mobile Home Park, Paunch watched Tex Wexler tinker. The day's highlight, Tex revving the engine of a meaty, demanding Plymouth Barracuda, rumbling the trailer park grounds, drawing ire and awe from trailer park residents.

Tex slept little, parented in spurts, and downed Dionysian amounts of budget beer while under the hoods of various reclamations. Casual observation implied he knew nothing of Teeny's whereabouts.

Still, Paunch observed actively, not casually. Through his binoculars, Paunch clocked a nod from Tex to the twins before the duo disappeared into the brush.

Every few hours, the Wexler twins trekked from the trailer. Once, the two carted a full-sized military duffle to and from the trailer. Later, the twins rummaged through their father's food delivery truck before sprinting into the brush.

Following the two proved a fool's errand. The twins traveled with youth's dexterity and experience's map of every tree, gully, ditch, and bush in their periphery. Paunch tried but failed to keep pace. When the twins returned home, Paunch attempted solo searches of the area. Each expedition proved unfruitful.

Paunch wiped his forehead, his body drenched in sweat, clouds mercifully drifting in front of the sun. He checked his Seiko; the sunset—and the cool relief it offered—remained ninety minutes away. Still, blue grays and soft oranges overtook the sky, as clouds blocked the falling sun.

A disturbance snatched his attention. The twins hurried from the brush toting the green military duffle again. The two struggled under the bag's weight, more so than on their previous trips. Paunch studied the twins gingerly placing the bag at Tex's feet. Paunch swore the bag jiggled. Shifting supplies, he reasoned.

Tex considered the bag before turning to the twins. The mechanic appeared irked, confused. The boy hopped on a car bumper and whispered into Tex's ear. The father whispered back, despite the fact that no one stood within earshot.

Paunch's attention returned to the duffle bag because it … squirmed.

Tex Wexler dropped to a knee, tugged open the duffle, and Teeny push-squeezed out, toting a stuffed animal with her. The corners of Paunch's mouth shot earward, a smile he forgot he owned, a smile not seen since before his daughter's death. Teeny Voix lived.

Then bedlam. Tex tossed vehicle keys to his twelve-year-old daughter.

"What the?" Paunch said out loud, baffled as Teeny and the twins sprinted to Tex Wexler's food delivery truck. Teeny hopped into the box truck's passenger seat and Tex's girl started the vehicle. Before she closed the driver's side door, her twin brother settled below her, manning the pedals.

"Holy mother … " Paunch said as the truck ground into gear and navigated womper-hazardly down the shell, gravel, and potholed drive toward his hiding spot. He jumped from cover and stepped onto the shell drive, making eye contact with the girl behind the wheel, waving for her to halt. She mouthed something, an order to her brother controlling the pedals.

Instead of slowing, the box truck tires spit shell from under them, plowing forward. Before Paunch dove to safety from the barreling box truck, he glanced at Teeny Voix. The girl failed to acknowledge him, her head turned back to Tex, engrossed by events behind her.

Paunch landed with a thud on the drought-hardened dirt surrounding the drive. He groaned, wiped dust from his face, as a box truck, piloted by twelve-year-olds, rumbled toward Interstate 10, one of the most trafficked thoroughfares in the United States.

He stood, calculating the distance to his car, wondering if his life could get weirder, when a pistol's *pumph, pumph, pumph* demanded his attention.

Paunch spun to Tex Wexler, who emptied the remaining bullets into brush surrounding the trailer park. The weekend mechanic shook his head and tossed the empty Colt toward his trailer. Paunch turned to the brush. Ten to fifteen heads popped up, like gophers timidly peeping out their hole.

Tex slid between two cars, dropping into a yellow '65 Barracuda. Tex turned the ignition, the 'Cuda complained, coughed, and contradicted, before roaring to life. Tex pumped the gas nurturing the metal beast. Trailer dweller's heads popped out, then withdrew to safety.

Next, the landscape teemed to life, as the brush dwellers stood, surveying the circumstances. Most sprinted away. But one man, Paunch remembered, built like a Greyhound, wearing nuthugger shorts and toting a pistol, chased after the yellow Barracuda as it peeled out and careened down the driveway.

The street racer skid to a stop, one door flying open as Tex Wexler yelled, "Get in, dumbass!"

Grabbing onto the swinging passenger door, Paunch jumped in as the Barracuda burned rubber, retching rubble, rock, and shell from the tires. The man in nuthugger shorts stopped, shielding himself from projectiles. All in a matter of seconds. Seconds that saved Paunch's life.

In his rearview mirror, Paunch watched the man plant his feet, as the Barracuda's rear window shattered. The *bink, binkity, bink, bink* of bullets barraging the Barracuda's backside broadcast throughout the chassis. "Shit, shit, shit," Paunch yelled as Tex peeled toward I-10 to follow his twins.

"What the hell's going on?" Paunch asked as the Barracuda exited the trailer park and gripped the street's asphalt. Tex whipped the car to the right.

"Now's not explaining time," Tex yelled over squealing tires.

Tex floored the gas as the road racer rectified. The Barracuda jerked forward, forcing Paunch's body back into the seat. As Tex power shifted, Paunch regained equilibrium, turned, and stared out the shattered back window.

"Don't worry, they ain't back there, but they will be."

"What?"

"Lexi found an army of white vans parked 'bout a mile back. Never seen 'em assembled in mass before. Dex said creepers were everywhere. My guess, most of the herd made a run for their vans."

"Okay," Paunch said, battling shock.

"Why didn't you take the shot?" Tex asked Paunch.

"I'm suspended, I don't have my weapon."

"Not much use. Thought you were lurking 'bout to protect us." Tex reached over and popped open the glove box. A box of shells, a bag of Mary Jane, and a Smith & Wesson 19, same model as Paunch's service pistol, filled the space. "Careful, it's loaded."

"Okay." Paunch inspected the weapon, then it hit him. "Wait, you knew I was staking you out?"

As the speedometer tilted toward 100, zipping past sedans, sports cars, and station wagons, Tex turned his attention from the road to Paunch, his look communicating, *No shit, Sherlock.*

The Barracuda barreled toward a Blue Bell ice cream truck's backside. "Eyes on the road, eyes on the road!" Paunch yelled.

Tex turned back to traffic, whipped around the Blue Bell truck, then foot-cranked the gas pedal again. He whipped off of I-10 onto US 90, following signs toward China, Texas.

"You know where the kids are headed?"

Tex nodded. "She only knows how to drive one place."

Paunch stayed quiet, awaiting explanation.

"Her grandmother's house in Cut and Shoot."

"Why the hell would you let your daughter drive a 10-ton truck to her grandmother's house?"

"Cuz she's a better driver than the boy," Tex said, as if his response answered the question in its entirety.

Paunch shook his head, then busied himself emptying and refilling the Smith and Wesson cylinder, ensuring the gun's readiness. Once he completed his ritual, Paunch said, "This is crazy."

Tex chuckled. "If you think you've seen crazy so far, brother, you jumped in the wrong car."

45

Each time Teeny glanced at the driver's seat, or the floorboard, an enthusiastic Wexler grin greeted her. The twins performed as one driver, Lexi captained, staring over the steering wheel, legs dangling over Dex's shoulders. Dex faced forward, butt on floorboard, feet on pedals.

Since Dex and Lexi found Teeny hiding in the trash trees yards from her trailer, they served as her caretakers. Dex hid Teeny in his fort, served as lookout, and retrieved food and supplies. Lexi accepted the toughest role, offering Teeny hugs and a shoulder to cry on. When necessary, the twins transported Teeny to pow wows with Tex in his army duffle. Dex and Lexi did not act inconvenienced. Instead, the situation invigorated them. Even now, especially now, the twin's relaxed and excited demeanor terrified Teeny.

To distract themselves, Teeny and Opie focused on the box truck's rearview mirror.

No one tailed them, not the twin's father, the porky man in the green sedan, or white vans. Teeny huffed. Adult supervision, even from Tex Wexler, offered comfort. Lexi rotated and saw Teeny's concern, "Dad promised. He'll be here." Teeny's eyes stayed pasted to the mirror.

"Teeny," Lexi called. "Hey," the driver's voice demanded. Teeny turned. Her chauffeur's chin barely cleared the steering wheel, hands 10 and 2, face forward, clocking every sign and vehicle. "It's gonna be okay." Teeny looked from her driver, down to Dex manning the pedals. He offered a snaggle-toothed grin.

Lexi's feet rested on her brother's chest. When the backside of her right foot bumped his chest, he dutifully pushed the gas with his right foot, enticing the box truck to creep from 46 to 48 miles per hour. Few automobiles shared the road with them since the box truck veered from I10 to US 90, then skid-bump-turned off US 90 onto Farm to Market Rd 770N. Teeny spotted the metallic green road sign for Daisetta and Batson. "Dad only let's me drive the backroads," Lexi said, as if Teeny required explanation for their gerrymandered route. Teeny nodded, then returned her attention to the rearview mirror.

Since the drive started, cars rocketed around the crawling box truck.

Another vehicle trailed behind them. Teeny restarted a silent prayer for the Wexler patriarch being the pilot of the car. Instead, Teeny clocked a tired, rusted, brown and wood paneled Ford Country Squire station wagon gaining ground. The rust bucket bolted by the box truck. The jalopy's driver, like most before, blared the horn, complaining about the box truck's pace.

"If them people that're chasing Teeny catch up, we can't outrun 'em," Lexi said.

"This'll be a blast." Dex said from the floorboard. The boy reached up and touched Teeny's knee. When she turned to him, Dex smiled again. Teeny understood Dex offered his expression to comfort her, but instead his turned-up lips communicated Wexler-batshit-crazy.

She decided to appreciate the intention and cradled his hand. "Teeny, when they catch up."

Lexi said, "And they will."

"It's gonna hafta be you," Dex added.

"We gotta drive."

Teeny nodded, accepting fate.

Dex explained his plan. Lexi lobbed ideas as well, two voices melding to one, finishing the other's sentences, adding minute detail, amplifying the other's insanity.

46

Paunch pointed to the sign for Daisetta and Batson as Tex's Plymouth Barracuda chewed up pavement.

"Why haven't we caught the kids yet," asked Paunch.

"Cuz I tried to lead the dogs away. Should be on 'em soon."

"What's the plan?" Paunch asked Tex.

"Get between the nightcrawlers and my kids."

Paunch nodded.

"You're the cop, any idea why so many scumbags're after her?"

"Not sure—something she witnessed or a piece of evidence she's toting around." Paunch sat in the passenger seat unconvinced of his own theories.

The suspended cop returned to his circumstance, checking behind them; no followers. He turned back to the front windshield as the white van caravan came into view.. "Shit, shit, shit," Paunch said pointing.

"Got 'em."

"Looks like—"

"Eight of 'em," Tex finished, jamming the gas guzzler's accelerator floorward. The Barracuda blazed past the caravan, without resistance. Paunch caught Tex studying the vans as he passed.

"They didn't even try to slow us down," Paunch said

"They want us close, brother. Easier to kill us all at once." Tex stared in his rearview. "Or, they were distracted." Ignoring the road, Tex flipped through CB channels. The Barracuda jerked toward the shoulder, aware its pilot's priorities lay elsewhere.

"Pay attention!" Paunch screamed.

"Okay, take over," Tex said, releasing the CB dial.

"What am I looking for?" Paunch asked.

"I wondered how they kept in touch, tracked down the kids' route so quick." Tex said. "Just spotted it. CB antennas. If we find their channel, we'll know their plan."

Paunch spun the CB dial.

Tex barked, "Slow down, spend a second on each transmission. It's an open channel. They gotta be vague."

Paunch flipped slowly now, and multiple voices greeted him. "Breaker, breaker one-nine; switch to our private; smoky on 10 at exit; pile up at … " but nothing about kids.

Paunch shook his head, ready to quit, but an icy stare from Tex kept Paunch turning. Static, crackling, more crackling, static, random voices, static, 'breaker-breaker', crackling, then … "We got 'em. Near Batson."

"That's them. Stop, stop!" Tex ordered. "Stay there!"

Paunch leaned back, jerking his hands from the dial.

Tex turned from the road and beamed at Paunch, "My girl's on course."

From the CB, "How far back … you, over."

"How many … ?" Paunch started. The cackling voices returned.

Tex shot a stay-quiet-imbecile death stare.

"If … ," crackling controlled the next ten seconds, "best chance … ," static, static, static, "before 59 and … " crackling, static.

Tex leaned forward and flipped off the CB, "It's starting."

"What?"

Tex skid-spun the Barracuda, turning back the way they came toward the eight white vans they passed. Paunch slammed against the passenger side door. Smoke squeezed from the asphalt-tire interchange blossoming around the 'Cuda. The distinctive scent of burnt rubber assaulted the detective's nose.

"The kids are the other way," Paunch screamed.

"Yeah, brother, we gotta thin the herd. Give the kids a chance." Tex jacked the petrol addict's pedal toward the floor, Paunch's body jamming back into his seat. The Barracuda begged for more, as Tex obliged, shifting with the synchronization of a familiar lover. Paunch watched the speedometer needle slam to the right.

The Barracuda basked in the moment, embracing the G-Force Tex coaxed from her. Paunch turned to Tex Wexler. The driver's lips pulled toward his ears, his eyes locked on the road ahead and the approaching caravan of white vans.

"What the hell?" Paunch started.

"Ever played chicken?"

47

"Shiiiiiiiiiiiittttttttttttttttttttttttt … !" Paunch screamed, as the Barracuda bulleted toward the battalion of white vans. The Barracuda took its half of the Farm Road out of the middle, daring interlopers to evade her wrath. The Barracuda bucked with each shift as Tex demanded his yellow American metal drive dead middle, offering moving vehicles two alternatives: death or destruction.

Paunch's eyes locked on the lead van; less than ¼ mile away it swayed from shoulder to shoulder. With each sway, Paunch noted the pack behind the lead vehicle slowed, now staying a hundred yards apart. The suspended officer turned to his left and watched Tex embrace, no, wrong word, revel in the moment. The driver's eyes expanded as the distance between van and Barracuda decreased.

Paunch, accepting the clarity of impending death, decided, *if this is how I die, I might as well enjoy the circus.* He turned vanward and embraced episode one of *FUN with Vans - starring Tex and Paunch.*

His life failed to flash before him. Instead, he found himself locked in one memory. American history, Coach Butler's class, and one specific lesson: the Battle of Bunker Hill. The American patriots lost that battle, but their pluck and determination set the tone for the Revolutionary War.

Colonel William Prescott, his ammunition stores empty, but his troops full of fight, set the tone with one command, "Don't fire until you see the whites of their eyes." Paunch suspected the story reeked of hyperbole.

Until today.

Life teaches lessons by allowing you to wallow in circumstance. As the last yards closed between Barracuda and lead van, Paunch studied the yellow T-shirted passenger and the black T-shirted driver. Paunch saw the whites of the driver's eyes, and the terror they contained, not staring forward, but whipping side to side. Even from his seat, the detective understood this play's ending.

RRRRRRR, the Barracuda screamed, offering no quarter.

At the last second, Van #1's black T-shirted driver jerked hard left, toppling the van, choosing a chance at survival over death. Paunch watched the van's first rotation from the Barracuda's passenger side window, then the second and third tumble from the rearview mirror.

Paunch's head whipped to the front as Van #2 pressed toward them, Paunch gauged still 75 yards out, then 50, 25 ...

Van #2 slammed its brakes and skidded to the left; Tex piloted the Barracuda, on a 70% asphalt/30% shoulder blend. In the 'Cuda's residency on the shoulder, Van #3 weaseled by them.

Seconds later, Paunch heard the distinctive sound of exploding metal, guessing correctly that Van #3 pummeled into Van #2. Paunch spun, staring out the shattered glass of the Barracuda's rear window.

Van wreckage spun, flew, blasted away, and helicoptered skyward. Remnants pelted the ground like hail. The chances of survival for passenger and driver hovered between zero and zero-point-zero. Van #2 exploded, blasting Van #3 off the side of the road.

Paunch spun back to the battle brewing out the front windshield. The rules of warfare changed. Van #4 pulled off the road, even off the shoulder, refusing to play. Ahead, Vans #5 through #8 followed suit, giving the Barracuda a clear path.

Smart, Paunch thought to himself, allowing himself to breathe again, as the Barracuda barreled past Vans #7 and #8. "Take the shot, take the shot!" Tex screamed.

"I'm a suspended police officer. I can't fire at vehicles," Paunch said. "We don't know who's driving 'em."

Tex kept one hand on the wheel, slamming the Barracuda's dash with the other. "Shit." Three more slams, then "Why'd you get in the car, asshole? Did you think I invited you to a garden party?"

Paunch swallowed the berating while staring out the back window. Vans #4 through #8 gingerly retook the road, avoiding the wreckage, but not stopping to check on their brethren. The remaining five vans restarted their pursuit. "Should've left your useless ass at the trailer park," Tex said.

The Barracuda break-skidded to a stop, "Get out," Tex ordered. Paunch stared back, baffled. "I said, get out."

"But … " Paunch started. He hung his head, complying with the order. He stared at the Barracuda, expecting the yellow beast to leave him in its wake. Instead, the driver's door opened. Tex marched into Paunch, standing belly to belly.

"The way I figure, there's three choices, brother," Tex said, towering over the detective. "Choice #1, stay here, useless as a Sunday school teacher at a kegger."

Paunch remained silent as Tex laid out the final two options.

48

"Relax, Teeny, we're 'bout half-a-way," Lexi said, offering encouragement.

Teeny breathed relief as the box truck passed a sign welcoming them to Batson. On their way to Grandma Wexler's house. No more running for her life. Safe.

"We're in a town, need to slow down," Lexi said, calmly tapping her left foot against Dex's left shoulder - brake side. Teeny's eyebrow raised silently, admitting her surprise at how smoothly the drive proceeded ... so far.

The box truck continued a perfectly-executed approach past oaks, telephone poles, and a country church, into Batson's city center. Teeny glanced at Opie, and he and she both sensed something amiss.

On Opie's recommendation, Teeny looked down the road. A pack of plain white vans, none featuring advertising or distinguishing marks, disguised by their generic nature, assembled at or near the intersection of FM 770 and TX 105. Teeny's hand shot to the driver, gripping Lexi's arm.

"Hey," Lexi said, before marking the vans herself.

Adrenaline, nature's fight-or-flight juice, pumped through Teeny's body, muscles tensed, reflexes heightened, fear raised. She turned toward Lexi, understanding the girl battled the same challenges. Challenges heightened by the fact that Lexi, an underaged driver, sans license, who barely peered over the steering wheel, piloted a ten-ton box truck loaded with dry goods.

Teeny's head snapped from Lexi to the front windshield and the army of vans. Two of the vans' drivers hopped out and walked calmly toward the intersection, stepping in front of the box truck, waving for Lexi to stop.

Teeny failed to recognize a fat, lumbering, bearded man in a baseball hat. For a moment, her brain processed the circumstances, and confusion overtook her. Then damning evidence of their situation was aroused when she recognized the second man, the Swizzle Stick, lollipop dangling from his mouth.

Teeny waved her arms forward, her body begging Lexi to keep driving as the men stepped forward, blocking the intersection.

"What's goin' on?" Dex asked. The two girls ignored him, drawn into the moment.

"Teeny, I can't run 'em over. I just can't," Lexi said as the box truck slowed toward the red-octagon. The Swizzle Stick man mouthed with adult authority, "Little girl, stop the truck, stop the truck right now, you stop this truck."

"What's goin' on?" Dex stared back over his shoulder at his sister, confused by the circumstances playing out above.

Lexi looked to Dex confused, afraid, triggered, looking for help from her twin, who shared far less information than the driver and shotgun passenger. Teeny's eyes, body, and expression, begging Lexi to keep the truck moving, no matter what.

Despite Teeny's pleas, Lexi answered, "I can't, I can't, I can't." Lexi's brain decided to brake, and brake hard.

Unfortunately for the two men in front of the moving box truck, the twelve-year-old's pumped full of adrenaline's feet got confused. Lexi told Dex to, "Stop, stop, stop," but her right foot pounded Dex's right shoulder, the GAS PEDAL shoulder, which told Dex to *jam, jam, jam* the accelerator.

Dex responded to the pounding foot, not the words.

Teeny's eyes widened as the Swizzle Stick Man leaped left into a ditch.

The bearded, baseball hat-wearing man, slow of mind and body, got tanked by 10 tons of metal. The sounds of cracking bone, squishing organs, and dying screams, "Ahhhh … ," reverberated through the box truck. Against her wishes, Teeny imagined the bearded man rolled up like a tube of toothpaste, innards spewing out his mouth.

Lexi, by rote, understood the need to turn left toward grandmother's house, but Dex's foot on the accelerator meant the box truck turned two wheels off the ground, slamming into white vans for correction.

Inside the box truck, grocery Armageddon ensued. Fifty-pound flour bags—launched from the floorboard—whipsawed into metal grocery racks, exploding, filling the truck with a white snowy haze. Punctured cola cans—spun like tops—spewed syrupy solution like lawn sprinklers. Teeny held up her hand—protecting her eyes—but watched cola spray across the windshield.

Next, clunks and crashes from the truck's rear. Teeny's head whipped over her left shoulder, as #10 cans of pumpkin, green beans, canned chili, and stew, slammed port side to starboard, denting, leaving 10-pound metal projectiles rolling across the floor now covered in flour and split bags of rice, beans, and cornmeal. Thousands of dried red, black, and pinto beans marbled around the rear of the box truck.

Lexi fought the steering wheel, but the dented truck corrected, heading west on 105 toward Cleveland, Texas, then Cut and Shoot. The driver's window remained clear of soda, so the white flour did not stick to it like the passenger side. Even through flour powdered passenger side front windshield, Teeny recognized two white vans now fronted the truck piloted by twelve year olds. Teeny stared in the rearview mirror and watched the remaining cadre of vans pull into formation behind them.

Teeny hoped—prayed—for the giggling sound, the sound that predicted the arrival of random, mysterious, deadly protectors. Her brain remained quiet. No saviors materialized.

Teeny looked at her driver(s). The three children were alone, outnumbered ...

Surrounded.

49

Paunch could not swallow Choice #1. *Stand on the shoulder, watching Tex drive off.* Or Choice #2. *Get back in the car, take the damn pistol, and prove useful.* Choice #3 offered the most palatable brand of nuts. *Driving.*

Paunch nurtured the Barracuda from the shoulder back toward the wreckage. Wreckage between them, the five remaining white vans, Teeny Voix, and the Wexler twins.

Tex now occupied the passenger seat, gripping the revolver. Paunch baby-tapped the gas pedal at first, getting to know the 'Cuda, who proved a wanting mistress. He pushed the gas and blew past smoldering remnants of Vans #2 and #3, a quick glance confirming Paunch's guess. No survivors.

As the driver, Paunch needed to focus on the next obstacle: Van #1's surviving occupants.

The van, six full up-n-over rotations off the road, rested clear of the two-lane asphalt. No issue. However, the two occupants had climbed from the wreckage and stood near the road. Both men wore jeans and T-shirts, one black, one yellow.

The yellow-shirted man toted a shotgun. "Shit," Paunch said. He guided the Barracuda directly toward the threat. The men smartly stepped from blacktop to grass-covered shoulder.

Tex, in tune with Paunch, leaned out the passenger side. The *click, phumph, phumph, phumph, phumph, phumph, phumph* six-shooter rhythm dared the shotgun-wielding man to hold position. The yellow- and the black-shirted men dove for cover, missing their opportunity to fire on the Barracuda from point-blank range.

Enjoying a brief moment of relief, Paunch jammed the gas pedal to the floor, not wanting to risk getting buckshot peppered at close range. In his rearview mirror, the two men bound up quickly. The man in yellow raised the shotgun.

"Get down, get down," he screamed. He reached over and shoved Tex's head toward the floorboard while lowering his own.

In his one retelling of the story, Paunch admitted he did not know if the *tinkity, tink, tink, tink* of the bearings peppering the Barracuda's backside, or the *chink* of three bearings plinking the front windshield— inches from Tex's ear—occurred first.

In the melee, Paunch allowed the Barracuda to slow.

"Drive, drive, drive, drive!" Tex shouted.

Paunch's foot floorboarded, and the Barracuda responded, ready to reengage. He looked ahead, but the five vans that passed them were no longer in sight.

Then the impossible.

"Hee, ha, hee, hee, ha, ha, ha … " bounced over the sound of the Barracuda's roar, from outside the car, inside the car, and inside his head.

He stared toward Tex, "Yep, heard it too."

Paunch felt the pull of a seismic sea wave charging toward shore. The change in atmosphere, the draw. Something zoomed—lightning- fast—mere yards above their heads, like a jet airliner approaching a landing strip without slowing. Too fast and too close to identify. Paunch's eyes tried but failed to focus on the object.

Air sucked from the Barracuda, hell, from the roadway.

"WHOOSH", followed by, "Hee, ha, hee, hee, ha, ha, ha … "

Tex shifted in his seat, staring skyward, to where the object was, not toward the destination.

Paunch heard it first, screams behind them. The rearview mirror offered an unexplainable mystery. The black T-shirted man and his yellow T-shirted shotgun-toting friend disappeared.

Even as the Barracuda barreled forward, he checked and rechecked the mirrors. No mistake, no movement, no T-shirted men. The two men had vanished.

50

"They're all around us," Lexi said. "Everywhere."

Dex looked up from the floorboard. "Teeny, it's time."

Fear captured her face. her head slamming side to side, letting her body, if not her mouth, scream, *NO!*

Teeny pointed to the front windshield repeatedly, motioning to Lexi.

"Teeny wants me to tell ya there's two vans in front of us. They're tapping their brakes, trying to slow us down," Lexi explained.

"Okay," Dex said, offering two thumbs up while pressing the box truck's pedal to metal.

"No, no, no," Lexi screamed as the vans in front of her tapped their brakes again. One white van blocking the street's right side, the other the left. Eight tons of metal carrying two tons of canned goods, charging toward the unsuspecting vans from their rear.

"Dex, no, no, Dex, Dex!" Lexi screamed.

"Just keep the wheel steady," Dex said back.

The left side van's driver must have peeked in the rearview mirror and spotted the box truck barreling up his backside. Having no time to accelerate and avoid collision, the driver jerked the van to the shoulder, allowing the box truck to pass unimpeded. The van to the right failed to adjust, mistakenly holding position.

Cruuunnnnch.

The box truck slammed into the van's backside corner, tilt-a-whirling the van toward a drainage ditch. The van clipped the ditch, flopped, severed a crepe myrtle, and wedged upside down between two pines.

Lexi smiled down at her brother.

"So, no one's in front of us anymore," he said, beaming back.

Lexi nodded, while peering over the steering wheel, regaining a modicum of calm. Tapping his right shoulder with her foot, he tapped the gas. The twins returned to synchronicity.

"Teeny," Dex said. She refused eye contact. "Can't let 'em get in front of us. You just can't."

Teeny pointed repeatedly to the truck's rear delivery door.

Dex answered her finger's question. "Dad never locks it."

Teeny looked at Opie in her lap. "We'll protect him," Lexi assured.

Teeny peered over her shoulder, into the food delivery truck's backside. Flour coated the groceries. Rice and beans shifted, rolled, and skittered along the floor. Busted sodas and #10 foodservice cans bumper-car battled for ground control.

Teeny hugged Opie, set him down, stood, and glanced at Dex again. He nodded, and the tiny, mute girl stepped into food mayhem. Gingerly dodging grocery shrapnel, the girl reached the box truck's roll-up back door. She breathed deeply, grabbed the handle, and tugged with all her might.

The door refused to budge. She stood, stared down, reassessed, breathed deeply, and pulled again. The door inched upward, but refused to give way. Rolling rice sucked through the slither of an opening, beans vacuumed against the crack, rattling, trying—but failing—to escape.

Teeny bent down, grabbing the handle once more, engaging arms, legs, back, and buttocks, then jerking the door upward. Light exploded into the truck's cargo bay.

She stared out the truck's backside, eastward down TX 105, wind whipping her shirt before ripping her bucket hat off her head. Teeny's cloth hat, the protector of her anonymity, drifted away.

She stared at an army of white vans, piloted by the devil's minions, grinning hyenas disguised as men. Teeny stood in the box truck opening, no hiding, fully Teeny. Closer to death and life than possible before, holding her battle position.

Slowly at first, then at once, beans, rice, and flour—sucked out by the wind—vacuum pelted the van directly behind her. The closest van adjusted to the rice and bean barrage as Teeny grasped the genius of Dex's plan.

51

After the wind sucked the flour, rice, and assorted beans from the truck, it gripped and ripped half-empty soda cans next, one flying by Teeny's ear and bouncing off the trailing van's windshield.

Teeny stared into the eyes of her pursuer, the closest white-van driver, a cue ball-headed man in a tank top, with thick, coarse, black arm hair, visible even from the girl's venue. The van's wipers whipped side to side to clear the assaulting flour, beans, and rice.

Even with the roaring engine and wind screaming in her ears, Teeny heard #10 cans—10 pounds of dented metal and food—bumper car behind her. Teeny turned, understanding the next assault.

The open truck door—and the box truck's momentum—pulled the huge cans like magnets toward the opening, rolling past a dodging Teeny toward their date with asphalt. The first two cans landed, and bounced innocently toward the road's shoulder, but not the third.

The third tapped Teeny's ankle as it passed, spun, and bounced off asphalt into the windshield of the tailing van. The can-grenade exploded, coating the van's windshield with chili con carne. The van driver jerked the steering wheel too quickly and it spun off the road, cleaving a small pine before tangling in a barbed wire fence.

Before Teeny could celebrate, the next van pulled behind her. The driver, now aware of the #10-can barrage, dodged the cans adeptly. He pulled the van closer and closer, positioning to pass the box truck. Teeny remembered Dex's orders. *Don't let the vans in front.*

Her head pivoted right, spotting a slit box of ketchup bottles. Reacting, not thinking, she snatched two bottles and tossed them toward the van, both bounding off the van's hood. The van's driver, a blazing redhead—not looking at Teeny—focused only on passing the box truck.

Teeny huffed and reloaded two more bottles, adjusting to the gust that misdirected her first two tosses. Instead of throwing directly at the van, she lobbed ketchup bottles in front of the van and let the wind take control. Both ketchup bottles slammed into the van's windshield; one cracked the glass, the other exploded, coating the windshield in muted red. The driver flipped the windshield wipers, spreading the mix of red ripe tomatoes, distilled vinegar, corn syrup, salt, spice, and onion powder—obliterating his view.

The van slowed—approaching the road's shoulder—but, with no vision clues, rolled into the ditch instead, seesawing back and forth. Encouraged by her success, Teeny lobbed more bottles at the next van. The van's pilot stayed back, out of throwing range, and sneered.

Teeny's brain recounted the battle's first success, can-grenades. She tugged and tugged, jerking a case of canned stew from the box truck's shelf. The box slammed to the truck's floor, cracking open. Teeny tilted the box, rolling cans from the truck onto asphalt; they bounced, bopped, and tumbled, but the van's driver nimbly dodged each.

"Mmm," she grumbled.

"How's she doing?" Dex screamed from the floorboard.

"Two down," Lexi screamed back.

Teeny paused, frustrated, but decided to channel her truck mates. *What would the Wexlers do?* became her motto. Teeny turned to grab the ammunition needed; tugging two boxes of #10 canned spaghetti sauce, they slammed to the truck floor. She snatched a box of green olives in glass containers. Tongue sticking from her lips, deep in thought, Teeny ripped opened all three boxes.

She turned to check. The van held position, not trying to gain yet, keeping a safe distance from Teeny's tosses. She huffed, using both hands to tilt boxes of spaghetti sauce upward. The twelve projectiles rolled toward the truck's rear, launching one after the other. Teeny tilted the box of glass-bottled green olives next. They rolled out behind their metal-plated lead soldiers, slower to battle.

The closest van dodged the first eight cans, but the ninth can bounced, cratering the windshield, sending glass into the van's cabin. The van now featured a gaping hole in front of the driver. The driver held position, undaunted. The remaining cans bounded harmlessly toward bordering ditches. The driver cleared windshield glass from his lap, not spotting the next onslaught.

Eleven olive bottles hit the asphalt and shattered, proving ineffective weapons. But the twelfth bottle landed lid-side, shot into the air, spinning toward the van. The flying bottle of olives cocktailed the van driver's teeth, exploding into his lower jaw, slicing his throat. Blood and pimento stuffed olives redecorated the van's fawn-colored seats.

The dead man-piloted van drifted off asphalt and tumbled toward the tree line. The next wave of vans approached.

Teeny turned to consider her arsenal, selected her next weapons, and tugged, tugged, tugged a sixty-pound box of pork and beans to the floor. She considered a second P-n-B box, when she realized her deadly mistake.

Using her need to reseed her ammunition, two of the vans revved their engines and pulled quickly within yards of the box truck. She grabbed at anything close and found herself holding a tin of shortening. She tossed it, and it bounced harmlessly off the van to the right.

The driver shook his head, smiled, and, like the van to the left, revved his engine to pass. Nothing she could do. The battle turned, she lost. Teeny looked back to the cab and her two heroic drivers, knowing she failed the twins, wondering what future awaited them.

She pictured herself surrounded by the Hawaiian-shirted man with the snake smile, the Swizzle Stick man, the Greyhound Man in nuthugger shorts, and the driver with thick, hairy arms. Picturing each of them stepping closer and closer—in her vision—she raised her hands to her eyes, blocking out the incoming horror.

Then the "BOOM," from above, the atmosphere announcing a new arrival. Teeny's head whipped back and forth, her eyes to the clouds, trying to find the upheaval's origin. Nothing, or at least nothing in her sightline.

She felt it next. Wind sucked the remaining flour residue, rice, and beans into the open air. Teeny grabbed the metal rack beside her, the disturbance threatening to rip her from the box truck.

"WHOOSH," followed by "Hee, ha, hee, hee, ha, ha, ha … "

In her head and all around.

52

The box truck jerked slightly as the driver(s) adjusted to new stimuli.

"What was that?" Lexi hollered back.

"Hee, ha, hee, hee, ha, ha, ha ... "

"They giggled in my head," Dex followed.

Teeny's head spun to the van on her right. The confused driver's head whipped right, left, then upward, trying to identify the sound. He, like the driver to the left, lost interest in passing the box truck, completely engrossed in finding the sound's origin.

Teeny—the only food-fight participant who understood the situation—smiled. *Allies arrived.*

Uncertain of the WHO or WHAT of her reinforcements, confused as to HOW or WHY, Teeny only needed one question answered.

WHEN would reinforcements arrive?

RIGHT NOW.

"Shiiiiiitttttt!" she heard their screams. Not one voice, two in unison. Screams of terror, approaching, intensifying. She looked skyward and her mouth dropped. Yellow and black projectiles bombed toward them. Her brain understood one fact: bombs don't curse. She shook her head, unraveling the information.

Time slowed; Teeny peeked to her right. The van driver's head jerked in the scream's direction. Vision blocked by his van's roof, the driver couldn't spot the falling ...

She turned back to the incoming yellow and black bombs, close enough now to offer answers.

Not bombs. Men plunging from the sky, one in a yellow T-shirt, the other in a black T-shirt, screaming, plummeting, understanding death awaited within seconds.

Teeny followed the path. Men … bombs missiled toward her.

"Shiiiiiittttt!" the screams continued. Teeny regripped the steel rack, dropping to the ground, preparing for impact, but unable to pry her eyes from impending chaos.

The black-shirted man/bomb arrived first, slamming into the van on the right, cratering the van's roof. The van jerked right, then flipped off the asphalt.

The yellow-shirted missile arrived seconds later, spearing the other van headfirst, slicing through the van's thin metal roof. The yellow-shirted man's head and shoulder, or the bloodied remains, dangled next to the van's driver. As the carcass jerked in the throes of death, the driver screamed at the upside-down corpse riding shotgun.

The second van decelerated as the driver's foot lost contact with the gas, lilting to the street's shoulder. The driver of the speared van, a man in leather pants and vest, sprinted from his van toward the tree line screaming, rechecking the sky every few steps.

As more vans approached, Teeny heard the "WHOOSH", then "BOOM!"

"What's happening?" hollered Dex.

Teeny studied the sky, realizing whoever—or whatever—assisted in her time of need departed. She stared down the final three vans, understanding they were hers to battle. She took a deep breath and turned to her arsenal: flour, wheat, beans, bottles of juice, cans of soft drinks, #10 cans of food, and jars of condiments. The girl categorized the death-dealing potential of each weapon at her disposal.

She turned back; another white van sped to join the fray. More pursuers. Not the greatest news.

Not the worst she would receive. "Teeny," Lexi called. "Hey, Teeny."

Teeny turned, hearing their rolling war truck's engine gurgle.

Lexi finished. "Hey, ahh, we're almost outta gas."

53

The Barracuda slowed as it entered Batson. Paunch drove while witnessing the bizarre occurrence in front of him.

One of the white vans they chased pulled to the shoulder. Two men efforted to pull an injured fat man, check that, dead fat man, into their van. A familiar man watched their efforts. Paunch eyed him, the Hawaiian-shirted man in shorts and huaraches. The man offered Paunch a jaunty wave that threatened replay in Paunch's nightmare. Caught off guard, Tex forgot the revolver in his lap, his voice pulling Paunch back.

"What're they doing?" Tex asked.

"It's Sunday, no one's around, looks like no church service tonight. I think they're trying to cover up whatever this is. Hide their existence before witnesses arrive. But honestly, I … don't know." Paunch studied the van collecting the dead body, now from his rearview mirror. "What do we do?"

"Find my kids, shithead," Tex said.

The Barracuda rumbled to the stop sign in Batson, where one van remained parked, driverless. Paunch assumed the men behind him loaded the vehicle's former driver into their van. Paunch refocused on his route. Tex did not need to direct him; he guessed the chase's direction. A seared rearview mirror, a hubcap, warped metal, and shards of glass coached him to turn left.

Paunch looked left. Before he could turn, Tex added. "That'd be the way."

The Barracuda left the body cleanup in its wake and sped toward what Paunch considered the strangest episode of his life. Two miles up the road, first a severed crepe myrtle—then an upside-down white van jammed between two pine trees—caused the two to rubberneck. As the Barracuda passed the strange site, the front two van tires spun, propelling the van nowhere. Paunch decided the dead driver's still flooring the van's gas pedal.

Paunch and Tex, in unison, "Hmm." Next, the Barracuda's tires crunched over dried beans and rice sprinkled over asphalt, the two men considering the roadway with raised eyebrows.

Tex spotted them first—dented and splattered cans of restaurant supplies spread across the road like food-landmines. "Watch out!" he screamed, pointing. Paunch adjusted the Barracuda, dodging each.

A few miles ahead, after dodging more can-mines, the scene offered the next mental puzzle. A van splattered with a reddish-brown substance, tangled in barbed wire.

"Good luck covering that up," Tex said, as he thumbed behind him. Paunch nodded. The visual buffet continued. A blazing redheaded man, trying and failing to push his van from the ditch, shot them the finger as the Barracuda passed.

"Was that?" Paunch started.

"Ketchup on the windshield, I think so," Tex said as they hurtled forward.

One of the vans in front of Paunch and Tex slowed, distracted by deaths diorama, not noting the Barracuda driving up its backside. The van drifted slightly to the right, Paunch using his years of training—and the van-driver's inattention—to bump into the van's rear right-side bumper. The Barracuda's headlight shattered as it spun the van into the ditch.

"Nice one," Tex said. Paunch glanced into his rearview mirror as the van's driver pounded his dash. "You owe me a front bumper and headlight," he added.

"Keep a running total. Bill me when it's over." Paunch right-footed the accelerator.

"Smart," Tex said, as g-force shoved his body back into his seat. Paunch skillfully jerked the steering wheel to adjust to dented cans in the road.

Once Tex's body adjusted, he screamed, "Be careful, be careful!" pointing toward jagged glass, busted jars, and more cans looming ahead in their wake.

"Are those," Paunch started, noting the busted jars and their scattered contents.

"Cocktail olives, yeah," Tex said as his head jerked backward, not believing his eyes. A quick glance to the left presented the next tumbled van. The spaghetti sauce-coated van resembled a horror movie scene.

"Nobody survived that," Tex mumbled. "Kids're holding their own, brother."

Embracing the ridiculousness, Paunch nodded as the Barracuda sped west.

This time Paunch spotted the next obstacle first, a piece of meat, a dead animal probably, lay across the asphalt roads yellow stripe. As they approached, Paunch recognized the roadkill. Twisted and bloodied, the jeans and black T-shirted man that disappeared. Paunch swerved to avoid driving over his carcass. He looked to the left, spotting another flipped, smoking van.

Paunch turned to Tex and found his passenger—Smith and Wesson in his lap—beaming. Paunch wondered, in the history of time did a father take pride in a stranger confluence of occurrences.

He turned his attention back to his job: driving. Tex pointed. A few hundred yards ahead a van angled 45 degrees, taking up part of the street and shoulder; only one narrow gap remained in their path.

"Can't be," Tex said as he and Paunch studied blue-jeaned legs and sneakered-feet jutting skyward from the van.

"What the hell?".

A suspended detective who witnessed bear-mauled, icicle-impaled, antler-gouged, and scissor-stabbed corpses might seem immune to surprise. However, every man, no matter how world worn, can be bamboozled. Flipped, crashed, smoking white vans, carcasses in the road, and asphalt-scattered groceries would propel most drivers to the point of stimuli overload.

An opportunity for ambush.

Paunch slowed the Barracuda slightly, like every driver trying not— but forced by morbid curiosity—to rubberneck the strange accident on the shoulder. He shifted his eyes from the road for a second to stare toward the legs jutting from the top of the van, while adjusting to the narrow gap left to pass.

"The feet, they're still, ah … moving," Tex said, pointing.

"Hmmm," Paunch sounded. He glanced into the van, recognizing the yellow T-shirt of the cadaver, before turning back to the road.

"Shit!" Paunch screamed. Two men pushed a van into the passing gap. A van, seconds earlier, obscured by the human-speared van. The two men used the vehicle as a mobile barricade.

Paunch slammed on his brakes, spinning the steering wheel, hoping, praying the Barracuda's backside sustained the majority of the damage, giving him and Tex a chance for survival. The last thing Paunch considered before collision, milliseconds before unconscious, *Teeny and the twins were on their own.*

54

Paunch's eyes drifted open, then closed. Not sure if seconds, moments, or hours passed. He shook his head groggily, begging for his snap to return. He glanced forward, the front windshield cracked but intact.

Smoke billowed from the Barracuda's engine, while gurgles, ticks, rattles, and clatters of the metal beast's dying gasp served as the situation's soundtrack.

Shattered glass covered the dash and Paunch's lap.

"Ugg." Paunch groaned, guiding his neck to the driver's side window, understanding the remains of that windshield covered his lap. Massaging his neck, he turned back, trying and failing to glance over his right shoulder. His neck did not currently bend in that direction.

Instead, he glanced in the rearview mirror. The Barracuda's back window, shattered by the gunshot at the trailer park, offered the view of an accordioned van, the one his ambushers pushed into the road, resting twenty yards away. The Barracuda's rumpled backside told Paunch he executed the spin before the crash, saving his life.

Not able to turn his neck, the suspended detective torqued his body instead, studying the vacant passenger seat. The door hung open. Out the same window he spotted the van with jeaned legs sticking out the top. An effective decoy, Paunch admitted. From his vantage point he confirmed the bloodied torso belonged to the yellow-T-shirted man.

Even in this moment of danger, Paunch's brain calculated how two men disappeared miles away, and reappeared as ... human projectiles destroying two vans. Paunch chalked up both bodies hitting moving targets to the case's impossibility tote board. Next, he checked the clouds. Nothing.

To survive this ambush, Paunch forced his head back in the game. His senses tingled as he listened for clues. Funny, the first thing he noticed. The van speared by the body idled. No one killed the ignition.

Then his ears tuned to the squeak of an opening van door. Next, voices. "Get him loaded."

"He's heavy," said another voice.

"Think he's heavy? Wait 'til we get the fat one," the first voice countered.

Paunch's hand drifted to his paunch as he shook his head. After seconds of self-pity, he considered the crippled 'Cuda and his circumstances.

The van the Barracuda slammed sat smoking yards away, undriveable. The human-speared van idled beside him. A third van must be hidden by the others. Two vans stopped to plan and execute the ambush, two voices; two people to deal with, Paunch postulated.

"Stop sniveling. Get over here'n help," said one of the voices.

"Okay," pouted a third voice. Paunch accepted … his battle just got tougher.

"Duct tape this one while we get the fat one."

Time for action.

He pulled the driver's side door handle. Stuck. He pulled again before turning to climb out the passenger side. His chest throbbed from slamming into the steering wheel, so his first move telegraphed the pain awaiting him. He turned and dog-crawled across the passenger side, keeping his head up, watching for enemies. He glanced down, seeing the steel tip poking from under the passenger seat.

Tex's body would have blocked it from their ambushers; carrying him off, they missed it, the Smith and Wesson. Paunch snatched the gun, rolled onto asphalt, as voices closed.

"This is gonna suck," said one approaching voice. Paunch rolled behind the van the ambushers used as decoy, the one the yellow-shirted carcass branched from. He pushed up to a kneeling position.

"Where the hell ... "

"Shit!"

"Get the shotgun from the van."

Paunch peeked around the van's backside. Tex was gagged with a strip of duct tape. A man in leather pants and a vest cut another strip from the duct tape roll with a pocketknife, preparing to bind Tex.

Paunch watched a man, he assumed one of the voices from earlier, reach into the van to retrieve the shotgun as ordered. Two voices accounted for, but Paunch did not know the third voice's position.

He looked to his right; the third man charged. "Get him!" the man yelled.

Thousands of hours of police training kicked in, Paunch's body performed not because of talent, but because of time on task and training,

Threat #1 - the guy retrieving the shot gun.

Threat #2 - the guy charging him.

Threat #3 - the guy in the leather pants with duct tape.

Paunch popped off two shots toward Threat #1 as Threat #2 tackled him. The shots were redirected by impact. Paunch heard two sounds in unison, "Mother Fu ... " from Threat #1, who clutched his arm and "Pumpf," from the punctured tire. Paunch and his attacker tumbled one over the other.

While fighting off his attacker, piglet-type squeals filled the air, then "Eek ... eek ... " and steps sprinting from the fracas.

Paunch glanced to the position of the absent Threat #3. Tex sat straight up, still gagged but not bound, in the back of the van they loaded him into minutes before. The leather-clad man, formerly considered Threat #3, sprinted toward the woods, pocketknife jammed between shoulder blade and spine.

Tex winked at Paunch and turned toward Threat #1.

Paunch fought over the Smith and Wesson as Threat #2 and he tornadoed on the ground. Spinning forth and back, sharp elbows slamming into cheeks and chins, head butting, knees slamming into groins and thighs, pinched painful pounding, both gripping the gun.

"Arr!" Paunch screamed as Threat #2's thumb pressed into his eye. Threat #2 focused on pressing his thumb, but did not account for how close his other fingers drifted toward Paunch's …

"Bastard," Threat #2 yelped as Paunch chomped the man's pinky, the attacker's thumb no longer in Paunch's eye socket, as the man focused on removing his pinky from jaws. Paunch clenched canines, incisors, and molars. The detective two-hand battled for the revolver, against his attacker's one.

Threat #2 pulled his teeth-locked hand, but Paunch powered his jaw shut. Then, like a gator, Paunch spun, dragging Threat #2 by the finger. Paunch's belly and rotund build forced the man to adjust; losing leverage. Threat #2 screamed in agony, then used his other hand to punch Paunch's eye.

Wuunk, Paunch's head whipped back, paying the price needed to force the man into an emotional decision, and amateur mistake. Threat #2's hand no longer battled for his revolver. By throwing the punch, Threat #2 lost the only battle that mattered, the battle for the gun.

Paunch received the beginnings of a black eye milliseconds before two muffled shots filled Threat #2's chest cavity.

"Uhh … ," he moaned, his last sound before dying.

Paunch's thought ran to his partner in the fiasco. "Tex, you okay?" he hollered from under the body.

"Mummph," his only response.

"Tex," he hollered again.

"Mummph," the return.

Bloodied, beaten, and bruised, Paunch rolled, pushing the body off of him, put one hand on the asphalt and pushed himself upright. He stood, steadied, regripped the blood-slickened revolver, and assumed a shooter's stance. He stepped around the van, prepared to face Threat #1.

Paunch rounded the corner slowly, finding a man with a gun.

But a different man than expected. Tex, duct tape spanning left ear to right, kneeled inspecting the punctured tire, the shotgun held casually by his side.

He turned to Paunch, and started to talk, "Mummph." He stayed in position but ripped the duct tape off his face. "You blew the tire out of the only working vehicle," Tex said with disgust.

Paunch's gaze passed from the van with a flat tire, the totaled van used as the blockade, the bashed Barracuda, to the van featuring a man's legs jetting from the top. The van's engine purring perfectly.

Paunch considered the jean-clad legs sprouting from the idling van. "Well … not exactly."

55

Lexi's words still fresh from her mouth, "Hey, ahh, we're almost out of gas."

Teeny decided, *well, then, I better get busy.* She jerked box after box of #10 canned food products to the floor. She split the boxes and rolled the 10 lb cans onto the street.

The van's drivers, learning from the errors of flipped, wrecked, and smoking vehicles before, slowed, allowing the cans to roll toward the shoulder. Teeny emptied box after box, but the vans easily dodged the arsenal they now understood.

She turned, realizing she spent her can-grenades uselessly. None left. Next, Teeny tossed bottle after bottle of olives, pickles, and beets to the blacktop, many shattered, some tumbled to the curbs and ditches. From their safe distance, the vans dodged each.

Her most dangerous weapons wasted, Teeny stood—arms at her side—alone. Miles passed, with the vans staying back, biding their time. Teeny wondered if the hyenas knew about the box truck's emptying gas tank, deciding that was impossible. The hyenas feared her arsenal—and the bomber from above scared them.

Okay, mostly the bomber; still, she owned a small part in the fear her pursuers carried with them. Pride swelled in her. Still, pride was an emotion. Pride could not save her now, but … *Thinking Teeny* could.

And *Thinking Teeny* looked right, left, then toward the box truck floor while formulating a plan.

. . .

Paunch kneeled on the floor between the passenger's and driver's seats of the white van.

The van featured only two seats. Tex Wexler drove the van, a man who Paunch, on his deathbed, would consider the craziest bastard who walked the earth. The yellow-shirted man, or the bloodied head, arm (singular), and torso, occupied the area above the passenger seat. Paunch tried not to stare at the carcass's face, more specifically, the lack of a face, shattered skull, and the blood, body fluid, and brain matter oozing onto the upholstery.

Paunch wondered why one arm remained on the torso and the other likely resided in a ditch. The detective turned, staring out the van's rear window, questioning if the arm remained on the asphalt behind them. Paunch found the question answered by the rolling bump-bounce behind him. A sound the detective never experienced but recognized in context. The dead man's arm completed its roll-journey, and bounded off Paunch's calf.

"Uhh," Paunch sounded, kicking the stump away.

"What?"

"Nothing," Paunch returned.

Tex raised his eyebrows.

"Nothing, comparatively," Paunch amended, not wanting to show weakness in the midst of madness. Not spotting a sidelined, damaged, or flipped van for miles left Paunch concerned. The van jerked left, then right, still dodging metal cans and shattered glass scattering the blacktop.

The detective watched an approaching Buick, the first car he had seen on the backroads since Batson. The Buick swerved. Paunch assumed the driver noticed the cadaver's leg thrust from the vehicle.

Tex laughed. Paunch understood the demented humor. If the Buick's driver considered that strange, just wait.

Paunch laughed too, despite himself, considering the menagerie of carnage awaiting the Buick's driver. Tex nodded back at Paunch. "We'll be dealing with cops soon. Surprised we're not already."

"It's Sunday, in the sticks," Paunch explained.

"You thought'a any way to, ah, explain this?"

"How the hell could anyone explain this?" Paunch said.

Tex nodded, then turned his attention to driving.

Paunch remembered Tex skidding up beside him, in the now abandoned Barracuda saying, "Get in, dumbass." That seemed eons ago, but Paunch checked his Seiko, yep, only an hour passed.

Concern coated Tex's face. "We need to get the kids and get scarce."

"We need to find them first, assuming they're—"

"They're alive, they're fine," Tex said. Paunch prayed the father convinced himself.

"Look, look, look … " Paunch yelled, staring out the front window. Tex's fist pumped, and, despite his bravado, a tear plikoed down the dad's stubble-covered cheek.

Paunch never asked if the tear represented relief Dex and Lexi lived, or pride they were winning the most bizarre battle in backroads' history. Even from this distance, Paunch counted four vans, jockeying for position, or more likely dodging foodservice obstacles. Then he saw her, the small figure guarding the truck's rear door.

As they closed on the vans pursuing the box truck, Paunch stayed locked on her, her defiance; locking that image forever. The LAST memory Paunch embraced before God called him home. Despite flipped vans, the cadaver in the passenger seat, and the craziness yet to come, that image remained.

56

Thinking Teeny unloaded what the trailing vans would consider deadly ammunition. She no longer possessed #10 cans, bottles, or jars. She stood in the truck's doorway, not reaching for food-ammunition, daring the vans to pass. A perfect plan, if the vans' drivers possessed an ounce of courage, which they did not.

The vans remained far enough behind to avoid her attacks, even though she stopped her assault due to lack of ammunition. If they would not come after her, she could not stop them. She slammed her foot to the ground.

The box truck would run out of gas, the White Van People would win, capturing her, Dex, and Lexi. Teeny needed them to have a reason to speed up, approach her, get close enough for *Thinking Teeny's* plan to work.

She prayed to see the tattooed graybeard man again or hear the laughter that marked the return of her strange allies. Neither came.

She looked around, considering the sky above her and the horizon. Abandoned.

She breathed deeply and looked to the asphalt below, the yellow lines zipping past her. She shook her head, gazed to the horizon. In the distance, Teeny spotted it, odd even by this day's standards. Another van approached, this one, with legs protruding from the ceiling. Another enemy to face.

She stood defiantly, ready for the battle, praying the enemy would retake the offensive, stepping into her trap.

•   •   •

"Vans are hanging back now," Tex said.

"Looks that way," Paunch answered.

"They got us outnumbered."

Paunch nodded before realizing Tex could not witness his agreement.

"You see this the way I see it, brother?"

"Unfortunately," Paunch answered.

"I'll ah … force the action." Tex floored the gas pedal and the distance between them, and the last van dwindled. Paunch understood, the white van he occupied acted as camouflage, the drivers of the vans ahead assumed an ally approached.

Tex pulled the van he piloted to the trailing van's bumper before whipping into the passing lane. Without delay, he slammed his van into the trailing van's driver's side rear wheel. The van turned into Tex and Paunch's, which slammed the van to the side while passing.

Paunch heard the unsuspecting van's driver overcorrect, skid, then flip.

"One down," Tex said confidently.

Over the van's CB radio, a voice cackled, "We got an enemy attacking from the backside. In one of our vans. They knocked Clarke off the road. I'll take care of 'em."

"Well, they know we're coming," Paunch said.

Each of the three remaining enemy vans adjusted. The third van slowed, Paunch assumed, to try to go toe to toe—or bumper to bumper—with Tex. The other two vans raced toward the box truck.

•   •   •

The confusing actions of the van with the legs protruding from the top enlivened *Thinking Teeny.*

That may be the strangest ally so far.

Then.

Why are they helping us?

After considering, Teeny realized the **why** failed to matter. The vans now trying to pass her mattered. They played into *Thinking Teeny's* plan.

The two vans pulled within yards of the box truck, the first van in her lane, the second in the passing lane. Teeny stared at the first driver, recognizing him, the Swizzle Stick man. She did not note the second driver, she only knew she must stop them both. She looked at the floor, making sure the open bag still lay by her feet. Then Teeny turned to grab her preselected weapon, apple juice.

•　　•　　•

The third van, prepared for the attack, cut off Tex's every effort to pass. The third van slowed, braked perfectly, sped up when needed, and thwarted every advance. Witnessing the past hours' action, Paunch did not worry about Tex and the ongoing battle. Instead, he focused ahead.

Tex tried the passing lane, shoulder, and attempted to bump the third van off the road. Each frustrating attempt followed by a cursing barrage, a barrage now so frequent it served as white noise. Tex and Paunch no longer possessed the horsepower advantage the Barracuda offered, and battled the white van on equal, or maybe inferior, terms. Paunch considered the head, shoulders, and torso dripping on the passenger seat, and assumed the legs protruding from the top hindered the van's aerodynamics.

Between views of the back of Van #3 and quickly approaching street signs, Paunch watched the first two vans close on Teeny's position. Paunch understood that, somehow, this girl and the Wexler twins outsmarted or outgunned pursuer after pursuer. So, he found himself strangely excited to watch the next foray unfold.

Paunch's van jerked to the right, in another attempt to pass; blocked again. Paunch's sightline improved for a moment. Strangely, Teeny opened two cans of beverage and sprayed the contents on the pursuing vans' windshields. The girl turned and grabbed more cans, repeating the process.

"What the … " Paunch started.

"Little busy here."

"She's spraying soda, or something on the van's windshield. That won't stop 'em."

"Not by itself." Tex slammed the gas pedal; blocked again, by the third van.

The distance expanded between Paunch's vehicle and the battle ahead, but his focus remained on the intermittent views of Teeny and her attack.

The pouring of canned beverages and the contents' lack of effectiveness offered the closest vans a swell of confidence. Even from this distance, Paunch watched the vans try to pass Teeny and the Wexler's box truck.

During Tex's next failed attempt to pass, Teeny repeated her process, can after can poured on her pursuers. Paunch lost his sightline as the van directly in front of him and Tex cut them off again. Tex adjusted to the shoulder, and Paunch spotted her again. Teeny held a bulging bag. She ripped it open as whipping wind tornadoed white powder from the top, even before Teeny tilted her weapon into place.

In that moment, Paunch understood the brilliance of the plan, and the demolition derby Tex must navigate to survive the next few minutes.

•   •   •

Teeny tilted the first bag of flour downwards, into the wind, and white fog clouds feathered behind her. She used her knee to tumble a bag of sugar, before kicking a bag of cornmeal off the rear of the truck. The bags exploded into the air, intermixing with the flour.

Cornmeal, flour, and sugar adhered to the apple juice-coated windshields. The van piloted by the Swizzle Stick Man drifted into the other. Both vans jerked.

Urrrrkkk, the sound of grinding metal on metal, followed by the sound of rubber stripping off a van's tire. The metal wheel ground against pavement. Sparks flew, one van twisted sideways before tumbling end over end toward the third van and the strange van with protruding legs.

The van piloted by the Swizzle Stick man, pulled slowly to the curve.

•   •   •

"Lookout!" Paunch yelled, as the van closest to the box truck jerked, sparked, then flipped toward them.

The van that blocked Tex and Paunch's pursuit failed to adjust. The incoming van bounded toward them before the "Cruuuuuuuuuuuuuuuuunch!"

Tex jerk-steered hard right to avoid joining the collision.

Tex's decision was simple. Join the pile up or overadjust to the right; he chose the second. Tex braked, spun, slowed, but momentum twisted the van into the dampened bog bordering the asphalt's shoulder. Paunch felt the van tires gloop into the mud.

The box truck topped a small bluff and disappeared. No more pursuers. Not yet. The skinny man Paunch remembered from the Pines Theater popped out the surviving van's door. Even from this distance, Paunch understood the van's driver was cleaning his windshield to reengage the battle.

"Let's go," Tex said, opening his door and stepping into the bog.

"Sure," Paunch said doubtfully.

Tex slogged through the bog. Paunch snatched the Smith and Wesson. A minute later, sans one mud-captured boot, Paunch joined Tex on the curve. Before he started to run—not Paunch's strong suit—he looked back at the van Tex piloted into the ditch and the two legs jutting from the top. The detective huffed before following Tex, already yards ahead, and jogged after him.

Paunch's belly bounced with each step as he stared toward the bluff the box-truck disappeared over. Huffing and puffing, the bluff now seemed forever away. Paunch trailed as Tex closed the distance to the van parked on the curve. The skinny man continued to wipe his front windshield but noted Tex's approach. The rail-thin man smartly used his van as cover.

Task completed, the skinny man hopped into his van, slammed the vehicle's door and pulled off. Tex tried and failed to run him down. Tex slowed, shouted curse words at the horizon, paused for a brief moment, put his hands on his hips, and continued his run toward the bluff, not accepting defeat.

Paunch's *run-jog* slowed to a *jog-walk* before transitioning to a *not so fast walk*. Seconds later, Tex disappeared over the bluff. Paunch stopped for a second, hands on his knees, sucking in oxygen.

"Heroes don't run out of breath two minutes into a chase," Paunch mumbled. He brought his hand up and wiped sweat off his forehead. Droplets rained to the ground. "And don't sweat like stuck pigs."

He stood wheezing, lambasting himself, reconsidering the shorter distance now to the bluff's top. Paunch studied his ridiculous camouflage outfit, which now slowed him. He considered keeping it on but accepted his only chance. He stripped the outer layer of clothes, and now stood in shorts, one boot, and wet T. He put one foot in front of the other—Smith and Wesson dangling by his side—and continued, dripping in sweat, after the van and box truck … on foot.

57

The box truck guzzled the last drop of fuel, coughed, then drifted to the curve, searing a 55 MPH sign from its base before settling to a stop. Teeny looked over the short bluff; no one followed … yet.

She took a deep breath, hopped to the asphalt, and Dex jogged beside her.

He pointed, "We need ta get to the woods, 'fore they catch up."

Lexi handed Opie to Teeny. Dex led the girls toward the pine forest. Steps short of cover, Teeny stared down the street. The white van driven by the Swizzle Stick Man topped the bluff.

"Crap," Dex said, spotting it too.

The sun conceded the sky, leaving the blood orange clouds as their companion. Dex jerked Teeny by the arm, following Lexi, who already disappeared into the pine's shadows.

•   •   •

Paunch passed two small houses as he approached the bluff. One woman stood in her front yard spitting curse words at him. He failed to register most of her diatribe, but caught her final words, "Calling the cops."

Paunch trudged forward. In his experience, Sunday slowed police response, especially in the country. Country folks, including local law enforcement, populated church pews or cooked their Sunday meals.

Paunch understood today's events occurred on back roads, miles from the interstate, delaying law enforcement's intervention.

He topped the bluff, spotting the box truck parked on the road's shoulder, the abandoned white van at its rear. Tex, maybe 100 yards ahead, sprinted to the two vehicles. He stopped, waving Paunch forward, before turning and disappearing into the woods.

The Smith and Wesson seemed heavier in his hand with each step. Paunch reached the van, leaned against its side and sucked in air. Sweat slimed his entire body. Paunch realized onlookers could count every hair on his chest and every inch of fat girdling his waist. Shadows and the evening's slow crawl to night embraced the woods.

Paunch entered the pine forest, readying himself for battle.

Pummf, the gunshot rang through the air. Birds scattered from their perch. Knowing a gunfight awaited, Paunch crashed through the woods toward bullets.

•   •   •

Teeny watched Tex spin as blood spurted from his arm. Seconds earlier, Lexi and Teeny hid behind an outcropping of pines, but, when Lexi spotted her father, she sprinted to him, screaming "Daddy." Teeny and Opie followed yards behind.

Tex spun toward his daughter's voice, raising a finger to his mouth to quiet her. Too late, the shot rang out. Teeny paused, but, instead of running for cover, Lexi sprinted to her father, covering his body. Tex Wexler twisted in pain, blood spouting from his left arm.

His body bucked in pain, but his eyes flash focused when he screamed, "Run!"

The Swizzle Stick Man burst from the woods and snatched Lexi into his arms. She spun, kicked, bit a chunk from his forearm, and spit blood before Swizzle Stick pointed his gun at Tex. "I'll put one through his skull."

Lexi's body went limp. The Swizzle Stick Man scanned the small clearing spotting Teeny and Opie. "Get over here before I gut your friend."

Teeny stepped forward. Swizzle Stick turned the gun to Teeny, then tossed Lexi toward her father. He jerked Teeny to him, placing the gun at his hostage's temple. Teeny squirmed under his grip, "Stay still, you little … "

•   •   •

"Arrrrrrrrrrrrrrrrrrrrrrrrrrrrrrrrrrrrrrrrrrrrr," Paunch registered from the gunshot's direction. Based on a lifetime in Southeast Texas, Paunch considered the sound's originator.

Coyote? Nope.

Wild dog? Again, no.

Cougar? Doubtful.

Bobcat? The most likely approximation of the scream. Still, probably not.

Haunting as shit. Yep.

He spotted the clearing ahead and trekked toward danger.

•   •   •

"Arrrrrrrrrrrrrrrrrrrrrrrrrrrrrrrrrrrrrrrrrrrrrr," Dex blared, bursting from cover behind the Swizzle Stick Man. Dex crashed into the man's knees from behind. Teeny tried to jerk away but her feet flew out from under her as the Swizzle Stick Man recovered, popped up, and jerked her collar, dragging her with him.

Tex rolled and pushed upward, slowed by his clipped arm, but started his charge before …

"Nah, unt, ahh," Swizzle Stick said, standing upright. The lithe man, understanding facts the others did not. He did not possess all the cards, just one card. The trump card, a gun to Teeny's temple.

Teeny's head turned upward, studying the man's sneer, knowing he killed before. More than that, he killed children before. Teeny allowed the feeling to wash over her, understanding the power inside her. She analyzed it, embracing the gift for the first time.

She saw HIM. Teeny did not suspect, she *knew* what he was.

Teeny recognized the Hawaiian-shirted man and the Greyhound man in nuthugger shorts for what they were. She thought back to the first time Sissie introduced her to Flick Hurt, her stepfather. She recounted him inspecting her up and down.

Teeny returned to her situation. *Thinking Teeny* processed the Swizzle Stick's ridiculous wardrobe, his denim vest and cutoffs. She planted, jerked, and spun in one motion, biting a chunk out of the Swizzle Stick Man's exposed hamstring.

He released her, turning his gun toward Dex, Lexi, and Tex when Teeny heard.

Pummf, Pummf, Pummf.

58

Swizzle Stick's body rocked backwards in rhythm to each shot fired from the Smith and Wesson. The bullets delivered chest, chest, chest, just like Paunch's thousands of practice rounds. The tall man wilted to the ground as Paunch stepped over and kicked the dead man's gun away.

He studied the girl, who snatched her stuffed opossum, then stared up at him. He understood the girl's brain would analyze his every move, every tic, every word. So, he chose carefully.

"Paunch Perez. Nice to meet you." He extended his hand.

•   •   •

Teeny stared up at the ridiculously-dressed, short, rotund, dark-complected man. One word, superball-bounced through her brain, "Safe."

Other less important words tickled her brain: messy, sad, depressed, alone, abandoned, loyal, determined. Teeny's head tilted slightly to the right, processing. She remembered her sweet dog Peanut, using his instincts to evaluate humans in his periphery.

Teeny's thinking and instincts merged. She embraced the synergy, a tool she would stock in her arsenal for the rest of her life.

A branch snapped as Teeny registered a tumbling sound. In a panic, Teeny turned to the spot Tex, Lexi, and Dex occupied seconds before.

They vanished. *High alert, high alert, high alert* pumped through her tiny body.

She recognized the hyenas the smug, Hawaiian-shirted man led.

Paunch could not see the threat, his attention turned to Teeny. She pointed, showing, not voicing her fear. Paunch lost valuable time in the translation.

The Greyhound man in nuthugger shorts pounced from behind. He swung a baseball bat that bounded off Paunch's noggin. The fat man's eyes rolled upward before he crumpled to the ground.

The Hawaiian-shirted man stepped over Paunch, snagged Teeny's wrist, and tossed her to his associate. A roll of duct tape circled his wrist.

Teeny stared at Paunch's crumpled body, pulled Opie to her, and heard the tape tear, before feeling the tackiness bind her wrist together. Tears streamed down her face. She failed him. If Teeny called out—or screamed—Paunch might have stood a chance.

She chose not to. Her choice. She failed.

59

The Greyhound man in nuthugger shorts removed her blindfold. She blinked, eyes adjusting. Her hands still taped together; her feet now bound as well. She peeked out the window, confirming the night's blackness, no porch lights, streetlights, or headlights. The White Van People held her somewhere remote, far from help. Opie, looking terrified, sat on the floor inches away.

She scanned her surroundings. Based on nights parked in front of her TV watching *Little House on the Prairie*, she guessed she occupied a log cabin. An unlit fieldstone fireplace with a matching hearth and split-oak wooden mantle dominated a majority of one wall.

Twenty-plus men loitered about, performing various tasks. As her gaze fell to each, her stomach turned, her pulse increased, her senses prickled. She realized the log cabin served as the headquarters of a large enterprise, the control center of a massive trading center.

Paunch's gun lay on a coffee table, feet from her, like an afterthought, impotent. No threat to the cabin's miscreants. She turned from wall to wall, studying the people and decor.

No satanic symbols, no signs of human sacrifice, no severed heads on stakes.

Instead, real evil greeted her.

Thumbtacked photos of children littered the walls, some featured check marks, some remained blank. Dollar amounts written on the borders of each photo.

Between the pictures, she noticed a register.

Blonde, Boy, <7, Dark Eyes, Athletic - $7800

Black, Girl, 12-16, Outgoing - $8200

Curly Red Haired, Girl <3, Green Eyes - $8400

Hispanic, Boy 6-8, Quiet - $8000

Teeny studied the register, realizing what the descriptions represented. Her momma kept a similar list on the fridge: oranges, flour, dog food. Teeny stared at a shopping list. Teeny looked from the list to Opie.

Someone mumbled next to her. The portly man drifted from unconsciousness. Teeny's abductors bound the Hispanic man to a chair beside her.

The Hawaiian-shirted man who killed Teeny's dog paced, screaming at the Greyhound man in nuthugger shorts and his other minions. "How the hell do we clean this up, you idiots?"

A man in an ill-fitting three-piece suit consoled, "Mr. White, none of the vans are trackable."

"Trackable? They're littering back roads from Beaumont to Houston, you idiot."

The three-piece suited man continued, "Vance, the vans, the men ... "

"Dead men," said the man in nuthugger shorts.

"None of the dead men can be tracked to you ... or us. We pay cash."

"We have to change vehicles, processes, pay out a fortune in bribes." Vance screamed as he turned to her. "Relocate six months ahead of schedule. Because of a kid and tub-a-lard." Vance marched to the Greyhound-shaped man in nuthugger shorts. "How the hell did this happen?"

The man did not answer. Vance's knee jammed into the man's privates. The Greyhound man crumpled to the ground in pain.

The minions stared at the floor or walked away. "And you ... " Vance spun to Paunch. "Chubby-pants, you couldn't leave it alone."

"For decades we moved in and out of … " Vance's mouth hovered over Paunch's face. Vance turned to the man in nuthugger shorts, still recovering, "Strap chub-muffin to the table."

Vance turned his attention back to Paunch, "One false move from you and I cut off the girl's fingers, pinky first. Understand?"

Paunch mumbled affirmation through the tape.

Four men cut Paunch from the tape and led him to the table. Paunch's stare locked on her. He shook his head. Kind eyes offered comfort incongruent with the circumstances.

The man in nuthugger shorts stripped off Paunch's taut T-shirt, exposing his hard-fat, bloated belly. A minute later the four minions duct taped Paunch to the table, belly side up.

"Plenty of raw skin. We'll take our time," Vance announced, staring at Teeny. The minions gathered tighter, familiar with the operation.

One minion, a man who hunched when he walked, reminding Teeny of a crab, handed Vance White a box of sea salt. Vance accepted the salt from the hunched Crab Man.

"Young lady, doubtful your elementary school teachers covered ancient torture methods in their curriculum. Disappointing. So much to learn. The saying, 'like pouring salt in a wound,' is overused today. People do not understand the historical reference. A shame. Pouring salt in open wounds is one of the most ancient forms of torture."

Teeny's eyes darted from Vance to Paunch, now wriggling on the table. The chubby man could no longer turn toward her or offer comfort. Vance stepped in front of Teeny, bent down, his hands on his knees. "The sodium hits exposed nerves, causing them to misfire, and the predictable result. Pain."

The smile wrapped around Vance's face. "Sure, sure, I know what you're thinking. Doesn't sound that bad. Let's try it out." Vance stood erect and waved his hand in front of her. She noted the length of his fingernails.

"Never had so much blubber to play with, Chub-a-dub," Vance chuckled.

Vance stood over Paunch, considering his belly. "You probably haven't heard, but there's a thing called a salad Chubmeister. Lettuce, tomato, onion, croutons, a little vinaigrette."

Paunch buckled under the tape, twisting his body back and forth, the table bouncing leg to leg, click-clopping, like a bucking bronco, under him. "Green vegetables, not your go-to food. I see that."

Vance smiled ear to ear, reveling in his work. "Well, to the task at hand. Don't worry, I've done this a time or two hundred." Vance's fingernails dug into Paunch's belly, ripping skin back, leaving four long marks. He brought his hand up, displaying blood-covered digits.

Blood leaked, drizzled, then poured from Paunch's wounds.

"I could use knives or razors." Vance smiled. "But to me … you lose the artistry." Vance tilted the box of salt over Paunch's belly and the bound man bucked. The table's rhythmic click-clopping dominated the room.

"There's two variations of the saying. The first we covered earlier—pouring salt in an open wound—is misguided. Oh, it does hurt. As Paunch here will attest."

"But the other variation has proven more accurate in my humble opinion. Rubbing salt in an open wound." Vance poured another salt layer over Paunch, the table rocked under him, accenting his pain. Vance pressed salt into the wounds, sandpapering the shards into the detective's belly lacerations. Paunch twisted the tape's limits, a millimeter more with each pain shockwave.

Teeny's head shot side to side, looking for help; none appeared. She listened for the giggles that marked the arrival of her strange allies; nothing.

Vance's minions fed off her fear, growing stronger. Shared cackles, elbow bumps, demented smiles passed monster to monster as Vance bongoed on Paunch's belly. The detective's belly jiggled, blood splattering with each slap. Vance danced; his face speckled with Paunch's O+. The room pulsated to the ancient rhythms of evil.

Instead of watching Vance's demented show, Teeny pictured her own death, allowing herself to view her tiny body on a cold slab, then a tombstone. She counted the attendees, Pru, the Wexlers, surely, maybe a classmate, or teacher. Teeny stared into the attendees' faces, listened to their whispers, *poor girl, never had a chance, a victim.*

A victim. She pictured those two words carved into the granite. *A VICTIM.*

Vance stopped drumming and returned to pontificating. "As torture goes, I'd label our efforts so far, Torture 101. Or Entry Level Torture. I've taught more advanced classes." The man in nuthugger shorts opened a toolbox. Vance's eyes lit up. The monster let Teeny inventory the toolbox's supplies: pliers, hammers, vices, razors, and screwdrivers. "I could write a 1000-page instruction manual on innovative uses of needle nose pliers alone."

Sweat puddled on the table under Paunch's body, draining to the floor. Vance and Teeny watched sweat waterfall together. When she turned back to Vance, he grinned.

She reached deep inside, not wanting those *two words*, *A VICTIM*, to be her label, at first accepting—then embracing—she must make the first move. Her. Teeny.

"There are hundreds of ways to die, Teeny, I've helped people experience most. Slow … fast. Painful … painless. You will not survive tonight, but you choose how uncomfortable you and your friend will be in your final hour."

Vance walked back to her. He bent over, his face now inches from hers. "Teeny, you may ask why you're here? Why all the fuss for one little girl?"

Teeny nodded, despite herself.

"Well, to me, it revolves around one question."

Teeny knew the question, before the icky-snakey-handsome man asked. She realized Vance White was not icky-snakey-handsome to most people, just handsome. The minions appeared normal to others: a runner, a businessman, a plumber. But not to her.

To her they looked like …

Vance's crystal blue eyes turned green, lime, lemon, and finally reptilian.

His icky-snakey-handsome face peeled back a layer at a time, seconds in reality, years of nightmare to unpack. Each micro layer of flesh ruttier, scabbier, oozier than the last, until a face that mirrored his soul stared back.

His scream reverberated as each of the men in the room covered his ears. "WHY CAN YOU SEE US FOR WHAT WE ARE?"

60

The Grant Wedding, Hotel ZaZa, Banquet Room, November 21, 2026

Harold and his "date" for the evening, Clarice Grant, both sat at the wedding party table. She, the sister of the bride and maid-of-honor, he, the second groomsman; both engaged in conversation with other tablemates.

Paired with Clarice tonight, not by his mother, but by his father, Senator Harold Edgard Reginald Oxford the VI, or H6 in Houston vernacular. Clarice's father spearheaded fundraising for H6's recent reelection.

Clarice, named by her movie-loving-mother for *The Silence of the Lambs'* protagonist, failed to display the movie heroine's gumption. The young social media star did possess millions of followers, the best liberal arts degree money could purchase, a wicked backhand, the hot-yoga sculpted body of a modern-Aphrodite, an infamous wit, a shower of suitors, and none of Harold's interest.

The bridesmaid to Harold's right babbled on, but he lost track, assessing the room's players. The mayor, a congresswoman, one Broadway diva, the Astro's left fielder, an ex-Texas A&M head football coach, two billionaires. Still, Harold comprehended who captained the room.

Harold's mother, Eunice, the legendary Houston and DC hostess, held sway over her table, each rapt occupant caught up in a recycled, revamped, and perfected story. His father, H6, exited Eunice's table as soon as etiquette allowed and held court under the banquet room threshold. Harold mapped the distance between his co-creators, yep, as far apart as the venue and social norms allowed.

He tasted the wedding cake, rich Mexican vanilla with a hint of lemon curd, and nodded approval to the bride. She smiled back.

He scanned the reception, hating that he ached for April, but understanding for the first time little else mattered to him. He watched her earlier, cutting her grandmother's veal piccata.

April's dress pure magic, azure near her décolletage and darkening every few inches to Prussian blue. The dress, longer than most of the wedding's beauties, featured a devastating slit from ankle to hip, accenting her sleek runner's legs and Christian Louboutin pumps.

When not accompanying her grandmother, great aunt, godmother, or nieces, April focused on dodging her date and the interest of suitors, single and married. Harold admitted to himself he spent a majority of the festivities observing her. "Shit," he said in his moment of epiphany. Clarice turned from her conversation.

"What?" Her smile perfect, teeth perfect, hair perfect. Perfect.

"Never mind," he answered. She took his hand, obligatorily it seemed, and returned to her conversation, something about transitioning followers into consumers, consumers to brand champions. YAWN.

When he turned back to the revelers, he caught April glancing at Clarice's hand resting on his. Harold's hand jerked away from Clarice's before his mind weighed the pluses and minuses of the move. April turned away, feigning disinterest, but Harold caught a smile's hint. *Wow.* He checked on April's date, currently chatting up the Connolly sisters.

Harold's thoughts drifted back to his first meeting with Val, and her words to him about April. "You're actually foolish enough to screw that up?"

He patted Clarice's hand to signal his departure. At that moment, he lost her. He prowled the banquet room, the halls, the hotel lobby, atrium, nothing. April vanished.

He returned to the wedding festivities or—more so—new networking opportunities. He studied the life everyone planned for him.

Complaining publicly about life as an Oxford echoed impotence. He accepted most people would kill—some had killed—for his family's status. Others did worse, sacrificing a child.

Harold studied his mother molding the latest gossip, his father shepherding a herd of hangers-on around the hotel.

Everyone … everyone told him how lucky he was, again and again, ad nauseam.

Clarice stood, bent at the waist, and whispered in the bride's ear. He and most male reception guests considered the perfection of Clarice's backside. He jammed his hands in his pockets, and studied the lavish wedding, the elegantly-attired guests, the incalculable wealth in the room. His eyes drifted to his tailored tuxedo, designer shoes, the plush carpet below him.

"Idiot," he said to himself. "It's all bullshit."

61

MD Anderson Cancer Center, Houston, Texas, November 23, 2026
The cream floor tile of Dr. Arthur's office featured brown accents. Val focused on the accents, and, like staring into the clouds, forms appeared. A curtseying elephant, a pirate receiving a spanking, and a dragon in drag. She shook off the images, returning to her dark situation.

Her nurse shepherded Val to Dr. Arthur's office, not her regular treatment room. The nurse did not weigh Val, log blood pressure or pulse, or draw blood. The doctor's last appointment of the day, Val predicted the news.

Val lifted the doctor's name placard again, returned it for the fourth time, and forced her hands back into her lap. After remaining still for twenty seconds, Val stood for another lap around the room.

Photo after photo featured the elegantly-gray Dr. Arthur with international luminaries, dignitaries, and sports gods. Some alive, most dead. She failed to recognize them all, but the ones she remembered barely survived bouts with cancer. Plaques, honorary degrees, and letters from former U.S. Presidents completed the doctor's décor.

She rushed to finish the last paragraph of a letter when Dr. Cynthia Arthur entered. Val turned and the doctor motioned for her to sit.

"Thanks for waiting," Dr. Arthur said.

"I'm dying for the news," Val lobbed.

Dr. Arthur ignored the comment, offering a different starting point, "I hired a new nurse."

"Okay," Val answered, not sure how the doctor's hiring practices pertained to her.

"Her name's Chelsea," the doctor led. Val did not follow the lead, instead she returned hands to lap. "She transferred to my staff when she found out I treated you. So, thanks for that, she's a fine, young nurse."

Val nodded.

"Chelsea told me … what you did for her, for lots of kids."

Val studied the tile floor again. "Val, you must name a caretaker for when we move you to … "

Val held up her hand, as if stopping the words stopped her cancer's spread.

"Chelsea offered to act as your caretaker."

"Dr. Arthur, I'll happily die in my living room alone. My kitchen's stocked with microwave meals, shelves full of cheap wine, hundreds of books I'm dying to read … "

Val paused for her doctor to appreciate the second attempt at humor. Dr. Arthur did not. Instead, the doctor gathered herself. Val pressed. "I'm here for the news. Spit it out."

Val's brain picked the keywords of Dr. Arthur's speech, metastasized, weeks … not months, while dispensing with the comforting words that did not matter.

When Dr. Arthur's words turned from medical condition to advice, Val's mind drifted to Devlin Maycare, and how to stop him, not allowing words like caretakers, hospice, palliative care specialist, herbal teas, and final plans to distract her thoughts.

So much to finish … so little …

She heard Dr. Arthur pounding the desk. "Come on, Val. Pay attention! You're facing something really scary here."

"Scary," Val laughed. "Dr. Arthur, I'm not belittling this, I'm not. But to me, this is … an inconvenience, interfering with my job. That's it." Val stood and marched to the door.

"Val, you're up against a real monster … "

Val paused, door in her hand. "No, Doc. I've shared rooms with monsters. I know exactly what they look like."

"Val, it's okay to ask for help."

62

Beeping car horns, blaring radios, and skidding tires greeted Val upon exiting MD Anderson during the height of Houston rush hour. Val tightened her vintage Burberry coat to her petite frame as she marched toward the parking garage stairs, the click of her tight, determined steps a tick faster than normal. Her pace comforted her, a subtle message to the grave diggers, *not today, assholes.*

She glanced at the elevator, considering—then eliminating—that option, and click-clacked toward the stairs. She loved heels from the day she discovered them. Heels helped her feel taller, appear taller to college classmates, then coworkers. Important to her because she topped out at five-foot-nothing.

As she climbed the stairs, she realized her affinity for footwear reached beyond love. Heels comforted her. Some people ate emotionally, Val shoe shopped passionately. Her taste in pumps, pedestrian at first, now bordered on extravagant. She explored the reaches of memory, for why, finding the exact moment.

The man who served as her closest proximity to a father brought her to Payless for her thirteenth birthday to purchase her first set of heels. The store banners announced a BOGO (Buy One Get One free, for the shopping novice). The saleswoman—and her sorta-father—encouraged her to buy one pair of heels and a pair of sneakers or boat shoes. She declined, instead selecting a pair of nude platforms and black slingbacks. Her love affair flourished. Val became the first girl in her class to master strutting the halls in high heels, and the least interested in boys or romance. Her maiden voyage invoked awe from female classmates.

Now, almost to the second flight of the stairs, a noise jerked Val to the present. A clue, an inkling, still, not able to recognize the origin of her concern.

Instead, she considered today's shoe selection. The perfect pair to confirm her fast approaching death: black stilettos.

"If a girl's cashing out, might as well wear Dolce & Gabbana," she said. She stopped, suddenly, two floors and forty yards from her car, when her brain flipped to full alert.

Val's ears worked differently than most. She possessed no superpowers, no sensory gifts, or hi-tech cochlear implants. Decades following the scum of the earth, and at times being tailed by criminals, other agencies' detectives, and street cops, taught her the beats and rhythms of on-foot pursuit.

There's a specific rhythm to footfalls—the pauses, the slowing down, the catching up.

Now that she clocked her pursuer, she needed to assess the danger. So, she continued up the concrete stairs, cataloging clues. In three steps she discerned only one person trailed. Two steps later, by the gate and the strike of the pursuer's shoes against the concrete, she determined the sex—male, the shoes—oxfords, loafers, or something with leather bottoms, not sneakers. Stupid.

She varied her pace, but leaned to speed, not to escape, but to confirm what she already knew. A stalker tailed. The person pursuing her possessed skills, not equal to hers, but substantial.

The pinks and oranges of early evening painted spaces between concrete and vehicles, as she turned and marched to her SUV. She stared straight ahead, not looking over her shoulder.

Her pursuer's ignorance of her knowledge offered Val an advantage. Decades of experience flowed through her brain. The informal rules of pursuit.

Rule #1: Wear soft-soled shoes.

Rule #2: If you can't follow Rule #1, hide your footfalls, if possible, on grass or softer surfaces (not possible in a parking garage).

Rule #3: If you can't follow Rules #1 or #2, don't match your target's pace. Even an amateur can guess they're being tailed by mirrored footfalls.

Rule #4: Stay far enough away to avoid being detected, but close enough to act quickly.

In this case, before a petite woman in heels opens her car door. She spotted her four-year-old Ford Police Interceptor—a huge car for a tiny woman—ten steps away. Funny her executioner would attempt to kill her in a hospital parking garage, when cancer promised to finish the job in weeks, not months.

Not today, asshole, she repeated to herself, hoping beyond hope Devlin Maycare himself pursued her, but knowing a minion most likely occupied today's menu. A quick glance at a mirrored metallic BMW offered Val the reflection of the bottom half of her pursuer, black dress pants, expensive loafers, argyle socks, just like …

When the footfalls behind her quickened, she loosened her jacket, sliding her semi-auto from holster to hand, stepped behind an ancient Dodge K-car for cover, spun, assumed shooter's stance, and faced her pursuer.

63

"Wa-wa-wa-wait," said the most annoying voice in Val's world, holding up empty hands.

Val studied the parking garage, making sure no one witnessed the exchange. Clear. She lowered her gun, returned weapon to holster, and secured her coat before addressing him.

"You're following me now, Harold?"

"You picked that up, all by yourself?" he asked, allowing his smart-ass smirk—the expression always a twitch-away—to cover his face.

"How long?"

"Long enough to know you're Dr. Cynthia Arthur's last appointment today."

"You know her?"

The smirk turned upside down. Harold shoved his hands in his pants pockets. "Family friend."

"So you … "

"Not tough to put the pieces together."

"Hmm."

They stood in the garage. She stared at his Gucci Ha Ha Ha loafers, scanned up to his bespoke pants, Saint Laurent cashmere sweater, then—finally—his punchable face. Reeking a life of privilege.

Yes, she loved expensive shoes, but she picked her battles. She harvested her designer clothes and heels from resell racks. She cooked at home when possible and dined at quality—but mid-priced—local eateries when not.

So, Harold's perfect-on-the-surface life and seemingly endless wardrobe annoyed her … and maybe tainted her against him, even with the shared …

Harold interrupted her thought, "So, I wouldn't become your protégé, I'd—"

"My replacement. Correct."

"So, you think I can handle it?"

"Someone does. Doesn't matter, you turned down the job."

"Yeah, I guess. But I need to hear the rest."

"I don't have time to screw around, Harold."

"You gotta eat, and I'll buy you dinner. There's a place on Kirby."

"Goode Company Taqueria," she finished.

"Best Pecan Waffles—"

"Sure, but I'm not checking out of this world without eating Buck Fever one last time."

•   •   •

Goode Company Taqueria

"Where did you put all that?" he asked, considering the empty plate formerly occupied by two fried eggs, jalapeno venison sausage, hash browns, and a biscuit. The two sat in the reddish-brown tile-floored patio, facing the fountain and the rear parking lot.

Dr. Arthur's prognosis contributed to her what-the-hell overeating. Having company, even Harold's, added to her indulgence. She stood, walked to the Bunn coffee urn, refilled her cup, and returned. After she sat, Harold seemed content to trudge through surface subjects.

"Do you meet anyone at a—"

Val derailed his question before he finished, "I seldom eat at a chain restaurant. Life's too short."

He raised his eyebrows.

"Funny how much that statement applies today." Val sipped her coffee, embracing the warmth.

"What I meant was—"

"To answer your question, I stay away from police stations, or another agency's office. My agency—"

"Again, when you say agency, you basically mean just you."

She sat brewing, letting her thoughts filter, percolate, drip. She raised her coffee cup to her cheek and let the warmth of the ceramic comfort her. She embraced the aroma, savored the moment.

Most people never appreciate the last time they hug loved ones, enjoy a plate of migas at La Guadalupana, a buttery croissant from the French Gourmet Bakery, or THE BAD pizza at Spaghetti Western Italian Cafe. Val understood the gift—or curse—of knowing this was her last trip to her favorite taqueria.

She also grasped the time to interview a dozen candidates to replace her passed months ago. Harold, despite his smugness, stood correct. She WAS the agency, not IS, not WILL BE, WAS – past tense.

For obvious reasons—well, obvious to her—adding dozens of recruits proved problematic. For better or worse, she stared across the table at her agency's option for a future.

A rich, spoiled, smug smart-aleck, spawned by meddling parents to be a congressman, senator ... or governor. Someone who turned down the job ...

Also, someone who, in limited time on the force, owned multiple, unexplained, instinct busts.

"Okay, but first, Harold. Why are you here?"

"Well, let's start at a wedding."

64

Harold caught Val up to the point of his pity party. "I stood at the reception, hands jammed in my pockets, listening to rich people complain about taxes and the inconveniences of wealth, realizing I was one of them. I hated everything, everybody. I blew my chance with April. I stared into a future I'd hate."

"I walked to the banquet room's wall of windows and stared out at Mecom Fountain. There she stood." Harold paused. "Standing in the grass, inches from the fountain. I sprinted, I mean SPRINTED, to her. Surprised how fast my feet moved under me."

Val nodded as Harold fell into memory.

•   •   •

The Grant Wedding, Hotel ZaZa, Banquet Room, November 21, 2026

Seconds later, he stood beside her.

"Hello, idiot," she said, staring at the fountain.

"Hey, brat," he panted from the run. He bent over, hands on his knees, recovering.

"You really are an idiot, you know."

"Yeah, got that."

Tears ran down April's cheeks. Harold offered his pocket square—between labored breaths. "How long?" he asked, not qualifying his question. He stared at the fountains, away from her, afraid her answer would accent his stupidity.

"My mom's lake house."

"That long." Yep, an idiot, he said to himself.

"We were water skiing," she started.

"You were great, I remember," he said, still huffing. He recalled other things too.

"The last trip of the day. The other girls tapped out. A boat loaded with four twenty-two-year-old boys and one eighteen-year-old girl trying to keep up. What could go wrong?"

He said nothing, wanting to hear her version of that day.

"I ignored you, like always. You were the least interesting person in the world to me."

"Thanks for that," he said, breath finally slowing from the run.

"Then … "

He relived the circumstances—too often, he admitted.

"Kent's dad's boat. He dared me to slalom without the lifejacket. I agreed. Stupid."

Harold stayed quiet.

"He drove way too fast, I tried to stay cool, hang on. When I tumbled, my bikini top and bottoms … well … "

"Yeah," Harold said, remembering the boat pulling up to April, the wake of a passing Chris-Craft, popping her topside like a fishing bobber. Her fighting—and failing—to stay below the surface. Kent circling. Herb and Lack lobbing innuendo after innuendo.

"He planned it."

Harold nodded, ashamed for not stopping it sooner.

"You dove into the lake, found my suit, brought it to me."

He nodded. "You were like my little sister, I … " he started, shutting up before his mouth buried him. She glanced at him. The sister comment hurt her.

"After we got back, I lay on my bed crying, the Connolly sisters comforting me. Stuff started breaking downstairs: tables, pots, chairs. Cursing, screaming. I tried to go down, but the girls stopped me. Later, they said you ordered them to keep me upstairs. Kent, Herb, and Lack left twenty minutes later."

"When I came down, you were gone. I remember being upset you left, then surprised I was upset. A strange mix of emotions."

She smiled; he nodded for her to continue. "You showed up later, with boxes of pizza, boxed wine, and a busted lip. Anyhow, that's when I knew."

She turned to him, he sighed.

"And when …" she started, daring him to answer the same question.

"At the event a few nights ago." He considered a passing maroon Dodge Ram before answering. "Tough to admit. I wish I figured it out, on my own, but it got explained to me."

"Excuse me?"

"Val—"

"The speaker from the other night?"

"Yes. She asked if I was stupid enough to screw up my chance with you. Something about her seeing it, calling me a dipshit. Now I keep thinking—dreaming—about you."

She smiled, and Atlas shrugged, rocking Harold's foundation. His old life crumbled. Promises of a lifetime, decades, years, or mere moments of her smiling that smile offered him salvation.

He pulled her to him, and they kissed for the first time. When he released her, April looked across the street to the mass of windows separating them from the banquet hall.

"You realize my date, your date—"

"The whole wedding party—" he added.

"Witnessed that. Our moms started planning our rehearsal dinner."

"Want to … " He motioned toward McGovern Promenade.

"I would love to take a walk with you, Harold."

They explored Hermann Park before he steered her toward the Japanese Gardens. They walked for hours. The conversation of a lifetime followed. Buzzing mobile phone calls from parents, text from dates, all ignored as they walked toward the Houston Zoo.

Harold barely remembered buying tickets. The two strolled past lions, orangutans, and elephants, he noted each, but failed to see any of them … just her. Later, when he bought April lemonade, little girls oohed and awed over April's dress and heels, not the usual zoo-goer's wardrobe.

Harold felt it, the natural rhythm of the person who understands you better than anyone becoming the person you ache to hold. The mechanisms locking into place. How could he miss this? "Idiot," he whispered.

On their return to Hotel ZaZa, she started, "Something always bothered me."

"Seems early in our relationship to consider my faults, but shoot."

"I mean, I need to understand this, if … " she paused, stuck.

"April."

"Yes."

"Whatever you need to ask, ask."

"I've known you since birth. Girls were around you … a lot, you dated a few, but always acted unsatisfied. You drove them away. You let your mom set you up, sometimes—"

"Mom's relentless."

April paused. Harold could tell, afraid her next question would crash everything. "Why, why drive them off? And how long before you push me away? Weeks? Months?"

He considered his answer as they walked, pondering, until they stood steps away from the reception. "The girls inside our circle calculate what a marriage to me would mean. I ahh … "

"I understand," she said.

"I've tried and failed to date outside the Oxford's scope of influence. I avoid telling girls who Dad is. But they find out. Pretty easy, they Google me. Days later they're planning to be Mrs. Harold Edgard

Reginald Oxford the VII and give birth to H8. They introduce me, like I'm a Hermes handbag they found at Blue Bird Circle resell shop."

"It's more than that—"

"Maybe." He took April's hand and electricity pulsed between them. "If I choose something, something other than what they've all planned for me—"

"I'd be right beside you, Harold, through it all."

•　　•　　•

Val let Harold finish. "Harold, even with a woman of April's caliber behind you—"

"This will suck. You mentioned that. I still want it."

"I doubt you'll believe me."

"Try me."

"On one condition. No matter what you hear or think, you stay 'til the end."

"Sounds ominous."

"'Til the end. Say it."

"Okay, okay, until the end. Does that make you happy?"

Val started where she left off at Simos. A half hour later, Paunch and Teeny were trapped in the blackness of Vance White's web.

65

July 11, 1976

"WHY CAN YOU SEE US FOR WHAT WE ARE?" Vance screamed.

Teeny looked to Paunch. The duct tape that bound him tested by his contortions. Teeny twisted, refusing to face the monster confronting her. Her eyes flashed to the children's pictures on the wall, understanding the evil here. She noted minions. A greasy overall-wearing smoker near an open window, the man in nuthugger shorts, the crab-walking creep.

Teeny understood the pain this collection of hyenas would continue to inflict upon innocents.

She gazed into her future, tossing aside the pathetic funeral, forever vowing not to die a victim. Embracing her selection as chaser, not chased. Understanding the terrors awaiting her chosen path. Thinking those terrors would dwarf this pathetic monster. Still, she accepted this mission—her mission, her *calling*, her *future*, her *fate*. But her fate demanded action.

Vance looked confused when a broad smile spread across Teeny's face. He jumped forward to stop her. Too late.

"Ahhhhhhhhhhhhhhhhhhhhhhhhhhhhhhhhhhhhhhhhhhhhhhhhhhhhhhhhh!" Teeny's scream shattered the night. Every head turned to the sound of her call.

Fate answered back.

"Hee, ha, hee, hee, ha, ha, ha …"

Heads whipped around the room. Every occupant experienced the giggle's echo. A few of the minion's stances communicated panic, most confusion.

Not Vance White. He laughed. "Really? Really?" He stood and turned away from Teeny toward the fireplace expectantly. "You show up here now?" Everyone in the room stopped, following his lead.

Teeny turned toward Paunch, and, in that moment, she heard *Woosh*. And she spun. Embracing the sensory explosion! Watching as flames engulfed the fireplace, burning like a scout nurtured it for hours. Witnessing the miracle, Teeny shook her head in disbelief.

The graybeard with the bear-claw tattoos on one arm, the interlocked antler ink on the other stood in front of the fireplace. He rubbed his knotty, calloused hands together.

"A little out of your pay grade, Nick," Vance taunted.

The graybeard sighed, popping his knuckles. Cracking his neck left—then right. The sound dominating the quiet room. He waited until all attention focused on him. "**Where is she?**" he demanded, his voice chilling the room.

Vance smiled. "She put her nose in my business, old man. So, she's been my guest … "

The graybeard's brow dropped. "I kept tracking you, but kept running into your B-Team."

Vance chuckled, "Even pawns play a role in chess, Nick."

A low, rolling mist or fog gathered at Nick's feet, then spread slowly at first, overtaking the room. Goosebumps covered Teeny's arms and legs as the frigid air spread and climbed, each breath now documented by whiffs of smoke.

Vance looked around the room, noting—maybe even counting—each minion, drawing strength from his army of acolytes. "Dumb," Vance said.

The graybeard arched an eyebrow.

"To show up here—by yourself," Vance said, smirking.

Nick started laughing, the infectious laugh of a grandfather. He put his hand on his belly, trying to contain himself, but failed. At first, the others in the room shuffled nervously, waiting for him to stop. Then one of the hyenas joined in, then another and another, until the room filled with laughter. Nick stopped first, his cheeks rosy from the effort.

A smile spread from cheek to rosy cheek. "Ahh, that felt good. Funny. I was thinking."

Vance waited for Nick's words to continue.

"Pretty stupid of you to put all your guys in one place," Nick returned. "With me."

The room's occupants remained focused on the graybeard and Vance. Everyone but Teeny's self-appointed, bleeding, bound, sweaty, exhausted, pudgy protector.

"And who said I was by myself," the old man stated, as "Hee, ha, hee, hee, ha, ha, ha … " filled the room again.

Click-clop-click-clop. Teeny recognized the sound from Paunch bucking under the salt, but more rhythmic now. *Click-clop-click-clop.* The table binding her chubby ally rocked back and forth, using the slack in the tape his bucking caused earlier. Everyone turned from the graybeard when Paunch's table crashed to the floor, collapsing under the fall and his weight.

Not free but loosened, bare skin ripped and pulled from duct tape as Paunch twisted his body away from table wreckage, one hand freed before he garnered the enemies' focus.

"Someone take care of Chubs," Vance yelled to his minions. A few started toward the partially-bound, bleeding, bare-bellied man.

The room's attention shifted from Paunch to a dying man's scream. "Uhh, uhh, uhh." Teeny's eyes riveted to the tattooed, muscled graybeard, holding the blunt side of an impossibly large icicle, an icicle impaling the dying man.

Every minion turned from the mound of a man freeing himself from tape and table to their cohort's final breath, none recovering from visual overload quickly enough to understand the dangers.

Thinking Teeny worked to process the data. How did the old man find an icicle in Texas in July? Did he carry it in a cooler? She didn't see a cooler.

Answers seemed less important than bearing witness.

The distraction offered her paunchy protector seconds to free himself. Shirtless and bleeding, he snatched the nearby Smith and Wesson.

"Stop him," Vance spun from the dying man to Paunch.

Paunch popped the revolver's last two shots, one each, into the chests of the approaching captors. They crumpled. The Smith and Wesson clicked as he continued to pump it before tossing it aside. Paunch did not await attackers, he rushed them, disappearing into a scrum.

"Hey, Teeny." She jumped, before recognizing the relaxed voice of Tex Wexler.

One bloody arm bound with Dex's shirt, Tex calmly kneeled below her, she assumed using the craziness to enter the fray unnoticed. Tex sliced through duct tape, as Teeny kicked free.

"Grab Opie, run outside," Tex stated. "Find the twins."

"Okay," she mumbled, her rusty vocal cords remembering the spoken word.

Tex smiled at the sound of her voice; he rubbed her head. "Promise." He pushed her toward the door. "Don't come back, no matter what, Teeny."

She hugged him, then turned as , "ROOOAAAAR," enraptured the room. Shattering glass, crashing, as a huge white paw burst through the window, ripping the closest room occupant—the smoker in greasy overalls—through the window. The man's scream, "Help, help, help me," echoed Flick's scream weeks earlier. Then the sound of crunching bones.

"Teeny, run, damn't," Tex said, before diving into Paunch's scrum.

As Teeny raced toward the door, chaos filled the room. Vance White screamed, "Come back, you cowards!" toward the exiting minions.

Six minions closed on the graybeard, one closer, cockier than the other five. Muscles rippled over the graybeard's body, but he was one man against six. Grappling, thudding sounds, then a scream filled her ears as she ran toward the door.

In her memory, Teeny remained unsure if the smell of burning flesh or the sight of the cocky minion roasting in the flames of the fireplace reached her senses first.

She bolted out the door, stepping into the darkness, racing toward the nearby woods, when the Crab Man snatched her, lifting her and Opie from the ground, holding her in front of him, a human shield. "Get back, get back," he begged, to something, someone, no, more than one—Teeny realized—surrounding him.

Her eyes failed to adjust to the night's blackness, but Teeny watched figures circle the Crab Man, establishing position, testing the limits of Crab Man's attention. The figures, the size of lawn ornaments, closed and circled half-steps at a time. The gleam of metal caught her eye, *knives* she thought at first, no, **scissors,** in each figure's hand.

Teeny realized her captor did have a gun, and he focused his weapon on the figures surrounding her. At the moment the Crab Man seemed most distracted, Teeny bit his thumb, gripped Opie, and twisted away. He failed to fire a shot before tiny bodies flowed over and around her, leaping onto the Crab Man.

His gun clattered to the ground and Teeny eyed it before the Crab Man's terror demanded her attention. "No, no, no," she heard from behind, drowned out by the stabbing sound she remembered from the woods days earlier.

"Hee, ha, hee, hee, ha, ha, ha ... " filled her ears, as she realized these tiny bodies originated the sound all along. Dying screams, spreading flames, and the sounds of battle poured from the cabin. Flames spread to the roof and Teeny worried about her friends inside.

Minion upon minion dashed out the door, fleeing from flames, the battle—or both.

Teeny turned to witness the wars in front of her. Caribou spread throughout the clearing, two twisted dead men on their racks, another cornered a man against the wall, two more chased Vance's deserters into the Piney Woods.

The clues slammed through her, *Thinking Teeny* jamming them together.

Everything went back to her letter.

The letter she begged Sissie to send, the letter Pru stamped and mailed. A letter millions of kids send each year. A letter to …

66

Goode Company Taqueria, November 23, 2026

Harold's mouth hung open. He vibrated anger, ramming his fists onto the tabletop, the plates and scant leftovers quaking in response. His chair screeched, tumbled backwards from the force of him bolting upright, and rocked on the floor.

"You proud now? You made a fool out of me," he snarled at her. "I believed in you." He shook his head and turned to leave, spotting his closest escape.

Val continued. "In America, hunters call them caribou. The rest of the world calls them reindeer."

"I spilled my guts to you," he said walking away. "You crazy bitch."

"I may be, Harold. But I have one question."

"Okay," he said, spinning, eyes burning, fueled by disdain, "out with it!"

"Are you a man of your word?" Val asked.

"Huh," he grunted.

"Because you promised."

"Before you proved you're nuts," he vented.

Harold marched toward the rear entrance, ignoring the other guests. A step past the three-tiered fountain, almost to the iron fence, he stopped. Val watched as Harold muttered to himself, then to the heavens, his words mostly four-letter.

Who thinks about dying early? In her 20s, 30s, and 40s she never considered death at all. Val never planned when, if, or how someone would commandeer her life's mission. Or **who**. Val assumed, **who** never resembled the well-dressed young man cursing to himself outside her favorite taco place.

She tallied his negatives dozens of times since Nick instructed her to recruit him. Val allowed herself a moment to consider the positives. He, or his family, nurtured connections to financial and political powerbrokers. She and Harold grew up much differently but shared the same skill; spotting monsters.

Val let Harold continue muttering, she rescued his chair from the tile, resetting it, and walked to refill her coffee, turning to him occasionally for entertainment. A busboy showed to rescue the plates from future attacks and wiped up the coffee spilled by Harold's outburst.

A guest walked past Harold, unseen by the young detective. The guest nodded at Val and walked to place his order. She laughed to herself, glancing at the menu on the wall; Nick never ate the venison sausage. Now, that's loyalty. He stuck to the sweet stuff.

Val shook her head as Nick returned to the patio; since no cocoa was on the menu, he had horchata in hand, nodded at her again, and took a seat in the corner, bear claw and antler tattoos displayed on his arms in full regalia. He nodded, opened a novel—*Politikill*—reading, while waiting on his order.

She studied the muttering young man, now sitting on the fountain's edge. Understanding she failed Harold, Nick, and the kids. From the corner, Nick nodded reassurance; as his food arrived, he held up his hand encouraging patience, then, after pouring warm syrup, shoveled pecan-loaded waffles into his mouth.

She snatched a *Houston Chronicle* from an empty table, returned to her seat, sat, and read—to distract herself. After learning about a new Container Store location, an I-10 expansion, and the new jobs hitting Houston over the next few months, she looked up, and there he stood.

Angry, bitter, perturbed, but there. He pulled out his chair and sat.

"Tell me one thing that would make me stay," Harold said.

"Sure."

He stared into her, daring her to lie.

"You know what happened to Paunch, you saw his statue. But the bronze little girl sitting on the bench represents Teeny. She was the first one he saved. If you stay, I promise I'll tell you how Paunch saved her, then got to 562."

He paused, wanting more; more was not offered.

"How can I believe you or anything you say?"

"That's your choice, Harold," Val answered. "But you already investigated my agency, Paunch, and this case. My numbers are real. If listening to the rest of my story helps you save one child, that's worth the risk, right? Even if I'm nuts."

He nodded.

67

"Teeny, Teeny," the Wexlers screamed, 30 yards away, 15 feet from the ground on the third limb of an ancient oak. Teeny turned to plot her path to Dex and Lexi, but, before she started, Lexi screamed, "Behind you!"

Standing in the fiery threshold, the Greyhound man in nuthugger shorts. She gauged her lead, fifteen—maybe twenty—yards. Nothing to do but run. She turned, holding Opie tight, pumping her arms, racing toward the sound of Dex's and Lexi's voices.

At her trailer park, she had watched the Greyhound man run down the margarine-haired woman, knowing she could not cover the distance—in her race toward Dex and Lexi—before he snared her. Lexi waved feverishly. The sound of the Greyhound man's approach, the quick and lengthy strides covering yards, not feet, filled her ears.

She breathed rhythmically, counting the steps to reach her allies, hoping, but understanding no scenario existed where she reached the tree before the Greyhound man tackled her.

Gunshots filled her ears. The Greyhound man fell, tumbling into her. They twisted together like static-laden socks in the dryer. The man's dead body settled on top of Teeny and Opie. She screamed.

With effort, she pushed the dead man off her, and grabbed Opie, now speckled in blood. Paunch arrived, pulled her up, and pushed her away from the battle. "This way, Teeny, this way," Lexi coaxed.

Paunch returned to the battle, unloading the Crab Man's abandoned pistol into Vance's men as they raced toward her, two more down. He waved for her to leave him behind in the battle's boiler room.

Teeny reached the oak seconds later, happy now for the craziness the Wexler twins offered so freely. Lexi waved her up the tree, coaxing Teeny to climb. Dex, now shirtless, monkeyed down and pulled her to the first limb, before she and Opie climbed to the twins' attack point.

Teeny surveyed the property, not a cabin but a compound or, more so, headquarters. A half-dozen smaller cabins and outbuildings surrounded the main cabin. More white vans, an eighteen-wheeler, and a few RVs cluttered the complex.

The Wexler twins stationed themselves above a circle driveway over a dozen white vans and a limousine, a parking lot of sorts, the seeds of the attack starting to grow in her mind

Teeny turned to the battle. A gigantic polar bear wrangled the man with the bad suit. Seconds later, the man's skull rested between the bear's jaws as the polar bear whipped the body back and forth.

Teeny turned back to her companions. Staring through binoculars, Dex watched the burning cabin intently. "Dad's still in there," he bemoaned to the girls.

"Dex, Dad'll take care of himself. You ready?"

Waving Lexi off with a "Yeah, yeah," Dex nodded to the bottle collection stationed on different limbs. "I soaked the wicks. We're ready."

White powder covered Lexi's hands and arms. She answered Teeny's unasked question. "I mixed flour in the bottles, to thicken it, like gravy," she said, shrugging.

Teeny asked herself whether the addition of flour would add to the success of the weapon, but appreciated the creativity. Beer, whiskey, wine bottles, and a few jars rested in the tree trunk's crooks and crannies. But the bottles didn't smell like whiskey, they …

• • •

"Gasoline," Harold said, pulling Val from her story. She looked around, forgetting for a moment she sat across the table from him.

"Yes, kerosene would've worked better, but Dex used bottles he collected roadside, and fuel he had."

"Before you go on, something's bugging me. The Wexlers, the daughter's name, Lexi."

"Sure, yeah."

"I've met an Alexis Wexler. Dad introduced me at a function in DC years ago. She's the Deputy Director of the FBI."

Val sat, stone faced, offering nothing.

"Same girl?"

Val smiled. He processed ahead of the story, trying to solve it. A good sign. However, Val understood he could not find his answers without more pieces. Instead of addressing his question, she returned to the story.

• • •

Teeny, like Dex, worried about Tex. Nothing to worry about. Crashing pulled Teeny's attention to the cabin as a flaming figure draped in a blanket dove through a window, rolling over the pine straw, dirt, and shattered glass to extinguish the flames.

"It's Dad. Dad's clear, Dad's clear!" Dex said, celebrating with Lexi.

Tex ran to his children's tree and screamed up, "Son, did you leave me something?"

"Near the sweet gum tree, Dad," Lexi hollered back to him.

The scum who escaped the scrum raced toward the vans under the Wexlers. A man jumped into one of the middle vans.

"Light 'em up, kids," Tex said before racing back to battle. Dex lit one wick and handed it to Lexi, lighting another for himself. Teeny remembered—from her time watching Dex and Lexi—they shared a pyro-fascination. Time to put their comfort with flames to good use.

Crazy crested in the Wexler twins' eyes—before tossing their Molotov cocktails.

68

"Teeny guessed Dex and Lexi would toss at the van the man jumped into."

"They took out the lead and last vans, creating a logjam," Harold said.

"Yes. The other vans and the limo bumpered out, giving the twins extra time to target them. Some of the vans exploded, taking out the closest vans; others burned out. Still, four or five vans escaped, most damaged, a few without taking hits."

"The Wexlers thought they positioned themselves far enough from the flames but underestimated their capacity for destruction. They led Teeny higher in the tree. Once they climbed to safety, Teeny turned back to the battlefield, now mostly cleared. The caribou, the bear, even the—"

"Elves," Harold added.

Val continued, "Teeny watched one straggler, a reindeer, turn into the woods west of the cabins while Paunch and Tex set the outer buildings on fire."

"Teeny assumed everyone inside the main cabin died, but the graybeard exploded out, driving two of Vance White's crew to the ground. One combatant dead already, the other man pinned under graybeard's girth. The man tried to wrestle free, but, even from the tree, Teeny heard it."

"What?" Harold asks.

"The sound of the graybeard snapping the man's neck. The graybeard looked up, his anger and fury unleashed. Still, even from the tree, Teeny understood something powerful honed his actions.

Then, the cabin's back door flew open. Vance White, a woman, and two of Vance's minions exited. Vance marched the woman, duct tape over her mouth, hands tied behind her back, black-eyed like a raccoon, bruised, cut marks up and down her arms, toward the van. Teeny's eyes welled with tears; she shook her head begging for it not to be true, but she recognized the woman, her distinctive margarine-colored hair.

Out of reach of Dex and Lexi's throws, Vance shoved the woman into his van and the foursome pulled away. The graybeard spotted the bound woman and ran toward the woods. Minutes later, the "whooshing" sound she remembered from the street battle before a sonic boom."

"A sleigh, maybe," Harold joked, but the words felt stale in his mouth.

Val ignored his cynicism. "Anyway, Vance's van cleared the property and stopped near the street, at the compound's exit. The monster death-stared Dex, Lexi and Teeny's tree. This is going to sound like bullshit."

"Really, just this part?" Harold sarcastically responded.

Val continued, "Vance waved his arms toward the sky. The wind picked up, like a fastball, or a snowball gathering size as it rolls downhill. Pine straw, pinecones, and leaves ripped from trees tornadoed into the mix, on their way toward us. It slammed into our tree. Dex and Lexi braced a half second before I did, so they didn't fall."

"The last thing I remember … falling. Snapping branches. I snatched one limb, delaying the inevitable, lost my grip, understanding from that height I'd break a leg, crack my ribs at least. But I didn't. My head bumped into something solid. That's the last thing I remember before Tex and Dex shook me awake. I woke on top of the man I landed on, Paunch Perez. He had sprinted under the tree and caught me, broke my fall. I rubbed my head, and I knew a massive bump would greet me the next day."

"Sirens blared in the distance, closing. I wobbled to all fours, then tried to stand upright and failed. Vance's crew littered the compound, dead. The smell of burnt flesh, you remember that," Val offered, turning up her nose.

"Tex shook Paunch, 'Wake up sleeping beauty, I ain't mouth to mouthin' on ya, brother. Wake the hell up. Look, I can't carry your ass.' Tex shook Paunch harder. 'Get to the truck,' he told Dex and Lexi. Lexi handed Opie to me. Dex tried to pull me with him. But I stayed with Paunch. Dex hung his head, but followed his father's orders."

"Tex shook him one more time, then stood up. 'Okay, dumbass, you explain this shit to the cops. We're out of here. Come on, Teeny.' He stood, holding out his hand."

"I stayed on all fours, climbing on top of Paunch. Now his protector. I'd wait, until he woke. 'Your call, Teeny,' Tex said, and walked away."

"I took Paunch's fat cheeks in my hands, staring into his closed eyes, and said, 'We have to finish our introduction. You're Paunch. And I'm Val, Valentina Voix, but everyone calls me Teeny.'"

69

Harold's whiplash seemed real, not metaphorical. He missed the story's blinking hazards, ignored collision warnings, refused to note the brake lights, and crashed into the cruel, dented bumper of truth. Val was not only insane, as he assumed earlier, but truly wrecked. His psyche jerked from the story, slammed back to this table. He blinked, breathed out, and used his rhythms to calm himself.

"Beer?" he asked, needing time.

She nodded; he assumed she understood his need to recalibrate. He returned with two Dos XX, dressed. Val wiped the salt from her bottle and set the lime aside. Harold said, "Of course." He squeezed the lime into the lager, and sipped, enjoying the salt, lime, and cerveza interaction.

Three healthy gulps later, he found himself staring at Val, Valentina, and Teeny, all three, only one. More complex than a Daedalus-level labyrinth. Sure, Val witnessed enough gruesome cases to drive her nuts. After listening to her, Harold understood the childhood abuse and trauma she experienced. So, he grasped her need to create a complex fantasy world.

Oh, and she was dying, grasping to find anything special, different, before she clocked out. He accepted that fact. Surprised he failed to identify Val's suspect grasp on reality at Simos Diner, Harold enjoyed another sip of Dos XX, admitting he enjoyed his time with the madwoman. He chuckled.

Mr. Poth, his colorful ENGL 100–Intro Literature professor, preached that apex storytellers straddle the borders of reality and insanity. The professor probed Poe's, Plath's, Lovecraft's, and Wolfe's struggles with internal demons: depression, nervous breakdowns, addictions, sleep disorders.

Following that warped logic, as a storyteller he never met Val's equal. The math equation formed in his head: Great Storyteller = Streaker at Cannibal Convention Crazy.

Harold focused on her story now. How did he miss the hint grenades throughout her tale? "Shit," he mumbled, not meaning to vocalize. Val shrugged.

Not just her storytelling, but her method of structure. Val's storytelling switched from third to first person, minutes before. Did Val plan that device to ease him to the truth?

Like the plot twist of *The Sixth Sense* or *The Usual Suspects*, he missed it … all. Again, how could she not be insane, based on what she witnessed, experienced? Val. A short name to hide complexity.

Even taking her insanity into account, a colossal woman in a teeny body. A woman who used 4-inch heels, not for fashion—he studied her outfit, okay, maybe a little for fashion—but mostly to face evil at eye-level for 40+ years. How could she avoid being jackknifed inside?

Harold let the story engulf him, cutting through the surface tidal waves, the cold-cool darkness at the story's ocean bottom. Val's tale: bullshit, crap, gross exaggeration, or likely fantasies of a damaged child. He sipped his cerveza accepting Val cha-cha'd on the cuckoo side of Cocoa Puffs.

Still, two numbers presented themselves as fact.

562–The number of children Paunch Perez saved.

1184–The number of children Valentina V. Perez-Maldonado saved to date.

He remembered seeing her full name before. How did he miss it? Harold reconsidered the story's details, understanding now how this woman knew facts, names, intimate details not in the report, remembering the glow in her cheeks when she mentioned Paunch and the Wexlers.

He took another sip of the cool longneck, letting his tongue experience the undertones of the German brew master Wilhelm Haase's masterpiece, created after he immigrated to Mexico before 1900. He admitted he intentionally distracted himself with beer minutia, to avoid diving into the problematic questions—when Val steered the conversation forward.

"I never hid who I was."

He shook his head, "Pff," he snorted.

"Okay, I was vague." Val paused, taking a sip. "I married a good cop, who died young, Hector Maldonado; I kept his name out of remembrance."

Val stared at her watch for a moment. To Harold, she appeared to study the time, the date, each tick. "We can either discuss this never or now."

"Sorry?" he asked, confused.

"I don't have much time left, so never or now," she demanded.

"Can I ask?"

"No. Never or now."

"Now," he answered.

"Harold, you know why you spot them too, right?"

He remained silent, but placed an elbow on the table, leaning forward.

Val continued, "The child molesters in the crowd, human traffickers like the McCluskeys, the two men who tried to kidnap the little girl at Paunch's statue's unveiling."

"What?" Harold's eyebrows raised.

"Yes, I heard about that."

He studied the floor, assuring that, despite the feeling, the tile was not crumbling under him. "I'm not sure why I—"

"Okay, so much for the easy tact." Harold's eyes darted around the room. Abandoned plates, sweaty half-emptied glasses with melting ice, discarded newspapers. Nothing materialized to delay this moment.

When his eyes returned to Val, at first she offered a softness—empathy—not offered before. She nodded encouragement.

The shockwaves blasted through him. He begged for **Harold Edgard Reginald Oxford the Seventh**, or just **H7**, the **FACE**—his cold smug protector—to step forward from his subconscious, to shield him from her, her questions, or more importantly the emotional shrapnel of their answers. H7, the smug, cold face he donned so easily, refused his call.

When Harold remained mum, her eyes tightened, and he noticed the soft wrinkles around her eyes for the first time. As if, in recognition of him spotting her failings—the beginnings of her end—she lobbed the grenade. "I showed you my monsters; show me yours?"

Instantly, natural instinct honed over thousands of years of human evolution to protect man's most vulnerable organs took over. In the wild, predators rip into the belly, to gobble the liver, kidney, and most nutritious organs first. So, without understanding the reason, evolution jerked Harold's hands to protect his abdomen. "You don't know what you're talking about," he tried.

"People think child abuse happens to the poor, the marginalized, the outliers. But, Harold, a family's money, neighborhood, influence offer little protection. They just draw cleverer predators. Child abuse happens on every economic level. The only thing that can protect children is vigilance."

H7, Harold's haughty, bullying, internal avatar, **again** refused to step forward, cowering in his subconscious. Harold felt something, no, SOMEONE else, stir inside him. "No," he begged that SOMEONE to stay tucked away, safe from harm.

Val seemed to understand the words were not meant for her and continued. "You stuffed it down for so long." She waited; he did not respond. "Trust me, Harold."

He sat silently, as the SOMONE inside him kicked toward the surface, swimming through the secrets, the forced promises, the slime, the muck, all four created from the same noxious materials.

She continued, "What happened left you bitter, a smartass. People who faced what we faced believe they can count on no one. Only themselves. You became your own protector. That's a tough job for a third grader, Harold. You must have felt so alone. I'm so sorry."

"But—" he started.

"How did I know, that's what you're going to ask, right?"

He nodded.

"Wrong question. All the signs were there. Every, single one. Happy child, great grades, then you stopped, you just stopped caring. When you picked a sport, you skipped baseball, basketball, track, football. And this is Texas, football is religion. You selected Muay Thai, becoming your own protector. **The right question**: how did your parents, your teachers, and your family miss it? Your friends."

"Listen to her, Harold," SOMEONE whispered.

Harold's thoughts, his soul, or an astral projection of himself, detached and now floated above his surroundings, watching Val talk to SOMEONE.

SOMEONE, *the boy,* sat in front of Val, a 3rd grader, so sweet, yet so fierce, the face of a battle-weary archangel, smiling and heartbroken, battered but determined. A 3rd grader forced to make adult decisions without the wisdom or lessons of age. A boy who created H7, the **FACE,** to make sure **IT** never happened again. A boy asked, or, more so, forced, leveraged, and guilted by inept protectors to keep **THE SECRET**.

The boy, the SOMEONE, the person Harold missed most in the world, stared into him, asking at first, then encouraging, and finally demanding. Harold nodded back. Agreeing to the path, consenting to the pain, the rawness necessary to solder the two parts of him back together.

"They knew," Harold said flatly, now back in his body, he and the boy stepping into the light, together.

"What?" she asked.

Freedom washed through him as he continued. "They knew. The person—"

"The molester," she clarified.

"Yes. He was like an uncle, held the Senate seat before Dad. He was Dad's political mentor, friend for twenty years."

"Oh," Val said.

"My mother caught him, with me. He—"

"The molester."

"Was staying in our guest house a few days. His wife kicked him out, I think, and he wanted to keep that quiet. He volunteered to watch me when Mom left for her tennis tournament. Fifteen minutes later, she circled back for her sunglasses." Harold allowed himself to sit in the last word of the sentence, "sunglasses." Ironic. A tool to hide your eyes from the light.

"I remember feeling so relieved, but ... "

Val nodded encouragement; he felt her passing strength to him.

"Mom took me with her to the tennis tournament, but she ignored what happened. When we got home, the Senator and my father drank Scotch in the library. Like nothing happened. I remember the sounds of ice cubes rattling around the snifters, while they laughed. **While they laughed.**"

"My parents, they, ahh," Harold stopped. "Didn't ask him to leave. He stayed another week."

He watched horror pass over Val, a horror darker than in the telling of her tale. "The night after my mother caught him, my parents sat on the edge of my bed. They explained that if I told anyone I would ruin my chances in the world. **I'd** be considered damaged goods. That night they told me I must keep **THE SECRET.**"

"But ... "

"Even then, I ah ... saw through it." He nodded.

Val nodded.

"My parents protected him—over me—to keep their position in line, their connection to the train of power ... and money."

"Most people didn't know the Oxfords were dead broke. The family, or, more specifically, my parents, squandered the last of the Oxford fortune. My dad bet what he had left on his startup, but it wasn't enough. The man who molested me, the Senator, put together the investor group that made the company's launch possible."

Val raised her eyebrows.

"The bet paid off; my dad's new company set the market on fire. The Oxfords are again worth billions. All on the back of **THE SECRET**."

"Say it, Harold."

"I was raped," he said. A weight he could not fathom before fell from his shoulders.

"Yes. And you can keep stuffing it down, or you can find help, start counseling, process what happened to you, and use it, Harold. Use what happened to you to save the kids who can't protect themselves. Some victims remain blind to the monsters, so the monsters chase them forever. Some of us can see them, fight back. I'm unsure of why, but it's the truth."

He studied her, and looked down, surprised to find his beer still in his hand. He swirled the contents, grasping onto the only three words that mattered. IN or OUT? His eyes floated in tears on the brink of escape.

"Want to hear the rest?" she asked, and offered her napkin. Harold took it, putting it to use.

Life's toughest decisions and greatest opportunities, marriage-divorce, investment opportunities, job relocations, all came down to those three words. IN or OUT?

He set aside the last swig of beer, leaving it unfinished. He stood and walked toward the front counter and grabbed three frosted Mexican Coca-Cola bottles from the icy trough. He paid, drank the first Coca-Cola, burped, and left the bottle on an empty table, before walking back. He plopped into his seat, set one of the surviving cokes in front of Val, and twirled his finger, encouraging her to continue.

IN.

70

Harold set his hurt aside, not forcing it down, or denying its presence, just allowing the past to sit with him. He understood that hearing the conclusion of Val's story offered the beginning of his healing.

"Paunch and I raced to Tex's truck bumping along the gravel road. We screamed for the Wexlers to stop. I remember the wail of approaching sirens, the crackle of burning buildings, the sight of floating, glowing ash lighting up the night sky, and the smell of roasting pines. Mostly, though, the memory of his hand in mine, how ridiculous he looked in his skivvies, his sweat, the slickness of his grip."

She paused, looking at Harold. He let her revel, wanting to point out the plot hole, but waited.

"Tex saw us in the rearview mirror. He stopped, reversed to us. We hustled to the truck. I sat in the back, flour everywhere, floor tacky with soft-drink syrup, Opie in my lap, and a huge smile on my face. On our way out, fire truck sirens lit up the night. Tex smartly chose to return on US 59 to I-10, avoiding the trail of destruction we left behind and the questions that might need to be answered at roadblocks."

"We made it back to Beaumont hours later ... "

Harold raised his hand like a schoolboy.

"Yes," she said, smiling at the uncomfortable stop in the story.

"I don't mean to call bullshit," he started.

"Sure you do, just spit it out."

"Tex's truck ran out of gas. Remember, during the getaway."

Val allowed Harold to celebrate his assumed victory. Seconds later, Harold understood she allowed his celebration for her entertainment, not his satisfaction.

"Two gas tanks," she said.

"What?"

"You grew up driving Porsches and Jags."

"Yes, so?"

"A lot of service trucks, especially ones that travel rural routes, have two fuel tanks. Tex just switched the truck's empty tank to his secondary tank. Lexi—"

"Didn't know about the secondary tank."

"I guess Tex hadn't taught her that yet." She paused, waiting for him to poke more plot holes; he chose not to, for now.

Val continued, "When we got back, we all pretended nothing happened. Paunch cut off communication with Fraley and Matthews, stopped answering his phone. The Wexler twins went back to terrorizing the neighbors, ant beds, and anything that crossed their path, Tex kept rebuilding cars."

"What about Teeny ... I mean, what about you?"

"Opie and I stayed at Paunch's. He took down the case files and pictures of dead and missing children, burned them in a trash can in a field next to his apartment. He built a pallet for me in his living room. He made me lunch and dinner at first, then I took over the cooking.

Paunch kept me hidden. We did everything outside of Beaumont, shopped for groceries in Lumberton, ate snow cones in Kountze, watched movies at the Pines in Silsbee. He gave me space to grieve for Sissie and found ways to be around if I needed him. Paunch didn't rush me. He allowed me to battle through the worst of it.

The following weeks remain the best of my life. I met his ex-wife, and she fawned over me, buying me dresses and shoes. Still, we could not hide in his apartment forever. The two of us had to emerge at some point from our shag carpet sanctuary.

The day Paunch's suspension ended he turned in his badge. Days later, I magically appeared at the police station. With no," she held up air quotes, "'memory' of what happened."

"The agencies took over. Opie and I got tossed into foster care for months."

Val paused. Tears ran down her cheeks. "No one ever really wanted me. Not Sissie even. So, I felt abandoned. Completely." She sat in her chair, distraught, back in Teeny's body.

"Then?" he pushed.

"A caseworker with a clipboard sat down with me. I forget her name, but she told me to decide."

"Decide what?" Harold asked.

"Which family could adopt me."

"What do you mean?"

Tex, not exactly a master of paperwork, the lady informed me, worked with her for weeks to complete the adoption application. Later, Lexi told me Tex forced them to straighten the trailer, hide all the liquor, guns, weed, and explosives from the case workers."

Tears streamed down Val's cheeks.

"And the crazy boys from Silsbee, their mother, Margaret, tried to adopt me too."

"The sweet old couple from Silsbee's daughter?" Harold pressed.

"That's her. Her paperwork, flawless, according to the case worker. Margaret worked for government agencies and understood systems. I wonder what life would have been, with those brothers, and a real mom."

"Molly wanted to adopt me too. So did the woman who ran the yard-sale, but neither completed the mountains of paperwork. For the first time in my life, I felt wanted, loved. But I wanted more. I asked the case worker if anyone else completed the paperwork, the case worker said yes, but would recommend against him."

71

"I embraced ecstasy as she stressed each flaw. 'A bachelor, unsuitable for a young girl.' I nodded right away."

"'Between jobs,' told her he was unreliable. I started to tear up, knowing it was him."

"'Out of shape.' How could a man care for me if he refused to care for himself? I screamed to the heavens, thanking them."

"Paunch?" Harold asked.

"Paunch," she said, beaming and crying in unison. "My Dad. The dream father, the man every girl deserves. The man I rate every man against."

"The caseworker fought against it. Her agency tried to place me somewhere else, anywhere else. Until Guillory got involved, used her connections, pulled strings."

Harold remained in stasis, Val guessed not wanting to rush her through her mental reunion. She nonchalantly lifted her Coca-Cola, rotating the bottle rhythmically, swishing brown liquid at the bottle's bottom, lost in thought. She took in the room, spinning ceiling fan, the recently mopped floor, and the bussed and nonbussed tables, sipped the cola, and set the bottle aside.

"After I moved back to his apartment, we steered clear of discussing … " Val paused, considering Harold. Despite his disbelief, she understood he possessed an affection for her. His smile encouraged her to continue. "We both needed time away … from **it**. He abandoned police work completely, he headed security at Parkdale Mall, and took odd jobs to augment his income. Every night he managed to be home, every morning he walked me to school, promising to take care of Opie, who I started leaving behind more and more."

"Weeks before Thanksgiving, I said, 'I wanna see him.' Paunch didn't ask who. He agreed but said nothing, did nothing. Days later, I pushed again. Paunch admitted he'd love to meet him too but had no clue where to find him."

"I told Paunch I could find him. He looked doubtful, but agreed."

"Wait," Harold interrupted, "You're saying you knew where to find—"

"I did." Val said, letting the word's seduction build. "I do."

"Even—" He started.

"Yes, Harold, even now."

"Bullshit."

Her disinterest in his doubt reached a new plateau. She watched his understanding of that fact fuel his laugh. "Okay, okay, just tell the damn story. I won't interrupt."

·   ·   ·

Paunch found the spot, following a few of my missteps. I could only navigate from Sissie's old trailer, so we restarted from there. Slapping him on the shoulder and pointing, I squeaked when I spotted the billboard again. I passed it hundreds of times with Pru or Sissie. "Speak out against Child Abuse."

Under the billboard that acted as my North Star stood my real destination: the rundown theme park, Santa's Summer Village.

"Really, Teeny?" Paunch asked.

I nodded, remembering Pru's comment about why Santa would pick this place for a summer home. Internally, I understood because I needed him there.

We entered the gravel road of the compound. As Paunch drove, weathered signs announced the attractions. The first faded, peppermint-themed sign announced, "Meet St. Nick." The next promised that you could, "Sample Cookies at Mrs. Claus's Bakery."

Paunch read the rest out loud as we passed. "Wrap presents with Santa's Elves." He looked at me for assurance. I nodded. He dodged the potholes of the cracked shell drive before reading the next, "Feed Santa's Reindeer at the Petting Zoo."

Next came a PARK HERE sign, indicating we turn to the left. Right after the turn, Paunch pointed to the next sign, "Take Pictures in Santa's Sleigh." Seconds later, we mustered a "Hmm."

We parked in the tour group's only section. A cottage retrofitted more than decorated to resemble a chalet greeted us. Shabbily-styled snowflakes and unrealistic icicles highlighted the gables and eaves of a home labeled only with "Velkommen."

As we stepped out of the car, the last peppermint-themed sign read, "Polaroids with Pétur the Polar Bear."

Paunch shook his head. We wondered about the wonders or disappointment the next minutes offered. Without knowing, we surveyed the parking lot in unison. Besides Paunch's Ford Galaxie, no cars populated the complex. An undecorated handwritten note announced, "CLOSED FOR THE SEASON."

Paunch shook his head and looked down at me. "Sure this is the place?" he asked again.

I nodded.

The first sounds I heard would not be appropriate for children visiting Santa's Summer Village. A clanking, before "Shit."

From my time living next to Tex, I understood when someone fumbled a wrench tinkering with an engine.

We walked toward the clanking and cursing, but found an eight-foot chain-link fence, with green slats blocking the view. Barbed wire topped the fence to stop intruders. A padlock.

I stared to the top, considering the climb. "Don't even think about it," Paunch said.

I'd made tougher climbs. But Paunch held my shoulder pointing to the aluminum sign. "Deliveries - North Entrance."

We walked to the north gate, which, like the other, featured an eight-foot chain-link fence, slats blocking the view, and a barbed-wire top. Paunch studied the setup, noting one key fact: no padlock.

My new father offered a 'what the hell' shrug and opened the gate. I turned the corner, walked ten steps, passing a shed, then froze. A reindeer stared back at me, inches ahead. Paunch bumped into my back; like me, caught off guard.

I stared past him to the strange surroundings. Five reindeer occupied a fenced area labeled Petting Zoo. Like the beast that greeted me, two others ranged freely. Erstwhile caretakers left the Petting Zoo gate unhinged.

"Hello," I said to the towering, antlered goliath. He considered me—mostly my lack of Swiss chard, lettuce, or cabbage—turned, and trotted toward his brethren. We paused, staring at the beast in awe, before returning to our mission.

Our path took us to a huge metal building. We entered through the service door. I remember the shock of the surroundings. Obviously, at night and during the season, thousands of lights illuminated the building. That afternoon, the lights remained impotently unlit, just green cords and glass. A sign announced, "Winter Wonderland," so we followed the peppermint-themed arrows.

The building featured life-sized diorama after diorama of Christmas settings, featuring cottonesque snow, slapped-on paint, glitter, and plastic pine trees. Most featured glossy, plastic, lawn-ornament height elf statues, almost—but not quite—lifelike, with black marbled eyes, hiding mysteries.

We studied each setting, focusing on the elves. Each elf staged, some building toys, others wrapping presents, a few holding scissors. I checked. None of the scissors were coated in blood.

"Hmm," we echoed. I stepped into one diorama, right to one elf. I bent to stare eye to eye. I waited, watched for the slightest tick. Nothing but disappointment.

The next sign announced Pétur the Polar Bear. We followed it to a second metal building.

The taxidermized polar bear dominated the other décor. Paunch guessed the bear towered twelve to thirteen feet above his cotton-snow-covered display stand. No sign announced the history of the bear, but missing fur and yellowed coat communicated decades on display.

I pictured Pétur lifting Flick in his jaws. Like with the elves, I waited for the bear to move, step, growl, or even blink. Again, nothing.

The final sign, pointing to Santa's Sleigh, coordinated with the clanking and cursing from earlier. We arrived at the third metal building a minute later.

As a younger child, I pictured Santa's sleigh. Like most children, I imagined it small, nimble. The sleigh in front of me? The size of the short bus from school or Tex's box truck.

The sleigh, huge, but strangely aerodynamic, featured three rocket-sized mufflers. I remember studying gears, like watch gears, peeking from the sleigh's underside, then I recognized his boots … boots attached to grease-stained blue jeans.

"Shit," the voice under the sleigh said again as a wrench clanked.

Behind me, I heard steps. I recognized the voice before turning. "Nick, I think … " a voice started.

We turned and watched the sparkly, margarine-colored-haired speaker from my class enter the room. The last time I saw her, Vance escorted her from the flaming cabin. I studied the woman, a soft cast still on her arm.

On the mend, I thought.

"Someone's here," the woman finished.

72

Harold held up his hand, "Restroom," he said, needing a bladder break and braincation.

He rubbed his temples, stood and walked away, making sure he passed hearing range before blowing air through his lips, creating the "Plaaaapppllaaaaa," similar to a horse snort. He entered the men's room, finished his business, washed his face, and shook his head in the mirror, before exiting. Upon return, he found her sitting patiently, as if talking to him represented the most important task in the world.

He considered her, everything he now knew, and understood that was exactly the case for her. He spoke before he controlled his mouth. "So, we stopped at boots dangling from under a sleigh," he said.

She waited for his sarcasm to dissipate.

"Sorry," he said.

Val started again.

•　　•　　•

A hand and tattooed forearm reached out and snatched an oil rag. We waited as the man under the sleigh wiped his hands and face. Next, light cursing, then a prolonged breath and muttering.

"Come on, Nick, you can't dodge her forever," the margarine-haired woman said.

"Thank you," I said, turning to see her again.

She smiled at the sound of my voice.

As if by incarnation or using the margarine-haired woman to serve as distraction, the tattooed graybeard stood 12 inches away, inspecting us. I stood under the oak tree of a man. So close I smelled his aftershave.

Val paused in the story, as Harold's face announced, *I gotta know.*

"Aqua Velva," she said.

"Ahh," Harold returned.

"Can I get back to it?" she asked.

Harold nodded.

He stared down, taking me in, before introducing himself, "Nick." His hand engulfed mine, then Paunch's when they shook.

"Hi Nick, I'm detective … " Paunch stopped, realizing his job no longer labeled him. "I'm Teeny's dad. Paunch."

"So, you're—" Paunch started.

"A retired auto mechanic and mall Santa. We set up this traveling … show, to make extra cash."

"Mmm hmm," Paunch said looking around. "Just a show?"

Nick smiled at his margarine-haired wife, marched to a mop sink, and washed his hands and forearms. An egg timer buzzed from the direction Nick's wife entered.

"Ahh, the cookies," she said, spinning and turning. "This way. Don't worry. Nick magically appears when the cookies come out." We followed the woman and the aroma to a small kitchen featuring café tables. She waved for us to sit, while pulling cookies from the oven. At first glance, they appeared undercooked.

The woman smiled at me. "Nothing's worse than overcooked sweets. Pull them out when they're soft in the middle, they'll finish baking on the cookie sheet."

"What do people—"

"Like Nick, people call me different names," she answered.

"I thought they might have killed … " I started, remembering her capture at the trailer.

"We're not allowed to kill each other, there are rules." She paused, "Even Vance—or whatever he calls himself this time—can't … " She stopped; pain shadowed her face. Paunch and I considered her words and stared at each other sadly.

I remembered Paunch's torture and considered the weeks of agony this woman suffered at Vance's hands. My eyes met hers, one cheek pulled toward her ear, a half grin. Her inner courage bolstered me.

She breathed out, then smiled, "But my Nick saved me. He tracked Vance's men but kept crossing paths with you." The woman winked at Teeny.

"After the fight at the cabin, Nick followed Vance. The coward tossed me out of his van to save his bacon." Before returning to her task, the woman looked around the room. "Nick found me in a ditch, brought me here to heal."

Seconds later, she clanked a platter of warm cookies in front of us, then opened the refrigerator and pulled out an iced pitcher of whole milk. After pouring three glasses, she plopped them on the table.

"Try 'em while they're warm," Nick said pointing, now standing beside her. He kissed the margarine-haired woman, scooping two cookies in his hand before sitting. I took a bite. Butter cookies, pure perfection, crispy around the edges, soft in the middle.

"Mmmm," Paunch sounded, next to me.

Nick wolfed his two cookies while he considered us. He glanced toward the woman, before starting, "She got your letter."

I remembered the morning Pru mailed it for me, staggered by the consequences one stamp set in motion.

Nick continued, "We get thousands of letters routed to us … " he started, then stopped. "The toughest thing," he gulped, looking for comfort from his wife. "Not every kid asks for toys."

"Oh," Paunch and I said in unison. I remembered my letter, asking, begging for someone to stop Flick … and … someone did. I pictured the postage bags of letters children penned not asking for a Slinky, Twister, or Big Wheels. Handwritten pleas, for a month without finding their parent in a drug-fueled daze, a week of sobriety for their mother, a day without being molested, a minute without fear.

"I'm," he looked to his wife, "we're, ahh … not supposed to get involved with that kind of thing. Like she said, there're rules for people like me … like us. But when she got your letter, she decided … herself to," Nick breathed deeply, "to do something about it. Things went sideways and kept leaning that direction."

"In for a penny, in for a pound," she finished, washing the buttered cookie sheet.

The three of us sat at the table, considering another cookie. I remember grabbing Paunch's hand when he reached for a fourth.

Val found herself staring across the table at Harold. "I'm not sure why Paunch's brain made the crazy leap in logic."

"What?" Harold asked.

She breathed deeply, tumbling back in time, enjoying the wafting smells of cookies, the warmth of the kitchen, cozying up to the memory as she continued. "So these, these, ahh … letters you get … " Paunch stuttered at first.

"Yes," Nick answered.

My father paused, cleared his throat, his face now that of the man he would become, "The ones not asking for toys … "

His voice deepened; the timbre of Paunch's voice filled the room. He took my hand, squeezed it, asking my permission. I nodded. "Could you send them to me?"

73

Nick pondered, looked to his wife for approval, then nodded.

In her mind, Val said goodbye to the defining moment of her life, before continuing her story. "A few weeks later, Paunch received his first packet. He pulled evidence from Nick's letters and used his experience and connections to track down three child molesters. He turned all his information over to Fraley. Weeks later, Paunch tipped Fraley about a child smuggling ring. Fraley became a true believer in Paunch's talents, and he brought in the big guns."

"Guillory," Harold said.

"Yes, Paunch's ex used her connections and pull to help Paunch launch the National Task Force to Stop Child Trafficking and Abuse."

"But no one else knew about, knows about—"

"Besides the Wexlers who proved reliable at keeping secrets. No one knows the source of the information, no."

"Wait, you were going to tell me—"

"The Wexlers. Tex died in a blaze of glory decades ago. Slim chance of living forever when you live that hard. You mentioned Lexi before. Yes, she is the Deputy Director of the FBI."

"Shit. And Dex?"

"You'll find out in time. Back to the story. I studied at Sam Houston State, criminal justice degree, and tried to join Paunch. He wouldn't let me. So, I worked as a street cop, then a detective against his wishes. As much as Paunch tried to protect me from the horrors he witnessed every day, I already survived monsters. I explained that, but he ignored me."

"In the end, Paunch didn't decide who succeeded him. Nick forwarded the letters to me when Paunch died." Val looked at Harold.

"Did Paunch catch Vance?"

"No."

"If Vance is still out there, he'd be an old man."

"Not exactly," Val answered. He awaited explanation; she offered none. For some reason, Harold remembered the slick-dressed man who Val met outside of Simos. The man surrounded by minions.

"Wait, did I, in the parking lot that day?"

"You'll decide for yourself, Harold. What's real, what's not."

"If I take over—"

"When you take over, you'll receive packets of letters every few months. You act on them."

"And?"

"You'll save lives, lots of them. That's all I'm asking. Can you do that?"

"I will."

"And sometimes, you'll see things—"

"Things—"

"Yes. And sometimes, you'll receive assistance in the strangest ways."

"I don't believe you. You know that, right?"

"For now, just wait for the damn letters. Read them. Act on them. That's all I'm asking." She paused, ensuring Harold focused on her, "Consider it my final request."

"But?"

"But what," Val said.

"It's too much. The van chase was so exaggerated, over the top. Santa's Summerland, elves, polar bears, reindeer, come on, Val."

"Maybe everything I said was just the overactive imagination of a little girl. Or it's all bullshit. Decide for yourself, believe what you want."

•   •   •

Harold's Home, Cypress, Texas, Four Months Later

Chelsea Lance—the purple-scrub attired nurse in the power ponytail—exited Val's room, and closed the door behind her. "Won't be long."

April held Harold's hand, lock-gripped. A shiny, but tiny, engagement ring adorned her finger. Val agreed to spend her final few weeks at Harold and April's new home. The modest one story purchased with Harold's savings and April's salary, stocked with surviving furniture from their apartments, served as the gathering spot for Val's well-wishers.

Harold provided the bed in which Val laid dying, but felt like a small cog in the production.

Chelsea Lance oversaw every aspect of Val's health care, rallied an army around her, ensuring someone oversaw the dying woman's every need. Another of Val's rescued kids, a current prosecutor, used his connections and handled Val's final legal wishes. A quiet, polite, thirty-something executive assistant set up a Meal Train and worked with families, restaurant owners, backyard BBQ connoisseurs, and want-to-be culinarians to arrange for meals to be delivered to Harold and April, the onsite volunteers, and the tiny woman fading away in their master bedroom.

Harold marveled at the people who cycled through to see his house guest: politicians, pastors, police chiefs, doctors, TV anchors, a Realtor who thought he was a writer, and one rock star. Still, the craziness elevated Val's final week. Three sturdy, intimidating men knocked at Harold's door. He greeted them, assuming the men wanted to see Val. He waved them inside.

"The Deputy Director's ready for you at Dragon Fly Park."

"Excuse me?"

"We'll escort you to her," the thickest of the three said, motioning for Harold to step outside. "We'll make sure no one follows." The man stepped toward the trail head, taking point.

"Seems over the top," Harold said. None of the three reacted. "One minute." He jogged back to tell April, "I, uh, gotta go."

She looked confused, mirroring his emotion, but nodded. A short walk later, he and his muscled escorts passed a stylish neighborhood clubhouse and walked to a short pier. FBI Deputy Director Alexis (Lexi) Wexler waited at the end of the pier, watching three Pekin ducks whimsically float along the surface.

Not turning, she said, "They can't fly, you know, or at least they suck at flying."

"I'm sorry," Harold said, unsure of why the Deputy Director chose such a strange starting point.

"Pekin ducks, they're too big for their wings. They grow fast, don't fly away, easy to tame. Raised for meat."

"Okay." He studied the surroundings, noting additional agents around the park. He counted eight. "Looking to start a softball team?" he asked.

Alexis Wexler turned and considered Harold. The FBI leader's expression reflected a woman tired of the weight of secrets, but understanding she must keep them … all.

Nothing of the mischievous girl Harold pictured in Val's story remained in the woman in front of him. Tailored Veronica Beard pantsuit, shiny hair, white teeth, rigid posture. Lexi nodded, and each member of the protection team faded into the surroundings.

"Nice trick," Harold said.

"I got a few," Lexi said. "So, Teeny … sorry, old habit. Val updated you on the nontraditional asset."

"Nontraditional asset?" He laughed at the appellation, before her stare forced him to match her seriousness. "Yes. You don't have much of a sense of humor."

"Of course I do. You're not funny."

Harold rocked back and decided to let the woman who brought eight bodyguards lead.

"You'll be the asset's mail contact moving forward. You'll get your first packet of letters soon. After Val passes. He's giving you time to take care of her arrangements. Still, the urgency of the victim's situations demands quick action."

"I'm not sure what to say here; I still don't believe this bullshit."

"Okay, but don't make me regret this. The asset did not select you."

"I'm sorry."

"I picked you," Lexi said, turning back to the ducks. "The agency placed undercover assets with the McCluskeys. Still, we were months away from compiling the evidence needed to crush their organization. You found a way."

"Thanks."

"After that, I tracked you. You spearheaded three busts I can't explain. Old-fashioned police work wouldn't cut it. You've displayed certain instincts, Harold. Val possessed those too. She saw the monsters in the crowd when everyone else just … "

Lexi tugged her jacket downward, correcting a miniscule imbalance in the jacket's venting. Harold understood she needed a minute to mourn her friend. "Anyway. I pulled all your files, talked to your commanding officer. I recommended you. The asset approved. He presented you to Val."

"I wasn't exactly her first pick, huh?"

"No," Lexi answered, before recovering, and reinhabiting the role of Deputy Director. "After today, direct contact will prove problematic. Going forward, I'll cover your backside, but you'll have a liaison working between you and me. He operates outside of the agency's jurisdiction. The liaison is clever, stays off the radar, comfortable working inside and … outside the law. He knows your asset's identity."

Harold assembled the hints, "Wait, you mean … your brother?"

Lexi smiled. "Possible I picked the right man." She paused, turning back to the Pekins floating across the lake. "Dex oversees several off-book programs, mostly the nontraditional assets."

"Assets, wait, there are others?"

Alexis smiled, not answering. "For obvious reasons, I cannot visit Val or attend her funeral. Tell her I love her."

"Sure," Harold said, staring at Lexi Wexler. She seemed sane, but suffered the same psychosis as the woman dying in Harold's home.

"I'll push through your funding requests, provide contacts to any local police force or agency, through the liaison, of course. I can't be connected with your program."

"Because if people find out about your nontraditional assets, they'll think you're nuts."

"Who said I'm not?"

Lexi Wexler turned and walked toward the waiting car. By the time she reached the door, a member of her detail held it open. She slid inside, then she and her team exited with efficiency.

"Maybe we all are," Harold said to taillights and exhaust.

74

Banquet Tent, outside of Houston's Youth Museum, Twenty-three Months Later

Harold tilted his chair back and forth on the stage, waiting for the mayor to finish his introduction. He surveyed the audience. April Andrews-Oxford, his best decision, rotated her head and mouthed, "Sit still."

He smiled and winked. She giggled. Three seats down, Harold caught a councilman sandwiched into misfitting pants ogle April's legs. Harold glared.

April mouthed to Harold, "PAY ATTENTION."

His role, as featured speaker, did not allow him to address the ogler. So, Harold grinned and followed April's direction.

The mayor finally steered his speech to the day's topic. "In his brief time as Director of the National Task Force to Stop Child Trafficking and Abuse, in cooperation with the FBI and other agencies, this native Houstonian oversaw the capture of thirty-plus criminals. Today he'll laud his mentor, the woman we assembled to honor. He'll also overview new broader initiatives for his agency. May I introduce Harold Oxford."

Harold exhaled, rose, and assumed his position at the podium. After months of counseling, rough conversations, torpedoing his mother's and father's plans for him, and selecting his own path, Harold stood erect, fully himself. He smiled broadly at the audience, while allowing himself a moment of melancholy.

A huge anonymous donation recently landed in the task force's account. Harold guessed the funds represented an olive branch, an admission, a request of clemency, from the Oxfords. He appreciated the good the money would do, but would await actions, not payoffs, before bridging the emotional valley between him and his parents.

Harold breathed out, adjusted the microphone, cleared his throat, and started.

"Valentina Voix Perez-Maldonado … " he paused after saying her name. "What a woman. A giant in a tiny body. Today, we're here to honor Val, not for the criminals she put away, but for the children she saved."

"Many of those children are here today." He stopped. "Hey, someone turn up the house lights?"

The event's technician hopped onto the stage and whispered, "We're not supposed to …"

Harold covered his microphone. "Turn on the damn lights." The technician hurried away. Seconds later, the shadows vanished. Everything could be seen.

"Can I ask, only if you choose, can those of you who … "

Before he finished, Chelsea—the nurse from MD Anderson—stood by herself. At first lonely, exposed, no longer in the shadows. Harold understood the difference one woman could make.

He finished. "Those of you who Val helped, can you stand?"

An awkward student, barely twenty, followed, then another, a few more, a dozen, twenty, then …

Harold reached up, wiping tears. Seeing them together, for her, cut through his practiced veneer. "Thank you, thank you all. Please sit." As they sat, Harold said, "A round of applause for Val's Valiant." The room thundered with applause. Harold waited.

"Val's husband died in the line of duty, a few years after their marriage. So, she lived most of her life solo. Alone, she chased monsters so heinous the mention of their names invokes nightmares. No one should have to face such monstrosities."

"But Val did. Challenged by childhood abuse, haunted by what she witnessed in her chosen work, she thought she'd die like she lived alone. But her Valiant army rallied around her. Led by Chelsea Lance, they sat at her bedside, cooked meals, and told Val, one after another, about the life they lived, because of her sacrifice."

He breathed to calm himself, set down his notes, then nodded to April. She returned his nod. "Let's do something fun."

Harold paused, smiling at the crowd, completely comfortable, maybe for the first time in his own skin. He quietly thanked Val for that gift. "As a child, Val had a nickname. Teeny. If you saw pictures of her at that age, the name fit. The cool thing is her last name was Voix. V O I X," he spelled out. "Rare last name. Not often seen in Texas. Look it up in your phones. I'll wait." He paused as phone after phone screen lit and attendees searched.

He continued. "Voix, the last name is French. As a word, or in conversation, voix means voice. Teeny Voice. Funny. The smallest voices, voices willing to stand, speak up, can change the world."

"In a moment, we'll unveil Valentina Voix Perez Maldonado's statue. Don't get me wrong. She'd be proud. But she would be proudest of the additional steps her agency will take moving forward. Along with continuing to put criminals behind bars."

"Not everyone can fight crime like Val. But everyone can help stop child abuse. In Val's name, a portion of our budget will be spent to supplement current programs to educate others on how to spot child abuse in schools, in our neighborhoods . . . in our homes."

He paused. "Just so happens, donation cards are making their way down your aisle right now." Harold's volunteers started their assignment moments earlier. "Most importantly, if you experienced child abuse, or if you see it, speak out. Don't look the other way because it's easier, don't let evil hide in the shadows. Val learned the hard way, to teach us all *it's okay to ask for help.*"

75

12:25 a.m. Christmas Morning, Seven-plus Years Later
April shook Harold awake. "You're up, baby."

"Just ten more minutes," he begged.

"You won't have time to assemble the bikes if you don't start now. We had a deal, I bought them, hid them, and wrapped every other gift. Assembling bikes rests within the borders of Daddyland."

"Huhh," he breathed. He turned to April, she pulled the cover over her, but some of his favorite assets peaked through. "How about," he said, moving toward her.

"After bikes stand in front of the Christmas tree, so Jeffrey and Little Val don't lose faith in Santa, you can open your present."

He tried to cuddle again; she held ground. "I left cookies out for you. Make sure you eat them. The alarm's set. Don't go into the garage without turning it off. Your toolbox is on your desk."

"Okay," he climbed out of bed, grumbled, then slipped on jammie bottoms and slippers. He snuck by the kids' rooms toward his office. He grabbed his tool kit and found the printed assembly directions with a note. *Thought you could use these, Love, April.* "You're the best," he whispered.

Surprised the fireplace roared as he approached, Harold decided April went all out this year.

"Well, at least there's cookies," he said aloud, toolbox in hand.

When he reached the den, the pink Barbie and green Hulk bikes stood fully assembled. Both sported huge bows, with matching helmets stylishly displayed on the mantle. Harold's jaw hung open. He looked to where he guessed April placed the cookies. Crumbs covered the red and green Christmas-themed plate.

"The bikes are a real bear, especially for first timers," Harold heard behind him. Based on the voice's location, he knew a butt rested in his recliner. He remained standing, not turning, wondering if he was still sleeping. *That's it. Dreaming.*

"Didn't think you'd mind the help," the voice continued. "Probably time for introductions."

Harold spun and saw ...

THE END

About the Author

While Texas's greatest storytellers Cormac McCarthy and Larry McMurtry focused on the western plains, Sojka focuses on southeast Texas's Big Thicket, Piney Woods, Neches River and the area's eccentrics. Few authors' voices more closely mimic the people and the rich environment they describe.

Sojka's plot twists often dare readers to connect the dots, but his devotion to character arcs and off-beat dialogue prompted critics to award his last novel *39: Your Last Birthday* the Maxy Award for Literature and Humor and a Readers' Favorite Silver Medal for Southern Fiction.

Sojka still lives in southeast Texas with his wife. He writes, runs, paddleboards, and aspires to smoke the perfect brisket.

Other Titles by Timothy Gene Sojka

Take A bribE, Meet yoUR MAKeR

MANY AWARDS WINNER

P litikill

Timothy Gene Sojka

Author of the #1 Political Thriller,
Payback Jack

Note from Timothy Gene Sojka

Word-of-mouth is crucial for any author to succeed. If you enjoyed *Claws*, please leave a review online—anywhere you are able. Even if it's just a sentence or two. It would make all the difference and would be very much appreciated.

Thanks!
Timothy Gene Sojka

We hope you enjoyed reading this title from:

BLACK ROSE
writing™

www.blackrosewriting.com

Subscribe to our mailing list – *The Rosevine* – and receive **FREE** books, daily deals, and stay current with news about upcoming releases and our hottest authors.
Scan the QR code below to sign up.

Already a subscriber? Please accept a sincere thank you for being a fan of Black Rose Writing authors.

View other Black Rose Writing titles at
www.blackrosewriting.com/books and use promo code
PRINT to receive a **20% discount** when purchasing.